For Pat

With special thanks to Brenda.

MR
BLUE
SKY

JOHN DARKE

Matador
9 Priory Business Park,
Wistow Road, Kibworth Beauchamp,
Leicestershire. LE8 0RX
Tel: 0116 279 2299
Email: books@troubador.co.uk
Web: www.troubador.co.uk/matador
Twitter: @matadorbooks

ISBN 978 1789017 618

British Library Cataloguing in Publication Data.
A catalogue record for this book is available from the British Library.

Printed and bound in Great Britain by 4edge Limited
Typeset in 11pt Adobe Jenson Pro by Troubador Publishing Ltd, Leicester, UK

Matador is an imprint of Troubador Publishing Ltd

PREFACE

VENEZUELA 1920, SOMEWHERE NEAR THE TARRA RIVER.

'*Esmuypeligroso! Esmuypeligroso!*' screamed the hysterical villager.

'What's he saying, Marcos?' Dr Cooper demanded impatiently.

'E's saying eets too dangerous, *Señor*,' Marcos replied.

'We must capture one alive, Marcos; tell him we must capture one alive.'

'But these men are not trained hunters, *Señor*. They are poor people, from the local tribal villages. They are only doing this for the money.' Turning to the terrified tribesman, Marcos babbled something in Spanish to him and a dispute erupted between them.

'Marcos, we don't have time to argue,' Dr Cooper yelled.

It was the dead of night and in the jungle the sound of gunfire crackled all around them followed by cries of terror. Crashing out from the thickets, a young man appeared wearing a cream shirt, khaki trousers and a beige panama hat. He was clutching a Lee–Enfield rifle to his chest. 'Cooper, they're all around us; there's too many of them,' Edwards bellowed.

Upon hearing this, Marcos and the villager abruptly stopped arguing and made a run for it. Dr Cooper curled his lip at their cowardice and treachery and turned his attention back to the young man, who stood before him. Sweat streamed from the brim of his panama hat and trickled down his suntanned cheeks. 'Edwards, we have to get them to the trap; it's the only way.'

His voice sounding hoarse, Edwards swallowed. 'I'll try,' he shouted as he disappeared back into the foliage.

Dr Cooper wiped his own sweaty brow with his cotton neck-scarf, his whole body tense with trepidation. In the dense jungle, the beastly roars continued, and the terrified tribesmen were forced to retreat.

Desperately, they popped off more panicky, random shots from their bolt-action rifles, fire flaring from their barrels but it did no good. The hunters themselves were being hunted by the towering shapes that stalked them in the shadows. The first to be attacked had his arm completely ripped from the humeral head of his shoulder, blood pumping out from the axillary artery like a fountain.

Then another man was attacked. His head was clamped by a set of thick, jagged molars that bit into his orbital cavity causing blood and vitreous humour to ooze out from his eyeball.

The huddle of men left, continued to fire off haphazard shots from their rifles as the two-legged beasts forced them back into a clearing. Suddenly, one of the beasts moved in for the kill and leapt at the nearest man but missed and disappeared into the trap that had been set for them. Boom! The jungle shook with the sound of an explosion and erupted in a blaze of red fire, the blast killing many of the beasts and sending the rest darting back through the forest. The MK2 pineapple grenade, saved only as a last resort, had finally been used.

When the air had cleared Dr Cooper, accompanied by Edwards and the last few tribesmen, began to edge closer to the trap to see what they had caught. The trap-hole they had dug was ten feet deep and had been covered by a criss-crossing of branches and sticks, topped with leaves.

'I think we've got a live one, Edwards,' Dr Cooper whooped.

Closer and closer they crept up to the hole.

'Can you see anything?' Dr Cooper asked.

Edwards twisted his Enfield to the side of his body so that he could squat down to have a peek.

'Careful, man!' Dr Cooper warned.

Edwards placed his hands on the ground so he could steady himself, then he craned his neck over the edge of the hole as two blazing orange eyes stared back at him from the murky depths. But he still couldn't see clearly and in the second it took for him to turn and ask for a light, the beast sprang from the pit. The last thing Edwards saw were its bulging eyes of fire and the drooling fangs of death.

CHAPTER ONE

Rebecca sat bolt upright gasping for breath, her heart drumming through her chest. In the darkness her eyes pinballed around her bedroom searching for that grotesque presence she knew was there. A moment ago, it had been standing over her, bearing down, watching her with its fiery orange eyes. She could even smell its foul, fetid breath against her cheek making her want to retch. And when the thing opened its mouth it was like a festering, gaping wound with a slug-like tongue making a sickening, sloshing sound as it slithered over jagged molars that were ready to bite and tear. A slow, raspy voice penetrated the darkness, whispering her name, but how come? How could this be happening? The thing did not have a voice; it could never speak.

The nightmares, those old, recurring nightmares had started once again. Why now? Why tonight? Drenched in sweat, she switched on the bedside light and sat up. Just how many times had she tried to work out what was going on and what it all meant over the years? Wiping away her tears and sinking back into her pillow, she asked herself the same old question. *Why am I still having to go through this?* She thought she had put it all behind her and moved on. But tonight, she wondered if she would ever be free from the torture of not knowing the answer.

According to Richard, her latest counsellor, that thing in her dreams wasn't real, didn't exist. It, or **Him**, as she had always described the monster, the cause of all her distress was, for complex reasons, fixed in her imagination. As the therapist put it, it was the manifestation of years of pent-up anger, guilt and remorse finally coming out. It was a clear case of post-traumatic stress disorder.

'We have to release such feelings at some point, Rebecca,' one of her previous counsellors had told her. 'You can't keep on cheating the mind. All of those repressed emotions are like links of a chain. The longer you try to run away from your problems the more links you add to this chain and the heavier it will become. In your case, these troubled emotions have moulded themselves into the form of this apparition, this demon. And like that chain that keeps on getting longer and heavier, this particular form, that you have given a dream-life to, will only add to your emotional burden. It will become more and more real unless you develop the courage to confront it. As soon as you start to accept what has really happened to you in the past your demons will start to grow weaker and weaker and finally, they will vanish forever.'

But this demon was real. Rebecca howled back at the professional voices of reason that swam around in her head. As she sat alone in her bedroom, she clenched her fists and repeated to herself, 'I know he was fucking real. I know he was fucking real.' She gave a resigned sigh as more memories came flooding back. 'I also know that they all thought I was crazy. None of them believed me. My mother, the police, the doctors; why couldn't any of them accept that I was telling the truth?'

'Of course he was real!' she shouted at the walls. 'I grew up with Him. He was a big part of my life. He was with me all the time. But when Dad died everyone tried to make me forget Him. Even when I told them that it was He who did it. He was the one who murdered my father, but nobody believed me. They thought I was just traumatised and making it all up. There was even a time when I was sure that some of them even suspected that I had something to do with Dad's death because of what I was saying. But it was Him, he did it.

'In the end, even my boyfriend turned his back on me. He thought I was crazy, they all did. I was only fifteen-years-old and I had to go through all that shit on my own. Now, the hell, the nightmares are starting again. Is he trying to punish me for abandoning Him all those years ago? Is he going to continue to haunt me forever? Of course he is,' she answered herself. 'Who am I kidding? Deep down I know it, these nightmares are never going to end.'

There was no point in trying to get back to sleep now, she was too shaken up. She dragged herself out of bed and looked in the dressing table mirror. There she was, Rebecca Samuels, thirty-four-years-old and no spring chicken anymore. Life was slowly beginning to pass her by. She was still single and lived in a one-bedroom flat above a newsagents' shop in the Welsh town of Benarth.

The flat was actually rented from her uncle, her dad's brother, who also owned a chemical distribution business in the town and Rebecca worked for him as his office manager. Rebecca had made the move away from her home town of Claydon when she was eighteen. After the death of her father, life around her quaint little seaside town held too many terrible memories for her and she became fed up with all the gossipy conspiracies surrounding her father's untimely demise. Living at home with her mother had also become unbearable due to the hurtful arguments they had on an almost daily basis. Rebecca always felt that her mother somehow blamed her for the death of her husband. In the end, she just had to get away from it all and start afresh and even more importantly, she had to get away from Him.

Fortunately, Uncle Jim gave her a lifeline and invited her to come and live with him and his family down in Benarth. Rebecca and her uncle had always been close, and she had seen him fairly regularly throughout her childhood. Even after the death of her father, they still kept in touch and he often went out of his way to try and make sure she was OK. Rebecca always looked forward to him popping over to Claydon to visit her and her mother at their old-farmhouse high up on Claydon Head. And when he left, he would leave a few hundred pounds to help them out. Over the years, Uncle Jim had become a father-like figure to her at a time when she really needed one. When she said that she wanted some space, he was the one who gave her a place of her own. He was her rock, her touchstone with normality.

* * *

The next morning, Rebecca felt drained and thought about not going into work but that would mean that she would just keep obsessing about the dream. Work was a better option and as she sat in front of her desk top she gazed idly out of the small, rectangular window of the office. Outside, the sky was grey and leaden, eking out the kind of gloom that reflected her own bleak mood. Bored, she slumped down in her chair and rocked back and forth, making it swivel and creak and her eyes drifted over to the models of Second World War spitfire planes that her uncle kept on the shelves near the doorway. In the background, she could hear the gentle humming sound of the electric heater in the corner of the office. She was tired and had trouble keeping her eyes open. The heater was giving the whole room a kind of soporific warmth as it guarded against the bitter February frost outside. Rousing herself, she turned back to the computer. She stared at the cursor bar on the screen as it blinked under a file of invoices, figures and monthly quotes. It was only mid-morning, but Rebecca's stomach began to rumble, and she wished she had eaten something before she had come to work.

She filled her lungs with the warm office air in a vain attempt to flush out the boredom.

Brushing back a greasy strand of his greying brown hair, Uncle Jim came into the office. Scratching his neatly trimmed beard, he leant down to open the bottom drawer of the filing cabinet. Rebecca watched as his portly belly spilled out over the top of his faded black tracksuit bottoms and she thought it looked like ready-mixed dough tipping off a cooking tray. In spite of the dark thoughts that were threatening to surface, she couldn't help but smirk at the image.

'You seriously need to get one of those treadmills,' she teased.

Jim gave her an indignant look. 'Sod off, Beccs. What's the matter with you this morning? Got the February blues, again?'

Giving him a cheeky grin, Rebecca stopped rocking back and forth.

Jim straightened up with a groan. 'I've already told you, you're just getting picky because you're getting broody again and you need to settle down. So, my question to you is, just what are you waiting for?'

Rebecca rolled her eyes despairingly; whenever she had a go about his weight he always came back with the same old personal attacks of his own.

'And I've told you I'll settle down when I'm good and ready.'

This time, it was Jim's turn for a victorious little smirk; he had got to her. Triumphantly, he slammed the drawer closed with a loud clang. Rebecca jumped and scowled at his deliberate heavy-handedness.

'How old are you, now; thirty-five?' he asked.

Rebecca gave him a warning look. 'Thirty-four.'

'Right, thirty-four; can't you feel that biological clock ticking? I mean, most women your age have at least one child by now.'

'You're a saucy sod, you are, and you are so chauvinistic. What are you trying to do? Get me married off so I'm out of the way?'

Jim threw her a superior smile. 'No, no, Becca, I just want to see you happy and content. I want you to enjoy a full life. I don't want you to miss out on some of life's great gifts.'

'But I'm not missing out. I'm quite happy just doing what I'm doing. I don't have to answer to anyone. I don't have to rush home to anyone in case they get suspicious. And I can go anywhere and do anything I like. Why is that so bad?'

'Just doesn't seem right to me, that's all,' Jim muttered as he hauled open another drawer.

'Perhaps you should have shipped me off to one of those Middle or Far Eastern Countries to marry some domineering restaurant owner. Would that have made you happy?'

But Jim didn't reply. Instead, he slammed the drawer closed again – just to annoy her. As he left the office he called out airily, 'Milk with two sugars please, my darlin.'

As soon as Jim had gone, Rebecca thought seriously about what he had said. Despite claiming that she was quite happy leading the proverbial single life, in truth, nothing made her more miserable. Deep down, Rebecca wanted to find that Mr Right, if he existed, settle down and have a family. But with all the emotional baggage she would have to carry into the relationship she knew it probably didn't have a chance of working.

Since moving to Benarth, she had dated twice; one relationship had only lasted for two weeks and the other just over a month. In both cases, the reasons for the break-up of the relationship came down to the fact that she had not been able to give them enough attention and the boyfriends just lost interest. Evidently, she was looking for something in a relationship that wasn't there. But what was that? Even she didn't know. Of course, she could never confide any of this to her uncle. He wouldn't understand and would start to think that she was even more emotionally damaged than he liked to admit.

* * *

At home in her flat that evening, Rebecca lay on her two-seater couch in her joggers as she watched some period drama on the TV. On the screen an intense love scene was being played out by the two young, attractive characters and Rebecca was pulled into the moment. She began to imagine what it might be like to be dating again. Now that she was going on thirty-five, she wondered if she was still young, or even attractive enough for the dating scene out there. Could she still pull a hunk? In a fit of paranoia she leapt off the couch and stood in front of the large mirror above the mantelpiece and stared hard and long at her reflection.

She was slim and just above average height. With her thick, shoulder-length locks of undyed, dark hair, sparkling brown eyes and the cute dimples in her cheeks whenever she laughed, she concluded that she didn't look too bad. She posed a smile to see how she looked to everyone else, then stopped because she just looked desperate and stupid. Rebecca glared back at herself.' Mirrors,' she snorted. 'They show you for what you really are and not what you think you are,' then she turned away.

* * *

That night, Rebecca dreamed but this time she had what started out as a regular dream, a dream of home. Claydon was a small peninsula that was sandwiched between two sweeping shores. And then there was Claydon Head, an impressive limestone mountain looming over the two shorelines. From the air, the mountain itself looked like a small island; an island with green plains, deep woods and steep, jagged cliffs that stared out over the grey-blue ocean. It was here, on Claydon Head, or Claydon Rock, as it was also known, where Rebecca had spent most of her childhood.

In her dream, she was a child once again, playing in the fields outside her parents' farmhouse. The farm animals had long gone, and they didn't even have a cat or dog. The animal pens had been knocked down to make room for parking and the only outside building was a small summer house and even that was dilapidated.

Rebecca was lying on her back with a grass stalk hanging out of her mouth and she squinted up at the sun, which beamed down on her from the summer sky. In the dream, she was reliving those times so vividly. 'Rebecca?' She could hear her mother's clear voice as it penetrated the drone of the honey bees and clicking of the crickets. In this dream, Rebecca would not answer straight away; she liked to play a trick on her mother and cause her a few moments of worry before replying. Then, she would spring up from the grass like a young hare and shout out back. Her mother would be standing in the front doorway, pretending to be cross with her mischievous daughter. She would shake her head and beckon Rebecca, the sunshine burnishing her auburn hair with streaks of gleaming red.

Her father, Rob, would always have his head under the hood of his Land Rover and when Rebecca shouted out to remind him of her existence, a dismissive hand would flutter out from under the bonnet. 'Yeah, that's great, Becca,' was all the response she would get out of him.

Rebecca would then stare across the summer fields carpeted with golden dandelions, towards the clearing leading into the woods; a place where the tall trees seemed to stand to attention like lanky wooden soldiers; a magical place where, she imagined, the plants and flowers would smell like the golden honey her mother spread on her toast in the morning; a place where shy creatures would hide away, too timid to come out and play with her. But this childhood dream would always become troubled as those woods would suddenly darken as if the night was rapidly falling. Now, she was sitting all alone in the field without the humming of the bees or the clicking of the crickets. But more importantly, her parents were no longer there to watch over her. They too had gone, along with the light.

'Mum? Dad?' she would cry. But nobody would answer. In this part of the dream, Rebecca would find herself drifting towards the entrance to the woods. She knew she was forbidden to enter the woods, but she was unable to resist. In the darkness beyond, shadows of small, nocturnal animals evading their night-time predators, took cover in between the gnarled roots of tree trunks.

Beside one extra-thick tree, one particular shadow always stood out and was the biggest and blackest of them all. There was a sense of menace in the air and Rebecca wanted to call out to her parents again. She wanted them to come and get her, but she was more worried in case she disturbed whatever was in there waiting. Then from somewhere she would manage to muster the courage to speak. This is where the dream became confusing. Rebecca knew that the thing in her dream could not speak but she called out to it and it answered her somehow. 'Who are you?' her voice a soft quiver. Two piercing orange eyes would glare back at her from the darkness.

'Rebecca,' it always growled.

'What do you want? Where are Mum and Dad?'

'Rebecca,' it would growl to her again.

Rebecca's breathing would become laboured, her chest heaving up and down.

'Rebecca, I'm waiting for you, come home.'

But she was too terrified to say anything else. Almost paralysed with fear she would begin to cry. She wanted her mum and dad. She wanted them to come and get her; to save her from what was waiting in the dark.

'REBECCA, COME HOME!' The voice would vibrate throughout the wood like a clap of thunder.

* * *

Then, it was over. The dream-turned-nightmare was over, and the alarm clock was beeping urgently on her bedside table. Struggling to wake up, she managed to lean over and whack the alarm off. While she waited for her heart to stop hammering in her chest, that last warning from her dream kept coming back to her; "REBECCA, REBECCA, COME HOME." *Rebecca, come home*, those same words reverberating through her brain again and again. It had been so overpowering this time. It had to mean something, something real. It was so vivid and intense, she was sure it was sending her a sign, telling her something – but what?

It must mean that He was telling her to come back home. Once more, she had felt Him coming through to her in the dream and she could feel Him again now. The last time she suffered a spate of these nightmares it took three months of therapy before she could finally have a fairly good night's sleep. She did not want to go down that road again, but she had to face the fact that she could not ignore what was happening any longer. 'Maybe I should go back home,' she said out loud, 'and maybe it's time to have another counselling session with Richard.'

* * *

Before setting off to work that morning Rebecca phoned Richard's secretary and was fortunate enough to get an appointment to see him early the next week. As she drove to work she thought more and more about the prospect of actually going back home and by the time she arrived outside the forecourt of her uncle's warehouse she had made up her mind to take the plunge. It was as if the decision had already been made for her. This command, this calling, was so strong that she seemed powerless to defy it, no matter what. Now all she had to do was persuade her Uncle Jim to give her the time off.

Her uncle finally rolled into work mid-morning and Rebecca called him to come into the office. He shuffled in with a weary sigh. 'I'll need to go on the computer in a minute, Beccs, I've got to update one of the accounts.'

'Before you do, Jim, can I have a word?' Rebecca asked.

'Do I need to sit down, or can I listen while I'm working?' he replied. This was his way of saying, is it serious or not?

Rebecca sat back from the computer screen. 'Can you give me some time off?'

Jim's face fell. 'Is that all? How long do you want; a couple of days, a week?'

'Actually, about a month.'

Knitting his brow into a row of deep wrinkles, Jim couldn't hide his annoyance. 'A month? What the hell do you need a month off for? You're not having a facelift or a sex change, are you?'

Rebecca gave him a withering look. 'No, I've decided that I need to go back home for a while to tie up a few loose ends, that's all.'

Jim squinted at her suspiciously. 'Such as?'

'Things to do with my personal life.'

'Is this something that your therapist has suggested?'

'No, I haven't even been to see him, yet. This was something I decided myself. It's something I should have done a long time ago.'

Jim eased himself into his chair and eyed her with an expression of fatherly concern. 'So, what's the problem then? Is it a family thing, or an old flame, or what?'

Rebecca felt that her uncle deserved some sort of explanation. After all, she was about to leave him in the lurch for at least a month. 'All I can really say is that my peace of mind may depend on it. I need to straighten a few things out and in order to do that I may have to confront some issues.'

'Sounds a bit cryptic if you ask me,' Jim replied. 'It doesn't have anything to do with Him, does it?'

Rebecca rubbed her brow awkwardly. Her uncle had said it, he had raised the issue; he had breached the taboo subject. Jim was fully aware of who He was. In fact, everyone in the family knew about Him and all the great adventures he and Rebecca had supposedly shared back in the days when she grew up on Claydon Head all those years ago. And they were also aware of the psychological damage all those so-called adventures with Him had caused her; the consequences of which had left their indelible mark upon everyone else in the family.

Rebecca thought long and hard before answering her uncle. The last thing she wanted to do was open up all those old wounds. If she did tell him the truth, he would only find some reason why he couldn't give her time off work. He would never agree to let her dig around in her past again. He had told her time and time again that it was too risky and could send her off the rails for good. So, for the sake of an easy way out, she decided to lie.

'No, of course not, all that nonsense is behind us now. I just feel that I need to spend some time with my mum. I need to clear the air and make peace with her; it's been over fifteen years and we've still hardly spoken to one another.'

Jim studied her hard for a moment, looking for any signs that she was trying to fool him. Finally, his expression softened. 'So, when do you need this time off?' he asked.

'In a couple of weeks. I want to get it sorted out as soon as possible.'

'In a couple of weeks, Beccs?' Jim protested. 'You know how busy we're likely to get over the next couple of months. I need you here to help me.'

'I know, Jim, and I'm sorry but I'll be back as soon as I can, I promise. I mean, I haven't had any time off for a long while so just think of it as having all my holidays all at once.'

'But in a couple of weeks!' Jim protested again.

Rebecca turned on her doe-eyed look. She knew how to play her uncle when she wanted to get her own way. 'Please, Jim, it means a lot to me.'

Jim glanced up, the heavy pouches under his eyes looking even heavier, and he gave a resigned sigh.

Rebecca rushed around the desk to give him a big thank-you hug. She wrapped her arms around him catching a whiff of the funny old carpet smell from his tatty work clothes.

With a fond grin on his face he said, 'You will be here for your birthday, though, won't you?'

'Of course I will.'

'Good, your Aunty Judith and I like to see you on your birthday.'

Rebecca stood back and gazed down at him affectionately. 'Shall we have a coffee then, or are you still trying to cut down on your caffeine?'

'Milk and two sugars please, luv,' he smiled, and he watched her walk out of the office.

But once she was out of sight, his warm smile faded like the sun suddenly disappearing behind a blanket of darkening rain clouds.

CHAPTER TWO

Rebecca eyed Richard, her therapist, as if it was she who was going to counsel him. Before their session began, he slipped into the same routine as he always did. He placed a box of tissues where she could reach it, asked her if she wanted a bottle of water, then he moved his chair, so he was close enough to hear if her voice dropped and made sure his body language was as open as possible. She guessed that Richard was in his early forties, but he didn't dress like a conventional forty-year-old professional. He favoured plaid shirts, worn unbuttoned, over designer T-shirts and designer jeans. In the whole year-and-a-half she had been seeing him he had never worn anything else. She waited as he glanced at her file of notes.

With his thick glasses, carefully styled haircut and his designer stubble, it was difficult to pinpoint him as a fully qualified cognitive behavioural therapist. He could have been anything from a teacher at a comprehensive school to an out-of-work actor. But Rebecca had seen enough therapists to know that it was a carefully constructed image, an image that was intended to break down barriers and create a sharing experience with clients.

Even the room that he worked in looked more like a cosy seating area rather than a formal consulting room: large, colourful cushions on a sofa, more cushions on the floor, two leather chairs with more cushions. Bookshelves lined the walls and a dream-catcher hung at the window. 'My God!' Rebecca muttered under her breath, 'I always feel like I'm waiting to be initiated into a whacky hippy commune when I come here.'

'So, Rebecca.' Richard cleared his throat and settled himself deeper into his seat. 'You've booked another appointment to see me; can you tell me why?'

Rebecca did a couple of quick relaxation exercises while she wondered where to begin. She breathed in to the count of four, held her breath to the count of four and breathed out to the count of four. Then, she came right out with it. 'I've started dreaming about Him, again.'

Richard's eyes narrowed, zooming in on her like he was using a pair of binoculars. He stopped moving and crossed his legs. 'OK, and why do you think that might be?'

Rebecca held out her hands. 'You're the doc, I was hoping you could tell me.'

'Maybe if you can tell me about these latest dreams, we can explore why they have restarted at this point. You've mentioned Him again. I know, from your previous therapists' records, that this particular problem tends to rear its head from time to time but I have to confess, since I took over your case you've never gone into great detail about it with me. Perhaps, if you start from the very beginning and fill me in, it's possible that we might uncover something that my colleagues have missed.'

Rebecca's eyes darted around the room while she tried to put her thoughts together.

'Right, from the very beginning,' she sighed. 'I suppose some things could have been overlooked or distorted. The fact that these dreams are beginning to plague me again suggests that there are still some missing pieces to that complex jigsaw that we've all been trying to solve. It's got to be worth a go.'

'I agree but I have to warn you how disturbing this might be for you. Sometimes, when you want to have a good clear-out, you have to go right down into the basement and get a little dirty.' Richard waited for her to respond.

Rebecca didn't think much of his ham-fisted analogy, plus, it sounded like there might be a sexual undertone to it. She did a couple more breathing exercises and looked down at her feet. To give her a head start, Richard read out some background notes from his file. 'I believe it started when you were living in an old farmhouse on Claydon Head.'

'Yes, that's right; me and my mother and father. I was the only child.'

'Tell me what the relationship was like with your parents.'

'I suppose I've never really felt like they were my true parents.'

'Why do you think that?' Richard asked and made a few more notes on the file.

'I don't really know. Sometimes they felt more like an aunty and uncle instead of a proper mum and dad. My father, in particular, was never really the paternal type. I know he tried his best, but I never thought he had the same kind of patience other dads had. Right up until he died, we used to fight like cat and dog.'

'Are you saying that your father wasn't prepared to spend quality time with you when you were a child?'

'No, he wasn't. I mean, we lived so far out of the way and I didn't really have any other children to play with after school so I suppose I needed more attention than most kids but he was always too busy.'

'What about your mother?'

Rebecca's face softened a little and she gave a slight smile. 'I could see that she noticed it too and at times she honestly tried to make up for what my father couldn't give but to me it still felt like it was all done more out of duty than genuine motherly concern.'

'Can you be more specific?'

'Sometimes, it was as if my mother didn't quite know how to behave with a child. When I was really little and needed a cuddle or some attention, she didn't seem to know how to deal with me.

She would look a bit lost and give herself murmured instructions, instructions of what she was supposed to do. But surely knowing when to give your child love and affection should come naturally, not from a set of self-imposed guidelines. Although, to be fair, I have to admit that she did get a bit better at it as I got older.'

'But things stayed the same with your father?'

Rebecca shifted her head to one side. 'Things didn't change much there but I still loved him and my mother dearly and I think, deep down, they felt the same for me; at least, I hoped they did. I suppose the only person who has felt like a proper parent to me is my Uncle Jim.'

Making more detailed notes, Richard asked, 'Tell me about your uncle.'

'Since I lost my father, he's the only one who has taken a real interest in me. He makes me feel like he really cares.'

'In what way?'

'He invited me to go down and live in Benarth with him and his family, he gave me a job and he looks after me like a father is supposed to.'

'And what was your relationship like with your uncle when you were growing up?'

'I never saw that much of him while I was growing up except when he came over to discuss business with my father. But when I did see him he always made a fuss of me. You see, just before we moved into the farmhouse, my father and uncle had a bit of a windfall. Apparently, it had something to do with some investment, or so I was told later by my mother. But whenever they talked business it was always done in a clandestine way, away from everyone. They didn't even want my mother to hear.'

'So, you've always got on with your uncle, ever since you were very young?'

'I suppose, yes, yes, I have.'

Richard continued to look at Rebecca intently, his eyes never leaving her face. 'OK, let's move on a bit more. When did this,' he chose his words carefully, 'unusual relationship begin with Him or Mr Blue Sky?'

Hearing that name again was like having a firework going off in the pit of her stomach. 'Mr Blue Sky.' Her voice fell to a whisper. 'I haven't even said that name out loud in years.'

'Can you tell me when and where you first met Him?'

Rebecca sat forward in her seat and clasped her damp palms together. 'I think it was that time of year when the summer was changing to autumn. Beyond the fields, surrounding our farmhouse, are dense woodlands almost covering the entire north face of Claydon Head and then, beyond the woods, there are sheer drops off the cliff edge into the sea below. You can be rushing through thick woods one minute and the next you can be toppling over the drop. I was eight-years-old and I remember I used to play in the dandelion fields where I could see the little bunny rabbits chasing each other in and out of the entrance to the woods. I can also remember how I always wanted to follow them into the woods and watch them play. But whenever I asked my mum if I could follow the rabbits she would tell me off and warn me never to go in there by myself.

'But one day, when I saw a group of bunnies disappearing into the woods, I just couldn't resist it. They looked like something out of a Walt Disney movie. Fortunately, my mother was busy with the housework, so I knew she wouldn't be checking on me for a while. I saw my chance to sneak into the woods to look for the rabbits. When I reached the edge, I peered through the trees, but I couldn't see them. Inside it looked dark under the canopy of leaves from the trees but some of the plants had bright berries and small white flowers.

'So, did you go in?' asked Richard.

'Yes, I did. Slowly, I crept inside and to me it was like a fairyland. The woodland was very dense and the tall trees grew tightly together like a regiment of giant wooden troopers. Although the leaves and branches formed a thick covering of shade, in between the trees you could still see golden shafts of sunlight pouring down onto the berries and flowers making them sparkle like jewels. Wherever you walked, the ground was carpeted by soft moss and overhead you could hear a chorus of birds singing in the treetops. I was enchanted by what I was seeing and hearing but I couldn't find those playful rabbits.

'I must have walked for about ten minutes, not knowing where I was going. In the end, I realised that I must be lost. Then, all of a sudden, I heard another sound and it wasn't anything like the other sounds I had heard. This sound was like a kind of whining. At first, I thought it was an animal in some pain; perhaps one of the bunnies had injured itself. Concerned by the noise, I set off to try and find what was making it and see if I could help. Not wanting to frighten the poor animal, I tiptoed through the foliage trying to avoid stepping on any dry twigs and give myself away. Closer and closer, I inched my way through until the whining became louder then I knew I was getting close. The thought of finding one of those little rabbits made my heart beat faster. If it wasn't badly injured, I would pick it up and feel its soft fur in my hands and its little heart beating against my palm. Perhaps I could take it back home and nurse it better, if my mum would let me.

'At last, I reached a large patch of ferns and I could see something moving in the patch, something black. Then a fiendish face shot up and glowered at me. This was no cuddly little rabbit and I screamed in fright and ran away. I didn't know where to run and it seemed as if the wood and everything in it, suddenly came to life all around me. The leaves, the branches, the thickets all began to cling on to me, making me feel like their prisoner. Perhaps I had trespassed into a sacred, forbidden place. As I ran, I winced as the spindly twigs and brambles whipped at my shins, arms and my face. Behind me I sensed that I was being chased and the fear felt like an electric bolt running from the top of my head right down to my plimsolls.

'Then, two things happened. First, I could see that the wood was thinning out and the ground was sloping steeply downwards. Second, a strong gust of wind propelled me forwards and I was slipping and sliding out of the wood across a short stretch of grass that ended at the edge of a cliff; a cliff I hadn't known was there.

'Out of blind panic and pure instinct, I grabbed hold of a low, twisted branch of a tree, jerking my whole body to a shuddering halt just before I reached the edge. When I looked down I couldn't believe what I was seeing. I was staring down at the ocean waves crashing against jagged rocks over a hundred feet below. Holding onto that branch was the only thing that had stopped me from falling to my certain death.

'Fear raced through me and I screamed and screamed for my life as warm pee ran down my leg and into my white socks. "Mum, Mum, Dad, Dad," I screamed as I tried to understand what was happening. 'Sobbing for my parents, I even promised myself that I would never take them for granted again. All I wanted was to be back in the safety of my bedroom with my teddies, my Madonna duvet and even my toeless pumps that I kept under my bed. As I crouched there, panting and hanging onto the branch, I knew that I didn't have the strength to pull myself back up the grassy slope and I wasn't even sure if the branch was strong enough to hold me for much longer. By now, my grip was beginning to weaken and I actually thought I only had minutes to live.

'I decided to test the branch to see how strong it was when something caught my eye and nearly made me lose my grip altogether. Some sort of hairy animal was rushing out of the woods and coming towards me. I couldn't tell what sort of animal it was but under the circumstances I didn't really care. "Help me, please help me," I sobbed to this thing and a second later a long, furry arm reached out. It curled its sturdy fingers around my wrist and clamped it like a vice. Then, it began to haul me up with one of its hands. It was so strong that it completely tore the twisted branch

I was holding, from the tree. As I was being hoisted back from the cliff edge, the wind dropped and I lifted my head and said a prayer of thanks to the cloudless blue sky above me. That's how I gave Him his name – Mr Blue Sky, because that was my first real sighting of Him, with his black hairy head set against the clear blue sky. Anyway, he lifted me out of danger and dragged me across the grass to a small clearing just inside the woods, woods which didn't seem so scary anymore.

'Completely bewildered, I stared across at this creature sitting before me. He was covered from head to foot in thick black fur, except for the face which was like a hairless mask. It was a normal, human flesh colour but it definitely wasn't human. Some of its features were similar to the features of a young person but not exactly. The forehead and cheekbones were different; they protruded outwards more like a primitive ape and his thumbs were as long as his fingers. But his eyes did not look like any eyes I had ever seen before; they were a bright, tangerine orange.

'I was so shaken up and confused by everything that had just happened, that I didn't have the energy to feel scared of Him. I just wanted to get a closer look so I leant forward, as much as I dared, but as I did he wound his head away from me. I was fairly sure this creature was a male and despite his reaction, I was sure that he was just as curious about me as I was about Him.

'As we stared at each other, I noticed that his eyes never stopped moving; they were constantly checking the area around us. I wasn't sure what he was looking for so I shifted my position to get a wider view. But my legs began to ache so I shifted my position again. It was this sudden movement that made Him flinch. Surely, I thought, he wasn't frightened of me?

"I'm not going to harm you," I told Him.

'The creature's nose began to twitch and he started to sniff the air around us as if he sensed something. As I watched Him, I wondered if he was smelling the drying pee on my socks. I also wondered what kind of creature he was as I'd never seen anything like Him before, not even in a zoo.

'As it was obvious that I wasn't in any danger, I began to relax a bit more and I tried to communicate with Him. "Thanks for saving me," I said. The creature's orange eyes continued to flick to and fro and his head tilted to one side the way a confused dog tries to understand its master. "Do you understand me?" I asked Him. "Can you speak?"

'The creature's only response was to make sniffing sounds as if that was the only way he could answer. I then became aware of a stinging pain in my hand and I opened my palm to inspect it and found a few deep red welts. I probably got them from my desperate grip on the branch. Then, the creature's furry hand reached over and with his fingers he gently dabbed at the flesh near my wounds. At first, I felt a bit uncomfortable and wanted to pull my hand back but I decided that such a move might confuse or scare Him. Actually, his gentle dabbing was quite soothing on my cuts. After examining my wounds closely the creature wet one of his fingertips and proceeded to dab them with his own saliva. I wasn't too keen on what he was doing and I found his touch a bit ticklish. In spite of my misgivings, I couldn't help giving a little giggle. But this new sound seemed to alarm Him and he snatched back his hairy hand.

"No, it's OK, nothing to be afraid of, I'm only laughing, that's all." I tried to explain but he just sat there looking totally bewildered. "I'm Rebecca," I introduced myself. "Rebecca," I repeated tapping my chest.

'The creature raised his head and with a vigorous grunt he tried to mimic the expression on my face. A bit unnerved by this, I stopped what I was doing and tried a different approach. I slowly pronounced my name and the creature studied my lips and then tried to imitate the shape my mouth was making. He wasn't doing a very good job of it and what came out of his mouth sounded like a cross between a low growl and the word "amber".

"No, silly," I corrected Him. "Rebecca, Rebecca." Over time, he made the growl sound like "Ecca".

'Up until that point, everything seemed to be going quite well then, suddenly, his mood changed and he began making aggressive movements with his hands. He was trying to draw my attention to his mouth and to my mouth. Initially, it scared me a bit but I eventually worked out that he was trying to get me to be quiet. I did what I thought he wanted and he tilted his head to one side and froze. I listened out for any sounds but I couldn't hear anything at first. Then, I picked up the soft murmuring of male voices so low that they sounded like talking on a TV with the volume turned right down. They were coming from some distance away. The creature's body stiffened and he looked as if an intense fear was running through Him. We sat there and waited until we couldn't hear the voices anymore and the only sounds left were the birds tweeting in the trees.

'Relaxing, the creature came back to life and sprang to his feet so I did the same. As we stood face to face I realised that he was a few inches shorter than I was but despite his size you could already see very powerful muscles beginning to develop on his chest, arms and shoulders. Catching me off guard and without any warning, he turned his back and ploughed through the thick foliage into the woods. I had no idea where he was going but I decided to follow Him anyway.

'Eventually, he led me back to the very same place where I had first spotted Him and he began a frantic search for something in the dense patch of ferns. Whatever it was had left a flattened imprint on the ferns and on the soft mulchy ground underneath. Suddenly, the creature became more and more agitated as he searched. "What are you looking for?" I asked, trying to help but he ignored me as his futile search ended in defeat and he slumped miserably to the ground.

"Show me what you are looking for," I repeated and he began to press his furry hands along the ground as if trying to show me the size of what had made the imprint. I shook my head indicating to Him that I didn't understand. The creature did his best to try and make me understand by clutching his fist to his chest and by sucking his thumb. Helplessly, I shrugged and he gave up. He made a kind of sobbing noise and laid down in the empty space left in the ferns. Immediately, I felt pity for Him as he was obviously deeply upset, as upset as I had been when I had called for my mum and dad. I desperately wanted to help, especially after he had just saved my life. But I also needed to get back home before my mother discovered that I was missing. God only knew what she would do if she found out that I had sneaked off into the forbidden woods.

"I'm really sorry that you have lost someone or something but I really need to get back home to my parents," I told Him.

'Of course he didn't understand what I was saying but I said it again anyway. This time, he stood up and looked into my eyes. The sadness in his face was heart-breaking. I mouthed the words, *Home; can you help me?* I think he must have worked out what I wanted because he reluctantly started to track back through the woods and I followed. It didn't take Him very long to guide me to a break in the trees where I could see the familiar dandelion fields that led back home. Before I left Him, I turned to say thanks again for saving me and showing me the way. There was a lost, longing look in the creature's orange eyes as he gave me the briefest of nods. Somehow, we had managed to communicate with each other.'

Richard cleared his throat and took a sip of water. 'So, was this boy-ape, as you called Him, perhaps an escaped animal?'

'I don't know where he came from even to this day and he certainly couldn't tell me because he couldn't speak.'

'You've mentioned that he was young; how old would you say he was?'

'I don't know but at a guess, maybe somewhere near my own age.'

'Do you think he'd been living alone all by himself in the woods all that time?' Richard asked.

'Perhaps he wasn't alone. He was looking for someone or something in the woods; maybe there might have been another similar creature or a keeper with Him?'

Richard rifled through his notes. 'Yes, that's right, you said he patted down an area indicating that something had been lying there. In the notes, made by my previous colleagues, you suspected that there might have been one or more with Him.' Richard screwed his eyes up as he looked through his thick-rimmed glasses. 'You said that maybe he had been searching for an injured sibling or a parent. But you didn't happen to see anything when you first startled Him?'

'No, the ferns were too close together and as soon as I saw Him, I ran off so I didn't have time to look.'

'Forgive me, but I know you have probably answered most of these questions before but sometimes, when you go back and review things, you might pick up on something you may have previously missed. And in your case, these valuable bits of information can turn out to be the missing pieces of your unfinished jigsaw.'

Rebecca creased her brow as she considered the possibility.

'And in all the time you spent with Him during those early years you never saw any sign of any other members of his family, if indeed, he ever had any?'

'No, but something must have given birth to Him; something had to rear Him. He didn't just pop out of a bush of ferns.'

Richard smiled at Rebecca's light sarcasm. 'Yes, the reports that you have given to my other colleagues have been quite informative and you have gone into some detail about his habitat and his way of life. But before we get into all that, I want us to take it one step at a time so we can give each aspect of your account a thorough going through. Perhaps if we try and approach it from a different angle we may get lucky and uncover something useful.'

'Why don't you just come out and say it? You don't believe me any more than all the other therapists – do you?' Rebecca blurted out.

'But the point is, you believe it, Rebecca, and until I, or anyone else, can prove otherwise, who has the right to say that you're not telling the truth?'

'It did happen, it did happen,' Rebecca insisted.

'OK, so just to recap, you do believe that other members of his family may have existed but you don't have the evidence to back it up. Do you know if anyone else saw Him? I mean, it's unlikely that an anthropoid, living in the woodlands for eight years or so, would have gone unnoticed.'

'Well, I do think that other people were aware that he existed. As I've already said in earlier sessions, in the weeks after our first meeting in the woods, I did spot people wearing white suits going in there every now and again. I had also spotted a horsebox parked on the road to the woods but I don't suppose that was anything to do with them.'

'So, were these people in suits the same ones you heard after he first rescued you from the cliff edge?'

'I don't know, I didn't actually see them clearly but I did hear them.'

'Who do you think the people in the white suits were?'

'I don't know and I never talked about it with my parents because then they would know that I'd been in the woods.'

'Well, don't you think that if these people went in to look for Him they would have found Him?'

'Not if he was hiding.'

'So, where might he hide from them?'

'His home.'

'How do you know he had a home?'

'Because I stayed there with Him.'

Richard glared at her over the rim of his glasses then his Adam's apple bobbed up and down. 'I think we'll leave it there for now and carry on in the next session.'

Nodding her head, Rebecca sagged in her chair. She was exhausted and felt as if she'd just run a ten-mile race.

CHAPTER THREE

Rebecca locked her car then strolled across the road to her uncle's warehouse. Just as she was about to pass through the gateway she glanced down the street and caught sight of a man watching her as he leant against the chain-link fencing that ran along the front of the other units. She stopped for a moment thinking that it might be someone she knew but she didn't recognise him. He was wearing a long, dark raincoat and his hair was short, slicked back and far too black to be natural. He was late middle-aged but looked as if he worked out. Rebecca stopped and waited for a second to see if he might look away but he didn't. With a swagger, he took a long drag of his cigarette and moved forward then stopped. He stared at her and his stare became challenging, even intimidating. Feeling uncomfortable, even rattled, Rebecca walked away anxious to avoid a possible confrontation.

In the warehouse office, her Uncle Jim was sitting at the computer with the mini heater switched on maximum, making the room sleepily warm. 'All right, Beccs?' he asked not even looking up from the screen.

Taking off her coat and dumping her oversized leather handbag on her chair, she blocked out his view of the screen with the splayed-out fingers of her hand. 'There's a man standing down the road. Do you know who he is? He was giving me a bit of the stares.'

'What man?'

'Down near the printing firm, there's a man leaning against the fence. He was just staring at me.'

'Get away! A man standing outside watching you? I'll get the cops on it straight away,' Jim scoffed.

Rebecca gave her uncle a questioning look. 'He definitely looked a bit suspicious. Maybe he's casing the joint, planning a robbery or something.'

'Maybe he fancied you or maybe he's planning to kidnap you and demand a ransom of a million quid.'

Rebecca ignored his facetious comments and moved over to the window to try and see if the staring man was still there but a van blocked her sight. 'No, I can't see him now, a van is in the way.'

Jim carried on making light of the situation. 'He was probably waiting for someone. I bet he was thinking, why does that nosey bugger keep staring at me?'

Rebecca snorted and gave up.

Jim closed the file on the computer screen. 'So, how did the session go with the psycho?'

Rebecca shrugged. 'OK, I suppose. I've booked another two sessions before I go back home.'

'Three sessions in three weeks. Better watch he doesn't have you sectioned.'

Rebecca gave him a long, withering look as she made her way over to the coffee machine.

The coffee from the machine was like dirty dishwater but she couldn't be bothered to put the kettle on.

Jim just grinned and laid back in his creaky seat. He knitted his fingers together across his hill-of-a-belly. 'What did you talk about then?'

The coffee machine gurgled and clicked as it filled the first plastic cup with a white coffee.

'Oh, he wants me to start right from the beginning all over again. Or, as he puts it, have a good clear out by starting in the basement.'

Jim leaned forward in his seat. 'You mean he's going to make you dredge up all that nonsense, again?'

'I suppose.' She shrugged her shoulders.

'Well, it's no bloody wonder you're feeling a bit paranoid then, is it?'

'I'm not paranoid,' Rebecca snapped as she placed two cups of coffee on the table.

Jim reached over for his drink. Changing the subject, her uncle reminded her about their night out. 'Hey, I intend to take you out for a meal before you go home. Don't forget it's your birthday soon.'

Rebecca's face lit up and she smiled as she blew into her coffee. 'Ah, that would be nice, thanks.'

'Just me, you and Judith; a nice little get-together. By the way, have you told your mother that you're going home, yet?'

Rebecca stopped blowing into her drink. 'No, not yet. I will, though.'

'Well, sooner rather than later, Beccs. You know she doesn't like surprises and she likes to know what's going on.'

'I know, I know, I'll tell her, don't worry.'

Jim's seat squealed as he relieved it of his weight. Taking his coffee with him, he made his way to the door.

'Where are you going?'

'Be back in a minute; just checking something that I forgot.'

Rebecca continued to sip her coffee and wonder about the mysterious man who had been watching her earlier.

* * *

The rest of the day was uneventful and after work Rebecca left the office and walked across her uncle's forecourt. When she reached the ten-foot chain-link gates, she peered across to check if the man was still there. To her relief, she couldn't see him. Feeling a bit silly she was just about to unlock her car when a figure jostled against her. Rebecca jolted back in fright and almost swore in shock as she saw it was the same man she had seen earlier. The man didn't stop or acknowledge her but kept striding away, leaving the smell of his heavily gelled hair behind him. Alarmed, Rebecca hurried back to her uncle in the office.

'He's still there, he's still there,' she wailed.

'Who? What?' Jim said absently. He was more interested in reading a text on his phone than in what she was saying.

'The man I saw this morning, he's just walked past the warehouse.'

'He's just walked past the warehouse, has he? I tell yer, girl, the depths society has plummeted to when people can just walk anywhere they want; it's absolutely criminal.'

'Stop teasing me, Jim. He's following me, I know it. Please, just take a look.'

Jim didn't move. He sat at his desk staring at her with a worried expression. 'Listen, Beccs, if this is what these therapy sessions are doing to you then I suggest you stop them right now.'

Dejectedly, Rebecca slumped down into her chair.

Seeing that she was upset, Jim got up and went over to her. He lowered his voice so that none of the lads in the warehouse could hear. 'Listen, Beccs, I don't want you dragging up all that shit again. And I don't want to have to watch you come apart all over again, either. You seemed fine until you went back to that therapist. What's going on?'

But Rebecca had to be careful about what she said. She didn't want to arouse any suspicions about Mr Blue Sky. How could she tell her uncle what was really going on? He wouldn't understand and it might make things worse. She lifted her head with a weary smile. 'Maybe I'm just a bit tired, that's all. Maybe I'm ready for that time off.'

Jim squeezed her shoulder fondly. 'Go home, luv, and have a good sleep. I'll see you bright and bushy-tailed in the morning, OK?'

Rebecca nodded back.

Sitting in her flat that evening, Rebecca stared at her mobile phone as if it was an unfamiliar pet sitting in her lap. The thought of phoning her mother to let her know she was coming back home was daunting. At present, her relationship with her mother was virtually non-existent. She had hardly seen her over the last fifteen years. Rebecca replayed the same old resentments in her head. Her mother would always hold her responsible for the death of her father. Of course, her mother had never come out and openly said all this when Rebecca lived at home but she had certainly insinuated it and that was why Rebecca knew that she had to leave.

The session with Richard had brought back so many unresolved issues; one of which being the fact that she and her father did not get along the way a father and daughter were supposed to, especially during the final years of his life.

Added to this was the fact that her father was a heavy drinker which made it impossible to reason with him during their heated disagreements. But what used to infuriate Rebecca more than anything was that her mother never supported her. Her father was a big man and when he used to give Rebecca a good verbal bashing he towered over her with clenched fists. But her mother never stepped in to try and stop him even when he was way out of line. And all the bad feeling that had subsequently developed between her and her mother had kept that bubbling cauldron of tension simmering over the years.

The mobile phone was still lying in her lap; she couldn't put it off any longer. With a deep sigh she snatched it up and punched in her mother's landline number. As she waited for the line to connect she felt her stomach knotting up. Just how was her mum going to react when she told her that she was going to stay for a short while? The dialling tone continued. *Perhaps she's gone to bed early* Rebecca thought, *a slight reprieve. I might have to try again tomorrow, I'll give it a few rings…* the line clicked and she heard her mother's voice on the other end of the line. Rebecca's heart sank.

'Hello…Mum, it's me.'

'Oh, Rebecca, I didn't expect to hear from you tonight.'

'No, I thought I'd give you a ring… How are you?' Rebecca winced at the phoney pleasantries.

'Oh, I'm fine, how are you?'

'Yeah, I'm fine, too.'

'That's good.' Her mother sounded guarded.

The conversation that followed between them was very tentative. They were just like two people trying to find their way through the rubble of a broken relationship. They remained distant and polite but when Rebecca finally plucked up the courage to broach the subject of her wanting to go over and stay for a few weeks, her mother actually sounded genuinely pleased. Rebecca couldn't have been more surprised.

She didn't know what to make of her mother's reaction. Ending the call, Rebecca dropped the phone back in her lap and played the whole exchange back in her head. Thinking about it, she thought she actually sensed vulnerability in her mother's voice as if she was reaching out to her. *That's a first*, she mused.

Outside, the wind suddenly began to rattle against the windowpane, startling her. She got up and went over to the window to check on the weather. Turning back the curtain she stared out into the inky black night. It looked cold and uninviting out there, especially with an eerie mist clinging to the tops of the orange sodium streetlights. Rebecca shivered and released the curtain then swiftly snatched it back; something had caught her eye. In the street there was a figure leaning against the brick wall opposite. Rebecca tried to get a better look, while holding her breath to stop it from clouding the window.

Yes, there was a figure. A Stetson hat hid the face and a floor-length raincoat covered the short body. Rebecca's eyes widened as she watched the crown of the hat slowly tilting up towards her. When the hat was removed a grotesque face stared back at her. It was sheet white and plastered with, what appeared to be, clown's greasepaint. It grinned up at her menacingly. It looked like something out of a travelling circus and it sent cold chills up and down her spine. The circus-clown figure continued to hold its grin while it performed a stage-show bow. But it didn't quite come off because its body seemed to be slightly twisted and one shoulder was higher than the other. It also had abnormally short arms. It looked as if it was making a formal introduction. Unnerved by this bizarre spectacle Rebecca wrenched the curtain back across the window and ran to the front door to make sure it was safely bolted.

'What and who the hell was that?' she panted. 'What the hell is a circus clown doing around here? It's me, I know it is, it has got to be me. I'm the reason.'

Fear curled through her and her imagination went into overdrive. She grabbed her phone to call her uncle but stopped herself as doubts raced through her mind. What would he think after she freaked out today? He obviously thought she was overreacting about the man who, she claimed, was stalking her. *He's probably already told John and Terry at work and they're probably having a good laugh about it. What, in God's name, will they all think if I start going on about a clown outside my flat, terrorising me? They'll think I've gone off on a real toot. No…I'll have a glass of wine and calm down. I'm probably being neurotic; I'm just getting carried away. The figure outside is most likely a person dressed up as a clown to go to a fancy dress or something and he's just waiting for someone. I'll wake up in the morning and realise that I was being manic.*

But, despite all her self-reassurances, Rebecca fetched her pillows and duvet from the bedroom and made up a bed on the couch. She filled her hot water bottle and hugged the white, fluffy cover to her as she wrapped herself in the duvet. But despite her attempts to relieve her fears, she left a lamp switched on and only slept lightly, just in case.

CHAPTER FOUR

'Are you sure you don't want to have these sessions taped? It might be very beneficial to you when you hear the playback,' Richard asked.

'No, honestly. Having to go through it all over again is more than enough for me. And I wouldn't want the tape to fall into the wrong hands.'

'That would never happen. Everything here is kept safe and in strict confidence.'

'Thanks, but no,' Rebecca repeated firmly.

'OK, then,' Richard said as he settled back into his leather armchair. 'You've already established how you and Mr Blue met so would you like to continue and tell me how your relationship progressed with him?'

Rebecca rested her head against the back of her armchair as she tried to jog her memory.

'Not very long after he saved me I can remember things started happening. At night he would come and stand outside my bedroom window and make this strange whistle. It was sort of high pitched, something like the pitch of a whistle a shepherd would use to control his sheepdog.' She tried to mimic it for Richard, but it came out more like a weak hiss. 'It wasn't anything like that and it did have a funny curl running through it. It wasn't very loud or anything but very clear and melodic; I thought it was so sweet and silvery sounding. It reminded me of one of those wind chimes or tubular bells. There were stretches when he would come most nights and announce his presence with this whistle.

'You see, my bedroom was at the rear of the farmhouse and there were plenty of bushes for cover. If someone was standing right outside you wouldn't necessarily see them. Blue, as I used to call him for short, would wait on the edge of the bushes and I would open my window, call his name softly and throw Him some food; he liked our food. Sometimes, I would even throw Him some of my father's old clothes that had been put in plastic bags ready to give to charity. I know Blue had a thick, hairy coat but he still shivered in the cold winter months and he would drape my dad's extra-large shirts, jumpers and jackets around his shoulders. He would only stay for a short while, in case he got spotted, then he would go back home. He looked very comical as he left. He would clutch my dad's tatty, old clothes around his neck, but he often dropped them and had to keep bending down to pick them up.

'It was a good job we didn't have any dogs; they would have barked and frightened Him off for sure. After he went home, I used to lie in bed and wonder where his home was and if he would be all right when the weather was bad. I would worry about Him getting wet, but the bad weather never stopped Him, and he would still come to the house and stand there, in the wind and rain, waiting for me to open my window. I wished I could have let Him in, so he could have warmed himself.'

'You didn't feel any danger from Him, then?' Richard asked.

'No, why should I have? He saved my life, remember. In a way it made me feel like I had a special friend.'

'And you didn't tell your parents about Him at that time?'

'Not in the early years. I didn't want to risk my father chasing Him off or calling the police. If he had, that would have meant that I probably wouldn't have seen Blue again.'

'So, was it just at night that you used to see Him?'

'No,' Rebecca retorted. 'In the spring and summer months I would sneak off to the woods to play with Him. I would try to do his whistle to call Him but most of the time he always seemed to know I was there. In the woods, we were careful where we played because we didn't want to get lost in case we ended up on the cliff edge again. Later, warning signs were posted all around the woods to let people know of the danger.'

'So, what sort of games did you and Blue play in the woods?'

'Hide and seek, mostly, or tip and run. I taught Him both of them. In the summer months, when the grasses were high in the dandelion fields, we could play there because no one could see us. Plus, it was easier for me to get my mum's permission because she didn't mind me playing so close to the house, just as long as I didn't stay too long. But I still wasn't supposed to go into the woods. Anyway, I preferred playing in the fields because they weren't as creepy as the woods could be.'

'And you still didn't feel afraid of Him?'

Rebecca shook her head dismissively. 'No, but I do remember one time when he scared me, though. A woman had let her big Alsatian dog off the lead and it came bounding over to us. It must have caught Blue's scent. Blue panicked and I'd never seen Him run so fast. In those days, he mostly scampered along on all fours like an ape. He soon disappeared back into the woods, leaving me following behind through the dandelion fields. The dog shot past me and went after Blue. In the distance, I could hear the dog's owner frantically calling and whistling. I remember feeling so frightened for Blue. I didn't know what the dog might do if it got hold of Him.

'When I got into the woods the dog was growling and snarling at the base of this great big chestnut tree and Blue was wedged up high in the branches. Then, when the dog saw me, it suddenly turned and began to go for me, its fangs showing and saliva dripping from its mouth. I was petrified and couldn't run because I knew if I did it would lunge at me, and I began to cry.' Rebecca paused for a moment.

'Then I saw a change in Blue; something awoke in Him, some kind of primordial instinct. A pure rage seemed to shoot through his body. Seeing me threatened and upset had triggered a strong, protective reaction. I didn't even see Him jump, I just saw this massive Alsatian crumble under his weight as Blue landed on him. The dog was too winded and too stunned to do anything about it as Blue sank his own fangs into the dog's neck. He began gnawing away at it like a tiger attacking its prey. I thought he was going to rip the dog's head off.

'Luckily for the dog, Blue's teeth weren't fully developed then. Of course, the dog tried to fight back but when it turned its head to try and bite Blue, Blue clamped its head more tightly in his mouth and twisted it, trying to break its neck. I didn't know that he was so strong, and I wanted to stop Him. 'No!' I cried… 'No'! He looked up at me with this wild, crazy glint in his orange eyes like nothing else was getting through to Him except the compelling urge to kill. 'Blue…No,' I shouted to Him again and this time the killing force seemed to die in his eyes. He stared at me and recognition slowly began to register and the old Blue, the Blue I knew came back to me. Still drooling, he swung away from the dog and bolted through the bushes.

'As soon as he'd gone, the dog staggered to its feet and began to limp off just as its owner arrived; a middle-aged woman, puffing and panting. Seeing its owner, the dog whimpered and flattened itself on the ground.

'The woman knelt down and gathered it in her arms. She asked me if I was OK. Although I was still a bit shaken I said I was all right. There was blood on the dog's neck and the woman asked me how he had been injured. I said I didn't know. Talking to him soothingly, she checked him over and told me that she would take him to the vet. She phoned her husband and let him know what had happened to the dog, but she said she didn't know how it had happened. She told him he needed to come and pick them up in the car. I said perhaps he had cut himself on a broken branch or something. I don't think she believed me, but she didn't get angry.

Instead, she suggested that I shouldn't stay in the woods by myself. She told me it was too risky, and she asked me where I lived. When she found out that I only lived a short distance away, she decided that it would probably be best if she saw me safely home before her husband arrived to pick her up.

'I didn't see Blue again for a couple of days after that. I think he must have been too shaken up and afraid to venture out.'

'But when you did see Him again, you continued to meet up on and off in the same way as before?'

'Oh, yes, as the years rolled by, I continued to see him regularly, although sometimes, he would disappear for a couple of months and I would start to worry that something might have happened to Him. But he always turned up in the end and even when he was gone for weeks and weeks, deep down I sort of knew that he was all right.'

Richard took a long sip of water and swallowed noisily. He then asked, 'How did you actually talk or communicate with Blue during the times that you spent with Him? Did he use some type of sign language?'

'Yes, a type of sign language; he would use his hands, fingers and facial expressions to communicate with me.'

'You can understand animal sign language?' Richard asked doing his best not to look sceptical.

'Only his sign language.'

'Did he teach you that?'

'No, not really. That's the strange thing; as time went on, we developed a way of letting each other know what we wanted to say. I always seemed to get what he meant when he made his signs. I never had any trouble understanding Him; it became second nature to me.'

Richard glanced at the previous notes then commented, 'I don't recall reading anything about this use of sign language in any of your other notes. Please give me a minute while I add this new information to your file, then we can carry on.'

When Richard was ready Rebecca continued. 'Besides the sign language we used, I tried to teach Him how to understand basic reading and writing.'

'Yes, all that information is here.'

'That didn't take Him all that long to get the idea, either. He appeared to pick it up quite quickly but only very simple stuff. In the summer, we used to sit in the long grass with half a dozen nursery books and I would read all sorts of stories to Him. He liked that a lot. He loved looking at the pictures and hearing me do different voices. Once he got to know about reading and writing he would copy short, easy words in my exercise book; words which I could just about understand.'

'What sort of things would he write?'

'To be honest, his writing wasn't all that great. He couldn't form proper letters and they were a bit unpredictable. Most of the time, it was much easier using our sign language.'

'It must have been an amazing breakthrough, though, to actually see Him trying to communicate with written words.' Richard sounded incredulous.

Rebecca chuckled to herself. 'One time, I think he wrote my name as B E G R. It was difficult to make it out because the letters were so wobbly. Anyway, it made me sound like a German.'

'He knew your name then?'

'He knew it, he just couldn't say it or spell it. As I have already said, he ended up signing Ecca.'

Richard obviously wanted to explore the subject of Mr Blue's extraordinary sign language ability much further and questioned Rebecca for another half hour. When he eventually finished, he glanced up from the folder and gave her the kind of smile that was difficult to decipher. 'OK, I think we'll leave it there for now. Next time, if you feel comfortable enough, we'll talk about the events that led up to the night of your father's death, if that is all right with you?'

CHAPTER FIVE

On Rebecca's day off, she liked to drive down into town to do some serious browsing. She did most of the clothes shops including the ones she couldn't afford. After trawling through the rails from Top Shop to Next, she always treated herself to a Starbucks' skinny vanilla latte and a fudge slice.

Cradling her drink in her hands, Rebecca sat at a window table staring out at the busy high street. She loved to people watch and the faces of some of the young guys with their girlfriends always entertained her. More often than not, they looked bored-to-tears as their persistent girlfriends dragged them from shop to shop, to shop, to shop. But some of the older couples had a different approach to the shopping thing; they had it sorted. The older men would kiss their wives goodbye and then scarper off, probably to the local, for a sneaky pint or two.

But the couples that interested her most were the teenage girls and young women out shopping with their mothers. In all of the fifteen years she had been living away from home, this was one of the things she thought about a lot and felt she had missed out on. She would have liked days out shopping with her mum.

As she reflected on past regrets, Rebecca noticed one particular mother and daughter couple happily strolling along the covered walkway. The daughter was a pretty, fair-haired girl of about twenty-five and the mother was in her fifties with well-cut, short greying hair. She had deep laugh lines around her eyes and mouth, but she was still an attractive woman. They looked like stereotypical, respectable, middle-class people. Probably had a nice house, nice family life with regular summer barbecues at the weekends and frequent holidays abroad. As they passed by the coffee shop, they were absorbed in a light-hearted conversation, chatting and laughing. Rebecca imagined what they might be talking about. Perhaps the hottest line of Pandora jewellery or the latest tangled plot in one of the TV soap operas. *What fun,* Rebecca thought, *what sweet, innocent, happy fun.*

Rebecca began to picture herself spending the day out with her own mother. But she didn't know if her mother liked the same shops as she did, or the same type of clothes or even the same type of jewellery. And what would happen when they visited a coffee shop afterwards? Would they pay for their own drinks or would her mother treat them both? If her mother was sitting opposite her right now, could they have a proper mother-daughter conversation? Would her mother be able to give her the kind of parental reassurance and guidance she needed? Would her mother reassure her and tell her not to worry and that everything was going to be all right? Would she tell her that she would always be there for her and she would do everything possible to help if she was in trouble?

How comforting, safe and secure that would make Rebecca feel. After all, she mused, girls never really grow up as long as they have a mother around to take care of them. They don't stop needing their mums, not even when they find a long-term partner and have children. Surely, that's the way it should be; the mothers of today paving the way and laying the foundations for the mothers of tomorrow? *But if that's true, where does that leave me and my mum?* she asked herself. Rebecca took another sip of her drink and once again faced the fact that her relationship with her mother had never fitted in with the so-called norm.

That's when she spotted him, sitting at the far end of the cafe: the man wearing a long raincoat, the man with short, slicked-back black hair, the man who had been staring at her outside work the other day. Rebecca felt her heart start to beat faster and she had difficulty catching her breath. Desperately, she mouthed a silent prayer that it was just a coincidence, a coincidence that he was here, in the same place. Trying not to look obvious, she peered at him out of the corner of her eye. As she did, he looked up and stared directly at her.

Quickly, she turned away and tried to get a grip on her fear and slow down the pounding of her heart.

The look said it all; this was no coincidence. That look was conclusive proof that she had been right to be suspicious. He had not just happened to be hanging about outside her work. Now, she knew he was following her. This was no chance meeting. What were the odds that he would turn up in the same town, same high street, at the same time and in the same cafe? She needed to think so she stared out of the cafe window.

Should she calmly get up and walk out and pretend that nothing was wrong, or should she walk over and confront him? Should she pluck up the courage to ask who he was and why was he following her? No, perhaps not. She chewed her bottom lip nervously. Maybe, she should threaten to report him to the police. But what if they didn't take her seriously, just like Uncle Jim? She would probably end up looking like a complete fool.

What if she played it a bit clever and told him that she thought that she knew him from somewhere? Yes, that might break the ice and give her the chance to work out why he was stalking her. But she must take it easy and be tactful. Rebecca thought about chancing another look, but if he caught her, it might encourage him to come over to her and then she would lose the edge.

But curiosity got the better of her and she couldn't stop herself. She stole another glance at him just as he was rising from his table.

It looked like he was heading over, and Rebecca panicked, her heart racing again. What do I do? What do I do? But she was too scared to do anything. She just sat there, eyes down, fixed on the table in front of her. She hoped that he would just walk past and out of the door. The seconds ticked by as she waited and waited and then he was there, standing beside her.

'Excuse me?' The sound of his voice made her jump so violently that she knocked her empty mug over. It rolled to the edge of the table, but his hand shot out and he caught it before it fell on the floor.

Jerking her head up, Rebecca saw the man's face close up for the first time. She gave a strangled scream, leapt to her feet, grabbed her handbag and bolted out of the cafe. She dashed back to the car park and flung herself into her car, slamming the door shut and locking it. Shaking from head to foot, she tried to pull herself together. But she couldn't get the man's image out of her mind: the carefully gelled black hair, the bloodless complexion, the cruel, thin lips and his piercing, pale grey eyes, eyes that were so pale they seemed to be almost opaque. But the strangest thing of all, was the fact that there was something disturbingly familiar about him.

* * *

When she went to work the next day, Rebecca couldn't wait to tell her uncle what had happened.

'That just goes to prove it, doesn't it? I wasn't imagining it.' Rebecca trailed behind him as he humped out boxes of supplies from the back of his van.

But Jim wasn't buying it. 'A strange coincidence, maybe. The fact that he was stalking you, I find doubtful.'

Rebecca yelled in frustration. 'What do I have to do to make you believe me? Maybe I should just wait until he takes me down some dark alley to rape me before I ask him why the hell he is following me, shall I?'

Jim stopped what he was doing and put his hands on her shoulders. 'And maybe if you hadn't done a runner on him in the cafe and stopped to hear what he wanted to say to you, you might not be standing here in such a state.'

'You must be joking, you don't know the half of it. The other night, when I looked out of the window of my flat, I saw another weird-looking guy, wearing clown's make-up, a hat and a long raincoat standing at the corner of the road staring up at me.'

'Well, I never, another man, this time a clown in a hat staring up at you. Don't go around telling anyone else that. They'll think you have really lost it. Keep it to yourself and put it down to one of the many great mysteries of life.'

Rebecca knocked her uncle's hands off her shoulders and stepped away from him.

'You just refuse to believe a word I say, don't you?'

Jim lifted another box out of the van and stopped again. 'It's not that I don't believe you, Beccs, I just think that your counselling sessions have triggered something in your imagination and it's playing strange tricks on you.'

'Just what the hell is that supposed to mean?'

'It simply means, that you need to chill out, relax, take a step back and try not to be so emotional. Who knows, you might see things a little differently?' Turning back to the boxes, he didn't notice how lost Rebecca looked as she envisaged the tormented days and nights that, she was sure, lay ahead of her.

* * *

As she made her way through the dark woods, her bare feet crunched painfully on the cold, wet twigs and foliage. All she was wearing were her polka-dot pyjamas, giving her no protection against the driving rain and blustering wind that lashed at her body. She stopped and stood there shivering, trying to decide which way she should go. By now, her pyjamas were so wet that they had literally become a second skin against her body. The wind was whipping the trees and bushes into a frenzy. It sounded like they were growling and cursing her. Were the woods angry at her intrusive presence?

Rebecca was trembling so much, from the cold and wet, that she could hardy move. She squatted down and hugged herself into a ball to try and generate some warmth and comfort. Through the rain, she thought she caught sight of a dark shadow beside one of the tall tree trunks. She squinted as tiny rivulets of rainwater ran into her eyes hampering her vision, and she wiped them so she could see more clearly. She wasn't sure if the shadow she saw was something real or just a trick of the half-light. But then, the shape moved, and an actual, tangible figure stepped out from behind the tree. Rebecca gasped as she recognised her father.

'Rebecca?' he called out to her, his voice almost drowned out by the raging noise of the storm.

'Dad?' she called. 'Dad?'

Her father came closer and she saw he was wearing a long raincoat. He held out his hand and beckoned her to him. 'Don't be afraid, Rebecca, come to me.'

But Rebecca hesitated. She didn't want to go to him; even though it was her father, something just didn't feel quite right.

'Rebecca, go to your father,' another voice ordered her.

Rebecca turned towards the direction of the voice and she saw a young boy with curly hair blowing in the wind.

'Patrick?' she gasped. It was her childhood sweetheart, her sweetheart from her schooldays, the only proper boyfriend she ever had.

Patrick stood there, in his school uniform blazer and grinned at her, his mouth stretching wider and wider until the corners almost reached his eyes. As the lapels of his blazer flapped wildly in the gale, Rebecca saw his grin slowly turn malevolent, making him look sinister.

'But how can you be here? Why?' she asked.

'Rebecca, you must go to him,' Patrick demanded, his voice taking on a man's deep tone.

Warily, Rebecca climbed to her feet. She should have been so relieved to see them both. Her father and Patrick were here, they had come to be with her. But then, Patrick lowered his head and fitted on a Stetson hat and straightened out the headband.

'Rebecca?' her father called out to her impatiently, his voice lowering to a deep boom.

'That's not my father.' Rebecca shook her head from side to side and as she did, she heard Patrick begin to chuckle. At first a creepy "tee-hee" that trickled down into an evil crow.

Slowly, she began to back away from the menacing figures and that was when Patrick raised his head once more to reveal an entirely different appearance. This one had a hideous painted face. It was painted in white greasepaint just like the clown figure she saw staring up at her the other night. It looked like the comic-book version of Batman's nemesis, the Joker.

'Go away, the pair of you, leave me alone. What do you want?' Rebecca stammered backing away, the bracken crackling under her feet.

'No, no, Rebecca, it's what you want.' The clownish grinner stabbed a bony finger towards her, a finger that had a long, pointed, blue varnished nail.

'What do you mean, what I want?'

'You want to see Him, don't you?'

'Him?'

The grinning clown rocked back and forth, back and forth and he let out a loud, demonic laugh. As he did, the gale ceased and the woods were silent. Rebecca glanced around in fear and astonishment, then turned back to face the evil presence before her.

'He's coming for you, Rebecca, he's ready for you now.'

'Who is ready for me? What are you talking about?'

'Aw, come on now…how could you forget Him after all you've been through together?'

The Grinner was edging towards her with tiny, determined steps, forcing her to back away. Then, he stopped. 'He's coming, he's on his way and he wants to see you, Rebecca. Oh, and he's big now, very big,' the Grinner crowed.

Rebecca knew only too well who he was referring to and in a hoarse voice she asked, 'What does he want from me?'

'He wants your SOUL,' announced the Grinner. As his words echoed through the woods Rebecca could hear all the branches in the trees begin to crack and snap. Terror-stricken, she searched desperately for a route to escape.

But there was no escape. All around her the woods were starting to fall apart. Trees and bushes were being uprooted. Thunderous sounds were attacking her ears, becoming more forceful. Rebecca could hear the death throes of tree trunks as they toppled and crashed onto the wet ground beneath.

'My God!' she gasped turning to the Grinner. 'What the hell is happening?'

But the Grinner seemed oblivious to the carnage and was shrieking and dancing among the fallen trees. Then, without warning, it all stopped. The wind dropped, and the woods shuddered into a silent surrender.

With her head and heart throbbing, Rebecca stared at the devastation around her. And then, when she thought she couldn't take any more, her worst fears were realised. It came out of the dank ruins of the woods and roared in her face, the thing with bloodstained molars the size of a shark's teeth.

* * *

Rebecca sat bolt upright and opened her eyes. The thing wasn't there anymore; her father and Patrick were gone, and the dark woods had disappeared. She was in her bedroom, surrounded by white emulsion walls and familiar furniture. Clutching her chest and hanging her head, she waited until she could breathe normally again. When she had calmed down she flopped back onto her pillow. The dream, the nightmare she had just endured had seemed so real, so vivid it was more like a prophetic message, a warning. But what was she actually being warned about? And why was Patrick in the dream? What did he have to do with it?

'Patrick?' she murmured in confusion.

She had not seen or heard from Patrick for twenty years. During their early teens he was her regular boyfriend and for a short while they met regularly for a quick snog. It was nothing heavy, even their kisses were only light and tentative, more like experimental lip-playing. Their adolescent courting only lasted for about four or five months but to a young, naive teenager it felt like a lifetime.

Then, out of the blue and without any explanation, Patrick dumped her and she never found out why.

Thinking back on the way he behaved Rebecca was more annoyed than upset. She wasn't even sure if she had actually fancied him. She just wanted to have a boyfriend and be like the other girls at school.

However, that first rejection from a boy did dent her confidence and she remembered that she had wept onto the head of her teddy bear that night. Maybe she had been more deeply hurt than she recalled after all.

CHAPTER SIX

Jim arrived at Rebecca's flat carrying a few birthday presents, and a bunch of flowers wrapped up in clear, plastic paper which crackled against his belly as he moved across the room.

'Heavens, thirty-five,' he teased as he gave his niece a fond peck on the cheek. 'By the way, these are from the boys,' he explained handing the flowers over to her.

Rebecca's face flushed with pleasure. 'Thanks so much, they're lovely,' she beamed and carefully placed them and the presents on her sofa. 'Are you sure you don't want me to come into work today? I know you have that big order coming in.'

'No, no, I wouldn't hear of it on your birthday. I've always given you your birthday off and I always will, no matter how busy we get.'

'Well, if you're sure?'

'Of course,' he said as he rattled his keys in his pocket. 'Right then, I'd better be heading off. Oh! ...and don't forget, me and Judy are taking you out for a meal tonight. It's booked for seven thirty so don't keep us waiting when we come to pick you up.'

'Thanks, Uncle Jim, that will be very nice. I'll be ready and I'm really looking forward to it.'

Jim led the way to the front door and Rebecca followed behind. As he reached for the door handle, he turned back to her. 'Are you feeling better now, luv? Things calmed down a bit after the other day?'

Rebecca leant her head against the smooth white walls. 'Yeah, I'm fine. Perhaps I just needed that rest. Anyway, you're going to be late for work.'

'But I'm the boss; I can get away with it.'

Laughing, Rebecca shoved him out of her flat.

'Seven o'clock,' Jim reminded her as he was propelled through the doorway.

Rebecca shook her head and closed the door behind him. Sometimes her uncle could be so irritating and insensitive but at other times he could be so nice, so loving. She went over and sat on the sofa to open her birthday cards and gifts. Before she started on the gifts, she picked out one card in a white envelope; it had arrived with the post that morning. Taking a deep breath, she tore open the envelope and took out a shiny card. She smiled as she saw a picture of a family of polar bears all huddled together on a single cap of ice. When she opened it, two twenty-pound notes fluttered onto her lap. Rebecca felt conflicting twinges of guilt and pleasure as she read the inscription inside. Her mum had written: "HAVE A LOVELY BIRTHDAY, LOOK FORWARD TO SEEING YOU SOON, LOVE MUM X".

'Always short, always sweet and always appreciated,' Rebecca said to herself. Once again, she began to wonder what it was going to be like going back home after being away all this time. How would the place look? How would she feel and most importantly how would she get on with her mother? Rebecca closed the card and leaned back; these were big questions without any easy answers.

* * *

As planned, Rebecca was picked up outside her flat by her uncle and aunt. She was ready and waiting and they drove straight to the restaurant. Like her husband, her Aunty Judith was very overweight and her large breasts squashed down onto her roly-poly stomach. She was sixty-four years-old and her main interest in life was food; shopping for it then cooking and eating it. As well as food, she had a thing about hugging everyone she knew and insisted on clasping them to her massive breasts at every opportunity. Jim would warn people that it was like being smothered by two massive mammary mountains. The orange and green floral peasant blouse she was wearing this evening didn't help. It made them look even bigger; like two enormous, overfilled cushions.

Chinese food was Rebecca's favourite, so her uncle had reserved a table at one of the most popular Chinese restaurants in town. During the meal, the conversation was light and jovial, helped by the bottle of wine that Rebecca and Judy shared between them. Jim was driving so he stuck to tonic water. He liked a drink but didn't see any point in just having one to stay under the limit.

During the main meal, the conversation turned to family matters and Rebecca braced herself for Judy's inevitable avalanche of questions about her mother. There was so much history between Rebecca and her mother that it was impossible for her to give her aunty any straight answers about their relationship.

Confusion, guilt, resentment and anger all played their part in the mix and she had never been able to work out how to get a handle on all these conflicting emotions. It meant that Rebecca really struggled whenever she was asked about her mother and would change the subject as quickly as she could.

Tonight, was no different. She steered her aunt towards the one subject Judy couldn't resist, the subject of marriage. She took the bait and started banging on about Rebecca finding a husband and having children. It wasn't the ideal conversation to have on her birthday, Rebecca had heard it so many times before, but it was better than being put on the spot about her mum.

After strawberry cheesecake and a liqueur coffee for Rebecca and Judy, it was time to call it an evening.

Sitting in the back seat of Jim's Range Rover Rebecca settled herself next to her aunty and was enveloped in one of her hugs. It was a ten-minute ride back home and as they were pulling away from the Chinese restaurant, Rebecca noticed a figure standing beside a bus shelter. It was wearing a hat and had its head bowed. Of course, she recognised the Stetson hat and as the car passed the face looked up and flashed a crazy, Cheshire-Cat grin at her. Rebecca felt sick, bits of the Chinese meal regurgitating in her mouth, but she managed to hold herself together, swallowing as she watched the figure receding into the night.

'You OK back there?' Jim was watching her through the rear-view mirror.

Rebecca didn't want to start anything, especially in front of her Aunt Judy, so she just murmured, 'Yeah, just thought I recognised someone from my school days.'

When they stopped outside her flat, she got out of the car. Rebecca badly wanted to fling herself back into Judy's arms and tell her everything that had been going on but like Jim, she probably wouldn't understand.

How could either of them understand when Rebecca didn't understand what was happening herself?

Instead, she bit her tongue and thanked both of them for a lovely evening. Reluctantly, she closed the car door and slowly left the safety of their company behind her.

Once she was inside her flat, she took off her coat, switched on all the lights and clicked on the TV for comfort. She didn't feel her flat was a place of sanctuary anymore and she went to the window to check that there wasn't any sort of scary figure standing outside. She made a small gap in the curtain and was relieved to see that no one was there; no sign of anyone.

She kicked off her boots but didn't have the energy to change out of her swirly burgundy-coloured skirt and figure-fitting cream silk blouse so she went and perched on the edge of the sofa, dropping her head in her hands. Oh God! Why, why was this mocking aberration stalking her? What did he want? Was there a connection between him and the man in the cafe? Or could she be imagining it? Was that possible? Could she be losing her mind? She kneaded her eyes with her knuckles. Her brain was actually hurting, and she knew she had to try and relax before she blew a gasket. With an effort, she sat up, placed her hands in her lap and started to do the breathing exercises that she and Richard had practised together.

There were no sightings over the next few days and no recurring nightmares. Rebecca dared to hope that her ordeals could be over, for now, anyway. The following week she was due to make that all important trip, back home to Claydon but first she had one final session with Richard.

* * *

As she walked into his office, Rebecca was surprised to see that he was wearing a different style of shirt; this one was pink with narrow navy stripes. Before he began their final session, Richard adjusted his glasses and looked over at her; he seemed concerned.

'You all right, Rebecca? You look a bit dark around the eyes and you seem a bit pale.'

Rebecca wanted to open up and tell Richard what had really been going on with her since she last saw him, but she couldn't. It was all too far-fetched to take in and although he was a trained counsellor, she was pretty sure that he would react the same way as all the others. So, she lied to the one person she should have been completely honest with.

'No, everything's OK.'

'Anything bothering you in particular?'

Rebecca shook her head.

'You getting enough sleep?' Rebecca nodded.

'Have you been using any of the techniques to help you relax?'

'Sort of, yeah.'

'OK then, let's pick up where we left off from last time. We've established that your friendship with Mr Blue continued throughout your childhood. You tried to teach Him to read and write and you also discovered a violent side to his nature when he stepped in to protect you from the dog that was going to attack you. Did you happen to see any other displays of aggression from him?'

'Not quite as intense as that with the dog but he would get frustrated when he couldn't do some of the things I was trying to teach Him and then he could get into a state and turn a bit nasty.'

'Towards you?' Richard asked.

'No, not towards me, but towards the things that he was trying to use and at the things he couldn't do.'

'Can you give me an example?'

Rebecca sighed. She had been through this same type of questioning so many times with other therapists.

'Well, I was fairly good at throwing when I was younger, and I was very accurate at hitting the things that I was aiming at and we used to play this game in the woods. I would wedge a small plastic bottle or a tin can in the branches of a tree then we would try and knock it out with a stone. But whenever I knocked it out first, Blue would roar and pound his fists into the ground like a little kid having a tantrum and he would storm off in a huff.'

'And didn't you ever feel threatened by this behaviour?'

'No, it used to make me laugh and I would call Him a bad loser, but I never used to rub it in too much in case he worked out what I was saying and turned on me. Instead, I used to try and help him practise at becoming a better shot but that didn't really work either because the more he failed the more he used to get frustrated. In the end, I would stop the game altogether but then he would come after me to carry on even though it made Him mad.' Smiling at the memory, Rebecca shook her head affectionately. 'So, I would tell Him, "no more" and he would stomp off again.'

Richard allowed himself a quick smile in response. 'Let's move forward: I want to talk about your father now, if that's OK with you?'

Rebecca shrugged. 'Yeah, OK.'

'When did you notice the relationship with your father deteriorating significantly?'

'It started at about the age of twelve; I started to notice that whatever I did was never right with him and he would find any excuse to start picking on me.'

Richard glanced down at his notes. 'He was a mechanic, wasn't he?'

'Yes, and every weekend he would have his head buried inside the bonnet of his Land Rover.'

'What happened to the business venture that he and your uncle planned to start after the windfall?'

'I think that sort of fizzled out and that's when my uncle started his own business distributing chemical products.'

'This picking on you; did it get worse when he drank alcohol?'

'Sometimes; you see, I was often awake at night because Blue would visit me and eventually, I think my parents began to suss that I was up to something. They never actually found out what I was doing but they probably thought I was misbehaving in some way. Perhaps they put it down to the normal behaviour of a child that didn't want to go to sleep.

'But whenever my father had drink in him and if I made the slightest sound he would storm upstairs to have a go at me.'

'What did he do to you, Rebecca?'

'He would shout and curse at me making me cry then he would order me to get back into bed before he gave me a clout. Sometimes, Mum did come up and tell him to calm down, but she didn't really stick up for me and she didn't come up very often.'

'How often did your father drink?'

'At first, it was mainly at the weekends, then it increased to a couple of times a week and eventually it became almost every night.'

'Why do you think he began to drink more heavily?' Richard asked.

'I don't know, I just thought it was because he wasn't very happy about something. Perhaps it was me or my mum.'

'Do you think he might have thought of himself as a failure as a father?'

'I really don't know. At first, I imagined that he might be getting tired of me and my mother and he wanted out.'

'What makes you think that?'

'He just never seemed happy with us, especially me, and as I got older things began to get worse, especially when I began to talk back at him. I just had enough of his bullying and Mum wasn't doing much to help so I stuck up for myself.'

'Was your father ever violent towards you?'

'He was towards the end of his life and I think Blue knew it because he started to keep away from the house at night in case he got me into any more trouble.'

Richard hurriedly scribbled down some notes in the file and Rebecca wondered what he was writing. He was still writing and didn't look up at her as he asked his next question. 'You say he looked for any excuse to come up to your bedroom and pick a fight with you. Was your mother always in the house when he did this?'

'Of course.'

'Were there any other reasons for him to come up to your bedroom or was it only to chastise you?'

Rebecca knew exactly where this line of questioning was heading, and she shook her head decisively. She had been asked the very same question by all her previous therapists and now Richard was going down the same old road.

'No, before you ask, he never put his hands on me in that way.'

Richard stroked his chin thoughtfully. 'I need to ask these questions, Rebecca, and I wouldn't be asking them if they weren't absolutely necessary.'

Giving him a dead look Rebecca muttered, 'That's what they all say.'

Richard didn't allow himself to get drawn in and carried on with the session. 'Do you think Blue ever heard your father shouting and cursing at you in your bedroom?'

'He probably did, yes.'

'How did he react to this?'

Sounding very matter-of-fact, Rebecca replied, 'Well, it's all down there in my file; what he eventually did to my father.'

'Yes, I know that it eventually led to your allegation that he murdered your father but before we talk about that, I would like to discuss the very first time your father attacked you?'

'The first time he attacked me was when I was fourteen-years-old. I was playing some music in my bedroom. It was a little bit too loud and a little bit too late at night. After my father shouted up to me to turn it down for the second time, I did as he asked. Apparently, I hadn't turned the music down low enough and he came thundering up the stairs. He burst through the bedroom door, kicked over my CD player and then he pinned me to my bed and started snarling in my face. "What's the matter with you, girl? What's the matter with you?" He kept shouting at me and I could smell the whisky fumes on his breath. I can remember it so vividly. I yelled at him to get off me and then my mother appeared in the doorway. She just stood there as if she didn't know what to do. Suddenly, my father lifted me off the bed and screamed at me, "Are you listening to me, girl? Do you bloody understand?" I remember looking right into his eyes and they didn't appear to be like human eyes anymore; he was looking at me, but he didn't seem to be seeing me. Does that make any sense?'

Richard nodded but didn't interrupt, letting her continue.

'Then he threw me down hard on the mattress and slapped me across the face. It really stung, and I cried out in pain. Finally, my mother stepped in and told him that that was enough, and he turned and raised his fists, telling her to stop interfering. That was when I spotted my chance. I knew I had to get away from him before he started on me again. I bolted past him, down the stairs and out into the night. Behind me, I could hear him crashing out of the house and bawling at me to come back. But in his drunken state he couldn't catch me and kept stumbling over. I raced through the dandelion fields as fast as I could and headed towards the woods. I kept looking over my shoulder to check that my father wasn't catching up then, all of a sudden, I tripped over onto the wet undergrowth. I remember feeling blades of grass going right up my nose and I could smell the damp ground in the cool night air.

'I also remember thinking to myself, *I'd better get up or I'm going to get caught.* But as I scrambled back to my feet I felt a hard tug on my arm. At first, I thought it was my father, but it wasn't; it was Mr Blue. He had heard my father shouting as he chased me, and he knew I was in danger, so he came to help. Blue dragged me through the dark woods. We were going too fast for me to see much but I could feel the low, spindly branches clipping my face and whipping my body. I was hurting all over and I wanted Blue to slow down.

'Suddenly, everything went black. I don't know if I'd been hit by something or what but the next thing I knew I was in some sort of cave with tiny bits of lighted candles placed in little crevices in the jagged walls. In a recess there was a fire burning. It was surrounded by stones and broken bricks to stop it spreading. In another recess, there was a pile of wood. Not just twigs and branches but broken pieces of shelving, gates, doors and chair legs. The cave wasn't very big; about the size of a living room. I would eventually call this chamber, this amazing place, the Sky Chamber.

'I was dazed, and my eyes didn't focus straight away. When they did, I saw that I was lying on a smooth stone slab. It was obviously some sort of bed with tatty curtains and rugs for covers. Stuffed away in the alcoves of the chamber were cracked, stained mugs, cups and kitchen plates. It looked like Blue had taught himself to be a good scavenger and a thief. In the centre of the cave there was a

rectangular rock with a flat surface. It looked like it was used as a
table. Next to it was a boulder which was just under the same height
as the rock–table so it could be used as a seat. On one side of the
cave there was a flight of stone steps that led up to an opening over
the entrance. I couldn't see where they went but later I found out
that they led to an outside ledge; later on, I named it Sky Ledge.

'I was too traumatised to think clearly after what had happened
with my dad and then waking up and finding myself in this unbelievable
cave. All I could do was stare at the tiny flames of the candles reflecting
on the shiny rock surfaces. I was mesmerised by them. Every now and
again a breeze would sweep in from the outside making the candles
flicker and throwing dancing shadows on the stone walls. When I
started to get my head together, I realised that this must be Blue's cave.
He must have brought me here, but where was he?

'He soon appeared at the cave entrance holding a metal dish.
It was like a large dog's bowl and was full of leaves and berries. I
was surprised; I thought he had those big teeth because he only ate
meat. I found out later that he was an omnivore. He ate everything:
meat, vegetables, cakes, everything. He lumbered over and put his
hand on my head. Then, he gently touched the red mark my father's
slap had made on my face. Making soft grunting noises, he patted
my shoulder and offered me some of the leaves and berries in the
dish, but I shook my head. Blue cocked his head to one side as if to
say he understood that I was too upset to eat anything. He went and
sat on his stone seat and began to devour his meal.

"Where am I?" I asked.

'Blue crinkled his forehead and he stopped chewing. Turning
his furry head towards me, he tapped his chest and splayed out his
fingers. I was pretty sure this meant that he wanted me to know that
this was his cave.

"Where is this place?" I asked Him.

'He rubbed his nose with the first finger of his left hand and
carried on eating. He wasn't going to tell me, it was his secret. I

turned to look at the candles again. "How did you get those candles? They look like the candles you see in a church, and how did you manage to light them?" I asked.

'Blue's mouth stretched into a cunning grin as he continued to eat. So that was to be a secret, too. I had actually worked out that he must use the fire to light them. It still didn't explain how he managed to light a fire in the first place, though.

'I gazed around the cave. So, this was where he had lived all those years, this was how he had survived. It was a brilliant place, but it did stink a bit and it was cold. I reached over and pulled one of the tatty bed covers over my shoulders to try and keep warm. It had a musty, mildew smell and I didn't really want to touch it, but I had no choice. Blue must have been cold too because he decided to copy me. He went over to a pile of clothes in a corner of the cave and draped a hooded jacket around his shoulders. I wondered if he had collected the clothes from recycling bins or stolen them from people's washing lines. But I recognised the jacket. Ironically, it was one that had belonged to my father.

'Blue finished his meal, stood up and stretched, the jacket slipped to the ground and he didn't bother to put it back on. I could see that his body had filled out a lot since I had first seen Him. His thick muscles were much more defined, and I noticed that he still had coarse black hair on his arms and chest but none had grown on his face. His face had changed over the last year or so and his forehead, cheekbones and jaw line protruded a lot more. I thought to myself, if this was what he looks like as a teenager what was he going to look like as an adult? Blue didn't like me staring at Him and grunted to distract me.

"What?" I replied.

'He stretched out a finger and pointed it away in the distance then he flicked his throat with the same finger. He wanted to know what had happened back at home.'

Richard broke in. 'It's difficult to understand how you got the hang of this sign language?' Although he was a counsellor, a professional, it appeared he had trouble hiding his doubts about what he was hearing.

Rebecca didn't seem to notice and went on with her account of the events that happened in the cave. 'Yes, whatever signs he made, whatever gesture or expression or grunt he made, I always knew what he meant. I've never had any sign language lessons and I'm certainly no Dr Doolittle, but I could make out everything.'

Richard couldn't help shaking his head but gestured for Rebecca to carry on.

'Blue glared at me and tapped the side of his cheek, once again drawing attention to the reddened flesh on my own cheek where my father had struck me. I told Him I had a big bust-up with my father. I told Him that my father had hit me and that was why I had run away and I didn't ever want to see him again.

'Blue glowered into the distance and his brow seemed to lower which made those orange-coloured eyes of his, appear even scarier.'

Richard could hardly contain himself. 'I find it completely astonishing that you managed to converse with Him like this, plus the fact that he also managed to pick up the English language so easily. The other thing I would like to know is if you had previously seen any pictures of cavemen in school books or books you had at home?'

Rebecca knew that this kind of question was his way of trying to cast doubts on what she was saying; to pick holes in her story so he could catch her out. He was suggesting that her description of the cave came straight out of a book. Irritated by his attempts to manipulate the conversation, she didn't answer but asked testily,

'Would you like me to continue?'

'Yes, of course.'

'After the meal, Blue gave me a brief tour of his cave using one of the candles to guide us. Beside the chamber we were already in, there was another entrance that led to a smaller chamber. Inside, there were a few piles of what looked like junk and some primitive drawings on the wall. They were drawings of Blue when he was much younger. He then showed me two other separate tunnels that stood side by side and he pointed to the right one. He wagged his finger, warning me that I must never venture down this one alone. I asked Him why, but he ignored me and instead he led me back through the Sky Chamber and took me outside. He flung out his arm and pointing, made the shape of a hole in the ground. Then he did a squatting movement; he was letting me know that was where he went to the toilet and I should use the hole, too. I was glad that the hole didn't seem to be too close to the cave because I didn't fancy the smell. But Blue let me know that when the shit-hole did become smelly, he would cover it up and dig a fresh one.

'We went back into the Sky Chamber and he guided me up the stone steps and out onto a balcony-like ledge, but it was too cold for me to go out even though I still had the bed cover wrapped around me, so I stayed put. Even though I wouldn't go outside I could hear the distant roar of the waves, so I knew we were somewhere high up on the cliffs. Blue seized my arm and urged me to step out onto the ledge with Him, but I pulled back, too cold and too afraid to do what he wanted. He turned towards me and made a sweeping motion with his arm. He was telling me that I wouldn't come to any harm. So, just to please him I plucked up the courage.

'We stepped out and sat cross-legged on the ledge, but I wasn't too happy with the fact that we were so close to the edge of the cliff.

'Blue appeared to slip into a kind of trance and I watched Him curiously as the sea breeze ruffled through my hair and chilled me to the bone. "Blue, what are we doing here?" I asked.

'Turning his head, he raised his palms to the glittering stars and thumped his chest. He was telling me that this was his way of trying to make some kind of spiritual connection with the universe. "But what is the point in that?" I asked. Blue leant over and touched my chest with his finger then he touched his own chest and looking upwards, made a together sign. But I wasn't going along with it.

"How can we be part of this universe? We're just standing here alone now millions of miles away from any other planets."

'The tone of my voice told Blue that I didn't agree with Him and tapping his chest again, he jabbed a single finger high up into the twinkling sky. He was trying to tell me that he believed that we are all one and the same with the universe. But to me, it all sounded a bit too convoluted and I was completely out of my depth. So, I left Him to get on with it and we spent the rest of the evening lost in our own thoughts.

'Eventually, it became too cold for me and I was so tired that I could hardly keep my eyes open. I crawled back inside and lay down on the stone bed, wriggling under the rest of the covers. I could still see Mr Blue meditating under the stars and I watched Him until my eyelids became heavier and heavier and I slipped into a dreamless sleep.

'In the morning, the rushing sounds of the waves below Claydon Head Cliffs woke me. I opened my eyes and saw brilliant sunshine pouring through from the Sky Ledge and the cave entrance, making the cave shine as if someone had turned on a light switch. I sat up and looked around for Mr Blue, but he was nowhere to be seen.

'Then I remembered last night and for one terrifying moment I imagined that he had toppled off the ledge while he was star-gazing and I began to panic. Where was he and how was I going to find my way back home without Him? All this, plus the worry of having to face my parents, especially my dad. But when I thought about things more clearly, I calmed down. Blue knew this place too well to fall off the ledge and tumble down the cliff, of course he did. Anyway, I didn't have to face my parents today. I could stay on with Him for a few more days and let them sweat it out. That would teach them a lesson. They may even treat me better, even appreciate me more and stop having a go at me all the time.

'Then, behind me, I heard a scuffling sound and saw Blue emerge from one of the tunnels with a cloth bundle in his hands.

"Where have you been?"

Blue unravelled the bundle on the stone bed and showed me what was inside. Somehow, he had got hold of half a loaf of bread, a few packets of crisps, two bars of chocolate, a bag of doughnuts and a full bottle of Pepsi. "Been shopping at Asda, have we?" I laughed. "You haven't stolen them, have you?" I asked.

'Blue must have thought I was telling him off because he looked like a guilty little boy caught with his hand in the biscuit tin. I told him I was only joking, he snorted and pointed at me. Then I looked at the food and realised how hungry I was. I ripped open a packet of cheese and onion crisps and crammed as many of them as I could into my mouth. While I was crunching away I mumbled to Blue that I had decided I was going to stay with Him for a bit longer so I could teach my rotten parents a lesson. I expected Blue to be pleased but he rolled his eyes as if he wasn't sure about me staying or about bringing me here at all. Suddenly, he gave a kind of chuckle – he was only joking, too. As I was finishing the crisps, I noticed that some food was lying on the ground near the entrance to the cave. There was some fruit, sausage rolls, cooked chicken legs and some big pieces of raw meat. I asked Blue if I could have a sausage roll but he shook his head and threw all the food over the cliffs into the sea. He looked so angry that I decided not to ask Him why he had done such a thing.

'So, I ended up staying at Blue's cave for another few days and at night we studied the stars. We sat out on Sky Ledge just like we did on the first night. Blue was my friend and I wanted to share his fascination with the night sky but I still found the idea of connecting with clusters of twinkling stars weird. It was worth humouring him though because he would bring me a bundle of food every morning, every afternoon and every evening; he was like clockwork. But he never let me have any of the food that was left by the entrance to the cave.

'The other thing I remember about staying there was this odd smell. It was everywhere in the cave and it got on my clothes; on my jeans, my T-shirt and hoody. Blue had rubbed this gooey kind of resin on everything. It was some type of earthy mixture that he used to hide the scent of his body. I think he was worried that he might be hunted by sniffer dogs.'

Richard made an arch with his fingers. 'But what about you going missing? Didn't your parents report you running away to the police or search for you?'

Rebecca threw him a stony stare. 'No, no, they did not.'

CHAPTER SEVEN

'They didn't even bother; they were my mother and father and they didn't even bother to look for me,' Rebecca spat out, 'although I did hear the whirring blades of a helicopter swooping around the cliff edges, but I don't know if that had anything to do with me. When I did leave the cave and went back home they both acted as if nothing had happened. Can you believe it?; they didn't even give me a rollicking. All Mum said was, "We were wondering when you would come back" and, "Would you like something to eat?" They didn't even appear to be the least bit worried about what could have happened to me.'

'Did you ask them why they were so unconcerned?'

'Of course I did. I even asked if they had even bothered to report me missing to the police and do you know what they said?'

Richard sat on the edge of his seat and stared at Rebecca. He was clearly absorbed and couldn't wait for her to tell him.

'They said that they knew I was all right and that there was no need to report it to the local police. What kind of supposedly responsible, caring parents would act like that?'

Richard raised his eyebrows. 'I have to admit that was extremely unusual. So, after things settled down a bit, did your relationship improve with your father?'

'No, not at all, he soon got back to picking on me again. Sometimes, when he'd really upset me I would go off the next day and lie face down in the dandelion fields and have a real blubbering session. Then Blue would turn up and lie down beside me, face to face, and press his forehead against mine.'

'Why would he do that?'

'It must have been something his own mother did to Him when he was young. I think it was a form of comforting or reassurance, I suppose.'

'Did it work?'

'Oddly, yes, it felt like someone giving you a big hug and making you feel better.'

'Going back to the time you spent in Blue's cave, was that the last time you visited it?'

'No, he took me there a few more times but whenever he did he would put this grotty cloth bag over my head, so he could keep the location a secret.'

'He didn't trust you?'

'He said to me, using sign language of course, that it was for my own good because if anyone ever found out about Him and me there was no way I could give Him away because I didn't know where his den was.'

Richard put down his pen. 'We have been going for quite a long time and I would usually stop the session at this point. But I want to talk about the events that led up to the murder of your father. So, shall we have a short break and then carry on if that's OK with you?'

'That's fine. Do you mind if I stretch my legs? The right one has gone to sleep.'

'Go ahead, I'll just nip to the loo.'

❋ ❋ ❋

Returning to his office, Richard asked Rebecca if she was ready to continue. 'Now, we will go over everything step by step and at a pace that you're comfortable with. But if things become too much for you to handle we will stop immediately. Are you all right with that?'

Rebecca nodded and leant back in her seat.

'You were fifteen years old at the time and things hadn't really changed between you and your parents. I presume that Mr Blue was still very much on the scene and this was what led up to the events of that terrible night when your father attacked you for the last time; is that right, Rebecca?'

Rubbing her temples, Rebecca sighed, 'Yes.'

'Can you describe what triggered this second violent reaction from your father?'

Rebecca stared ahead for a few seconds before her lips moved. 'The month or so leading up to this point, I began to suspect that my parents knew I was up to something because they had spotted me hanging around the woods so often. At that time, there happened to be a spate of burglaries occurring on the farms and houses on Claydon Head. The blame for all these break-ins fell on a group of tramps, or travellers, who were camping out in Claydon Woods. My parents had warned me to keep away from the woods in case I got abused or injured by them.' Rebecca snorted. 'Apparently, going missing for a couple of days didn't worry them; that was fine, but me getting too close to a group of down-and-outs was far too dangerous. Does that make any sense to you?'

Starting a new page in Rebecca's file, Richard didn't answer.

'My father had even borrowed a twelve-gauge shotgun from my uncle just in case they tried to break into our farm. Anyhow, my parents were watching me very closely.

'On the very week that the attack took place my father had become even more stressed and uptight and he was drinking more heavily. I thought it was down to the fact that he was worried about our house getting broken into. At the same time, my Uncle Jim was making quite a few trips over to visit us. He and my father would spend a lot of private time together and they were always arguing about something.

'The actual night, the night it all happened…' Rebecca stopped for a moment to compose herself. 'It was early evening and I was pottering about in my bedroom. Outside, I heard Blue's calling whistle, so I went to the window. It was chilly, and he was standing there wearing a heavy coat like a cape. The coat was one that I had given Him, it was another of my father's cast-offs. I opened the top window and told Him to go back to his cave because it wasn't safe to come around at the moment. But Blue couldn't understand what the problem was at first and I literally had to shoo Him off. He must have thought that I was in a mood but finally he went. Then, just as he disappeared, my bedroom door burst open and my father stood there with the twelve-gauge in his hands with my petrified mother standing behind him. Well, I was rooted to the spot. I was speechless and didn't know what the hell to do.

"Right then, what's going on?" my father barked.

"Nothing," I stuttered.

"Who's out there?" He marched over to the window and cupped one hand against the glass to look out.

"Nobody, nobody's there," I cried.

"There, I see him. Who's that?' he snapped. I didn't know if he'd actually seen Blue or if he was bluffing.

* * *

"I've seen him. I've seen him. Right," he roared and headed out of the bedroom.

'I was so scared that he might go after Blue that I made a grab for the barrel of the gun to try and stop him. That's when my father seized me by the throat and began to scream in my face and I could feel my windpipe begin to tighten.

"Who is he? Who is he? Nearly every night he's been coming here, hasn't he? Oh, we've been watching you, girl, we've been watching you. But he's early tonight, isn't he? Trying to fool us, is he?"

"Rob, Rob, please let her go," my mother begged.

'It was becoming more and more difficult for me to breathe and I remember trying to get my dad's hands away from my throat, but I couldn't. My father took no notice and wouldn't let go of me.

"Well, he's not going to make a fool of me. He comes from the woods, does he? Right then, I'm going to sort this out right now."

"Rob, no!" Mum pleaded. "Please wait for Jim, please wait for Jim."

'My father finally released me. He dropped me back on my bed and thundered past my mother and out through the bedroom door. Rubbing my sore windpipe, I turned to my mother. "What is he going to do?" and without waiting for a reply I went to go after him, but my mother stepped in front of me, blocking the way.

"No, Rebecca, you stay here," she said. "Your father is going to put a stop to all of this once and for all."

"What? No." I was crying my eyes out by now. My mother tried to pin my arms to my side to restrain me, but I was too strong for her and managed to wriggle free. In desperation, she made a lunge for me, but I was too quick and was already out of the bedroom door. I leapt down the stairs and I was out of the house before my mother had left the bedroom. I tore down the driveway and across the dandelion fields in pursuit of my father. Then, as I ran, I remembered seeing the glare of a car's headlights turning up the driveway to our farm and wondered who it could be, but I didn't have time to find out. Behind me, I could hear the distraught shouts from my mother but nothing on earth was going to stop me.

'BANG! I heard the shot and it sounded like one of those Chinese firecrackers. The noise disturbed the birds in the trees and they all squawked into flight. "No!" I yelled. Fearing the worst, I felt a surge of adrenalin giving me more strength and speed. I burst through the woodlands slashing at the bushes and branches with my bare hands until I came to an abrupt halt… I saw Blue standing over my father, who was lying on his back in the undergrowth.

'In Blue's hand was a large hunting knife with dark red blood dripping from the blade. Our eyes met and I whispered to Him, "Oh what have you done, what have you done?"

'Blue's mouth opened like a mute trying desperately to speak then he began making frenzied hand signals as if he was trying to explain. But I had seen enough, I had seen all I needed to.

'Then I heard the voice of my uncle calling and I turned to warn Blue. He sensed the gravity of the situation and bolted away through the trees with the dripping knife still in his hand. A second later, my Uncle Jim appeared puffing and panting heavily. As soon as he saw my father lying motionless on the ground he cried out, "What's happened? … Rob, Rob! No! No!"

'A few seconds later, my mother caught up and stumbled onto the same horrific scene. I remember seeing her clasping her hand to her mouth, her eyes sticking out of her head like protruding golf balls. I just stood there, shocked and wondering what was going to happen next.

'Jim and my mother rushed over to my father and frantically tried to rouse him but there was no response. Jim shook him again and again until he realised that his hand was covered in my father's blood and that he had been stabbed.

'In blind rage my mother turned on to me. "What have you done? What have you done?"

"Nothing, I found him lying there," I protested. I couldn't believe I was actually being accused of attacking him.

"I can't find a pulse, I can't find a pulse," Jim cried in desperation.

'My mother's accusation had put doubts in my tortured mind and I found myself muttering over and over again, "What I have I done, what have I done?"

"Sandra, get an ambulance, quick," Jim ordered tossing over his mobile phone.

'I stood there, numbed by shock and the terrible thought that my dad might be dead. If only he hadn't gone after Blue he would have been all right. Now, all I could do was just stand there, by the bloody body of my father, not knowing what was going to happen. I have never been so scared in all my life.'

'Unfortunately, your father did pass away that night.'

'Sadly, yes, he did,' Rebecca gazed up at her counsellor, 'despite the fact that he was actually alive when we found him and he did still have a weak pulse. But when the paramedics finally arrived they couldn't do anything because his injuries were too severe and he died on the way to the hospital. Later, it was confirmed by the pathologist that his death was caused by a single stab wound to the heart and he wouldn't have survived even if they had got him to the hospital.'

Richard bowed his head and consulted his notes. Giving Rebecca a moment or two he paused before carrying on. 'At first, the police, your mother and even your Uncle Jim suspected you had something to do with your father's death, isn't that right?'

Rebecca covered her mouth with her hand then took it away again. 'Of course, they all thought I had the right motive because of the way he ill-treated me. But they never found the murder weapon. To be honest, even if I had done it, I would have thrown the weapon into the bushes to hide it. Anyway, there was no evidence of any other murder weapon I could have used to attack him, it would have been covered in blood and they didn't find one. So, it was impossible to say what had been used to kill my dad and impossible to prove that I had done it.'

'That must have been a terrible ordeal for you to have gone through. You were only fifteen; a very traumatic experience at such a young age. The kind of experience that can leave emotional scars for life.'

'Yes, very traumatic indeed. What made it worse was having to convince everyone, including my own mother and uncle, that I hadn't murdered my own father. Then I had to deal with the mixed feelings I had about losing him.'

'You blamed the death of your father on Mr Blue. That was when you finally exposed Him?'

'I had to, Blue gave me no choice. I wasn't going to take the blame for Him. After all, he left me alone to deal with the whole thing. I know he only did it in self-defence but it was me who had to suffer the consequences, wasn't it? Thinking back, though, I always wondered why Blue couldn't have just knocked the gun out of my dad's hands. Why did he have to stab him and where did he get the knife? You think of so many ifs and buts, but even so, at the end of the day, it doesn't change what has happened.'

'How would you have felt if it had been Blue who had been killed?' Richard asked. 'Do you think you might have grieved more for Him?'

Rebecca's eyes flickered from side to side. 'I really don't know.'

Richard scribbled down some more notes on another fresh page. Then, tapping the tip of his pen on the sheet of paper he looked up at her. 'So, how did everyone react when you tried to tell them about your secret friend?'

'Well, that was the strange thing. They all knew I was hiding something from them and I guessed that my mother had probably told the police investigators about secretly watching me for the last couple of weeks. But even my parents didn't know what I was actually hiding from them. They must have thought I had made friends with one of the homeless people, who were hanging about the area at the time. They probably believed I had found a boyfriend who came to visit me outside my bedroom at night. So, they decided something had to be done. I imagine that that was when they asked my uncle to come up to the farm and together, he and my dad would tackle this person.'

'But you don't think that your father was actually going to shoot this person, do you?'

'No, I'm positive it was only meant to scare him off. He wouldn't have shot someone just because they were trying to lead his daughter astray.'

'Your father would have seen Mr Blue just before he was killed. Your father was the only person who could have proved that your story was real?'

'Yes, but I'm sure he never would have imagined that there was some primordial ape-boy roaming about in the woods on Claydon Head, not in a million years. I don't think he would ever have been able to come to grips with the very idea that such a creature existed. As far as he was concerned, the only explanation for my behaviour was that I was giving some disreputable vagrant the come-on.

'Of course, nobody believed what I told them about Mr Blue anyway. They all thought that I had fabricated this ridiculous story to try and get out of any blame. But, as I've already said, nothing could be proved. There was no actual evidence they could use to pin anything on me. There were no witnesses and the evidence they had was only circumstantial. Not only that, I was a juvenile and that would have raised all sorts of complications if they had gone ahead with a prosecution. And if the press had got hold of my statement about Blue together with what had happened to my dad, they would have gone into overdrive.

'But they couldn't leave a murder case unsolved, not in our respectable little town, could they? Someone had to be blamed. So, in the end they pinned it on some poor drugged-up-to-the-eyeballs young lad. To make it believable the police cooked up some story about my father going out with his gun and threatening this gang of travellers who were camping out in the woods. And one of the gang, fearing for his life, stabbed him in self-defence and made a run for it. In the end, the police just grabbed the most likely looking vagrant they could find and now some poor innocent had to rot in some jail down south. My dad's murder was reported on the news and in the national press as drug related and so it didn't stay headline news for very long.'

'And was that the very last time you saw Mr Blue?'

'I think I saw Him one more time after that. He came outside my bedroom and I heard his whistle but I just ignored it. I did peep out from the side of the curtain and he was standing there on the grass waiting. I think he waited for about ten minutes then he wandered off into the darkness. I think he understood that I didn't want to see Him anymore. After that, I never saw Him again.'

'How did that make you feel?'

'Sad, very sad, I knew that I was going to miss Him very much; after all, we grew up together. We had laughed, cried and played our hearts out together. But he killed my father and I could never forgive Him for that.'

Richard studied Rebecca for a few moments; he had watched her body language, and he had listened to the tone of her voice. During all their sessions he had looked for any signs of deception, denial or fabrication on Rebecca's part. That was what he had been trained to do. As a cognitive behavioural therapist, he was on the alert for any telltale signs that might suggest she could be in denial or lying. The specific signs he was looking for were involuntary body or eye movements, face and upper chest flushing, or crossed arms and legs or even scratching any part of the body. He hadn't seen Rebecca display any of these signs.

Richard set his notes down on the table in front of him and leant forward in his seat. He was now ready to give his professional evaluation based on the evidence he had gathered over the last couple of weeks and from Rebecca's file. He smiled up at her and let his hands dangle leisurely in between his knees. He wanted his body language to be open, without any barriers between them. 'Rebecca… every child growing up requires plenty of love and support from its parents or primary carers. Every child also needs to develop certain bonds with its parents, or primary carers, which are essential to that child. During its earliest formative years, it's these particular bonds that set firm foundations so the child can eventually grow into a mature, confident, communicative and responsible adult. Unfortunately, in your case, you were never given the opportunity to develop any of those essential bonds with your parents. You've even stated that you never felt that type of closeness with your parents. You have told me that, deep down, they didn't feel like your proper mum and dad. If a child has never been shown how to love, how to care, or how to communicate effectively, then that child will grow up unable to express their own natural feelings to anyone else.

'Many will become stunted in their emotional growth and they will tend to repress many of their feelings. Now, how can any adult in that position ever engage in a proper relationship? How can they ever socialise or interact with anyone successfully when they have few fundamental communication skills and little understanding of social relations? To you, the only person who came anywhere near to being a true, loving family member was Mr Blue. According to you, he was the only one who was really there for you. He comforted you when you were sad and understandably, you became emotionally dependent on him. Then, tragically, after your father was killed you felt responsible in some way.' Reading from his notes, Richard quoted… 'I stood there looking at the body of my father and thinking what the hell have I done?'

'You were not emotionally equipped to process or accept the responsibility for the devastating situation. You did not have the emotional tools to deal with what had happened. So, although you briefly doubted your own innocence after your mother had accused you of killing your father, you passed all the blame onto Mr Blue. But you still felt guilty and responsible. You believed that if you had not befriended Blue in the first place then your father would still be alive. Your conscious mind presented a way to deal with the guilt. It came up with a solution… "Hey, I don't know what the hell to do with all this so what shall I do? I know, I'll pass them onto Blue, no longer my problem." However, that didn't address what was going on in your subconscious mind.

'Then, later in your life, your uncle stepped in and tried to fill the gap that your father left. It was your uncle that took you in and made you feel a part of his family, the kind of family you never had. In a way, he was the one who filled the gap left by your father and to a certain extent, your mother, and of course, Mr Blue. And once you began experiencing this type of stability, once you started experiencing a near-to-normal life, you began to gain in confidence, you even began to express some normal adult emotions. You were on the way to developing into the kind of mature, well-rounded adult you should be. But once you started becoming a mature adult, you started to have a sense of right and wrong. You began to take responsibility for some of the things that happened in the past, i.e. acknowledgement of your own decisions and mistakes, blame and GUILT.'

'Guilt?'

'Guilt,' Richard repeated. 'Remember how convenient it was to dump all that guilt onto Mr Blue after your father died? Well, Mr Blue, in the form of your conscience, is now standing right in front of you and saying, "Hey, I've been carrying all this crap all around for you for the last twenty years and now I think you're strong and grown-up enough to carry them around yourself. So, here they are, take them all back."

'This is the reason why you are still suffering from all these terrible nightmares about Blue. It is the subconscious part of your mind that is saying to you… "By the way, you sort of misplaced all that blame. You repressed it down here all those years ago when your dad got killed. But you are ready to do something about it now."' Richard paused. 'Are you with me?'

Rebecca's head nodded mechanically. She had much the same diagnosis dished out by all her previous therapists. Why couldn't she convince any of them that Mr Blue Sky was real? He was not a convenient stowaway drawer for all her repressed feelings of guilt and resentment.

Seeing the look on her face, Richard asked, 'What is troubling you, Rebecca? Tell me, what are your feelings right now?'

'You don't believe in Him, do you? You're just like all the rest. None of you will ever believe me.'

Richard's professional smile slipped. 'Like I've already explained to you, the very fact that you believed in Him, the very fact that you have experienced all those emotions associated with Him, doesn't exclude the fact that he is not real, to you. You shouldn't dismiss Him as of no consequence, you shouldn't treat Him any less. You believed that he was real and you developed a real bond, a connection with Him and he was what you needed at that time in your life. He has been the direct result of a symptom of severe post-traumatic stress disorder.'

'But you're still telling me that Mr Blue was only a figment of my imagination, something I created to fill in the gap of a lonely, emotionally-damaged young girl. I created Blue so I could conveniently direct all my trauma and guilt onto Him. But none of what you say in your analysis adds up. At the end of the day, it was Blue who killed my father and not some drugged-up, drunken tramp.' Rebecca sighed deeply. 'I just wish I could prove it to you all.'

'You don't have to prove anything to me, Rebecca, all I want to do is help you.'

'Yeah, help convince me and your other clients, that there is always a rational explanation for everything. Keep telling us that this is the way we are supposed to think. If we don't conform to whatever explanation you trot out, you will recommend mind-numbing medication, and brainwash us until we accept it as the truth and surrender.'

Richard smiled at her little rant but Rebecca didn't miss the condescending glint in his eyes. 'Next time,' he continued, 'we will review all these sessions and then break each one down. What we have to do is isolate every part that is associated with a bad memory and then tackle them individually. Systematically, we will then dissemble every negative thought and try to replace them with more positive thoughts.'

Richard's voice trailed off into a meaningless prattle. Rebecca had switched off, she couldn't stick anymore of his predictable psychobabble. And as for the next session, well, he could stick that right up his arse; she wasn't going to waste any more time or money with any of these bloody smug, stupid, short-sighted sods ever again.

CHAPTER EIGHT

Driving back home, Rebecca felt angry and resentful about her last session with Richard. She should have known what the outcome would be, but she hadn't been able to stop herself hoping that this time, a counsellor might take what she said about Mr Blue seriously. No chance; Richard had just trotted out the same old post-traumatic stress disorder stuff. The same old stuff that all the other therapists had told her. Mr Blue was merely the product of an over-imaginative and severely traumatised teenager.

Contemptuously, Rebecca shook her head. What did they know? OK, she admitted that she had many of the symptoms of post-traumatic stress. Anyone who had been through what she had been through as a teenager would. That didn't automatically mean she had fabricated a whole history between her and Mr Blue.

But she had to admit that it was difficult to dismiss all those professional opinions and as she pulled up at a junction, her certainty about Blue began to dissolve. Oh God! What if they were right? What if I really did imagine Him? What if Blue was never real at all?

If he wasn't, then I must be deranged? I must have imagined Him, and he never existed; that means that the therapists have been right all along. I mean, how can they all be wrong? How come none of them has even considered the possibility that I might be telling the truth? But why would I be so sure? Why would I carry on making the same claims all these years later? Then, becoming infuriated with herself, she slammed the steering wheel hard with the heel of her hand and shouted out aloud, 'No! It did happen, everything I have told them happened, he does exist, he does and I'm going to prove it. I'll show them and they'll all look like idiots when I rub their noses in the truth about me and Blue.'

* * *

After finishing work at the office, the day before she was leaving for her trip home, Rebecca logged off the computer and filed some invoices into a folder and then stacked them on the shelf with all the others. Grabbing her coat and bag she threw a backward glance at her workstation to make sure she hadn't left anything behind. Satisfied, she went to search for her uncle in the warehouse. Jim was just about to climb up onto his old Daewoo forklift truck to stack some pallets when Rebecca called out to him. 'Jim, I'm going now.'

Jim wheeled around. 'OK, luv, what time are you heading off tomorrow?'

'About 10 am, I don't want to leave it too late.'

'Right, I'll pop over to see you before you go.'

Rebecca smiled back. The fact that he cared and did his best to make her feel loved and secure gave her a warm feeling. 'OK.' She blew him a kiss as she set off with her car keys jangling in her hand.

* * *

In her flat that night, Rebecca managed to stay in a fairly happy mood. She refused to let herself dwell on her last therapy session or let herself worry about the trip back home in the morning; in fact, she persuaded herself that she was quite excited about it. She was so chilled out that she didn't even peek out through the curtains to check if anyone was hanging about in the street. Later, when she went to bed, she propped herself against her pillows, did her breathing exercises and actually slept quite well.

In the morning, she was up early, and it didn't take long to finish packing her suitcase and check that the wheels were working properly. At around nine forty-five Jim arrived to bid her *au revoir*.

'All ready for the off? Got all your bits and pieces?' he grinned, standing in her hallway breathing heavily, his voluminous belly wobbling under his grey polo shirt.

'Pretty much,' she answered, tucking a lock of her hair behind her ears.

Jim sighed deeply. For some reason, he looked worried. 'Are you sure you're making the right decision about this?'

Rebecca frowned. 'Yeah, of course, I've made up my mind and I thought you were all right about it.'

'Right then, if it's what you need to do, it's your choice.'

Squeezing his hand under his bulging belly and reaching into the pocket of his tracksuit bottoms, Rebecca watched as he pulled out a wad of twenties. He held them out to her.

Rebecca shook her head. 'No, no, you've already spent too much on me, I can't.' She tried to push the money away but Jim crammed the notes firmly into her palm so she couldn't refuse. Rebecca had no choice but to accept, and besides, she knew he would be hurt if she didn't take it.

'If you get into any trouble, call me,' he instructed.

Rebecca threw her arms around her uncle and kissed him fondly on the cheek. 'I will,' she murmured, swallowing the lump in her throat.

Jim turned away and brushed his greying hair with the back of his hand. After one last mega sigh he opened the front door. 'I don't really want you to go, Beccs, but if you really have to, then so be it. I'll see you in a couple of weeks.'

'OK.' Rebecca nodded back at him.

With nothing left to say, Jim wagged his finger at her. 'Don't forget to ring me and let me know how everything is going and don't talk to any strangers.'

'Oh, go on with you.'

* * *

Before setting off Rebecca needed to fill up with petrol so she shot across to the Tesco filling station on the outskirts of town. As she stood in the queue waiting to pay, she thought about her mother. How on earth had she managed, all by herself, in that isolated farmhouse for all those years? Rebecca was so deep in thought that the customer standing behind had to nudge her to pay for her fuel. She handed over her credit card, took her receipt and then she was on her way.

Leaving the filling station, she turned left and drove through a small village so she could reach the junction to the motorway. When she was about two miles down a narrow, leafy back road she suddenly became aware that her steering didn't feel right and her driving felt bumpy. There was nothing coming behind her but she indicated anyway and pulled over to the side of the road. The moment she climbed out of the car she spotted the flat back tyre.

Cursing her luck, she wondered what she was going to do now. She wasn't a member of a breakdown service so she had no other option but to phone her uncle for help. 'Jesus!' she seethed, 'I haven't even made it more than a few miles; Jim's going to think I'm a right airhead.'

Diving back to fetch her mobile phone from her handbag, she heard a car pulling up behind her. Relieved at the thought of some help she watched as a black Discovery wagon stopped and purred in neutral, its Pirelli tyres crunching on the pitted road surface. The passenger door clicked open and a tall man with raven-black hair, and wearing a long mac, climbed out. Rebecca recognised him immediately and she caught her breath. It was the man who had been stalking her. She had her phone in her hand and started to punch in 999 but the man held up his hands, making her pause.

'Miss Samuels,' he called over to her.

'How do you know my name?'

In a low, measured tone, he replied soothingly, 'I'll explain but first, let's sort out your flat tyre.' Pointing at the two other people in the car he smiled. 'These kind men will take care of it.' Without a word, the two smartly dressed men got out of the Discovery, took off their jackets and rolled up their shirt sleeves.

'Can we talk inside my car while we wait?' he asked.

Rebecca was rattled. She didn't know what was going to happen but she definitely wasn't going to make things easy for him. 'No, we can talk out here.'

The man smiled again, a kind of understanding smile that was probably intended to let her know that he understood why she wouldn't get into his car. 'Of course. By the way, my name is Samuel, too. It's my first name.' Holding out his hand he introduced himself. 'I am Samuel Olsen.'

Watching him like a hawk Rebecca asked, 'What do you want?'

'I'd be more comfortable sitting down, but maybe we can lean on the end of my car's bonnet while they fix your tyre,' he suggested.

Reluctantly, Rebecca agreed and followed Olsen to the Discovery.

Parking her behind against the bonnet and putting on a brave face, Rebecca turned to him. 'I suppose it was just chance that you happened to pass by like this and I suppose it was just chance that I happened to get a puncture at the right time.' Up close, she could see that his dyed black hair was showing a few grey roots at the temples and his pale eyes looked more cunning than piercing and together with his thin lips it gave him a cruel, superior appearance.

'You are a smart girl; I knew you would be. Please don't be alarmed; all I want to do is ask you some questions, that's all.'

Behind them, there was the reassuring clang of metal tools as Olsen's silent accomplices set about replacing the flat tyre with her spare.

'What kind of questions?'

Rebecca sprang to her feet as Olsen slipped his hand inside his mac. Was he going for a gun? But he simply asked, 'Do you mind if I smoke?'

Feeling foolish, Rebecca leant back on the bonnet. Olsen flashed a grin and produced a pack of Silk Cut with a foreign name on the front. He offered the pack to Rebecca but she shook her head. He popped one of the cigarettes between his lips, lit it, inhaled deeply and let the curling smoke roll languidly out of his mouth. Rebecca found the smell quite pleasant and it reminded her of her headmaster's office when she was in primary school.

Sounding much more self-assured now, Rebecca decided to challenge him. 'So, when did you tamper with my tyre? Was it at the petrol station? I could have you charged with interfering with my car and potentially causing a serious accident.'

Olsen squinted as the smoke stung his eyes. 'Please let me explain. You probably don't remember me but I remember you as a very troubled teenager after you had just lost your father.'

Rebecca regarded him, dumbfounded. She was at a loss, totally bewildered.

'I'm a professor of anthropology which, as you may or may not know, is the study of human societies, cultures and their development.'

'And what does that have to do with me?'

Olsen took a long drag of his cigarette and watched as a car whizzed by. 'Back then, when you were giving your statement to the police, the statement that gave the details of how your father was murdered, I was very interested in the strange ape-like creature you described. To an anthropologist like myself, your description raised the possibility that, if you were telling the truth, the creature could have displayed humanoid characteristics. However, when you claimed it was responsible for your father's death, I had to also consider the possibility that you were just fabricating a scapegoat to save your own skin.'

'How would you…?' Rebecca paused as Olsen's words began to unlock the shackles of long-buried memories. 'Wait a minute, I know why you looked so familiar to me. When I was being put through all those police interviews you were the man always lurking in the background, listening.'

'Wow! You do have a good memory and yes, that is correct, that was me. I have certain connections with the police force; they provide me with, shall we say, prerogatives and access to certain cases.'

'In all those interviews you never asked any questions yourself, you just stood there listening and making notes.'

'You were very observant. You were always a bright young girl.'

'So, what do you want from me after all these years?'

'I've never really been away, Rebecca, I've just been waiting for the right moment. You see, back then, the notion that such a creature could exist and commit such a terrible crime stretches even the broadest of minds. But someone in my profession might look at such a claim in, let's say, a much more open-minded light. To someone in my profession the very idea that such a species might exist is not as far-fetched as it sounds.'

'You're telling me that you believe that I was telling the truth?' Rebecca cried in amazement.

'Miss Samuels, through advances in science, researchers are constantly discovering many new species and even rediscovering many old ones.'

'And what exactly do you want from me?'

'An hour or two of your time, that's all. We just want you to provide us with all the relevant information we need.'

'Information? What information?'

'We need a detailed, physical description of this creature, its characteristics, its type of habitat, how it eats, etc.'

'But, why? Why do you want to know all this information now? What's it to you?'

Olsen stood up and moved in front of her. 'If it exists and we are able to observe it in its own habitat, I can't begin to tell you what that will mean to the field of anthropology. It will be phenomenal.'

'You mean to try and capture Him and make shed loads of money from your discovery then subject Him to all sorts of tests for the rest of his life.'

Olsen dug his hands into pockets. 'No, of course not, money is not the issue here. My team are all humanitarians and passionate animal-rights campaigners. We would protect Him from all that and protect Him from being captured by unscrupulous people who would exploit Him.'

The two silent men finished changing her tyre and Rebecca took the opportunity to wind the conversation down. 'That all sounds a bit rich coming from someone who has just sabotaged my car just so they can pick my brains. Oh! One more thing, just for your information, there was no such creature, anyway. I made it all up.'

Then she swung herself off the bonnet and went over to her car. As she got in she called, 'Oh, and thanks for changing my tyre for me, even though you were responsible for the damage, anyway.'

Olsen didn't react. His face was impassive as he watched Rebecca slam her car door shut. Tapping the ash from the end of his cigarette, he blew a perfect smoke ring while Rebecca started her car and accelerated away.

When she looked back through her rear-view mirror, Rebecca saw that Olsen and his two companions were not making any attempt to follow her. They stood unmoving as they watched her tail lights disappearing in the distance.

For the umpteenth time that week, her mind was whirling, trying to absorb yet another dramatic turn of events. She gave a hollow laugh. If she wasn't already bonkers, she soon would be. At least she now knew where she had seen Olsen before. True, it was twenty-odd years ago and he was much younger then but it was him all right. She could see him now, trying to look inconspicuous, hanging about in the background. She had just assumed he was another police officer or maybe, some sort of psychologist.

So why now? Why after all this time is this Olsen interested in me and Mr Blue? Why does he think I could have been telling the truth when all of the other trained counsellors, police and even my parents have dismissed my version of events as a symptom of PTSD? Why would this supposed anthropologist go to such lengths to track me down and want to question me about something that occurred such a long time ago? And why tamper with my car so he could put me on the spot and cross–examine me about Blue? There is a lot more to all this than meets the eye. She confronted herself in the rear-view mirror. 'I don't trust him, there's definitely something sinister about the bastard.'

Realising that she was doing fifty-miles-an-hour in a forty speed limit Rebecca eased her foot off the accelerator pedal. She had to concentrate on her driving and not allow herself to be distracted by her speculations and her plans for her next course of action.

As soon as I get home, I'll phone Jim and tell him what has happened. On second thoughts, that's probably not a good idea. He'll go ballistic and phone the police straight away. Then, he'll insist upon coming down to keep an eye on me. Shit, no, the last thing I want at the moment is Uncle Jim faffing about while I am in the middle of all this mess.

Needing some music to ease her clattering mind, Rebecca turned on the radio. As she did, a motorway sign loomed ahead and she read it out aloud, 'Claydon, thirty-eight miles.'

CHAPTER NINE

As Rebecca drove through the streets of her home town she was keen to see how much of it had changed since she'd been away. A few of the older buildings were still there but most of the high street stores she had known, were gone. Many of them had been replaced with charity shops and a Poundland had taken over the old Woolworth site.

On the climb up Sirius Hill to Claydon Head, her pulse began to quicken in anticipation. As her Mini Coupe crested over the hill, the engine began to whine and strain so she switched down a gear. Peering through the windscreen, she could see acres of woodland stretching out before her; the woods where she had spent so much time when she was growing up. Nothing had changed here, it all looked the same; it was as if she had never been away. Dropping down into Bishop Road, she then snaked around a few sharp bends until she was coasting towards her mother's farm. As Rebecca neared the house, she caught sight of the dandelion fields and they conjured up happy images of herself playing chase with Mr Blue; Rebecca couldn't resist a rueful smile. But enough of that for now, there would be plenty of time to have a sentimental wallow later on. First, she had to brace herself for the daunting reunion with her mother.

Reaching the old farm gate, her car chugged up the dog-legged driveway with the low, dry-stone walls on either side. She pulled up beside her mother's red Toyota and wondered if the house would look any different after so much time. But she wasn't all that surprised to find that the farmhouse also looked exactly as she remembered it.

She climbed out of her car and quickly checked the spare tyre that Olsen's men had changed. After giving it a kick, to test that it was sound, she grudgingly had to admit that it was. Then she realised that her mother was standing at the front door, waiting for her. There was an uncertain smile playing around her mother's lips.

Her mother had clearly spruced herself up for her daughter's arrival. She was wearing smart navy trousers with a navy fleece with turquoise piping on the cuffs and collar on top and she had even pencilled on a lick of rose lipstick.

'Hello, Rebecca,' she called, her smile not quite reaching her eyes.

'Mum.' Rebecca replied in a tone that sounded colder than she had meant it to be. To make up for it, she walked over to hug her but that didn't work out either. The hug didn't feel warm, it just felt the way it used to.

Her mum let her arms fall away and turned to go indoors and Rebecca followed.

The kitchen smelt of roses and Rebecca guessed that her mother had gone on a mad air-freshening spree before she had arrived.

'What about your suitcase?'

'Oh, I'll wheel it in when I've got my bearings again,' Rebecca replied giving the kitchen the once-over. Nothing had changed in here either: the same tired oak units; the Formica worktops and the stainless-steel sink and taps. The only new addition to the kitchen seemed to be a white kettle-jug. After Rebecca had fetched her suitcase her mum made them both a coffee and they sat in the living room with the TV switched on but with the sound turned down. Pointing at the television, Rebecca chuckled. 'I didn't think that would still be working.'

'Yes. It does still work but I don't have it on that much. I prefer the quietness. So, really there's not much point replacing it with an expensive one.'

'Well, what do you do in the evening to pass the time away?'

'Oh, not that much. I read books, newspapers, magazines and then it's usually time to go to bed. I don't stay up very late.'

'Right,' Rebecca nodded. 'Oh, by the way, thanks for the birthday money.'

Inclining her head, her mum acknowledged her thanks with a thin smile and set her mug down on the glass-topped coffee table. 'So, have you come down to see me in particular or are you just staying here while you sort out some other things?'

'A bit of both as it happens. I came back home to see you, plus, I also need to sort a few things out as well.'

'I'm pleased. It's good to know you wanted to see me after all this time but what things do you need to sort out?'

Rebecca couldn't tell her mother that she had come back to try and prove that Blue had actually existed so she dodged the question. 'I just needed a break, I've been working so hard over the last six months and things were beginning to get on top of me.'

Her mother didn't look so convinced. 'Are you sure that's all? That doesn't seem like too much of a problem. Jim phoned me and said that you were seeing a counsellor again.'

'Thanks Uncle Jim,' Rebecca muttered under her breath. 'It's nothing serious, I just get these minor set-backs every now and again, that's all. Anyway, I find it easier to talk about things nowadays instead of bottling them up like I used to do. It's better than taking all that medication.'

'You haven't come back because of your previous problems, have you?'

'What do you mean, Mum?'

'Rebecca,' tutted her mother.

'Seriously, I just need a break and I want to spend some time here with you. Is that such a crime?'

'No, of course that's not a crime. I just want to know that you're OK and that you've moved on with your life and put all that Mr Blue business behind you.'

Rebecca held onto her mug tightly and thought, *Christ! I've only been her five minutes and we're already at each other's throats. What are we going to be like after a month?* Needing to stop the situation getting out of hand, Rebecca stood up. 'I'll just go and unpack.'

Pushing her old bedroom door wide open, she could smell that familiar smell, sending her back to her teenage years. She put her suitcase on the bed and slid off her backpack. Her mother had left everything virtually untouched except for the posters on the wall. The posters of all her teenage heart-throbs, all gone now. Yet, it still felt as if she had stepped back in time.

She went over to the window, drew back the net curtains and stared across at the grass embankment, half-expecting to see a young Mr Blue standing there waiting for her. Rebecca let the curtain fall and thought about what her mother had said about her problems; of course, what she had meant was her imaginary friend. 'I will prove he was here,' she told herself. 'I will prove to them all that he wasn't a figment of my imagination. I have to, even if it means that I have to put my own sanity at risk.'

✱ ✱ ✱

Her first evening at home was spent watching the TV and chatting to her mother about Aunty Judy, Uncle Jim and work. Despite the fact that there were so many unanswered questions waiting to be asked, neither of them wanted to push things. They were like two adversaries, not wanting to challenge each other but knowing that some sort of showdown was inevitable. It was the only way to get things into the open and they both knew that the time had come to do just that.

The following morning, her mother had to nip into town to do a bit of shopping so Rebecca was alone at the farmhouse for the first time. She walked from room to room, touching ornaments and furniture. Just how long would it be before she started to settle back into her old habits? Then, she opened the front door, as wide as it would go and stood there with a mug of hot coffee cupped in her hands. She stared out towards the dandelion fields and the woods, the woods where she had first tried to communicate with Blue.

Outside the sky was clear and a cold snap had drifted in off the south coast making the air quite chilly.

Rebecca lifted the hot mug to her lips and enjoyed the warmth of the steam on her face. She paused before taking a sip and asked herself, *Does he know I'm here? Can he feel me? Is he even still here?* She took a mouthful of coffee, gulping it down. *There's only one way to find out. Mum is out of the way, no better time than the present to find out once and for all.*

Wearing her hooded black jacket, purple scarf and gloves, she set off down the driveway to begin her momentous search. As she walked across the grass, she noticed a horsebox parked at the far end of the road that led to the farmhouse. She squeezed through a gap in the hedgerow and stumbled into the dandelion fields. Of course, at this time of the year, there were no dandelion flowers and the grass was short and damp.

It was only during the hot spring and summer months that the grass was high and the fields festooned with bright yellow dandelion heads.

When Rebecca reached the edge of the woods, she stopped dead in her tracks. It looked incredibly bare in there, most of the shrubs and trees had lost their leaves and they lay on the ground like a thick brown carpet.

It was difficult to believe that this was the same place she had spent so much time as a child; most of her memories were of summer scenes. She remembered the woods as a place full of all types of fauna and flora and bursting with life. Now, it looked so dead. Of course, her memory was being selective, she had come here throughout the year; she must have. Taking a tentative step forward, Rebecca advanced into her past.

Pushing her way through the sparse undergrowth she heard the dried-up twigs crunching under her feet. At first, it was difficult to find her bearings but she soon began to recognise certain areas, then it hit her. She had reached the very spot where she had found Mr Blue standing over the body of her fatally-wounded father.

Rebecca stepped over a small heap of broken twigs. This was it, this was the place where her life had changed forever. There was nothing to suggest that it was once a murder scene. Nothing to suggest that a man had been stabbed here, stabbed by an ape-like creature that nobody believed existed. If only the trees could talk, Rebecca thought, as she steeled herself to leave.

The clump of ferns where she had first communicated with Blue had a special place in her memory but it was difficult to tell where it was. Ducking under some low-hanging branches she was sure she was close but it was impossible to identify the exact spot. She stopped and gazed up into the trees half-expecting to find Blue balanced on one of the branches. But all she could see was the tawny winter sunshine filtering through the stiff, corpse-like boughs.

After a while, Rebecca became worried that she was venturing too deeply into the woods. Best to call it a day in case she got lost; after all, it had been twenty years. Anyway, there was no guarantee that Blue was even around anymore. As a last resort, she decided to try the whistle they used to call each other. Maybe that would do the trick. Rebecca scanned the area just to make sure she was alone, then she cleared her throat.

She pursed her lips and blew softly at first then increased the force until the sound pitched up and then trailed away as the air drained from her lungs. She waited and waited but the only responses she got were the squawks of a couple of blackbirds in the distance. Nothing, no reaction. 'It looks like I've come all this way for nothing!' she told the trees.

Exasperated, she started to shout angrily. 'Look, you, I know you've been calling me. You've been doing my head in. I know you wanted me to come all the way here, the least you can do is show up if you've got the guts? Don't you dare go all shy on me now! I'm here, so what the hell do you want?'

The only reply she got was the crows squawking.

'Well, come on, I'm here; answer me! I'll even give you the chance to explain to me why you did it.' As a last throw of the dice, Rebecca tried the whistle one more time – again, nothing; he wasn't going to show.

Accepting defeat, her shoulders slumped and she headed off back home kicking the dead leaves as she went. But after a few paces, her anger boiled over again. 'I know you're fucking here,' she yelled into the stark woodland. 'I will find you,' she warned and still yelling, she stormed out of the woods.

By the time she got back to the dandelion fields, she was more upset than angry and it took her a while to become aware of something rumbling in the sky. When she looked up she saw a helicopter circling the area. Not thinking anything of it, she continued on home.

Her mother was in the kitchen busily unpacking the shopping and putting it away so Rebecca offered to help. Outside, she could still hear the helicopter swirling overhead. 'What is that helicopter doing?'

'You get used to it; they're always flying over here. At first, it used to be once or twice a week but now it's almost every day.'

'Why? What's going on? They never used to do that when I was living at home.'

Her mother shrugged. 'No idea. Perhaps they're using Claydon Head for training exercises.'

It seemed a plausible enough explanation and picking up a can of tomato soup, Rebecca thoughtfully placed it in the cupboard.

Eying her daughter with some misgiving her mum asked, 'So, where did you go?'

Rebecca froze and thought of a quick excuse. 'I went over the meadow towards Grove Farm then I turned back.'

'You didn't go anywhere near the woods, did you?'

Rebecca wheeled around. 'No, why?'

'The woods are out of bounds now. It's something to do with all the poisonous plants that have been discovered. There are council and environmental warning signs ordering people to keep out, so keep away from there.'

'Oh, OK,' Rebecca replied and carried on unpacking the shopping.

Her mum lifted another bag onto the worktop then stopped to massage her lower back.

'Tell you what, Rebecca, after we've finished here, how about going into town for a coffee?'

A possible mother and daughter bonding opportunity, Rebecca was pleased. 'Yeah, OK.'

* * *

They went to a popular coffee shop, just off the high street. While Rebecca ordered, her mum went to find a table. As Rebecca sidled along the counter with her tray, she gazed at the various cakes and pastries that were on offer in the display cabinets. Taking a fancy to a couple of scones she added them to her tray with some jam and butter. As she was deciding whether to get a pot of cream as well, she felt a tap on her shoulder. She turned and her mouth fell open.

'Hello, Becca.'

'Patrick! I can't believe it,' she cried.

It was Patrick Farrell, the same old boyfriend Patrick who had appeared in her nightmare only a few days ago. But he didn't look the way he did in the nightmare. This Patrick no longer had a mop of unruly ginger hair; his hair was short-cropped and fashionably styled. Gone were the chubby cheeks that Rebecca used to love tweaking. His face had become more angular with a strong jaw. Now, twenty years later, here he was standing right in front of her. He was all grown up and looking smart in an expensive, padded grey jacket with a white shirt and patterned tie underneath. But all she could think of was the day she had had to stare at his black bubble jacket as he walked away, after telling her he wasn't going to see her anymore.

'What are you doing here?' he asked.

Flustered and blushing very slightly, Rebecca posed a false smile. 'I'm here having a coffee with my mother. She's sitting over there… but fancy seeing you here.'

'Actually, I should be saying that to you. I come here more or less every day to get something to eat. You're the one who was supposed to have moved away forever.'

Rebecca inched towards the till with her tray. 'Yes, I moved about fifty miles away to Benarth but I've come over to visit my mother. I'm only down for about a month, and then I'm going back. So, this is your local?'

'Yes,' he replied moving along with her. 'I teach at the Thomas Morris Secondary School, just off the expressway and I come here for a break.'

'I don't remember that school, it must have been built after I left. So, you're a teacher? I'm impressed,' she remarked as she reached the till.

"Fraid so, and what do you do when you're back at home at Benarth?'

'I work as the office manager at my uncle's chemical warehouse.'

Patrick returned the compliment by looking equally impressed. Reaching for his wallet, he took out a ten-pound note, ready to pay for his chicken baguette and apple juice.

'Two coffees as well, please,' Rebecca ordered as the assistant totalled up her tray. Then, she turned back to Patrick. 'Christ, has it really been twenty-odd years?'

'Yes, it must be.'

Rebecca finished paying and waited for him. 'Patrick, would you like to join us?' she asked praying that he wouldn't.

'No, no, thanks, I've only got time for a quick bite and I don't want to intrude.'

Rebecca tried to hide her relief. 'OK then, no problem. Enjoy your meal and maybe we'll get the chance to talk again before I go back home.'

'Yes, I think I'd like that very much,' he grinned. 'By the way, you look well.'

Taken aback by his eager response, Rebecca stared into his blue eyes for a couple of seconds longer than she should have. 'See you, Patrick,' she smiled sweetly.

'See you, Rebecca,' he replied watching her walk away from him.

When Rebecca reached their table, her mother whispered, 'Who was that?'

Rebecca placed the tray on the table in front of them. 'That was Patrick.'

'Who's Patrick?'

Pleased and puzzled about the way Patrick had behaved but not wanting to show it Rebecca replied, 'Oh, he was just an old school friend, that's all. I haven't seen him for over twenty years. He's a school teacher now.'

Her mother didn't say anything but Rebecca sensed her disapproval. While they had their coffees and scones Rebecca couldn't resist glancing over at Patrick. He was sitting at the far corner of the cafe and eventually, her mother became irritated with her daughter.

'Are you listening, Rebecca?'

'Um… no, sorry, I missed that. What did you say?'

'I said I hope you're going to visit your father's grave while you're here.'

'Yes, of course I will.'

As her mother prattled on Rebecca saw that Patrick was getting ready to leave his table. Pretending not to notice and nodding mechanically at whatever her mother was saying, she desperately hoped that he wouldn't leave without saying goodbye. She wasn't disappointed.

'Hello, again.'

Rebecca feigned surprise. 'Oh, hello again, Patrick. By the way, this is my mother.'

'Hello,' Patrick nodded courteously.

'Nice to meet you.' Her mother looked at him with indifference.

'Nice to meet you, too,' Patrick replied as he unfolded a slip of paper. 'I've written down my mobile number just in case you might want to meet up again before you head off back home.'

Taking it, Rebecca said quietly, 'Thanks very much.' Her mother ignored the exchange and stared out of the window as she briskly stirred her coffee.

Patrick gave them a brief salute and left.

Once he had gone, Rebecca turned on her mother. 'God, Mum! Did you have to look so po-faced when he came over? It wasn't very polite.'

'I don't know what you mean, Rebecca. I thought I was pleasant enough. So, will you be calling him then or are you going to wait for him to call you? In my day, that was what any self-respecting young woman was supposed to do.'

Rebecca answered with a teasing shrug. 'We'll just have to wait and see what happens, won't we?'

CHAPTER TEN

In St Bartow's Cemetery, Rebecca and her mother stood looking at the granite headstone of the grave belonging to Rob Samuels. While her mother knelt down to clear away some dead flowers and replace them with a fresh bouquet, Rebecca took the opportunity to gaze at the panoramic view from the summit of Claydon Head. On one side, the North Sea stretched out for miles and blended into the horizon. On the other side there were acres upon acres of rolling hills and patchwork fields. Further down, she could see her mother's farmhouse and the woods. From her vantage point, the woods looked as if they were edging closer and closer to the house, threatening to engulf it in a tangle of bushes and trees.

Her mother straightened up, her eyes never leaving her husband's last resting place. Rebecca turned back to her father's grave before her mother caught her daydreaming. As she stared down at it, the bitter resentment that she had tried to stow away in the deep recesses of her mind began to surface.

'Why was he so mean to me?'

This was not the kind of question that her mother wanted to be asked; not here, not now. Rebecca watched her eyes drop from the headstone to the gravelled grave. A sharp breeze eddied through the quiet cemetery pulling at her scarf and lifting the lapels on her woolly coat. 'I'm sorry, Rebecca.'

Rebecca gazed at her, astonished. 'Why should YOU be sorry?'

'I'm sorry for…I'm sorry for the way things turned out and I'm sorry for the way you were treated.'

Rebecca couldn't believe what she was hearing; was this an actual apology? After all the years of accusations, denial, blame, was this finally an admission of guilt? Hell, it had only taken her twenty years. If only she had said something years ago.

'Your father didn't hate you, Rebecca, and he wasn't a bad person, either. He honestly did love you.'

'Well, he had a funny way of showing it,' Rebecca retorted.

'I know he did, but it was very difficult living under those conditions at that time.'

Rebecca raised her eyebrows questionably. 'How were they difficult? We weren't struggling for money or anything, were we?'

'Not exactly; after that business venture fell through with your Uncle Jim, Rob resented the fact that he had to go back to work as a mechanic. You see, your father was a very proud man; he had so many plans for us. He wanted us to have the best in life. When all his dreams were shattered he turned to drink. Drinking was his escape. He needed it to cope with all the bitterness and disappointment. In his mind, he was a failure and that for him, was very hard to accept.'

'But, why did he only ever take it out on me, then? I mean, I never saw him having a go at you all the time, not that I ever wanted him to, that is. But if someone was under that much pressure, surely it would affect everyone around them.'

Avoiding eye contact, her mother hugged her coat more closely to her body as if she needed the comfort. 'It's not quite as simple as that, Rebecca.'

Rebecca's alarm bells started to ring, and she had a funny feeling that her mother had a lot more to tell her.

'What do you mean, Mum? It sounds as if you're trying to hide something.'

Her mother looked away and shivered as the breeze turned into a short blast of cold wind.

'Mum?' Rebecca pressed her.

Spinning around, the words came spilling from her mother's mouth; it was as if she couldn't wait to get them out fast enough. But she was only repeating what she had already said. Then, just as she was about to say more, she abruptly broke off. Something had caught her attention near the entrance to the cemetery.

Rebecca glanced over and spotted a black transit van creeping slowly past the graveyard gates. No sooner had she clocked it when it screeched off down towards the west side of Claydon Head, disappearing out of view.

'Who was that?'

'No idea, Rebecca,' she stammered uneasily. 'Let's go, it's starting to get a bit cold up here now.' Without waiting for her daughter, she hurried along the footpath towards the exit gate. Rebecca had no choice but to follow.

* * *

Back at home, Rebecca wondered what her mother was going to tell her before the black van had shown up. She also wondered why she was so spooked by it. Desperate as she was to hear an explanation for her father's behaviour, this was not the right time to put her on the spot. Her mother was still in a strange mood; she would probably get more out of her later. Besides, as far as Rebecca was concerned, she had already achieved an apology from her. At least that was a start.

That evening, while her mother was downstairs reading a magazine, Rebecca decided to phone her uncle to give him an update on everything that had happened so far. Speaking to him in a hushed tone so her mother wouldn't hear, she mentioned the mysterious black van from the cemetery and the fact that her mother might be trying to hide something from her.

'I don't know, Becca,' Jim replied. 'I mean, what the hell would that have to do with anything? Maybe she was just feeling a bit down because she was visiting your father's grave with you. I honestly think it was just a coincidence that the van drove by when it did. You know how paranoid you have become lately.'

'Ah, that's where you are wrong, Jim,' Rebecca butted in. 'You know that man I told you about, the one I thought was stalking me? Well, on my way to Claydon I had a flat tyre and I had to pull onto the side of the road. I was just about to phone you when this black Discovery showed up and he got out. It was him. I couldn't believe it. He said his name was Olsen and he offered to change my tyre. While the two men with him were putting on my spare tyre, he started asking me all sorts of weird questions about my childhood. I was actually quite scared.'

'Why, in God's name, didn't you give me a call? I would have been straight down there with the lads,' Jim raged.

'I know, I should have done but I didn't think properly at the time.'

'What sort of questions was he asking you?'

'Just things about my past; the bad things.' Rebecca avoided mentioning that it was *Blue* who Olsen was most interested in.

'And are you definitely sure it was the same chap who you've been seeing around?'

'Absolutely, he also claimed he was one of the investigators on the case of my father's death.'

'What?' Jim bellowed. 'Right, I'm calling the police. I don't like the sound of this.'

'No, no, Jim, I can't deal with all that official fall out right now. I haven't got the energy and it will only make matters worse. Besides, he doesn't know where I am. I'm safe here. Let's decide what to do when I get back to Benarth.'

Jim gave a sharp intake of breath. 'Look, do you want me to come down there to Claydon and keep an eye on you just in case he does show up again?'

'I'm sure that he won't show up, Jim. I've told you, I left him back in a country road on the outskirts of Benarth. I kept checking that he wasn't following me so there's no way he can possibly know where I am. I'll be fine here, honestly. At the moment, I'm more worried about Mum and what's on her mind. I've never heard her talk like that before. For her to apologise to me, about the way I was treated, was definitely the last thing I expected.'

'No, maybe not, Becca. Listen, your mother has been living up there all alone for many years and she's not getting any younger. People in situations like that have a lot of time to reflect on what has happened in their lives. It sounds to me like she's actually trying to reach out to you now. And I don't think it'd be a good idea to use her vulnerability as an excuse to dig up all the dirt from the past. Why don't you just draw a line in the sand and start afresh. She needs you right now, and you need her. Don't spoil that by opening up old wounds.'

What he said made sense but not the kind of sense Rebecca needed to hear. She was still determined to find the truth. She needed to know everything there was to know about her dad. 'But wouldn't it be best for the both of us if she just got everything off her chest and we were able to move on?'

'Becca, haven't you both gone through enough over the years? Just leave it be now. Look, do you want me to have a chat with her?'

Humouring him for the time being, Rebecca answered in a conciliatory tone. 'No, no, that's OK, I know what you're saying and maybe you're right. Anyway, I'd better go now before she hears me on the phone.'

'OK, Becca, but if you get anymore hassle from this chap asking all those suspicious questions keep me posted and phone the police straight away and I'll come down to help you handle everything.'

Rebecca smiled. Her uncle was her rock; he was always there when she needed him. 'I will, thanks, Jim.'

❋ ❋ ❋

That night Rebecca tossed and turned in bed trying to get to sleep as all those unanswered questions and suspicions clamoured for solutions. They invaded her mind like buzzing bluebottles trying to find their way out of a room with closed windows.

In the end, she had to try and think of something to stop the turmoil. Ironically, the only thing which helped was to focus on the happy times she had spent, whiling away the summer days in the dandelion fields with Mr Blue.

Once again, she was there with Him as they lay in the long, waving grass, both of them exhausted after a hard game of hide and seek. After getting their breaths back, they would share the bottle of orange squash she had brought. Then, they would scamper over to sit under one of the shady bushes, which fringed the fields, to escape the hot afternoon sun. Sometimes, a cool breeze would stir the air and fan their sweaty faces. The summer heat was much more uncomfortable for Blue because of his fur and he loved rolling around on the ground while Rebecca squirted him with her mega-sized water pistol.

As she slipped further and further into the reverie Rebecca could actually smell the scent of dandelions and the earthy, herb-like aroma of the bell heather. She even heard the droning of the bees as they swirled around the flowers. It was all so real, the way she would pretend that they were the only two living creatures around, marooned on a desert island with nothing else to do all day but play and eat coconuts. Freedom, with nobody to tell them what to do or what not to do, or when they should go to bed. One time, after closing her eyes to concentrate on the desert island fantasy, when she opened them again Blue had gone.

Alarmed, Rebecca squinted in the glare of the sunshine, and her eyes darted this way and that looking for Him. Then, just as she began to think that he had left her there and gone back to his cave, a handful of soggy earthworms dropped into her lap making her squeal in horror. With the joke on her, Blue broke into a chugging laugh and danced around victoriously.

Other times, when they didn't feel like playing any games, they would just sit. Rebecca would watch as Blue stared up into the summer-blue sky as if he was in one of his trances. The times they spent together, the fun they had and the games they played, forged a strong bond between them and Rebecca felt so much closer to her secret friend than she did to her own parents. To her, he was family and spending time in his company was like having her very own big brother. While she was with Him she forgot all about the problems and tensions at home.

When she ran away from home and spent a few days in Blue's cave, that bond became even closer. Not only did she begin to learn about the incredible way he survived but also about the way he thought about the universe. The nights they spent sitting on the Sky Ledge, watching the glorious sunsets together, was when she realised that she had a lot to learn from Him. At first, watching sunsets was a bit boring but after she persevered she began to get a sense of wonder at all the spectacular colours on the horizon and she could understand why Blue was so enchanted by it.

Another memory surfaced, and she recalled a time when Blue had gone off to scavenge or steal. She went out onto the Sky Ledge, daring herself to get as close to the edge as she could; she wanted to see how high up she actually was. That was the day when she discovered the two iron handles bolted to the side of the cliff. Rebecca remembered being puzzled by them and tried to work out what they were used for and why they were there. When Blue got back, she showed him the handles and asked Him about them, but he only signed that he had no idea who had put them there or what they were there for.

I never did find out what those handles were used for, Rebecca mused, as the images of her childhood started to melt away into the darkened walls of her bedroom. She heaved a long, regretful sigh. *Why couldn't I have told Mum and Dad about Blue? Why did they make it so difficult to be honest about Him? If only they hadn't made me feel that it would have been too problematic to tell them.* But before she could think of any answers her eyelids became heavier and heavier and at last, she drifted off into a fitful sleep.

* * *

When it came to helping her mother tidy the house, Rebecca always opted to do the kitchen. After she emptied the bin and tied the plastic bin liner into a neat bow she took it down to the wheelie bin at the bottom of the driveway.

On this particular morning, a north-westerly wind found its way down the front of her fleecy top and she shuddered as she dropped the rubbish into the empty container. It landed with a loud clump and she shut the lid. As she turned to hurry back to the warm kitchen, something caught her eye. She stopped and looked towards the corner of the field beyond the wire fencing. Narrowing her eyes to sharpen her focus, Rebecca saw what looked like a roll of old carpet left beside a gorse bush. But was it a roll of carpet? Something wasn't quite right; it almost looked human-shaped. Intrigued, Rebecca hugged herself against the cold wind and jogged out of the drive and across the field to get a closer look. Her first impression was that it might be a dead animal but as she drew closer, the bundle proved to be rags, not carpet, and it was definitely human. Dreading the thought that it might be a dead body, Rebecca stopped jogging and swallowed. Edging slowly towards it with her hand clasped over her mouth the rags suddenly moved.

Realising that it was a person, Rebecca called out, 'Are you OK?'

A muffled groan was the only response so Rebecca squatted down and peeled back the rags at the top end of the bundle. A grimy face beneath a dirty black beanie hat emerged. It was the face of an old woman.

Initially, Rebecca was revolted by the features of the unfortunate woman. Years of neglect and ingrained dirt were embedded in the furrows of her wrinkly skin, making her appearance even more unsightly.

This woman would still have been a frightening sight even if all the top make-up artists in the country had spent all day working on her. Whatever they did, they would not have been able to disguise her bloodshot eyes and sagging mouth. To Rebecca, she looked like a witch from a classical fairy tale. Rebecca asked her again, 'Are you all right?'

'Yus, luv, I'm all right,' she croaked, revealing a set of broken and blackened teeth.

Seeing the feeble woman struggling to get to her feet, Rebecca held out her hand to help. She didn't relish the prospect of getting close and touching her, but she had no option. Once she was standing, the woman staggered, and Rebecca had to steady her.

'Do you want me to call you an ambulance?' Rebecca asked.

'No, I'm fine. I just need some food, that's all.'

'Do you want to come to my house and I'll get you something to eat?'

The old woman's bloodshot eyes locked into Rebecca's and for a second Rebecca feared she was going to put a spell on her. The childhood memories, that had been occupying her recently, must be triggering childhood reactions. She would have to watch that. Her grown-up self knew she was being ridiculous and she felt even sillier when the woman spoke.

'No, no, dear, don't worry yourself, I'll be as right as rain in a minute.'

'Tell you what then, you stay here and get yourself together and I'll go back and fetch you some food.'

'That's very kind of you, young lady.'

Rebecca helped to lower her back onto the rags lying in the soft grass and left her there while she went back to the house. When she got there, her mother was in the kitchen.

'You've been out there a long time, Rebecca. What have you been doing?'

'There's an old woman who's collapsed by the corner of the field. I don't think she's eaten for a while so I'm going to take her some food.'

More curious than concerned, her mother peeked through the kitchen window to try and see where the old woman was. Meanwhile, Rebecca rummaged about in the kitchen and managed to make up a couple of ham and pickle baps. She also remembered the tin of tomato soup she had stored in the cupboard the day before.

'Can I have this?'

Her mother nodded. Rebecca opened it and poured it into a small plastic flask then she heated it up in the microwave. She added two packets of crisps, and a small packet of chocolate digestives. Dropping them into a plastic shopping bag she pointed at the fridge. 'Oh, and a couple of bottles of mineral water; she has to drink, too. By the way, she was shivering. Have you got any worn blankets that you want to get rid of?'

Her mother glared as if she had been asked to donate all her blood. Taking that as a resounding no, Rebecca headed off back to the old woman.

When she returned, Rebecca was relieved to find that she was still conscious and sitting up. As she started to hand over the supplies the old woman snatched the bag and began to devour one of the baps. 'Thank you very much, dear,' she rasped between gulping mouthfuls.

'Are you sure you don't need anything else?'

Between her mouthfuls, the woman smiled, flashing her rotten old teeth again.

'Yus, I'm sure, luv, I'll be fine, now.'

Hoping that she had done everything she could to help, Rebecca was about to leave when the old woman gripped her hand tightly.

'You've helped me, now I'm going to help you, luv.'

Rebecca became alarmed but resisted the urge to snatch her hand away.

'I know who you are looking for.'

'Pardon?' Rebecca replied.

'I know who he is, but I don't know where he is. Nobody does.'

'Who are you talking about?'

'I saw you in the woods yesterday – you know they won't let anyone in there anymore, not since…'

'Not since what?'

The old woman avoided the question with a high-pitched laugh.

'I've seen Him all right. I've seen Him wandering through the woods at night. Nothing stays in there while he's around; not even the animals will go in there. Nobody goes into the woods at night, that place is unholy. None of us goes in there, not anymore, not since that horsebox turned up.'

'Why is that?'

The woman wagged her finger. 'No, no, those who talk, disappear. So many of us have vanished over the years and now there are not many of us left.'

'Tell me who you have seen?'

Finishing the bap and wiping her mouth with the back of her hand, the woman gave Rebecca a knowing nod. 'But you already know who he is, don't you? The thing that passes through the trees like the breath of death. He's an abomination; everyone who sees Him, sees Him once and then they're gone.'

Despite the cold, Rebecca could feel perspiration forming on her top lip. Then, feeling queasy, she felt herself breaking into a clammy, nervous sweat.

'We know all about you, Rebecca dear, we used to watch you play with Him when he was a youngster.'

Rebecca gawped, 'You saw?'

'We've all seen lots of things, dear, that's why we don't last around here all that long. Poor Rebecca, we know what you went through and I feel so sorry for you but in the end, it was one of our own who got the blame for what happened. You know what I mean, don't you?'

Rebecca didn't know what to say and her mind flashed back to the aftermath of her father's murder, and the headline in the local paper. "Claydon Head Tramp Charged and Imprisoned." 'You knew the guy they pinned it on?'

'He was a brother of one our group and he saw what happened that night. The thing is, if he hadn't spoken out about it he might still be alive.'

'What did he see? What did he see?' Rebecca's voice was barely louder than a whisper.

'It went badly for him; the drink loosened his tongue then he knew his time was up and it wasn't long before the noose. That noose he was supposed to have made when he was in his cell broke his neck like a twig.'

'Who really killed him?'

'They did, they made it look like suicide, but they did it.'

'Who?' Rebecca persisted but the woman thrust a grimy, talon-like finger to her cracked lips.

'We keep our tongues still… shhh.'

'Are there any other people who know what happened the night my dad was murdered?'

'Only one.'

'Who?'

'He lives in the cave beyond the forest. They've been after him for ages; he's the only one left who knows the truth.'

'Tell me where I can find him, please, he might be of some help.'

'Look for the rock that's formed like a snake.'

'A snake? I've never seen a rock like that.'

'That's all the help I can give you.' The old woman poured some of the hot soup into the flask cup and as she waited for it to cool, she warned, 'Please take care, dear, they will let you into the woods because you are very special. The Gas Mask Men won't touch you while he's around.'

'The Gas Mask Men? Who are the Gas Mask Men?'

'They wear old-fashioned gas masks over their heads. They wear them to deter people from going into the woods. They want to frighten people by convincing them that the ground has been polluted; that the ground has been poisoned by the exotic plants. But you and I know there aren't any exotic plants in the woods. It's just a cover-up to hide the real reason they want to keep people out.'

With Rebecca's support, the old woman struggled to her feet. Swaying slightly and breathless from the exertion, she gripped the bag of food tightly. 'Look out for the flying wasps, dear. They swoop over here at least once a week but now you're here they'll be watching all the time. Take care, dear, and thanks for the food and here's your flask,' she added as she started to hobble away.

'What are the flying wasps?' Rebecca called but the old woman didn't reply.

Was it a coincidence that the old woman had turned up when she did? What she had said was mind-blowing but there were too many details for it to be dismissed as the batty ramblings of a weirdo. Frustrated, and astounded Rebecca watched the woman slowly making her way over the field. Then, roused by this startling information she headed back home, turning to check on the progress of the old woman every now and again.

Rebecca reached the driveway to the farmhouse and checked on the woman one last time, but she had already disappeared from view. She stopped in her tracks and attempted to absorb everything she had been told. *So now there's a witness to my father's murder. But how could there have been? With the exception of Blue, there were only Uncle Jim, Mum and me there while Dad lay dying. Just who is this other eyewitness?*

Who is it that the old woman was on about? And if there was someone else there what can they tell me about what actually happened? Also, if this person did witness everything there is someone else who can prove the existence of Blue. Up until now, I thought I was the only person who had seen Him. But, according to this woman, he has been seen by her and other tramps. *If only I had known that then. Maybe, I could have got one of them to testify for me.* Rebecca snorted to herself. *But who's going to believe a bunch of homeless vagabonds? Nevertheless, it might be a good idea to try and track down this other tramp, the one that is supposed to live on Claydon Head. Maybe he could provide me with some valuable information about what happened that night. Maybe this person can fill in all the gaps? And who the hell are these Gas Mask Men the old woman tried to warn me about? I've never seen any people wearing gas masks hanging around Claydon Woods.*

Rebecca reached the front door with the questions and the riddles still running through her brain. With her hand poised on the door handle, she stopped once more. *Wait a minute, should I be taking the word of a deranged, homeless person seriously? She probably doesn't know what's going on half the time because she is so zonked out on drink and drugs. But then again, how does she know about Mr Blue?* Giving herself a mental shake to try and clear her mind, she pushed the front door open and went inside.

'My God, Rebecca, you've been gone for ages,' her mother grumbled. 'What on earth were you doing? Having a party with the tramp?'

For the time being, the subject of Mr Blue was off limits with her mum, so she decided to be a touch economical with the truth. 'We were just chatting, and she was telling me about the history of the place. It was quite interesting.'

Her mother lost interest in what Rebecca was saying and she went over to the sink to fill the kettle with water while Rebecca leant back against the Formica worktop.

'Mum, do you know who that horsebox belongs to? The one that's sometimes parked over on the road?'

'I'm not sure but I've heard that one of the children at Grove Farm has a pony. They could be using it to bring it to the fields to graze and exercise it.'

'One more thing, Mum, have you ever seen any strange men wearing old-style gas masks hanging around the woods?'

'Men in gas masks? What in God's name has that old tramp been telling you?'

CHAPTER ELEVEN

Returning from a quick trip into town, Rebecca pulled into her driveway and grimaced when she saw Patrick waiting beside his metallic-grey Golf. It wasn't because she didn't want to see him, she just wasn't prepared for an unexpected visit. She put on a welcoming smile as she got out of her car. 'Hello, Patrick, what are you doing here?'

'Sorry to drop in on you like this. The thing is, I didn't know when I might get another chance to see you, so I thought I'd pop up for a quick visit. I still remembered where you lived. Hope you don't mind?'

Rebecca wasn't sure what was coming next, but she forced herself to carry on smiling. 'No, not at all, it's good to see you again. Would you like to come in for a drink?'

'You know, Becca, it's such a lovely day, how about we take a nice stroll through the fields?'

Rebecca was surprised but pleased that he sounded so friendly. 'Great, I'll just pop my bag in the house and we'll go.' Her mum was in the bathroom, so she just shouted that she was going for a walk and would be back soon.

They strolled across the lower fields of Claydon Head, the damp grass saturating their shoes but neither of them mentioned it even though they must have felt the moisture coming through. An awkward silence hung in the air while they both tried to think of something to say to one another.

Rebecca was the first to have a go. 'So, have you got the day off school today?'

'Yes, teachers' training.'

Rebecca gave him a teasing look. 'Is it required teachers' training to visit old friends?'

'Not necessarily but teacher training days can be taken as days off as well.'

'Oh, of course, it must be hard to know what to do with them all. Especially with something like fourteen weeks' holiday a year to fill as well.'

'Rebecca, I've come all this way to see you and you're giving me a hard time already.'

'I'm sorry, Patrick, I'm only kidding you.'

'Still got that sledgehammer humour, I see.'

'It's the only thing that keeps me going.'

Patrick was obviously in the mood for some straight talking and asked, 'Are you married? Single? I just don't want anyone getting the wrong idea about me dragging you up here, alone.'

'No, there's nobody,' Rebecca answered. She couldn't keep that damn note of bitterness out of her voice.

The truth was, even after all this time, she was still smarting over him dumping her when they were kids.

'And you?' she asked him.

'I was married for a couple of years, but we drifted apart when we became involved in different interests. We realised we didn't want the same thing and finally came to the conclusion that we didn't have any kind of meaningful relationship anymore.'

Rebecca kept her head down. It wasn't easy hearing that; the only boy she had ever cared about, had been in a serious relationship with someone else after her. Patrick must have sensed her discomfort because he quickly changed the subject.

'Becc, it's been such a long time since we did anything like this. Do you remember us going on long walks over Claydon Head?'

Rebecca's expression changed, and her eyes became tender as she travelled down that particular memory lane.

'But you would never go anywhere near the woods, would you? No matter how often I tried to persuade you that we'd have such fun messing about in the trees. Do you remember that, too?'

Within seconds, Rebecca's tenderness vanished, and she felt as if she had been wrong-footed. Why was he churning up that particular bit of the past?

'We'd go to all the other places; Spartan's Rock on that little hill and the pool nearby.'

'How do you remember all those places?' Rebecca asked.

'Well, I am a history teacher and I have lived most of my life here. It wouldn't look very good if I didn't have at least some background knowledge of our local area.'

'Are you familiar with all the caves on Claydon Head, then?'

'Sort of, I guess, although I'm not an expert and I'm no local historian. Why do you ask?'

'Just curious.'

They continued their walk up the field until the land flattened out into a broader field, bordered by dry-stone walls, with flocks of sheep idly grazing together in small groups. As Patrick seemed so intent on bringing up the past and risking opening up old wounds Rebecca decided to give him a taste of his own medicine.

'Tell me, Patrick, why did you dump me all those years ago?'

Clearly embarrassed, Patrick cleared his throat. 'Believe it or not, Becc, it all started when I began to have really scary nightmares.'

'Nightmares?'

'Yeah, honestly, I would wake up in the night and sense something standing at the foot of my bed. Oddly, I only ever had those nightmares after I had been out with you.'

Rebecca didn't know if he was being serious or if he was taking the Mick.

'I didn't know what was causing these scary dreams but the more I saw of you the more intense these dreams became. After we had spent time together, the nearer this thing would come up to the head of my bed. Sometimes I would wake up screaming and my parents would rush into my bedroom. Finally, I worked out that whatever it was that I was seeing in these dreams was something to do with you; it was trying to warn me off you. Then, when the dreams started affecting my schoolwork I told my mum and dad and they told me I had to stop seeing you. To be perfectly honest, they were never comfortable about me seeing you in the first place.'

Rebecca rounded on him. 'You really expect me to believe that lot of old crap?'

'But it's true. After I dumped you, the nightmares stopped completely.'

'I can't believe that your parents got you to dump me because of your bad dreams – is that the best you can do?'

Patrick gently placed his hand on her shoulder. 'It wasn't just that, Becc.'

Rebecca waited for him to go on.

Patrick took a minute to compose himself. 'It was also because of all the publicity you got after your father was murdered and then when you started claiming that some kind of hairy Bigfoot had murdered him, everyone thought you had lost it…' Patrick's voice trailed off.

Rebecca couldn't deny that she was more than a little disturbed by Patrick's startling explanation but at least she had got him to tell her why he had chickened out.

'Things became even stranger, Becc. This creature that you described, it was exactly the same as the one I saw in my nightmares.'

Rebecca was incredulous. 'You saw Him?'

'Only in my dreams, only in my dreams Becc, it wasn't real.'

'But Patrick, it was real for me, believe me. I was telling the truth, I wouldn't make up something like that to explain how my father died.'

'Come on, Becc, you don't seriously expect me to believe all that, especially now, here, after all this time?'

'Patrick, listen to me. Lately, I've been having the very same dreams that you had. I believe they are some kind of warning and that's why I have come back to Claydon, to sort it out once and for all.'

'Dreams, Becc, nightmares and dreams; that's all they are.'

'Patrick, I know what happened to me was very real. It wasn't just dreams for me, I actually did have an ape-like friend when I was young, and we grew up together.'

But Patrick's expression made it clear that he was having a real problem believing what Rebecca was saying.

'Patrick, I know it all sounds highly unlikely, but on my way here to Claydon, I was waylaid by this man called Olsen and he wanted me to tell him about Mr Blue.'

'Mr Blue? Who the hell is Mr Blue?'

'That's the name I used to call my ape-friend. This Olsen chap knew the name because he was involved in the investigation into my father's murder case.'

'And…?'

'So, why would he suddenly pop up twenty years later to ask me questions about Blue if it was all such nonsense? Why would he go to such lengths if it was all in my imagination?'

'Becc, Becc, just because a strange guy wants to know about some mythical beast on Claydon Head, doesn't prove your story is true. Hells bells, he's probably one of those crazy monster hunters like the ones who spend their lives sitting on the banks of Loch Ness waiting for some prehistoric sea serpent to pop its head above the waves.'

Patrick sounded just like her Uncle Jim and Rebecca decided that it was not a good idea to say anything else about Blue. All she could do was to try and salvage some credibility.

'Patrick, I'm sorry for going off like this. I shouldn't have opened up about all this to you, it's really not fair. I wouldn't blame you if you wanted to get in your car and drive away at a hundred miles an hour. I'd probably want to do the same.'

'Rebecca, I've always thought you were a bit of a crackpot but that's what I liked about you. But when your dad was murdered, and I started to get those nightmares, plus the things you were claiming; it all became too much.'

'Why are you here, then?'

For a moment, Patrick seemed lost for words. 'I suppose I always regretted dumping you when I did. Back then, I could see that you were in great pain and you didn't seem to have anyone around to help you when you needed it. I felt sorry for you, but I wasn't there for you. I took the easy way out, but I was only a kid.

'Then, when I saw you again in the tea shop the other day, you looked great, like you had moved on and got on with your life. That made me feel better inside but I wasn't completely sure you were OK. I still sensed there was a sadness about you. A sadness that didn't show on the surface. I sensed that it was a deep-down sadness and I thought to myself if she wants someone to talk to or confide in while she's here, then I'm going to try and help. This time I'm not going to run out on her.'

'You don't have to do that, Patrick. It's not your concern and it's not your fight.'

'But I want to help, Becc, I want to try and make it up to you and hopefully, when you go back home, we can still keep in touch. I'd like us to become friends again. I'd like that very much.'

Rebecca gave him a weary smile. 'Patrick, I've come here for a specific purpose. I've come here to try and get some peace of mind. I need closure in my life, so I can move on and live normally, or as normally as possible. But there are things I need to find out first and to be frank, I don't think it'd be something you would want to get involved in.'

Trying to lighten the mood, Patrick touched her hand. 'You make it sound like you have the starring role in some TV mystery.'

'No, seriously, things have been happening since I arrived back home. The other day I helped an old woman, a vagrant or traveller who collapsed by my house. I think she felt that she had to repay me in some way so, in return for helping her, she told me something unbelievable. She told me that there was a witness to my father's murder. It was another homeless person who still lives in one of the caves on Claydon Head. She said I could find the cave by keeping an eye out for a rock shaped like a snake. She also said that Blue has been spotted many times over the years. Other tramps have seen Him in Claydon Woods.'

'A vagrant told you this? Someone who lives under the stars and probably gets pissed out of her head with drink and drugs every night and talks about a rock like a snake? You're honestly going to take that seriously?'

'But how did she know about Blue then? I didn't mention Him – she did – I didn't tell her anything. She couldn't possibly have read my mind, could she?'

'So, that's why you wanted to know about those caves. Anyway, how do you know that the old woman didn't read about Blue in the papers all those years ago? Anybody could have. Come on, Rebecca, don't be so naive.'

'I have to at least try, Patrick. I know it's a long shot but if there is anything anyone can tell me about that night and if there are other witnesses who claim to have seen Mr Blue, then I need to check it out.' Rebecca stepped closer to him. 'After all the shit that has happened to me this could be the only chance I will have to get some peace of mind. This could be the only chance to get the answers that I need to move on. I've already told you why I need to do this. It could be my closure. Wouldn't you want that too, if you were me?'

Nodding, Patrick let out a long breath. 'What do you want to do?'

'Are you saying that you will help me?'

'I can't believe what I'm letting myself in for. Where do you want to start?'

'I need to find that homeless guy who lives in one of the caves.'

'A needle in a haystack,' Patrick retorted.

'Not if you know the geography of Claydon like you do,' Rebecca countered.

'OK then, I don't know the exact location of the caves but if we do find them, just promise me one thing? Once we prove that there is no conspiracy surrounding your father's murder and that this Mr Blue doesn't exist, will you promise to drop it for good and start living your life?'

Rebecca looked him straight in the eye. 'I promise, Patrick.'

'OK, great, now I know how I'm going to spend my half-term off school next week.'

* * *

High on the ridge of the nearest hill and out of sight, someone watched them as they headed off back down the field. Through the long lens of a camera the photographer clicked off a series of high-speed snaps then, crouching down, he moved stealthily down the other side of the hill.

* * *

'Is that Patrick's car outside?' Rebecca's mother asked, craning her neck out of the kitchen window.

'Yes, he just popped round for a bit of a catch-up.'

'So, how did it go?'

'OK, I suppose. We're only old school friends, you know; it wasn't a date or anything.'

'Yes, but he was your old boyfriend, wasn't he?'

'He was but we were only kids then, Mum, and that was a long time ago.'

Randomly stacking plates in the cupboard, her mother clearly wanted a chat. 'I've been thinking, Rebecca, and perhaps it is a good idea that this Patrick has turned up after all.'

'Why do you say that?'

'Perhaps a friend is what you need right now. It's not good to be alone for too long; it's not healthy.'

'What do you mean by that? You're on your own most of the time.'

Her mum lifted out the plates she had just stacked and clattered them into a small column. 'It's different for me, Rebecca.'

'Why is it different, Mum? It wasn't your fault what happened so why do you stay by yourself?'

'Like I've said, it's different for me. In life, some paths run in completely different directions than you thought they would. Sometimes fate provides a different route and there's nothing we can do about it; that's life.'

Rebecca shook her head. 'No, Mum, I believe we can map our own destinies but we need our families and the people around us to be open and honest.'

Placing her hands on her hips, her mother turned to face her daughter. 'Tell me, do you ever plan on having children?'

Rebecca wasn't ready for the abrupt shift in the conversation and stumbled over her words. 'I hope so, one day. Why do you ask?'

'The thing is, you're thirty-five now and before you know it you'll be forty. Having children in middle age can be quite risky. Maybe the time for having children has passed you by.'

Rebecca scratched her head. 'Loads of middle-aged women are having children these days. Back in the old days it might have been risky but not now with all the advancement in medical technology.'

'Technology isn't always a good thing, Rebecca.'

Rebecca was becoming increasingly confused by the way the conversation was going but there was no way she could stop it; her mother was determined to have her say.

'At least in the old days things were more straight forward. They didn't have these manufactured families. Nowadays, everything is grown in laboratories; human beings are being groomed to accept these government-sponsored programmes.'

'Mum, what the hell are you going on about?'

Backing off, her mother shrugged. 'Oh, it's just what I've been reading in the papers, you know how these things play on your mind.' And without finishing to stack the plates she turned on her heels and walked out of the kitchen.

Rebecca didn't know what to make of her mother's odd line of questioning and while she continued to mull over it she heard a distant rumbling coming from the sky outside again. She moved over to the window and peered out through the wooden-slat blinds and saw a helicopter hovering over the northern cliffs. The helicopter remained stationary in the air for a moment, then it swooped down in a side arc and disappeared out of sight. As she let the blinds flick back something clicked in her mind, something that the old woman had told her…"Watch out for the flying wasps."

CHAPTER TWELVE

The ache in her bladder was becoming painful and Rebecca knew she would wet the bed if she didn't go to the loo. Yawning, she reluctantly left her warm duvet and pillows and shuffled to the bathroom. As she shambled back into her bedroom she could hear the wind rattling through the ill-fitting wooden window frames. Going over to make sure the windows were fastened as tightly as possible, she peered out. There was someone out there, a figure in the shadows and as the light of the moon came out from behind a cloud, it shone down on a face, a face behind an old World War II gas mask. Rebecca clapped her hands to her mouth to prevent herself from screaming and waking up her mum. Almost immediately the figure, realising that it had been seen, darted away into the darkness. Rebecca blinked and rubbed her eyes. The sight of the figure had been so fleeting. Did she really see it? Outside, the ghostly wind whistled even louder. The eerie sound and her tiredness, together with that clown figure she had seen outside her flat in Benarth, made her doubt her own judgement. After all the nightmares and that figure she had seen outside her flat, it would be understandable if her imagination was running away with her.

She climbed back into bed, pulled the duvet right up to her neck and lay there. She wouldn't be getting much sleep tonight. She dozed on and off until she decided it would be better to get up rather than stay in bed tossing and turning.

* * *

Closing the lounge door and switching the television on for company, Rebecca packed her small backpack ready for her trek with Patrick over Claydon Head. They were going to start the search for the elusive vagrant who was supposed to live in one of the caves. As for the unnerving incident that occurred during the early hours of the morning, she made up her mind not to mention it to Patrick. Not today. There was enough on the agenda without making things even more complicated.

Later on that morning, the weather woman on the TV was about to deliver her regional forecast for the day. Rebecca stopped to listen in case she needed to pack a waterproof jacket.

The attractive woman with a Scottish accent pointed at the giant, superimposed map behind her. 'Today has begun with some sunny spells but all that is going to change. Clouds will appear by mid-afternoon, but it will largely remain dry. However, very unseasonal thunderstorms are expected to develop early this evening, especially over the coastal areas.'

Rebecca switched the television off complaining, 'That's all we need. Looks like I need to take a waterproof jacket then.'

* * *

Making their way through Claydon Woods, their footsteps squelched in soggy mulch. All around them they could hear the squawks of crows as they circled the high treetops. Rebecca glanced across at Patrick and couldn't stop grinning at what he was wearing. He had on a wax jacket and beige, corduroy trousers which were neatly tucked into his thermal socks and he also wore big brown clumping boots.

'God, Patrick, you look like Sir Edmund Hillary, the mountaineer who climbed Everest back in the 1950s.' She choked back a laugh.

Patrick gave her a twirl and then minced up and down on an imaginary catwalk. 'You're saying that now but don't blame me when the weather turns, and you end up getting soaked. You saw the forecast.'

Rebecca couldn't stop laughing out loud but managed to gasp, 'I'll be OK, don't you worry about me. You just concentrate on where we are going. You do have a vague idea where these particular caves are, don't you?'

Patrick dug a map out from the pocket of his jacket. Rebecca leant over his shoulder and tried to trace a route to the caves with a spindly twig.

'It'd help if we knew the names of all these damned caves.'

'Just how many caves are there on Claydon Head?'

Patrick held up his hand and wiggled three, then four fingers. 'Well, I've heard there are only a few; three or four, maybe.'

'No, there should be more than that,' Rebecca corrected.

Patrick looked up at her. 'Are you sure, Beccs?'

'Don't forget Blue's cave.'

Patrick waved the map at her. 'Yeah, well, hopefully by the end of today we will be able to debunk that particular theory.' Stuffing the map back into his pocket he scanned their surroundings. 'So, this is where the two of you both played when you were little?'

'Here, and in the dandelion fields,' Rebecca replied almost tripping over a fallen tree trunk.

Patrick caught her and asked, 'How did you actually meet Him?'

'When he saved my life.'

Patrick glanced across at her, intrigued.

'I was wandering through the woods, without my parents' permission and I eventually got lost. Then I heard this strange kind of whining, so I went over to investigate and as I got closer a hairy head suddenly popped up out of a clump of ferns. Obviously, I was scared, and I ran off to try and get away from whatever it was. But I fell headlong through some bushes and started to roll down a grassy bank. I nearly toppled over the edge of the cliff, but I managed to hang onto a branch. I was terrified because I knew I wouldn't be able to hang on for much longer. It was Mr Blue who came to my rescue, he pulled me back up. That's how he got his name – Mr Blue because all I can remember was seeing this great big blue sky behind Him.'

'He must have been very strong to lift you up all by himself.'

'He was very strong. He always was, in lots of ways.' Rebecca suddenly stopped in her tracks. 'Come to think of it, the very spot where I first saw Blue isn't too far from here.'

She gazed up into the tall trees. 'Sometimes, he would hide right up there in the trees and when they had all their leaves it'd be very difficult to see Him. And when he did pop out he would show off by dangling from one of the high branches with only one arm. Now and again, he would even try and get me to climb the trees with Him, but I was always too scared to go that high up.'

Leaning against an old oak tree, Patrick threw a stick into the air. 'By the sound of it, you were very close.'

'We were.'

'Christ, you certainly kept all that well hidden from me when you were my girlfriend.'

'Back then, I was trying to protect Him from everyone. I couldn't even tell my own parents.'

'But you did come clean about all this, eventually.'

'Yes, he killed my father, Patrick, I had to in the end. I had no choice and knowing that he was capable of doing such a thing made me aware that he would always have that killer instinct in Him which could be triggered off at any time. After that, I thought it wouldn't be safe to be around Him again.'

'You still miss Him, don't you?'

Rebecca's expression became sad. 'We were literally like brother and sister; without Him I probably would have ended up in a correctional institution or something. Being with Him, playing, fighting, I was able to let off all that pent-up stress and emotion that I was suffering at home.'

'Oh, I wasn't fooled, I could tell you were a bit of a psycho,' Patrick teased.

Rebecca wasn't offended and flicking a leaf at him, she picked up where she had left off.

'The fighting wasn't all one-sided, you know. I really used to give it back to Blue as well. I would punch him, kick and bite him and he would love it. I could never hurt Him, and he never hurt me. He always held back when it was his turn, perhaps it was because he knew I was a girl. Although, on some days, when he was having a bit of a moody because I annoyed Him, he would throw twigs at me and would bare his teeth, but he never went any further than that, he never attacked me.

'But as he got older, I could see a change in Him. I couldn't seem to read his emotions as well as I could when he was younger. As he grew, he became grumpy and didn't want to play as much. But despite all that,' Rebecca paused reflectively, 'the thing that scared me the most, more than any fear that he might attack me, was the terrible thought that one day I would have to say goodbye to Him. We were from two completely different worlds. I mean, it was OK then, we were young, and it was our time, our playtime and we didn't care.

'But even then, I would sometimes wonder when our long playtime together might be over. You see, even then, I was aware that nobody stays young forever and eventually everyone has to grow up. But it wasn't just that we were two different species; we both knew that it would mean that we would have to go our separate ways one day.'

Patrick was surprised to see Rebecca's eyes turning to liquid and he noticed that her voice had become husky.

'When you're young, life is all about dreams and when you grow up those dreams tend to get quashed by the harsh realities of adulthood. And once that has happened we start turning into human robots, going through the motions of everyday life and forgetting all about those magical times. As soon as we reach that particular age, everything changes and we get lumbered with responsibility; we're told just to shut up and do our job. Don't you remember having such a great time with your friends when you were young? Didn't you think it was going to last forever and that you would never part? Then you grow up and those very same friends become husbands and wives. They start families of their own and that promise you made to each other, when you were children playing in the woods and fields, is finally broken.

'As I said, Mr Blue Sky and I were from such separate worlds and right from the very beginning our childhood was always going to be short. As we got older we both knew it wasn't going to last forever. It was like playing with a child who has a terminal disease and having that terrible, empty feeling knowing that you would soon have to say goodbye. It was a cruel game that nature played on us; letting two innocent souls bond together and knowing full well that at any time fate was going to split us apart. It was like some sick experiment.

'In the end we parted sooner than I thought we would, but I never imagined we would part the way we did. I never imagined that he would murder my father. Now, I'm not sure I did the right thing when I told my parents and the police about Him. He had saved my life and when he killed my dad it was because he was protecting me. These days, I sometimes feel that I betrayed the best and most loyal friend I could have had.'

Patrick peeled himself away from the old oak and rubbed his back where the bark had dug into his spine.

'Either you're telling the truth, or you have one of the most vivid imaginations I have ever heard and being a schoolteacher, I have heard them all.'

Rebecca smiled. 'I'm sure you have but, Patrick, I know he's real and I know he's still here somewhere, I can feel Him. He's drawn me back here for a purpose. For some reason he wants to see me again probably for the last time.'

'What do you think he wants, then?'

'I honestly have no idea yet. Look, I've brought some tuna sandwiches and crisps. I've got a couple of small cartons of orange juice as well. Shall we have them now and then we should get going? Time is getting on and it's going to rain later.'

'Good idea, thanks, Beccs.'

It didn't take them long to finish their packed lunch and begin to make their way through the woods again.

They decided the direction they should follow was to take a tangled but pretty straight forward path until they reached a fork. When they reached the fork, they had to make up their minds about which path to follow.

They could either climb up until they reached an outcrop of rock, which overlooked the dizzying drop to the sea, or they could dog-leg it, going further through the woodlands, which would lead them up towards the summit of Claydon Head.

Rebecca suggested that they could climb up the rock, so they could scan the coastal cliffs for any sign of a jutting ledge that could indicate the location of Blue's cave. However, Patrick was more concerned about tracking down the vagrant, so they could find out what he knew about Rebecca's father.

While they argued the toss about what to do, a dark band of clouds gathered overhead. The storm was on its way. In the end they went with Patrick's plan. They trudged on for about another thirty minutes when they came across an unexpected rocky mound but this one looked much higher and steeper and would mean much more of a challenging climb.

'I'm not going up there,' Rebecca announced firmly.

Patrick took out his map for another look. 'We won't have to.' He pointed to a cleft at the base of the rock. 'We can access it from the beach and we can get down to the beach if we carry on along this path and turn right.

'It's got to be one of the caves. See that tiny writing there? I didn't see it before but it's the name of the cave. It's actually called Bishop's Cave. There's even a little bit of blurb about it. Apparently, at the turn of the century, it was one of the caves used by smugglers. They would come straight from the ships in rowing boats and ferry their contraband in there.'

'Are you sure that's the cave we want?'

'If this guy lives in a cave, then yes. The others are on the east side and the only way to reach them is to abseil down the cliff. This has to be it.'

Scrambling down from the woods onto a narrow bar of shingle, they crunched towards the cleft. As they reached the entrance, Rebecca stared around her. 'Well, I can't see a rock or anything that looks much like a snake here. It's a bit overcast though and maybe I just can't spot it. I don't suppose you remembered to bring a torch, did you?'

Patrick sucked air through his teeth. 'No, I didn't. What an idiot.' Taking Rebecca's hand, he led the way.

As they ventured through the entrance they both turned sideways, to stop their jackets catching on the jagged walls.

Inside, Patrick used the LED light on his mobile phone to guide them. Cold, dank air replaced the smell of the sea as they went further in. Patrick swung the beam of his mobile around the interior. 'Hello?' he called, his voice echoing around the cavern.

As they carried on, the light revealed an opening, about the size of a small room. Patrick trained the beam over the floor. The place was unoccupied and empty except for some litter strewn on the ground and a filthy old sleeping bag.

'Someone has been living here, that's for sure,' he whispered.

Hanging back and peeping over his shoulder, Rebecca felt jumpy. 'Maybe we should go back outside and wait for him to come back?'

'Well, we're here now so let's have a good look, eh? Anyway, it doesn't look as if anyone has been here for a while.'

'Yes, but what if he does come back and finds us in here rummaging about in his hideout? We'll get off on the wrong foot and he won't want to talk to us, will he?'

Patrick grabbed her hand and put his finger to his lips. 'Wait!' he hushed her.

They both listened, and Rebecca clung anxiously to the arm of his jacket.

'Can you feel a draft?' he asked.

'No.'

Patrick loosened her hold and took a few steps forward, leaving Rebecca where she stood.

'Patrick, don't leave me here,' she hissed.

But Patrick had seen a shaft of light coming from somewhere deeper in the cave. 'I think there may be a way through,' he whispered.

'No, don't go, stay here,' Rebecca pleaded but he didn't listen.

She threw a small stone at him for ignoring her then, rubbing her cold hands, she followed him.

'Here,' Patrick announced. 'I can see some light coming from around this bend.'

'Wait for me,' Rebecca cried.

They turned up a steep passage and had to use their hands to feel their way. The beam of the torch just about guided them towards the source of light yet the light was becoming stronger with each step and soon they wouldn't need the torch to guide them at all. The passage opened up again, but this space was much lower and narrower than the first and they both had to hunker down and scrape along. Gradually, the sound and smell of the sea became unmistakable.

Finally, Patrick came to a sudden stop.

'Whoa!' he cried as he found himself emerging towards a sheer drop. It plunged down to the shingle shore below; the movement of the waves pulling and pushing at the wet pebbles in a never-ending cycle. Patrick thrust his hand back to warn her. 'Stay where you are, it's over a hundred feet all the way down.'

'Let's go back, Patrick, it's getting too dangerous,' Rebecca begged.

Patrick craned his neck over the edge.

'Patrick, what are you doing?'

'Hang on, I just have to check on something. Wait a minute, what's that on the rocks down there?'

'What?'

'It looks like a jacket or something, I can't really tell.' He glanced back at her and she saw the alarm on his face. 'I think it's a person.'

'A what?'

'Do you want to have a look?'

'No way, I'm not going anywhere near the edge. Come on, Patrick, I've had enough. Let's go before we end up down there, too.'

Patrick pulled away from the edge quickly and ushered Rebecca down through the passage until they were back where they had started. As they stumbled out of the cave, the weather had changed dramatically and in the distance they heard the ominous rumbles of thunder.

'Shit, we've got to get back before this storm really sets in,' Rebecca said.

'What the hell was that at the bottom of the cliff?' Patrick asked.

'Maybe it was just a jacket.'

'It could have been a body.'

'Oh, don't, Patrick.' Rebecca looked as if she was going to freak out.

'Maybe it was that guy we were looking for. Maybe he did have something important to tell us, but somebody got to him.'

'Patrick, you're scaring me now. Stop it.'

Patrick didn't pick up on how panicked Rebecca was and made things worse. 'Maybe it was Mr Blue.'

'Patrick, that's not funny. No, it was just a jacket, an old coat that someone has thrown away so let's just leave it at that.'

In the distance there was another rumble of thunder making them both looked skyward.

Patrick, finally realising he was being a bit of a prat, tapped Rebecca lightly on the shoulder and said, 'I think it was just a jacket. Come on, then, let's go.'

Leaving the cave, they headed off back through the woods. Suddenly, two tall, bizarre figures burst out from the bushes in front of them and blocked their path. Patrick and Rebecca froze. Before them stood a couple of men in long raincoats and full-face gasmasks. The gasmasks they wore were the old rubber Brearley covers with the sealed filter and the fog-lens eye pieces. The figures just stood there, motionless.

Patrick was just as scared as Rebecca, but he tried to put on a brave face. 'Hello, can we help you?'

Rebecca remembered the old woman's warning about men in gas masks and an icy shiver rippled through her body.

'Can we help you?' Patrick repeated.

The two men didn't respond and remained as still as statues.

'OK.' Patrick had had enough, and he steered Rebecca off the path so they could sidle around them.

Once they were on their way they quickened their pace and Patrick turned every now and again to make sure they weren't being followed. As they hurried forwards Patrick kept his hand on Rebecca's back to keep her moving then he cried out, 'Shit! They're right behind us.'

Rebecca's legs turned to jelly, and she almost fell. Patrick grabbed her and almost carrying her, increased their speed. But the deeper they got into the woods the darker it became making their progress difficult. All at once, an intense bright light turned the woods a brilliant white. Seconds later, thunder boomed in the sky adding even more drama to their already terrifying situation.

'Where are they now?' Rebecca whimpered as they smashed through a row of bushes.

Patrick chanced a backward glance. 'I don't know, I can't see them anymore. Maybe they've gone.'

They both stopped for a breather, their chests heaving. They frantically scanned their surroundings, but it was becoming so hard to see anything; the two men could have been hiding anywhere.

'I think they've gone,' Rebecca gasped.

'Maybe, but let's keep going. I don't want to hang around and find out.'

They hadn't taken more than a few steps when a gloved hand seized Rebecca by the throat. She let out a blood-curdling scream and Patrick sprang over to try and help. As he did, a steel-like grip locked around his neck and held him tight. He couldn't do anything as Rebecca was hoisted up by her throat and pinned to the trunk of a nearby tree.

Because of the immense pressure on her throat, Rebecca's eyes were almost popping out of their sockets. She hadn't been able to see what had happened to Patrick and she desperately tried to call to him for help. Patrick fought as hard as he could to get to her but the grip from his attacker was just too strong. Breathing in raspy-gasps, Rebecca struggled against the waves of unconsciousness that were overtaking her. In a moment or two she would black out and then she would choke to death.

Patrick, she called out soundlessly. He would be the last person she thought about before death would take her. But then, the pain and the stranglehold vanished, and she slumped back down to the ground coughing and spluttering. She opened her eyes and her focus slowly returned as the thunder continued to rumble around the wood.

Before her the Gas Mask Man was on his knees. His head was bowed and only the top of his mask was showing.

Behind him, she saw Patrick in the clutches of his attacker but then, something snaked around the neck of his captor and Patrick was released. The Gas Mask Man scrabbled frantically at his neck which seemed to have some type of thin wire wound around it. Rebecca could just about see the line of the wire, which trailed up into the trees and was looped over a thick branch. The tension seemed to be taken up by the movement of something in one of the trees.

Once the pressure on Patrick's neck was released, he dived towards Rebecca, he lifted her up and held her tight in his arms. She pointed up into the tree where the wire came from and as she did a rapid succession of blinding white lightning revealed a hulking shape. It was squatting in the fork of two thick branches and holding the line.

Paralysed with shock, they watched as the shape steadily shifted forwards and with one huge hand leant down and gripped the Gas Mask Man by the neck and hauled him up. The second she got a better view of Him, Rebecca's heart nearly burst out from her chest and she gasped, 'Oh God! Oh God!' From where she stood Rebecca could see that this was a familiar shape; a beast with deep-set orange eyes wearing human clothes.

He was also wearing a man's long raincoat but instead of a gas mask covering his face, a Stetson hat was crammed down over his ears.

Then, he lifted his head and let out a threatening growl, as it twisted the Gas Mask Man's head from his body, snapping the neck from the cervical spine. Rebecca clasped her hand to her mouth and turned away repulsed and nauseous. The corpse was then dropped to the ground like a sack of potatoes and the beast leapt down from the branches as more thunder boomed through the forest.

Rebecca and Patrick shrunk away from this terrifying sight and pinned themselves up against the trunk of the nearest tree. The beast stood looming over them and it was only then, that they both saw that the raincoat he was wearing was exactly the same as the rain coats the Gas Mask Men had on. Although she was too terrified to think clearly, it dawned on Rebecca that the raincoats and even the hat were very similar to the ones Samuel Olsen and the clown figure had worn.

Straightening the rim of his Stetson hat, the beast stared at them before another flash of lightning illuminated a long, gleaming blade flicking out from the sleeve of his raincoat.

With one silent swish of the blade, the head of the kneeling Gas Mask Man was sliced off and it plopped onto the ground. The cut was so precise and so neat that the body remained in the same kneeling position. The butchery was too much for Rebecca to handle and she passed out. Although he was horrified himself Patrick managed to catch her limp body as it sagged to the ground. Towering over the mutilated bodies the beast retracted the blade of the knife and it disappeared back into his sleeve with a clink. Holding Rebecca close to him Patrick could do nothing but pray. But the beast ignored him as he gently prised Rebecca away from his arms. Patrick knew that there was nothing he could do, and it would be fatal to even try. With great care the beast lifted Rebecca up and straightening his massive torso turned to walk away with Rebecca lying unconscious against his chest.

'Blue, Mr Blue,' Patrick stuttered.

Hearing his name called the beast stopped dead in his tracks and Patrick suddenly wished to God that he had kept his big trap shut. Slowly, Mr Blue turned his massive head around to face Patrick with a contemptuous expression. Had it not been for the raging storm, Patrick would have been spared such a spine-tingling stare.

But another streak of sheet lightning lit up those demonic eyes and they penetrated into Patrick's soul, making his legs turn to liquid. As the booming thunder continued to roll all around the woods Mr Blue turned his back and carried Rebecca away.

* * *

Rebecca's eyes flickered open. Her pupils were dilated, and it took a few moments for her to take in her surroundings. She was in some kind of cave, softly lit by candlelight. The candles were placed in small apertures in the rock walls and their dancing flames made flickering patterns on the limestone ceiling. No, it wasn't some kind of cave, it was his cave, the cave she shared with Him when she was fourteen-years-old.

He was sitting at the table, the same table made from a flat slab of rock with chunky, round boulders for the legs. The sight of Him, with his powerful adult body and the long, dark fur that grew from the crown of his head, made Him look so different from the young friend she had known. Age had changed Him, and he looked even more astonishing than he used to. The head fur was more like hair and he wore it tied back in long dried-out braids which reached down to his shoulders. His face had also altered quite a bit since she had last seen Him. The ridge of his brow was heavier, and his cheekbones were more prominent; the eyes were more deeply set inside the skull. To Rebecca, his face looked much more ape-like. However, the skin of his face was still paler than the dark, wrinkled flesh of an ape. Blue's face was more like the colour of a human face. He had discarded his bloodstained raincoat for what appeared to be a wrap-over type of poncho, made from an old canvas sheet.

Mr Blue had obviously learned new skills over the years because he was busy making quite good letter shapes on heavily creased paper curled up at the ends. He was grasping a large novelty pencil in his huge hands. Rebecca inched closer to try and see if he was trying to make words when she felt an icy breeze nipping her ears. It made her look up towards the Sky Ledge where she had once spent so many evenings watching the sunset with Mr Blue. Feeling the chill spreading, she tried to pull her weatherproof jacket around her, but her jacket was hidden beneath a cover made up of animal skins stitched together. Was this another new skill? Had Blue stitched them together himself? If he had, how had he managed it? She turned to Mr Blue. It was about time she got some answers. 'So, here you are.'

Blue stopped writing and lifted his head. Rebecca could clearly see his glowing orange eyes, the eyes she remembered so well; the eyes that had terrified her in her nightmares. He leant back on his seat and attempted to pronounce her name. But he had not developed his speaking skills and he gave up, making the old sign of "Ecca".

'Yes, it's me, Rebecca,' she corrected. Why was she even bothering to communicate with Him? This was the creature who had murdered her father. True, her father had been a violent drunk, but he had still been her dad. Sitting up she felt the same anger and resentment she had felt after Blue had killed her father all those years ago. Her feelings were torn. She thought that she had come to understand and accept why he did what he did but she couldn't stop the old bitterness surging through her. She wasn't going to thank Him for saving her life again, she wasn't going to be grateful and she spat out, 'Why have you brought me here?'

But Mr Blue ignored the tone of her voice and angled his body to face her. He made a fist and with his finger he drew a circle around it. Rebecca hadn't forgotten their special sign language and knew exactly what he was saying. Despite the time apart and the recriminations, a connection was still there. 'You want me to help you? Why?'

Blue opened up his palm and traced a finger around it.

'We might be in danger?'

Blue puckered his lips and shook his head.

'No, no, tell me,' Rebecca demanded but Blue had clammed up.

'You have to tell me. You've brought me all the way here so what the hell is going on?'

Blue turned away, making it clear that he wasn't going to give her any more information.

'Blue?' Rebecca wasn't going to let Him get away with that.

Blue made the shape of a beak with his first finger and thumb. 'No, not yet. Why?'

Blue wagged his head.

Rebecca sighed back at Him. 'Well, I can't stay here for ever, can I? Patrick will probably go back and…' she froze in mid-sentence. 'You didn't harm Patrick, did you?'

He sniffed the air.

'Blue, tell me you didn't harm him, did you?'

He glanced back at her and made a chattering noise with his lips. It was his way of letting her know that he hadn't harmed Patrick.

Rebecca blew out her cheeks. 'Thank God for that. So, who were the other two men in the gas masks and raincoats and why did you have to kill them?' She pointed at Him, 'And tell me why you were all wearing the same type of raincoats.'

Blue sat there, a mix of emotions flitting across his face. Then, he made a series of defensive hand movements.

'They're after you? Why?' Rebecca asked.

Blue drew a finger across his throat.

'Who is after you and why do they want to kill you?'

Blue picked up a book from the floor and started to turn the pages and he beckoned Rebecca over. Rebecca still didn't feel so good, but she got up and went over to the table. Shivering, she folded the fur blanket around her tightly. Standing beside Him she experienced a twinge of unease. But it only lasted a couple of seconds; he wouldn't attack her, he never had. In all the time she had known Him, he had only tried to keep her safe and she felt her bitterness towards Him ebbing away. She gazed over his shoulder. 'What is that? A kind of diary?'

Blue tapped the side of his desk with his fist. *Yes.*

Rebecca turned the book towards her and noticed that the cover was encrusted with some type of dried, lumpy resin. 'What is this made of?'

Blue signed a reply.

'Dead animal flesh.' She recoiled in disgust.

It makes for a good binding cover. Blue replied with exaggerated hand signals and his body rocked with amusement.

Rebecca tried her best not to get too near to the book, but she needed to lean quite close to read his child-like writing. But she couldn't make out what was on the paper and he had to sign what he had tried to write.

We were brought here from a long distance. Many men wearing white coats looked after us and they brought us here. Some of us were separated but they left me with my mother. These men had guns and then they killed my mother and took her body away and left me alone.

Rebecca placed her hand on his shoulder as she cast her mind back to that fateful day when she first encountered Blue in the woods. She recalled seeing the young Blue's head bursting out from the ferns and startling her so much that she ran away. After Blue had rescued her from the cliff they both sat at the edge of the woods fearfully listening to the distant voices filtering through the trees. Once he thought it was safe to move, Blue took her back to the patch of ferns. When they got there, he began frantically searching for something or someone. That something or someone must have been the body of his mother who had been murdered by the men with the guns, the same ones Blue was trying to write about in his diary.

'So that was your mother you were looking for?' Rebecca asked.

Blue nodded his head vigorously.

'Why did they kill your mother?'

Blue's enormous shoulders lifted into a shrug.

'Well, where did you both come from?'

Back in the days when they were playmates, Blue had to take his time to sign even a simple sentence. But now he was able to sign all the answers to her questions, questions she had waited so long to have answered.

Rebecca felt guarded and exhilarated at the same time.

A place where there were lots of people in white coats and lots of machines.

'Like a laboratory, you mean?'

Yes.

'You and your mother were brought here from a laboratory and then she was killed. But why was she killed and why didn't they kill you, too?'

Blue growled and shook his head.

'Now, after all this time, they send these men in the gas masks to kill you. It doesn't make any sense.'

You will help me? Blue had never appealed to Rebecca for help before.

'Me, what can I do to help?'

Find out.

'Find out what?'

Why have these men come for me, who sent them and why? I sense danger for me and you.

Alarmed, Rebecca pressed Him further. 'Danger for me; how am I in any danger?'

There is danger for everyone.

Fear and confusion made Rebecca indignant and she moved away from Him. 'You drag me all the way back here after everything you've done, and you expect me to risk my life to do all your dirty work for you? Do you realise what I have had to go through all these years? All the self-denial, the medication, the therapy I have had to endure, and the ridicule. Can you even understand?'

Blue stared back at her in the same way a pet dog tilts its head when it's trying to figure out what it's done wrong to upset its owner.

Calming down, Rebecca lowered her voice. 'Why should I help you after you killed my father?'

Blue let out another growl but this one lingered in his throat like blocked water in a drain.

'How do you ever expect me to trust you again after that?'

I didn't kill him.

Rebecca took a few steps towards Him. 'Look, Blue, do not insult my intelligence. I know what I saw that night so don't try to deny it. For the last twenty years I have had to live with what happened that night and the only way I have managed to accept it is the fact that you did it in self-defence and it was not a cold-blooded murder. So, don't you sit there and say you didn't do it otherwise I will leave and never come back.'

Blue leapt to his feet and with one mighty blow of his fist he smashed a nearby wooden crate into tiny splinters. Cowering back by this display of primitive aggression Rebecca decided to choose her next words more carefully. It wouldn't be a good idea to make Him angry; after all, he did just murder two fully grown men with his bare hands. Seeing the fear in her eyes, Blue sat back down at his stone table and he signed out another message. *Ok, I did kill him.*

Rebecca's eyes filled with tears and in a tone barely louder than a whisper she asked, 'Why?'

* * *

Avoiding the misery in her eyes, Blue replied, *I didn't want him hurting you anymore.*

Rebecca slumped down onto the stone bed. She couldn't think of anything to say to Blue's explanation for killing her dad, so she just curled herself into a ball. Not wanting to see her so distressed, Blue roughly pushed his writing to one side, rose to his feet and stormed out of the chamber.

* * *

Rebecca awoke from a light doze, her eyes hypnotically drawn towards the flickering flames of the candles in the rock walls. Through the entrance leading out onto the Sky Ledge she saw Blue standing there gazing out into the crisp, clear night. Raising herself on her elbows she began to wonder how her life might have turned out if she had never met Him. Would she have lived a conventional life with a husband and children? Would she have been any happier and more emotionally stable than she was right now? Perhaps not, she concluded. Even if her life had taken an entirely different route she would still be searching for a purpose and she would probably be just as insecure and uncertain about everything.

Feeling sorry for herself she stared at the cave walls and cried plaintively. *Who in their right mind would want someone like me?* Then her thoughts turned back to Patrick. She had almost forgotten about him. *God! I hope he got back all right. At least I've proved to him once and for all that Blue isn't just a figment of my imagination. He does exist, and I am not crazy after all. Now, there's a chance that Patrick and everyone else will be able to see for themselves.*

But then she had another thought. *Shit! I hope he hasn't gone to the police or anything.* No, he wouldn't; she trusted him even though he had only just come back into her life. It occurred to her that, with the exception of her uncle, he was the only other person she did trust.

Something else occurred to her. She was surprised at how completely at ease she was in Patrick's company. Despite the fact that they were on a potentially dangerous hunt she had felt happy and comfortable as they had waded through the woods in search of the vagrant's cave. Even when they were in mortal danger from the Gas Mask Men there was something about Patrick's demeanour, something about his presence that heartened her and made her believe that he would do everything he could to save her. *I wonder,* she mused to herself, *does Patrick have thoughts about me, or am I just being stupid again?*

Outside, Blue was sitting cross-legged on the Sky Ledge, just like he did when she had lived in his cave. No longer annoyed, Rebecca felt the sudden urge to join Him, so she clambered off the bed, taking the fur cover with her. Soundlessly, she climbed the steps up to the Sky Ledge and stood beside Him.

Blue was aware of her presence, yet he ignored her, so she didn't break the stillness. As they both gazed out over the horizon the dawn sky was gradually radiating fingers of light on the landscape and the sea beyond. Rebecca lowered herself into the same sitting position as Blue and as the fresh morning air bit her face she burrowed herself deeper into the warm fur.

Every now and again she glanced at her old friend as he gazed aimlessly over the horizon. After a while she saw his gaze drop as if he was delving deep into his own private thoughts. Then she saw Him stealing a look at her. He seemed to be wary of her presence and unsure of how she was going to treat Him.

Wanting to reassure Him, Rebecca smiled. She tried to imagine what he might be thinking and wondered if his mind always followed the same thought processes. *I bet he's been doing the same thing every night since we were young. I wonder what he thinks about while he's here all alone all day and all night? Before he became convinced that he was in danger, did he ever wonder why he was here and what the future may hold for Him? Did he think about living out the rest of his days here alone and did he ever long for a companion to share his life?*

He must be sad, lonely and bewildered. He doesn't know if he has a purpose in life and he has learned not to trust anyone. Rebecca gave a wry chuckle as she realised that such depressing similarities mirrored her own private life. *Here we are, both alone, both with no purpose, both of us like leaves on a tree bending to circumstances beyond our control. Blue doesn't have anyone to care about Him, no one he can really trust.*

Although I have Uncle Jim and maybe Patrick, I do understand how that feels. So, what does fate have in store for two lost souls like us? Perhaps, in the end, we may only have each other just like we did when we were kids playing in the dandelion fields.

Watching Blue in the dawn light, she began to sense a deep melancholy in Him. She had never really considered his feelings up until now. Perhaps all that counselling had blocked her ability to take them into account. Her counsellors had only been interested in the way she felt; they never encouraged her to explore the feelings of others; it was like being the star of her own reality show.

Sitting there every night gazing out over the horizon this hulking figure may have the combined strength of ten grown men and he may look invincible, yet he had nobody to care about Him. Since his mother had been killed he'd had no one to look after Him and no one to share his pleasures and disappointments. For years, nobody knew he existed; nobody, except for her. If he died or was killed, the sun would still rise, the wind would still blow, and the woods would still grow. Nobody would mourn, nobody would grieve. The people who killed Him would be the only ones to witness the death of this unique being.

Rebecca's heart was full of pity for Him and she had a sudden urge to reach out and touch one of his colossal shoulders. She wanted Him to know he was not alone. Now she was there to share his doubts, fears and emptiness. Her hand moved out from under the fur blanket, but she drew back. Why did she hesitate?

Perhaps it wasn't the right time to show that she cared for Him, not yet. It would be like trying to sooth a deep wound that was still too fresh and too raw. First, it needed time to begin the healing process.

The sun was rising on the east side of Claydon Head and the sky was suffused with yellow and pink curling tendrils. Rebecca turned back to Blue. She was pleased to see that the sight of this glorious spectacle appeared to lift his mood. *The dawn of a new day,* she said inwardly, *a day of new hope.*

'Blue?' she called gently.

Blue gave a soft grunt and stretched out his hand towards her.

'I don't know what you are expecting me to do to help or what you're expecting me to find out but if I do uncover something, how can I find you again?'

Blue raised his hand, and the fur on the back of it gave off a golden sheen as it caught the rays of the sun. He fingered his response. *I'll find you when I need you.*

Still troubled by what he had said earlier she asked him again, 'Could I really be in danger?'

This time Blue didn't respond and as the day finally broke, Rebecca again was left wondering what the future held for them. What dangers would they face, and would they survive them? Resolutely, she squared her shoulders. Whatever lay ahead, she would not desert Him this time; they would go forward to meet what was to come, together.

CHAPTER THIRTEEN

When she eventually returned home, Patrick's car was still parked outside in the driveway. Exhausted, cold and dishevelled she dragged herself through the back door and noticed that the slats of the window blinds in the kitchen were still shut. Curiously, she went through the hallway and headed towards the living room and that's when Patrick appeared in the doorway; the relief on his face was apparent.

'Rebecca, thank God,' he gushed breathlessly.

Rebecca only had the energy to give him a glimmer of a smile as she walked past and into the living room. Inside, her mother was sitting in the armchair holding a steaming mug of tea and she looked up, her face deathly pale and drawn. She looked too tired to show any relief at her daughter's safe return.

'Mum, I'm sorry for putting you through all that worry but...'

Patrick cut in. 'Becc, your mother and I have had a very disturbing talk and I really don't know what to make of it.'

'Patrick.' Mrs Samuels hushed him. 'I need to talk to Rebecca alone, if you don't mind?'

Patrick looked unsure but nodded his head.

'What's going on?' Rebecca asked unzipping her heavily stained jacket and perching herself on the edge of the couch.

Patrick shrugged. 'Like your mother said, she needs to speak to you alone and now I know that you're all right I might as well shoot off, if that's OK?'

'You're going?' Rebecca protested.

'I think I should. I really need to get my head around everything that has happened in the last twenty-four hours and I need to get some sleep.'

'But, Patrick, I…'

'Don't worry, just give me a call later on and we'll…' Patrick's voice trailed off. He was too tired and confused to finish the sentence and he didn't really know what he was saying anyway. Reaching for his jacket he took out his car keys and stopped in the middle of the room. 'Look, I have to go.'

Reluctantly, Rebecca let him go and turned back to her mother to hear what she had to say.

'Rebecca, why don't you let me get you something to eat and drink, and for heaven's sake sit down before you fall down; you look completely done in.'

* * *

Patrick was exhausted and took care as he drove carefully back down Bishop's Road. He was just about to reach the crest of Sirius Hill, over-looking Claydon town, when he spotted an odd figure. He was very short and was standing on the grass verge at the side of the road. But what struck Patrick was the fact that he was wearing a raincoat and a Stetson hat, the same sort of raincoat the Gas Mask Men and Blue had been wearing and the hat was exactly the same as Blue's. The odd figure tipped his hat as the car passed. Too washed out to pay much attention to the gesture Patrick drove on. But as the tail lights of Patrick's car started to disappear down the hill the short man danced a tiny jig and flashed a wide, psychotic grin at the back bumper.

* * *

Wearing a pair of jogging pants and a warm hoody, Rebecca sat down in the living room. Wiping the crumbs from a couple of slices of cheese and bacon on toast from her mouth with one hand, she cupped a mug of hot tea in the other. Relaxing against the sofa cushions she did her best to tell her mother what had happened in the woods. Her mother waited for her to finish, then she dropped her bombshell. 'We knew all about Mr Blue Sky.'

Rebecca's face contorted into a mask of fury and her mug of hot tea spilled slightly onto her thigh making her wince in pain.

'We've known about Him for years, ever since you were a child.'

For a moment, Rebecca could not speak and when she did her own voice was strangled and accusing. 'You knew, you knew all about Him all along and you made me think that I was crazy. Dad even made me believe that he didn't know who was outside my bedroom window on that night, the night he was killed. Why, Mum, why? You've stood by and watched me almost tear myself apart battling with my own sanity over this. You all tried to convince me that Blue was a manifestation of my own guilt for what had happened to Dad. All the therapy sessions I have had over the years, all the mind-altering drugs I have been given to stop me getting at the truth, to keep me quiet; why did you allow me to go through that, Mother? WHY?' Rebecca was screeching now. Her voice had risen to such a high pitch that it could have splintered glass.

Her mother leaned over in her armchair. 'We had to, for your own sake.'

'For MY own sake?'

'And for your own safety.'

Rebecca snorted. 'All this was for my own safety? My God, are you serious? If that's what you call protecting me, is it any wonder that I turned out the way I did?' Rebecca sprang to her feet and clenched her fists. She wanted to strike out and she actually had to stop herself from slapping her mother.

'Rebecca, sit down,' her mother said tonelessly.

'No, Mum, under the circumstances I think I'm entitled to be just a bit miffed, don't you?'

'Rebecca, please.'

Rebecca needed to find out what had been behind the unforgivable behaviour of her parents, so she took four deep breaths and tried to focus on her relaxation techniques. Finally, she composed herself enough to ease back down on the couch and with a deliberate, ice-cold delivery she asked again, 'Why did you put me through that, Mum? Why?'

Shredding the tissue she was clutching, her mother spoke in a monotone, 'When you were a child we first began to notice that you were disappearing off by yourself a lot. One day your father followed you and saw you playing in the dandelion field with some type of monkey-boy. At first, he thought it was some kid dressed up in a costume but the more he saw of you together the more he figured that a child wouldn't be wearing the same monkey costume every time you played together.

'He knew he should have stepped in and done something. He should have stopped it there and then but seeing you both together he said you looked so happy and so innocent. Even though we didn't like the fact that this monkey-boy wasn't a normal playmate we were sure you'd be safe with Him because your dad said that he was never rough or nasty. You see, when you were young, we were so worried that you didn't have any kids to play with after school. When you came home, you didn't mix with anyone your own age. Your dad and I talked and talked about what to do. In the end, it seemed cruel to deprive you of the only friend you had and so we kept quiet and allowed the friendship to carry on.

'Besides, we knew that if we had tried to stop you from seeing Him you probably would have sneaked off behind our backs anyway. You would have started being secretive and taking risks, like slipping out at night. I know it was irresponsible of us but at the time it seemed to be the kindest thing to do for you. Then, as the years went by and you both started growing up we started to have second thoughts about it. To be honest, we both hoped that you might have grown out of your childhood games with Mr Blue, but you didn't. Our biggest concern was that we weren't sure what this monkey-boy might grow into. He was getting so big and so strong and we were worried that he might hurt you. He might even...' Her mother's cheeks became flushed and she couldn't look Rebecca in the face.

'What, Mum? What did you think he might do?'

'You know, interfere with you. That's when your father suddenly became very strict and he started to feel guilty that he had allowed things to go on for as long as they did. That was why he was so mean to you at times. It was because he was trying to make you come to your senses and when it didn't work he took all the blame on himself even though I had gone along with it as well. He drank more and more to try and blot out the guilt he felt.

'That night, when he slapped you and you ran away for a few days, we knew where you were. We knew you were with Mr Blue. But how could we report you missing? If we had gone to the police, they wouldn't have believed us. It would have looked as if we had done something to you and made up this fantastic story to explain your disappearance. Anyway, when you came back they would have charged us with wilful neglect and social services would have got involved. You could have ended up in care and there could have been an all-out search for Mr Blue.

'So we decided to wait a few days and if you didn't turn up we would have reported it; honestly, that's what we agreed. But after you came home, and things settled down again we realised that your friend was beginning to visit you. We saw Him waiting outside your bedroom window during the night. That was when your dad decided to put a stop to it once and for all. Maybe, if we had stopped it sooner, your father might still be alive today.' She paused and reached in her pocket for another tissue.

Rebecca's eyes were as hard as flint as she waited for her mother to collect herself.

'Well, if you knew about Blue murdering Dad why didn't you back up my story?'

'Rebecca, how could I? First of all, nobody would have believed me. Second, if they did believe me, I would have been taken to court and given a custodial sentence for allowing this creature to have regular contact with our child for all those years. I had to keep quiet about it, I didn't have any choice.'

'And what about Uncle Jim; was he in on it, too?'

Her mother nodded miserably. Rebecca was now past all feeling. She couldn't even feel outraged or betrayed – she was numb all over.

'So you all left me to deal with it by myself?'

'Rebecca, we all have to accept the consequences for the choices we make in life. I know we should have intervened and I know we are to blame for the way things turned out. But it was difficult. If we had stopped you having contact with Mr Blue you would have ended up hating us and you might have run away for good.

'Just spare a thought for the people who loved you before you condemn us and remember what I have lost too. I lost my husband and I lost my daughter for the best part of twenty years. I can't do anything to change the past and if you want to cut me out of your life I can't stop you and I probably deserve it. It's your call.

'Rebecca, I will respect whatever you decide to do. I just want you to know that I have missed you so much.'

Rebecca had heard enough; she couldn't listen anymore. It was too much to take in all at once. All these revelations on top of everything else she had been through lately. She needed to be alone, she needed some fresh air. She got up and without a backward glance, left her mother sobbing into a whole wad of tissues.

* * *

After walking in the fields for a while, Rebecca went to find her mother. She was still sitting in the living room. She had stopped sobbing but she hadn't moved. Rebecca sat back down and put her arm around her mother's shoulders.

'I don't hate you, Mum. You're right, we could go on hating each other for the rest of our lives but all that's going to achieve is more pain and anguish and cause even more damage. Anyhow, I'm too tired to go on feeling like that, it's time to let go and move on.'

Rebecca's mother slumped forward. For a minute, Rebecca thought she was having a heart attack. 'Mum, Mum, are you OK?'

With tears streaming down her cheeks, Mrs Samuels straightened up and enfolded her daughter in her arms, holding her as if she would never let her go. Rebecca wasn't sure how long they hugged each other but her mother eventually disentangled herself. Stroking Rebecca's hair she murmured, 'I have something to show you, Rebecca.'

'What's that?'

'Wait here.' Her mother got up from her armchair and dashed out of the living room.

When she came back she was carrying a small, shoe-sized cardboard box. Rebecca watched fascinated as her mother placed the box on the coffee table beside her chair and sat down. She lifted the lid off the box and it was almost full of pressed flowers.

'Where did they all come from?'

'They're all yours.'

'All mine? ... Who from?'

'Ever since you left home, every year on your birthday, a different flower has been left on the driveway.' Her mother plucked one random flower from the top of the pile. It was a pink carnation and she handed it to Rebecca.

Rebecca took it and sniffed the dried petals. 'Tell me, who are they from?'

'Who do you think?'

As Rebecca glanced up from the petals, the penny dropped. 'Blue, they're from Mr Blue?'

'Who else could they be from?'

Rebecca put the dried petals to her nose again and imagined she could smell the fresh scent. 'Why would he leave me flowers on my birthday? He never did it when I used to live here.'

'Perhaps it was his way of letting you know that he was still here waiting for you.'

'But why would he risk it? Why would he take such chance he might have been seen and exposed?'

'You'll have to find that out for yourself, won't you?'

'Have you ever seen Him around here?' Rebecca asked as she put the carnation back in the box.

'No, and there haven't been any sightings of Him on Claydon Head in the last twenty years that I know of; he has obviously learned how to remain hidden from the public eye.'

'Up until now,' Rebecca corrected.

'Yes, Patrick told me all about what happened. Of course, if the authorities believe he exists and he really did kill those men in the gas masks then, that's murder and they're certainly going to hunt Him down.'

'But who were those men chasing us and what might have happened if Blue hadn't saved us?'

'Well, I've never seen any strange men hanging around the woods wearing gas masks, Rebecca. Are you sure they were really after you?'

'Oh, yes, Mum, they were trying to kill us all right and I think it must be down to some official organisation. They must know about Blue's existence. I mean, why else have those woods been off limits to the general public for the last twenty years? And why were those two gas-mask weirdos patrolling the woods in the first place?' Rebecca paused. 'Do you happen to know a man called Dr Olsen?'

Her mother looked flustered. 'I've never heard of him, who is he?'

'He's got some sort of agenda and it's all about Blue.'

'Well, how does he know about Him?'

'He doesn't for sure, I think he just suspects. He's probably one of those Bigfoot-legend-fantasists just trying to get lucky. Back when Dad was murdered he told me that he was one of the investigators on the case. He said that he remembered me claiming that it was Blue who killed Dad. I think he's been obsessed with what he heard me say about Blue ever since. I think he's trying to capture Him so he can be famous and then sell Him off for scientific studies. Are you sure you don't remember a Dr Olsen at the time of the investigations?'

Rebecca's mum gave a firm shake of her head.

'Why is he so interested in Him now, all of a sudden? Why not ten, fifteen years ago? It certainly seems as if he has some connection to all this.'

Not answering her daughter's questions, Mrs Samuels tried to change the subject. 'I'm just relieved that you didn't get hurt last night, Rebecca. I mean, what on earth prompted you to wander off into the woods until all hours, anyway? And if you are sure about what you witnessed yesterday then you need to go straight to the police and report it.'

'Oh yeah, Mum, and what do you think they will say when I try to tell them what happened and who did the killing? I tried that the last time with Dad and where did that get me? Even if they did investigate, which I'm pretty sure that they wouldn't, I bet they'll be no bodies there now. I'm certain that they'll have miraculously vanished. And then I'll get charged for wasting valuable police time.'

'But you can't just sit back and do nothing, Rebecca.'

'No, you're right, but I'll need to be as rational as I can and pray that no more Gas Mask Men come out of the woodwork in the meantime.'

'What if Patrick has already gone to the police?' her mum suggested. 'Perhaps they might take his account of what happened more seriously.'

'No, he said he would phone me before deciding to do anything. But Patrick has got to be careful. There are definitely dark forces at work here. Firstly, this Olsen chap, then the woods being closed off, those Gas Mask Men and the helicopter hovering over Claydon Woods. It all adds up to something far-reaching and ominous. I have got to find out what it is; it could be a matter of life or death.'

'Rebecca, please, please, please don't get involved, I couldn't bear the thought of losing you, too.'

'I can't just bury my head in the sand, Mum; it won't just go away and you have just said that I have to do something. Whatever is going on definitely involves me as well as Blue. If I run off back home to Benarth they, whoever they are, will follow me. And you can bet your boots that this Olsen character has no intention of taking no for an answer. He'll be back. If I did go home I would be on my own. Who would I have to protect me there? I know Uncle Jim would try but what could he do? At least if I stay here I know Blue would lay down his life to keep me safe.' Rebecca mused, 'It's ironic, isn't it? For the last twenty years I've been running away, trying to get Blue out of my life, and now it looks like I'll need Him in my life to try and save it. The thing is, should I be so selfish? Should I be putting such a loyal friend in that kind of danger?'

* * *

That afternoon, Patrick sat in his favourite cafe, the very same place where he had bumped into Rebecca barely a week ago. As usual, he sat near the window where he could gaze out and watch people passing by as he drank his coffee.

Sitting there alone with his thoughts he leant his forehead against the cool plate glass to try and stop his head from trembling.

He didn't notice the two girls at the till giggling at him. All he could think of was the horror that had taken place in Claydon Woods yesterday and he couldn't stop his head and hands from shaking as he relived it. 'Jesus, what the hell have I gotten myself into?' he mumbled under his breath. 'A week ago the most dramatic thing in my life was handling a group of boisterous kids in the classroom.

'Now, all of a sudden, I'm involved in the death of a couple of gas-mask murderers and as if that isn't enough, I get confronted by a seven-foot monkey-man wandering around the woods. Christ, it sounds like a Stephen King novel. All I wanted was a quiet meal with Rebecca to discuss old times and apologise for the way I dumped her. I certainly didn't bargain for being dragged into the fucking *Frankenstein Chronicles*.'

He raised his mug of coffee to his lips. *If only I had taken a later lunch that day.* Taking a mouthful of the creamy latte, he closed his eyes as he savoured the comforting warmth. But when he reopened them he found a man with slicked-back black hair sitting at his table. The man was wearing a long raincoat and he regarded Patrick with his hard grey eyes. Almost choking, Patrick gulped down his mouthful of coffee.

'I'm sorry to barge in on you like this, Mr Farrell, but I really need to speak to you.'

'How do you know my name?' Patrick asked.

The man smiled ruefully. 'Please, allow me to introduce myself. My name is Samuel Olsen, Dr Samuel Olsen; I'm an anthropologist.'

Olsen, wasn't that the guy who had been stalking Rebecca? Patrick asked himself under his breath. 'So, what can I do for you?'

'I need your help, Mr Farrell.'

'In what way?'

Olsen put a finger to his lips as one of the girls who had giggled at Patrick came over and placed a fresh mug of coffee on the table. 'Thank you,' Olsen called after her as she went back to the counter. She turned and smiled back at him. He started to raise the mug to his lips but stopped before taking a sip. 'I believe you and Miss Samuels happen to be in great danger.'

'You don't say.' Patrick gave a mirthless laugh.

Olsen ignored the sarcasm and drank his coffee. 'I understand that you both went into Claydon Woods yesterday?'

'That's right, we went for a walk.'

'You do know that Claydon Woods have been closed off to the general public for quite a number of years, now?'

'Really; and why is that, Dr Olsen?'

'Apparently, there are extremely delicate plants and flowers in the woods that need to be preserved. Also, some of these rare plants may be poisonous to humans.'

'I thought you said you were an anthropologist. Isn't that the study of human origins, the development of the human race, not the study of plant life?'

Olsen's mouth twitched at the corners, a glimmer of a smile suggesting he was enjoying the verbal challenges Patrick was throwing out. 'Of course you are correct, I am an anthropologist and my interests extend to the many great fossilised caves in that area, too.'

'Isn't that archaeology?'

'No, not necessarily, fossils can give us invaluable clues into the study of human culture, past and present.'

Patrick muttered, 'Touché' and drank a mouthful of coffee but he pulled a face as he tasted it. His coffee had gone cold.

Olsen continued, 'I know why you both went into Claydon Woods, Mr Farrell.'

'I've already told you, we both just went for a walk.'

'No, you both went in there to look for Him.' Olsen sounded almost disinterested as he turned down the collar of his mac.

Patrick continued to play dumb, 'For who?'

'Mr Farrell, please,' Olsen said in a patronising tone.

'We just went for a casual stroll. What's wrong with that?'

Olsen leaned forward. 'Mr Farrell, there is much about Miss Samuels that you are not aware of.'

Oh, here we go, classic dividing strategy, Patrick thought. *Now, he's trying to drive a wedge between me and Rebecca so that I'll trust him and believe what he says.*

'Are you aware that she is currently under the care of a cognitive behavioural therapist?'

'Of course, she suffered a lot of trauma when she was a child; her father was murdered. That's bound to have a profound effect on any child.'

'That's right, being a school teacher you have quite a lot of background experience with children. And yes, I agree with you but do you know who she actually claimed was her father's murderer?'

It was blatantly obvious that Olsen was trying to manipulate Patrick but Patrick was determined not to take the bait. 'Yes, apparently it was some traveller or vagrant, wasn't it?'

Olsen leant further forward in his seat. 'No, Mr Farrell, she blamed the murder on an ape-like beast who she befriended as a child. She called Him Mr Blue Sky.'

'Is that right? She's never told me.' Patrick shrugged innocently.

'An ape-like, bipedal beast with human-type intelligence,' Olsen added dramatically.

'Well, I never knew that.'

'Do you believe it?' Olsen asked.

'Do you?' Patrick retorted.

'Of course I do, otherwise I wouldn't be here right now and I believe you know all about Him, too.'

Patrick sat back with his arms folded. 'How can I believe in something I know nothing about? Anyhow, how come you believe in Him? Have you seen Him for yourself?'

'Mr Farrell…'

'You can call me Patrick.'

'Patrick, we have been studying this creature for the past thirty-five years. At first, we wanted to study him in a controlled environment but in an environment close to a populated area to see how this might affect Him. We wanted to explore his survival instincts and test the power of his instinctive fears. In other words, would his instincts prevent Him from interacting with human beings even if those human beings had become very familiar to Him? Familiar because he had the opportunity to secretly observe them over a crucial period in his physical and mental development. In the right environment, he would have had the opportunity to watch them regularly, their behaviour patterns, etc. Therefore, it was essential to our research, to establish if he could survive living so close to a well-known, civilised, populated area without interacting with the humans who lived there. We also wanted to study the impact of these conditions on his habits.'

Patrick decided to tread carefully. 'You are telling me that this creature does exist and it exists because you put it in Claydon Woods on purpose?'

'Of course.'

'Bullshit! What is this? Some kind of government experiment? Is Rebecca aware of all this?'

'Mr Farrell, you really need to listen to what I have to say.' Olsen leaned even closer and Patrick could feel his breath brushing his cheek. Olsen made an arch with his fingers. 'I am here to help you both, you have to trust me on that.'

'Trust you on that, trust you on that. What about those thugs in the gas masks who tried to murder us last night? Were they part of all this, too?'

'They were there to protect you.'

'Really?' Patrick bristled. 'I'd hate to think what they would have done if they were there to harm us. And why were they wearing gas masks?'

'Like I have tried to explain, Mr Farrell, sometimes these rare and toxic plants in Claydon Woods have to be sprayed with a special compound to try and reduce their potency but the compound itself can be just as poisonous if inhaled when it is being applied and immediately after.'

'Bullshit,' Patrick snorted.

Olsen sank back in his seat. 'I think we're getting a little side-tracked. Getting back to what I was saying, it was not the wandering transient who the police claimed to have killed Rebecca's father, it was Rassimus.'

'Rassimus? Who the hell is Rassimus?'

'I'm sorry, I should have explained. Rassimus is the name of the bipedal ape whom Rebecca befriended as a child. I'm sure she has told you the whole story about Him, Mr Farrell, so let's stop playing games.'

'So, what do you want from me?'

Olsen smiled but the smile did not reach his eyes. 'We now know that Rassimus can be very dangerous. He has already shown this by murdering Rebecca's father when he was only half-grown. Rassimus is now fully-grown and is more powerful than an adult silverback gorilla. He literally has the strength to tear the average human being into pieces and what makes him even more dangerous is his high level of intelligence.'

'And why is that, Dr Olsen? How can such a primate develop that kind of special intelligence? Is there something else you're not telling me?'

'Mr Farrell, I am trying to give you the basic facts. I really do not want to confuse things with scientific explanations at this time. Suffice it to say that when Rebecca was a child she bonded with a Hominoidea and over the years that bond grew stronger and stronger. We hoped that our experiment would establish if Rassimus would interact with humans but we were not expecting our study to reveal anything so momentous.

'It had far-reaching implications for anthropology. You can imagine our frustration when Rebecca moved away and that connection with Him grew weaker but we were excited when we realised that it did not sever completely. Now, for reasons best known to herself, she has returned and I strongly believe she is going to be manipulated by Rassimus.'

'In what way?'

'It is my belief that he is trying to break free from his controlled environment and he wants Rebecca to help Him. Although he has many human characteristics, he is still a wild animal and any wild animal does not like to be confined. Its natural instinct is to escape and escape it will, by any means possible. But Rassimus has the mental capacity to plan his escape very carefully and eliminate all the dangers first and then leave no traces behind, whatsoever.'

Giving Olsen the impression that he was prepared to hear him out, Patrick asked, 'So, what can I possibly do?'

'I need you both to help me capture Him before it is too late. I can't impress upon you enough how vital this is. The kind of carnage an animal of his immense size and intelligence could create if it was to attack members of the general public would be catastrophic.'

'But if he is so powerful and intelligent, why does he need Rebecca to escape? Why doesn't he just do whatever he wants to do?'

'Because Rebecca must be a part of his overall plan. She must be, otherwise she would not be here.

'Somehow, he has a great influence over her mind. For the time being, we must monitor his actions and the reasons for them, until we can figure out what he is planning.'

It was clear that Patrick wanted no part of this so-called anthropological experiment and Olsen realised that he wasn't getting anywhere. 'Mr Farrell, please.'

But Patrick had already made up his mind. 'I don't know if I can help you, Dr Olsen. After all, you are talking about eliminating this creature, not simply capturing Him; am I right?'

Avoiding Patrick's eyes, Olsen's words came out in a rush. 'No, of course not, we do not want to kill Rassimus, we simply want to move him to a secure unit so he, and everyone else, will be much safer.'

Patrick wasn't taken in and he suspected that Olsen was lying. Back when he was doing his teacher training, he took a short course in psychology. It was part of the syllabus and it focused on body language and signs to look for when people were being untruthful. Patrick recalled that one of the signs, amongst many others, was that a person will look downwards or move their eyes when they are lying. A way to test them is to ask a simple question that they will answer truthfully. If their eyes move to the right that suggests that the right movement indicates a truthful answer. If the eyes move to the left when answering then the answer is probably untruthful. Just to confirm this theory, Patrick asked Olsen what he called Mr Blue. His eyes moving to the right, Olsen answered, 'Rassimus.'

'You're saying that you don't want to kill Him?'

Olsen's eyes moved to the left as he lied, 'Absolutely not.'

'I'll have to think about all this, Dr Olsen.'

Olsen smiled to hide his frustration and reaching into his pocket, he took out a small white card. 'Here, Mr Farrell, this is my private number and you can reach me any time of the day or night.' He rose from his seat and straightened out his long mac. 'I'll await your call, Mr Farrell, please don't leave it too late.'

And he slipped away as silently as he had appeared.

Patrick watched through the cafe window as he got into a black Discovery. He turned away from the window and studied the card in his hands. The name was indented in bold black capitals: DR SAMUEL OLSEN and underneath was his contact number.

CHAPTER FOURTEEN

'Olsen is here,' Patrick blurted out as soon as Rebecca opened the front door. Instead of texting or calling her he wanted to give her his news personally and on the same day. So, he drove up to her mum's house as soon as he had got his head together after Olsen had left the cafe.

'He's here?' she gasped.

'He tracked me down and caught up with me at Strauss's Cafe this afternoon.'

'What the hell is he doing here?'

'He wants Blue.'

Rebecca checked behind her to make sure that her mother was out of earshot. 'It's a nice day, let's go for a walk.'

Reaching the meadow above the farmhouse Rebecca felt they were far enough to talk without being heard or observed. 'I know he wants Blue, but what for?'

Patrick kept his voice down. 'According to him, he wants us to help him to capture Blue so he can transfer Him to a safer environment. He and his team have been studying Blue for thirty-five years and they know how intelligent he is. Olsen tried to convince me that Blue is going to use you to help Him to get away from his captors so he can disappear. Although I have to say, I don't think Blue can disappear. Where would he go and how would he get there? Olsen also said that Blue is very dangerous.'

'It's true that Blue has asked me to help Him but he hasn't let me know if he has an escape plan; he hasn't let me know anything really, except that he and I are in danger.'

Patrick interrupted, 'By the way, Blue's real name is Rassimus.'

'Rassimus? Rassimus? Are you sure?'

'That's what Olsen told me. Blue is part of some anthropological experiment. They have been monitoring Him all his life, observing him in Claydon Woods to see how he developed and reacted to living in a specially selected environment.'

'And was part of that experiment to kill his mother?' Rebecca retorted.

'What did you say? They killed his mother?'

'Yes, they did. They killed her when Blue was an infant and they left Him to fend for himself. I also found out, from Blue, that he came from some kind of institution or laboratory and then some strange men took Him and his mother to Claydon Woods. Blue did let me know that he was being hunted now and he wanted me to find out exactly why and who was after Him because he doesn't want to be hunted anymore. So, what do you think? Is Olsen trying to capture Him so he can experiment on Him or worse.'

Patrick kicked the ground. 'Well, Olsen didn't look very convincing when I asked whether Blue would be safe if they ever captured him.'

Rebecca tossed her head. 'I bet the first thing they would do is to conduct all sorts of experiments on Him.'

'But Olsen did say he believed that Blue killed your father and I think he is using that to prove how unpredictable Blue can be. He said he believes that you may be in very serious danger.'

Rebecca fell silent for a moment.

'What did your mother have to say to you earlier? Did she tell you everything?'

'Yeah, she confessed that she and my father knew about Blue all along and they'd allowed me to play with Him because they thought

I needed a friend to keep me company. But she swore that she didn't know where Blue had come from.'

Patrick sighed heavily. 'Christ, Becca, what the hell have we gotten into, here? All I wanted out of this was a meal out so I could spend some time with you. I certainly didn't expect to be plunged into a death-defying plot from a horror movie.'

'Look, Patrick, I'm really sorry for dragging you into all this but I have to find out what's going on. I can't explain it but when I was back home in Benarth and those nightmares started up again, I could feel something calling me. It was like one of those strange prophetic messages that tell you that you have to do something; you don't know what it is but you know you have to do it. I had no idea that, if I did follow it up, it would lead to me being stalked by a crazy anthropologist or being attacked by men in gas masks, or even having a seven-foot old friend pleading for me to help Him. I honestly imagined that when I came back here all I would find would be empty woodlands and forgotten memories and then I would have made myself accept that. It would have taken a big effort but I would have come to terms with it after a while. There would be no such thing as Mr Blue and eventually I could have convinced myself that everyone else had been right and I had been wrong. I could have put everything down to childhood fantasies. I would have been able to try and get on with my life at last. But now, with all this, I don't know what I'm going to do.'

Patrick gently took both of her hands in his. 'I'm sorry, Becca, I didn't realise how tough this was for you. I just never expected all this either. I mean, just think what it's been like for me, too? I've now seen indisputable proof that Blue does exist and I almost got killed in the process. The closest thing I get to any kind of drama these days is marking a pile of composition work from a class of delinquent fourteen-year-olds. Do you know, as I sat in the cafe this afternoon, before Olsen turned up, I had made up my mind that I didn't want to get involved any longer?'

Rebecca glanced up at him; her eyes dulled with disappointment.

'I mean, up until now I've had a fairly stable and predictable life and I have a good, secure career at the moment.'

Here we go again, Rebecca thought to herself, *another brush-off. Back when we were teenagers he dumped me because of my crazy, delusional fantasies; this time, he's going to dump me because I'm telling the truth. It seems as if you're damned if you can't prove that you are telling the truth and damned if you can. Patrick isn't going to stay around to help after all and to be honest, who could blame him?*

But Patrick hadn't finished. 'When that damn Olsen appeared and I heard what he had to say I felt very scared for you and I knew I couldn't walk away. I couldn't leave you to fight all this shit on your own.'

Confused, Rebecca stepped away.

Patrick followed her. 'If I walked away and something bad happened to you I would never be able to live with myself and what kind of man would that make me?'

'Let me get this straight, you haven't been scared off then?'

Patrick smiled. 'I suppose I can hang around for a while.'

Rebecca wasn't completely convinced but she still threw herself into his arms and gave him a big squeeze. At least, for the time being, her doubts about Patrick were set aside. However, Patrick wasn't expecting such a show of appreciation but he soon warmed to the moment and very tentatively he curled his arms around her waist. Their embrace lingered and when Patrick kissed her, Rebecca didn't pull away.

The kiss kindled overwhelming surges of desire in both of them. Patrick buried his face in her hair and whispered, 'You are so beautiful, Beccs, even more beautiful than you were when you were fifteen. I love your dimpled smile and the way your brown eyes seem to have tiny pinpoints of rubies in them when they catch the sun.'

Rebecca was too breathless to answer but she kissed Patrick hungrily. He took her hand and led her over to a dip at the edge of the meadow; it was partially screened by thick bushes. Without speaking, he took off his jacket and spread it on the ground. They sank down and fumbled with each other's clothes. As the naked parts of their bodies came into contact and Patrick started to touch her, Rebecca felt as if she was being whirled away on a high fairground ride that sent all her senses into overdrive. Patrick moaned and groaned as he thrust himself inside her but just as she was about to reach cloud nine, it was over. It had only lasted for a few minutes and it was over. Patrick shuddered and collapsed on top of her and whimpered, 'Sorry, sorry.'

Rebecca broke away saying that it was, "OK". But it wasn't OK. What had she done? What, in God's name, had she been thinking? What had she risked for a few minutes of disappointing, unprotected, casual sex in a field?

She must have been out of her mind. She didn't want to make Patrick feel bad, after all it was as much her fault as it was his, but she also wanted to let him know that what they had just done had been a mistake. She held him in her arms and blurted out, 'Patrick, this has been a reaction to the horrors of yesterday. It was our way of dealing with the bloody murders of those Gas Mask Men. We needed to release all that fear and confusion so that we can go on. We had to relieve our pent-up feelings but please don't think that I didn't want you, because I did. But now, now we have to put this behind us and get back to weighing up what we should do.'

Pulling up his trousers, Patrick avoided looking at Rebecca. He was obviously embarrassed and hurt and as anxious as she was to move on. 'You can tell you have been having counselling, Beccs, you sound just like a counsellor yourself. But I will go along with what you say and for now we can pretend that this never happened.' Brushing the grass from his knees, he did his best to regain his composure. 'OK then, so what are we going to do about Olsen?'

'What do you suggest?'

'Maybe it's a case of better-the-devil-you-know type scenario. Who are we more likely to be safe with, Dr Olsen or Mr Blue?'

'You're putting Blue in the same category as Olsen?'

'All I'm saying is that you were very young when you had that special bond with Blue and even though he was only an infant he still murdered your father. What do you think he's capable of doing now, as an adult? We've already seen what he did to those gas-mask freaks. Can you honestly say that you can still trust Him with your life?'

'Patrick, he's not going to hurt me, I do know that. He saved my life and he risked his life to save me yesterday.'

'OK, then, what if he really did want to escape from Claydon Woods; how long do you think a creature of his immense size would last before he was spotted by someone? And, if that did happen they would probably send in the armed forces to destroy Him, not capture Him. So perhaps Olsen, as dodgy as he is, is the lesser of two evils.'

Rebecca bridled, 'Do you think I would trust Olsen with Blue's life? Absolutely no way. At least if Blue does get out and away from those bastards he's got a chance and I owe Him that.'

'But, Becca, you can't let Blue loose to roam around the Welsh countryside, come on! What about all those innocent people you may be putting at risk?'

'Blue wouldn't harm anyone, he'd just keep himself to himself and hide away somewhere. He'd probably just find another wood or forest to hide in once he's escaped from Olsen.'

'Fine, let's say he doesn't harm anyone at first but if he does become exposed then all hell will break loose and Olsen is not going to take any chances. He's not going to risk any of this falling back on him. Believe me, he will want to destroy Blue and all that incriminating evidence connected to this so-called experiment. And I remember something else Olsen said to me in the cafe and it stuck in my head. He said that any trapped, wild animal has a natural instinct to escape but any intelligent, wild animal will first eliminate all threats to its life before it makes its move. In other words, everyone around it could be in great danger.'

Rebecca needed time to think before she could come up with any answers but she was sure of one thing. 'I want to see Blue before I can decide what to do next.'

'Are you going to tell him about Olsen's plan to capture Him?'

'Of course, that's what Blue asked me to do.'

'Are you sure that's wise? I mean, what if Olsen is right about Him? What if Blue is manipulating you into helping Him so he can kill us and get rid of all the witnesses?'

'You're not listening, Patrick. I have already told you that I don't believe any of that, I know Him too well.'

Patrick grabbed her shoulders firmly. 'Do you really know Him, though? You didn't even know his real name until today and before yesterday you hadn't seen Him in twenty years. Twenty years he's been all alone in that cave without any interaction, any contact with any other humans. That's a hell of a long time, Becca. What's been going on in that unique mind of his in all that time? All he has ever known is that humans are the enemy; they killed his mother and betrayed Him and now they are trying to hunt Him down. And you say you can trust Him? Perhaps, for Him this may be the ultimate revenge on his captors, he might want to lead us all into a trap then kill us and make his escape.'

But Rebecca still wasn't prepared to go along with Patrick. He didn't know Blue the way she did. 'I still don't believe he'll harm me,' she insisted.

'Becca, I think you're being a bit naive. OK, just for argument's sake, let's say you're right and he doesn't harm you, but what about ME and anyone else who's involved? We could be in real danger. We would be like insects that get too close to an electric fly catcher and end up getting zapped.'

'No, you'll be OK, Blue knows you're with me.'

'Somehow, I don't think there's any guarantee that's going to make any difference, do you?'

Deep down, Rebecca suspected that he could be right; at this stage she couldn't guarantee his, or anyone else's, safety.

'Last night in the woods, when he was carrying you off, he turned back to look at me. I saw a look that I don't ever want to see again. As he gave me that stare, I honestly believed he was trying to decide whether or not to kill me there and then or save it for another day.'

Rebecca became indignant. 'That's mad. It was your imagination. He has no reason to kill you. He wouldn't even bother about you.'

'Yeah, and that's what worries me.'

Rebecca had heard enough, they were getting nowhere. She suspected that Patrick was letting his humiliation over their pathetic fling in the grass colour his judgement and she stuck to her guns. 'I need to see Him and I need to see Him now.'

CHAPTER FIFTEEN

Rebecca was glad that she and her mother had confronted the complex problems which had been the cause of their long estrangement. Under the circumstances, the outcome could have been so much worse. But her mother's honesty and abject apologies had made it possible for Rebecca to put their past behind her. Not only that, Rebecca now felt closer to her than she had ever done. Tonight, Mrs Samuels had gone to bed early and Rebecca was downstairs drinking a steaming mug of hot chocolate in front of the TV. Even though she had the television on she couldn't concentrate on any of the programmes. Her mind felt like a rotating tumble dryer full of jumbled thoughts and emotions. And after what had happened between her and Patrick earlier, well... thank God her mother didn't know.

She sat, staring into space, absently stirring her chocolate drink. As she made circles in the froth with the teaspoon it took a minute or two for the sound to pierce through her muddled thoughts. Perhaps that was because the sound was not continuous; it came from outside the house and it came in short, regular pitches. Rebecca was inexorably drawn to it as if it was pulling her by an invisible cord. Dropping the spoon back in her mug and placing it on the coffee table she walked out of the living room and made her way to the front door. She opened it and peered out into the night but she couldn't see anything. Then, in the distance, she heard the whistle once more. This time, it had a sharper tone which carried a sense of urgency.

The compulsion to follow the sound was growing stronger and without even slipping on her coat she left the house and walked down the driveway without a backward glance. The open front door spilled out its welcoming light on her retreating figure until she was consumed by the enveloping darkness. Where she was going she didn't know; she was guided only by the sound that resounded in her ears. What's more, she was not afraid. She sensed that she was being watched and she knew she was being protected.

* * *

For the second time that week Rebecca opened her eyes to find she was lying on the familiar stone bed, snugly wrapped in the familiar animal fur. The Sky Chamber flickered with the warm glow of candlelight and she knew instantly where she was but her sight was slightly blurred and she rubbed her eyes as she sat up.

'How come I can never remember how I get here?' she mumbled. 'How come I always black out?'

She looked around the cave but there was no Mr Blue and she rose to her feet clutching the fur blanket to her neck to ward off the cold draughts.

'Blue?' Rebecca kept calling out until she heard a soft scuffling coming from behind her.

In a halo of candlelight Blue emerged from the forbidden passage, the one he had told her never to enter all those years ago. He was dressed in a long brown robe, a bit like a monk's habit. In one hand he held a candle in an ornate silver candlestick. In the other, he carried a round clay dish filled with food. He moved past her grunting a friendly acknowledgement.

'You were beginning to scare me. You look scary dressed like that,' she complained sinking back down on the stone bed.

Blue ignored her and went to sit at the table to eat his meal. Irritated by his manner but more curious about his food she craned her neck to see what he had in his dish. It looked like some a sort of thick paste mixed with wild mushrooms and red berries.

Making a face she asked, 'Just what is that muck? It looks revolting.'

Blue lifted his dish to offer her some but she threw up her hands and turned her head away.

Blue gave a playful snort indicating that he found her squeamishness amusing. Then, he put the dish back on the table and carried on tucking in.

'Revolting,' she repeated.

Even though he had offered to share his food and she had refused, Blue watched her as if he thought she might snatch it from Him.

'Don't worry, I'm not going to nick any of that horrible stuff off you,' she told him.

Blue continued to finger out the disgusting paste and shovelled it into his mouth revealing his large yellowy incisors. Just as Rebecca was beginning to wonder what she was doing sitting there this time, she felt something hit her shoulder. Blue had tossed over a small stone to get her attention.

'Did you just chuck that at me?'

Blue blinked his eyes at her and began making finger signs, asking if she had anything to tell Him.

'Yes, I have found out some things.'

Blue rapped on the rock table impatiently.

Rebecca gave Him the sort of look she used to give Him when she thought he was being annoying and rude. In response, Blue snarled the sort of snarl he used to make when he was irritated with her. Then, as they remembered, they both grinned and Rebecca threw the stone back at Him before she shared the information he wanted. 'There's this man called Olsen and he intends to try and capture you.'

Blue's glowing orange eyes narrowed as he listened.

'It sounds like you were part of some scientific experiment. I don't quite know what type of experiment yet. But this Olsen thinks that you may be planning to escape from Claydon Woods. He refers to Claydon Woods as your planned, controlled environment and he wants to take you away to a safer place before you cause any harm to yourself and others.'

Blue made some more question signals asking for a full name and description.

'Olsen, Dr Samuel Olsen, he's tall with jet-black hair and he is supposed to be an anthropologist,' Rebecca replied.

Blue pointed his finger at Rebecca as if the name meant something to Him.

'Do you know who he is?'

Blue frantically signed, *I remember a man, a man with black hair, holding me in his arms when I was taken away from my mother. I did not like this man. He gave us all a happy smile to try and comfort us but he still gave us a lot of pain.*

'Was it he who brought you here?'

He gave me to some other men then they brought me here with my mother because I would have been very sad without her. After we got here, the other men killed my mother and left me all alone. I was confused and didn't understand why she wouldn't wake up. I needed her. I remember crying but she couldn't hear me. It was like she didn't care and didn't want to touch me. I felt alone, frightened and water ran down my face and onto my fur.

You, Ecca, helped me then went home. I didn't know what to do or where to go and I roamed the woods for days and when I came across this cave, I hid here and made it my home. Every day I ate the food that I found outside the cave but it made me ill, hurt my stomach, so I threw it away and had to find better things to eat. My fur kept me warm and I made more fur from dead animals but sometimes their meat was not nice to eat. I ate plants and berries and I learned how to steal some chicken and meat. I felt much better, stronger.

Although she felt sorry for Him Rebecca tried not to let her pity distract her. 'But why didn't they kill you, too?'

I don't know but they're trying to kill me now. Maybe they don't like me because I have grown so much. Maybe they only liked me when I was young. I know I can't stay here any longer. If I don't get away they will kill me and I need Ecca to help me, now.

'But I don't know what I can do.'

After you went away from here for a long time they began to hunt me every day. They would capture me, hurt me and then let me go again. They did the same thing many times but when I grew big and strong they started to play the game much harder and would hurt me much more before letting me go.

'What do you mean, play harder?'

It was like a big hide and seek game, like we played when we were young. Only when they caught me I got a big stick of pain. Now the games are for real.

'For real?' Rebecca questioned.

I mustn't lose the game anymore or they will kill me. Now, I have to kill them to live. They make the game much harder so I have to be much smarter. I can't play this game forever, they will get me in the end.

'But where do you plan on going? Where can you go where you'll be safe?'

I can't stay here in this cave. They will find me in the end.

'But, Blue, tell me, where will you go?'

Live with Ecca, Blue joked, barking short pants of a laugh.

'Oh, yeah, I'm sure that'd work out very well. The man from the energy company might get a bit of a shock when he comes to read the gas meter, though.'

Gas man, like the men in the woods? Do the Gas Men come to your home? Blue signed.

'No, no, they don't come to my home but never mind that now. You have to tell me where you want to escape to?'

Blue tapped his barrel-sized chest and burped after his meal. *Berries make me shit better.*

'Charming and succinctly put,' Rebecca remarked. 'Well, if berries give you wind, wait till you taste my home-cooked bean casserole.'

What the fuck do you mean? Blue signed.

'Fuck is an offensive word, Blue. You didn't learn that one from me. Where did you hear that word before?'

One of the men I caught when we were playing the hiding and seeking game. I stole his clothes while he was hanging upside down in the tree. He said, "Fuck You" to me when I ran off with them. I thought they were special words that were part of the game. Then another man came and I shoved my spear into his shit hole and he howled and said, "Fuck You," before he limped away. This time, I thought he was using the special words to thank me for letting him go.

Although Rebecca was at her wits end she couldn't stop herself falling about giggling. Blue had learned so much about humans but in other ways he had learned so little. She had no choice, she had to help Him to escape. Between her fits of giggles, she gasped, 'I really don't want to hear about any of that now, I just want to know where we can possibly get you safely away from Olsen and his team.'

Eying her solemnly Blue signed slowly, *Maybe you can help kill me?*

Rebecca suddenly got serious and frowned back at Him. 'Kill you; what do you mean, kill you?'

Maybe it is my only chance to escape.

'Don't be stupid. That's no way to think. You can't just give up like that.'

You don't understand. I have a plan.

'No, I don't understand and I think you'd better start planning something else.'

Blue made a sign she couldn't make out.

'What?'

Want to play hide and seek?

'Hide and seek? Here? Now? Are you joking?'

Not here, now; tomorrow in the woods just like we did when we were little.

'Blue, don't be a moron. I thought you wanted to stay hidden from those men who are after you?'

They don't come on scraping day.

'Scraping day?'

Sometimes, they give me days off to make scraping tools so I can set new traps for the game then they come back with a big, noisy flying thing.

'Yeah, I've seen the big, noisy flying thing too. How often do they hunt you?'

Most days but because you taught me hide and seek game they find it very hard to catch me.

'Blue, hide and seek is a child's game; you don't play it when you grow up.'

Blue shrugged his heavy shoulders. *I think it keeps me alive.*

'OK, maybe we'll play it some other time. But for now, we've got more important things to sort out.'

You're going to stay here until the sun comes up, Blue commanded.

'No, I can't stay here. It's too cold for me. I need to get back home. By the way, how come I can never remember how I get here?'

Blue pointed over to an old glass jar, shoved in a corner amongst a pile of half-burnt church candles.

Rebecca could see that the jar was nearly full of dark liquid. 'What's in that?'

Sleep juice, Blue replied pushing his empty clay dish away from Him.

'Sleep juice? You mean, you've actually been drugging me?'

I had to. Where I live must stay a secret. If they catch you and torture you to tell them where I am, you can't because you don't know.

'Oh, well, thanks for thinking of me in that way, and what may I ask is in it?'

Who knows? Not me. The men left it by mistake when they first brought me here and it works on small animals, too.

'Brilliant, that's really great, Blue. For all I know you could be giving me something poisonous. Just don't give it to me again. How do you get me to drink it anyway and has this sleep stuff got anything to do with the way you can send me those telepathic messages?'

Blue rose to his feet and looking a bit shamefaced, he avoided the questions and signed out a light-hearted reply instead. *It only gives you a bad taste for about half hour; that's all and you might blow from your back hole a bit.*

Rebecca decided not to push it. Blue wasn't going to give anything else away. Maybe there were some things he would never tell her. Patting the seat of her jogging bottoms, she drawled, 'Oh, that's very nice.' And she stood aside as he headed past her towards the forbidden tunnel. 'Where are you going now?'

Always nagging, you give me more trouble than a bellyful of bad berries.

'Yeah and I missed you, too. Tell me why I can't go down there.'

Too dangerous, too many holes in the ground and you don't know the tunnels like I do.

Then he made a sound of an object falling from a great height. *You need me to help you, guide you.*

'So, why don't you take me down there now then?'

Not yet, but soon, when it's the right time.

'When is the right time?'

Blue shoved his hairy hand towards her mouth to stop her asking anymore questions.

Perhaps it was because he didn't want to answer any more of her questions that he changed his mind about her staying with Him and he agreed to let her leave the cave there and then. Not taking any chances with the sleep juice she refused to eat or drink anything so Blue tied a blindfold around her eyes before he led her back through the woods.

* * *

When she arrived home, her mother was at the door waiting for her. 'Where have you been? The front door was wide open and I thought you had been kidnapped.'

'Sorry, Mum, I was quite safe. I've been with Blue. He needs my help and I have to work out what to do. You look exhausted. I'm sorry you were worried. Let's try and get some sleep now, shall we?' Putting her arm around her shoulders, Rebecca led her mother into the house shutting the door behind them.

Rebecca knew that it would be another sleepless night but for her mum's sake she went to bed anyway.

There wasn't much of the night left and as the hours and minutes ticked away she lay awake staring at the ceiling of her bedroom and it became a listening ear for all her anguished reflections.

Damn, I forgot to ask Blue about all those flowers that he's been leaving me every year on my birthday. Damn, why didn't I tell Blue that Olsen warned me that I could be in great danger for helping Him? Why didn't I ask Blue to reassure me? Was it because Olsen has sowed seeds of doubt in my mind. Doubts about whether or not I would be safe around Blue after all this time? Or was it because, after everything that has happened, I don't trust Blue anymore?

What if Olsen is right? What if Blue doesn't genuinely care about me at all? He might be programmed to follow his instinctive, primordial instincts in order to survive. That might mean that he will destroy everyone else in the process. What if it did come down to a life and death situation? Will that special bond, that strong bond that we once had, actually make a difference?

Perhaps I should make some self-preservation plans of my own just in case things do go wrong. Or, on the other hand, maybe I should pack my bags tomorrow and shoot off back to Uncle Jim in Benarth and leave them all to battle it out amongst themselves. Rebecca drummed her fingers on her chest. *In the long run, it might be safer if I just opt for the simple, humdrum existence that I had before. At least I would be safe. Only, is it safe enough?*

Despite all her uncertainty, deep down Rebecca knew she couldn't run out on Blue now even if she wanted to. She also knew that she shouldn't give in so easily, especially after all those years living as a prisoner shackled to her confused fears, regrets and doubts. No, she couldn't go back home and endure all that again. It would finish her off, although she had to acknowledge to herself that either course of action could finish her off. This was it then, the ultimate test. This was the mountain she had to climb so she could reach those peaceful green pastures she longed for. As tough as it might be, the only way to make it was to grit her teeth and get on with it.

✱ ✱ ✱

At the bottom of the driveway Rebecca was doing her rubbish duties, dumping another heavy, plastic bag into the wheelie bin, when she caught sight of a group of black-clothed figures striding into the woods. She gazed over and from what she could make out there was one figure in front. She stood watching apprehensively then headed back indoors. In the kitchen, her mother was about to take a sip of freshly brewed coffee. 'Mum, who are those people going into the woods?'

'What people?' her mother frowned.

'I thought Claydon Woods was closed off to the public, no trespassers.'

'Oh, they must be those health and safety officials checking the toxicity levels on the plants or something; I don't really know for sure.'

'But don't health and safety officials wear white uniforms, not black?'

Lifting her shoulders in a tired shrug, Rebecca's mum stuttered, 'I don't know. Perhaps they're conducting some experiments; who knows?' She sagged onto a kitchen chair and swallowed some coffee.

Rebecca leant against the worktop and thought back to what Blue had told her about the *scraping days*, his days off from the hunting game. If this was a scraping day then who were these people going into the woods?

But before she could come up with an explanation she heard the familiar whirring sound of a helicopter swooping over the cliff tops. Rebecca made a dive for the window. Flinging it open, she craned her head out as the same helicopter hovered overhead for a minute or two then dipped down beneath the cliffs and out of sight.

That afternoon Patrick called Rebecca from his mobile. He sounded a bit wary, as if he wasn't sure if she would bring up their clumsy fumble in the fields. When she didn't he sounded relieved and told her that he had tried a Google search on Olsen to see if he could find out any information on him. But all that came up was a list of businessmen and entrepreneurs. There was nothing on a Dr Olsen– Anthropologist; he had drawn a blank. Rebecca suggested that he should try searching Covert Government Animal Experiments and this gave Patrick an idea. Patrick remembered that he had an old friend who was a bit of an expert on conspiracy theories and if he contacted him he might be able to come up with something. Rebecca thought it was certainly worth a try and told Patrick to ring her back that evening to let her know how he got on. Now they were back on track and seemed to be getting somewhere, Rebecca decided it was time to give her uncle a ring and tell him the truth about Mr Blue Sky.

Sitting in the little summerhouse, well out of earshot of her mother, Rebecca dialled her uncle's number.

His gravelly voice barked, 'Hello?'

'Hi, Jim, it's Rebecca.'

'Becca, my love, how are you? How's it going down there?'

'Fine but I'm in a spot of bother.'

'Not again; what's up?'

Rebecca eased herself into a more comfortable position on the dilapidated wooden bench. Before answering, she checked to see that her mother wasn't about. 'You're not going to like what I'm about to say to you.'

'That sounds a bit ominous, but that's nothing new,' Jim replied.

On the other end of the line Rebecca could hear the office door being closed. He obviously wanted to talk in private.

'So what's it all about?' he asked.

'He's real.'

'Who's real?'

'Mr Blue Sky.'

The line seemed to go dead.

'Jim, are you still there?'

Jim's sigh was so loud that Rebecca could almost feel it over the line. 'Yes, I'm still here and I just can't believe what I'm hearing, that's all. Not this thing all over again, Rebecca, please; we've been through all this already.'

'But I know he is real, I've seen Him and now I can prove that he does exist.'

'Becca, this is really…'

Rebecca cut in before he could finish. 'Mum knows he exists, too.'

'You've involved your mother in this as well?' Jim protested.

'We had a long talk and she told me things I should have been told years ago. She confessed everything to me, after…'

'After what?'

'You probably won't remember Patrick; we dated when we were teenagers and met up again when I got back home. The other day Patrick and I went into Claydon Woods to look for some proof that Blue was real. Anyway, we were attacked by these two men in gas masks and it was Blue who saved us. Patrick saw Him too and I even visited the cave where Blue lives, the same cave he took me to when I was fourteen. When I eventually got back home and told Mum what had happened, she finally admitted to me that she and Dad knew all about Him all along. By the way, she said you were in on it, too. Were you?'

'No, Rebecca, I wasn't in on anything.'

'Are you sure you didn't know anything about it? Mum told me you did and that on the night that Dad went after Blue in the woods he was supposed to wait for you to go in there with him.'

'Well, your mother got that wrong, I didn't know anything about it.'

'OK, but they both knew all about Blue right from the start and now I have the evidence I needed to prove that I am not a crazy fantasist.' Rebecca took a breath. 'The problem is, this Olsen chap has turned up again and he wants us to help him capture Blue so he can take him away to a more secure unit. According to him, Blue was part of a scientific experiment and he believes that Blue is out of control and we might all be in great danger.'

'Becca, are you seriously expecting me to swallow all this?'

'Jim, listen, I've seen Blue with my own eyes and I have witnesses to back it up. What more do I need?'

'This is madness,' Jim snorted.

'But Blue wants me to help Him escape from Olsen and his men. He thinks they are trying to kill Him.'

'Oh, and he's told you all this, has he? He can speak English?'

'Blue doesn't speak, he uses sign language and for some unknown reason I can understand it. Blue is very intelligent, much more intelligent than the average primate, because it looks like he has been genetically engineered for this experiment.'

'That's marvellous,' Jim scoffed. 'I suppose he can bake cakes and sing like a canary, too, can he?'

'Jim, will you just listen? I've phoned you up in the hope that you might give me some advice because you're the only one I feel I can truly trust to do that.'

'Rebecca, I just don't want to see you go through this all over again. Just look what it did to you last time. And I have to say I'm very disappointed in your mother for encouraging you like this.'

'Jim, I'm not crazy, I'm not imagining it; you just need to have faith in what I am saying. You have done so much for me and I wouldn't lie to you.'

'OK, OK, let's just say for a moment that he is real but let me ask you this. In all the time he's been wandering around Claydon Woods how come no other person has ever seen Him?'

'Because Claydon Woods has been closed off to the general public for the last twenty years and Blue has learned how to keep hidden from most humans. He has to because he is being hunted by the same men on a regular basis. They are probably Olsen's men and they are probably carrying out his orders.'

Jim fell silent again as if he had given up trying to argue with her. 'OK, Rebecca, if you really want my advice then I advise you to pack your bags and get as far away from Claydon as you can. That's my advice.'

'Jim, I was hoping you could give me some advice on how I can help Blue, not run off and abandon Him. I've already thought about that and I can't do it.'

'Why?'

'Because the very reason I came back in the first place was to face this thing head on, no matter what. Believe me when I tell you that when I got back here to Claydon I wanted to find that Blue was just the imaginings of a deluded and mixed-up child. But now I know he is real, that I wasn't mentally ill and that means I can find some closure. Something is telling me that I really need to be here because the entire course of my life depends on it.'

'Rebecca, for Christ's sake,' Jim sighed.

'Nothing is going to change my mind, Jim, and I need your help to sort this thing out.'

Rebecca could hear Jim putting the phone down on his desk.

'Jim, say something.'

Coming back on the line, he sounded guarded. 'Becca, I don't know what to say. You've obviously made up your mind.'

'If you can come down here and help I will prove to you that I am telling the truth.'

'Rebecca, you know how much work I have on at the moment. It was touch and go whether I could even spare you. But I did because I wanted you to sort yourself out. I just haven't got the time to come over and play silly buggers like this.'

Rebecca's heart sank. No matter what she said she wasn't going to persuade him to come to Claydon. Of all people, she wished he understood how important this was to her. Her Uncle Jim had always been her rock, her protector, her mentor and he was always there to mop up the tears when things got too much to handle. Even when she threw his fatherly advice back in his face and told him to keep out of her business, he still supported her. Deep down, she knew he had her best interests at heart when he lectured her but she never admitted it to him. Yet now, when she really needed him the most, when she needed that reassurance and guidance, when she needed him to believe in her and give her the benefit of the doubt, now, he was going to let her down. It felt as if a door had been slammed in her face leaving her in an empty room.

That safe pair of hands she had always depended on, those hands she had bargained on always being there to catch her when she stumbled were not going to be there to catch her this time.

'Rebecca, are you still there?'

'It's OK, Jim, I understand if you're far too busy.'

'Listen, love, just forget this silly nonsense and hurry back to Benarth. We all miss hearing you whining.'

Feeling as if an impenetrable barrier had come down between herself and her uncle, Rebecca felt cold and alone and she wasn't able to listen to him anymore. 'OK, Jim, I'll speak to you soon,' she mumbled ending the call before he could say anything else.

While she sat there, with her phone held against her chin, she tried to stop herself from having a knee-jerk reaction and hating her uncle. Hate him? *No, that would be childish. I couldn't hate him. After all, he is only trying to protect me and if the situation was reversed I would probably have a hard time believing such a story.*

If he genuinely knew what was going on he would have raced down like a shot. That was what she told herself. She had to defend him because that was the only reassurance and support she was likely to get.

CHAPTER SIXTEEN

That night Rebecca waited for Patrick to call. She was dying to know if he had managed to contact his old friend but the call never came. Impatient for news she thought about phoning him just to check that everything was OK. But she didn't want to give him the wrong message, especially after what had happened between them. So, she decided to play it cool by turning in early and waiting until tomorrow.

* * *

On the west side of Claydon Head, in a tiny alcove beneath an outcrop of limestone rock, Helen sat huddled beside her crackling campfire. Sometimes she socialised with the other travellers and sometimes she preferred her own company. It would depend on whether she was willing to share her booze, mostly cider.

The drinking had started when she was in her early twenties. Back then, she was an attractive, popular young woman. She was the only child of well-to-do parents and was married to Stephen, a successful merchant banker who provided her with a comfortable lifestyle. They lived in a five-bedroomed eighteenth-century vicarage set in the heart of the Surrey stockbroker belt. They had lovingly renovated the vicarage and restored the gardens to their former glory. As well as having a lovely home, she drove a flashy BMW and enjoyed expensive holidays. On top of all that, she loved her job as an assistant editor of a women's magazine.

However, as things turned out, all this good fortune wasn't enough to make her happy. The one thing Helen desperately wanted was children. She couldn't wait to hear the sound of kids laughing and running around in the vicarage. At first, she and Stephen thought it was just a question of time. When nothing happened after five years of trying they went to see a consultant. It turned out that Helen had a medical condition known as uterine fibroids. This meant that she could never conceive because inoperable tumours in her uterus were the cause of her infertility.

When they learned what was wrong Stephen was understanding and didn't blame her at first. He hid his own disappointment and seemed to accept the fact that they couldn't have children together. At one stage they discussed a course of IVF or adopting but Helen wanted to experience the natural birth of her own baby.

She told her family and friends that if Mother Nature had denied her the right to conceive then it just wasn't meant to be.

But her heartbreak began to eat away at her and she started to drink. Gradually, her drinking increased until it began to get out of control. Stephen was also drinking more than he was used to and it was during those alcohol-fuelled episodes that the arguments would start. Losing all restraint Stephen would let his true feelings show and end up blaming her for her inability to get pregnant.

But Stephen knew that he couldn't let his drinking dominate his life. He had to keep his wits about him at work. He couldn't afford to lose his job, whereas Helen didn't know when to stop and eventually she did lose her job. Stuck at home the only way she could get through the day was to start drinking in the morning and carry on until she passed out at night. She tried to conceal how much she was drinking by driving to different supermarkets to buy her supplies and taking the empty bottles to the local recycling centre instead of putting them in her own recycling bin. On one fateful night she miscalculated a sharp bend on her way back from a supermarket. She had finished off one of the bottles of wine she had just bought in the car park and crashed the car, writing it off. It was the last straw for Stephen and he told Helen he was leaving. Not only that, he intended putting the vicarage up for sale so he could buy a flat in London. When the sale had gone through, Helen went to live with her parents but after a while her behaviour became so out of control and they told her that they couldn't cope any longer.

From then on, she lived her life in a blur of drunken stupors and telephone arguments with Stephen; the rows were always about money. But Helen couldn't hold herself together long enough to string coherent sentences together, let alone argue effectively, so she gave up fighting for her financial entitlements. She still had proceeds from her half of the sale of the vicarage and she was able to afford to stay in bed and breakfast accommodation but when the money ran out she slept in doorways and parks.

She no longer cared anyway, nothing mattered anymore. She had fallen in love with someone else and he was taking very good care of her now, thank you very much. He didn't bitch about her drinking; in fact, he was happy to feed her addiction and most importantly, he didn't mind that she couldn't have any kids. She even loved his name, Jack Daniels; it had such a ring to it.

Mr Daniels had played a big part in her downward spiral into destitution. Because of him, she had nowhere to live and no money to rent a place. Because of him, she had always refused to go into a hostel for homeless people; hostels did not allow alcohol on the premises and she couldn't cope without her Jack by her side. But she did collect benefit payments; how else could she pay for her booze? Not the classy Jack Daniels though; cheap wine and cider was all she could afford to drink these days. Nevertheless, it still blanked out her past heartaches and was how she had ended up with a bunch of homeless dropouts. Dropouts who, like herself were bombed out of their minds most of the time. To be fair, none of them ever attacked or abused her but more importantly none of them lectured her or tried to derail her journey on the road to self-destruction.

Tonight her tipple was in a large plastic container; it contained some thin, cloudy liquid. It did the trick but she had no idea what it was, only that it smelt of ammonia. She had no money until her next benefit payment so one of the travellers shared what he had with her.

Leaning back against the jagged rock, Helen laughed as she realised that she had a problem remembering her own name. The sharp edges of the rock should have made her wince with pain but the effects of the poisonous concoction had deadened the nerves. Yet even as it dulled her senses and ravaged the major organs in her body, it did trigger a kind of euphoria to help pass the night away.

'What does anything matter anymore?' she slurred to the stars.

Over the last few months that deep, gnawing pain in her kidneys and the blood in her urine told her that she was fast approaching the end of the line. It was the best reason there was to keep drinking, of having another and another mouthful. A gentle breeze ruffled through her cobweb hair and drifted over the flames of the fire. 'What a lovely, burny smell,' she sang. 'Why not have another drink; don't mind if I do. So what if my liver packs in; what does it matter, they'll get me anyhow.' Then she chorused, 'Oh yes, they're trying to bump us all off, oh yes, they're trying to bump us all off.' Dropping her voice to a dramatic whisper, she pointed at the fire. 'They got poor little Mick already, they threw him off the cliff into the by and by but who's gonna care?' Helen's chin began to tremble with self-pity so she took another long swig.

'Who's gonna care? That poor girl down on the farm, she doesn't know what's going on. She doesn't know what plans they've got for her. They'll get her in the end, too, and they'll get that abominshion, aboinaton, that ape thing that stalks the woods at night. 'S why I had to warn her. At least I tried to give her a chance, poor girl.

'Doesn't matter about me, matters about her, though, she's only young and she shouldn't have to…' Helen's monologue trailed into a snore as she passed out.

When she came to she gazed up into the heavens and marvelled at the twinkling diamonds that were sprinkled in the black velvet sky. 'If only I could touch them.' She reached out as if to try and catch one but her line of vision was suddenly blocked by a shape; a gross, dark shape, darker than the night. Exhaling deep, throaty pants the shape loomed over her.

Helen's hand dropped limply to her side and she cackled triumphantly. 'I've been waiting for you, knew you'd come for me in the end.'

Before the end did come there was just enough time left for one more swig.

* * *

The following morning Rebecca and her mother watched an ambulance and a line of police cars swerving past the farm and heading up towards the summit of Claydon Head.

'What's going on?' Rebecca asked.

'Well, I don't know, Rebecca.'

For one dreadful moment Rebecca suspected it might have something to do with Blue, especially after seeing those strange men in black overalls entering the woods yesterday and the helicopter swooping over the cliffs. 'Christ, I hope they haven't captured Him.' She was working herself up into a panic. Then, pulling herself together and unclenching her tight fists, she turned to her mother and asked as calmly as she could, 'Do you think we should go and take a look?'

'Oh, no, let's not get involved, Rebecca.'

'Well, I'm going to have a look,' she said adamantly and went upstairs to get her car keys. When she came down her mother was waiting in the hall with her coat on. 'I'll come with you, I can't let you go on your own.'

As they drove up towards the summit of Claydon Head there was no sign of the police cars but as they continued down the road on the west side, a uniformed officer halted them in the middle of the road. The officer, wearing a reflective jacket, approached her car and Rebecca wound down her window.

'I'm afraid you'll have to turn back, miss,' he told her.

'Why, what's the problem?'

'There's been an incident and we have had to cordon off the area.'

Rebecca tried to make out what was going on up ahead but she couldn't see anything.

'Oh, OK,' she complied, and made a short U-turn ready to head back the way she had come.

She drove about a hundred yards further up the road then curved around a slight bend. Once she was out of sight she pulled up and stopped.

'What are you doing?' Mrs Samuels protested. 'I didn't bargain for this, I'm not traipsing over that steep hill.'

'It's quite safe, you only have to walk along a winding footpath; there's no real climbing involved.'

But her mum had made up her mind and stayed sitting in the car, with her arms folded across her chest.

'I won't be long,' Rebecca said as she handed over the car keys and wound her purple scarf around her neck. She scrambled up the grassy embankment and followed the narrow footpath that took her to an elevated point where she could see directly over, what appeared to be, a crime scene. There was an army of plain-clothed and uniformed officers milling around the area. On closer inspection, she spotted a tent with white-suited figures slipping in and out. To Rebecca, they looked like police forensics which must mean that this was a murder scene. A murder, but who's murder was it?

Of course, Blue was still her main concern. Again, she felt that familiar churning feeling in the pit of her stomach. 'No, it can't be Blue,' she told herself. 'They wouldn't have caught Him that easily, not Blue.' Shielding her eyes from the glare of the early morning sun, as she checked the area she spotted the last person she expected to see and her eyes widened in astonishment.

Standing beside one of the uniformed officers was a tall man in a long mac with raven black hair. Rebecca remembered the pair of sunglasses in her pocket and put them on. Yes, she was sure now; it was definitely Olsen.

'What the bloody hell is he doing there?' she muttered.

Seeing him there stirred up those anxieties about Blue again and her fear that something had happened to Him resurfaced. Resisting the urge to dart down to find out she decided to head back to the car instead; she couldn't afford to act without thinking of the consequences these days. When she got back, her mother had got out of the car and was standing on the footpath. 'Did you see what's going on?'

'It looks like they've found a body.'

'Oh my God! A body, are you sure?'

'Well, there's police forensics and a white tent so they have something in there; can't imagine what else it could be.'

They both fell silent as they got into the car. Rebecca turned on the ignition and drove them back home.

Later that morning Rebecca prowled from room to room. She just couldn't stay still and desperately needed to know that Blue was all right. At lunchtime she turned on the TV to watch the regional news. She hoped she might hear something. Fortunately the news was just beginning and the female newscaster delivered the breaking headlines.

'Early this morning a badly mutilated body was discovered on Claydon Head in North Wales. At this time the police have only confirmed that the body was that of an elderly woman. We will have more details in our six o'clock news tonight.'

Rebecca felt a mixture of guilt and relief as she called through to her mother, 'Mum, it's on the news. It was the body of an old woman.'

Mrs Samuels opened the living room door. 'What did you say? An elderly woman has been found dead? That's terrible; do they know who it is?'

'No, that's all they said. They'll give more details in the six o'clock news tonight. Wait a minute, I hope it wasn't that poor old, homeless lady I helped the other day.'

'Why would anyone want to harm an old lady?'

'Maybe she knew too much,' Rebecca said in an undertone.

'What was that?' her mother queried.

'Nothing.'

Her mum started to get uptight. 'I bet the whole area will be infested with TV reporters by now.'

'You know what the media is like,' Rebecca replied. 'They'll all clear off when something more sensational happens. Go and sit down and watch TV, Mum. I think there's an old black and white film on BBC2.'

As soon as she had gone, Rebecca swiftly punched numbers on her mobile phone and waited for Patrick to pick up.

'Hello.'

'Patrick, have you heard the news about the body being discovered on Claydon Head?'

'Yeah, it's all over town,' he replied.

'I've just found out about it now. It sounds like it may be that woman, the vagrant. You know, the one I spoke to the other day outside the farm.'

'You don't know that for sure.'

'Who else could it have been? I think she's the only old woman who hung around on Claydon Head.'

'Yeah but the identification is going to be a bit tricky, isn't it?'

'Why, what do you mean?'

'From what I've heard, she was decapitated; the head was ripped from the body and they haven't found it yet.'

Rebecca was horrified. 'Decapitated? Are you sure?'

'That's what I heard from a guy who knows one of the officers on duty at the scene.'

'Oh, Patrick, who or what did that to her?'

'Dunno, but it would have taken someone or something with immense strength to inflict that kind of violence.'

Rebecca's stomach did another somersault. 'You think it might have been Blue, don't you?'

'No, no, calm down. All I said was only something or someone with tremendous strength could kill like that.'

'Blue would only kill in self-defence, Patrick. He wouldn't go out and murder a defenceless old lady in cold blood, so let's not go there.'

'Yeah, OK, OK, Becca, keep your hair on. Besides, I have some other information that you might want to hear.'

'Oh, what's that? Could it be the info you were supposed to tell me about last night?' She couldn't resist a little dig about him neglecting to call.

'I didn't get the chance to ring you last night, it was too late. But never mind that; do you remember Richie Dixon? He went to the same school as we did.'

'Richie Dixon?' It took Rebecca a second or two to jog her memory then she guffawed. 'Not the Richie Dixon, otherwise known as Dick-fell-out-of-the-window? The friend you used to go around with?'

'That's the one, yes,' Patrick chuckled.

'The same little podgy Rich who had a droopy eyelid and was always into ghosts and monsters?'

'Hey, he's not so podgy any more. In fact, he's quite the opposite. He's a complete fitness fanatic. Plus, he's got himself a job as the manager of 'The Computer Clinic' in town. We have kept in touch on and off and believe it or not, he's still into all that supernatural and conspiracy theory shit. I managed to get hold of him on the phone and I asked him if he could do some research on Olsen and find out if there was a connection with any secret or illegal animal experiments in the UK.'

'You didn't tell him about Blue, did you?'

'No, I just said that there's been a spate of sightings of some strange creature on Claydon Head recently and I asked if he could check it out for me.'

'And what did he say?'

'He called me up today and said he's come up with some very interesting information that he thinks we should hear.'

'God, that was quick. What is it?'

'What are you doing this evening?'

'Not much, why?'

'Fancy taking a trip over to his house tonight, so we can find out?'

'Why couldn't he just tell you over the phone?'

'Because he believes all our phones are being tapped by MI5.'

'He believes what? OK, Mr Bond, try keeping me away. Can you pick me up around seven o' clock tonight?'

* * *

They got to Richie's at twenty past seven and pulled up outside a secluded Gothic-style house, set on the slope of a brooding wooded valley. Rebecca couldn't believe her eyes. In this light it was just like a house in a horror film. Peering out of the car window, she curled her lip. 'You have got to be joking; he doesn't actually live here, does he?'

Patrick yanked on the handbrake. 'Yep, ten years ago his aunty left it to him in her will; it's a family heirloom. She left him quite a bit of money as well. Apparently, his great-grandfather was a bit of an eccentric and built this place so he could indulge his fantasies about being an alchemist or something.'

Rebecca glared back at him. 'Jesus, this is too much, I hope we don't get another thunderstorm tonight or I'll be having more nightmares.' Rebecca got out of the car and as she stood looking over the building she got a funny feeling that it was waiting for them to enter. In some ways it looked like a small mediaeval village church with heavy stone walls and pointed windows. It even had a little tower sticking out of the roof.

'I wouldn't be surprised if Dracula had a room here,' Rebecca smirked.

'He's probably watching and listening.'

'Well, if he is, perhaps he can help us out.'

They reached the solid front door and Patrick lifted the black lion's head knocker. A deep booming echo could be heard resonating inside.

'I'm half-expecting Vincent Price to answer,' Rebecca quipped.

'Shush, someone's coming,' Patrick told her.

The door slowly creaked open and they were greeted by a lanky, grinning person with a bushy red beard and octagonal glasses. The biceps straining against the sleeves of his Godzilla T-shirt were evidence of his regular workouts.

'Guys,' Richie cried stepping out and sweeping Rebecca off her feet in a rib-breaking bear hug.

Rebecca coughed as the wind was squeezed out of her body. Then it was Patrick's turn, but he was too quick and thrusted out his hand like a fence. 'That's OK, Rich, I'm good.'

Richie shook Patrick's hand while he nodded back at Rebecca. 'Becca, how long has it been? Twenty years?'

'Yeah, possibly, Rich. Wow! What the hell have you been eating? Last time I saw you, you were a couple of inches shorter than me.'

He gave her a buddy-slap on the shoulder and she teetered backwards.

'Guys, come in, come in.' He swivelled on his toes and led the way inside.

'Said the spider to the fly,' Rebecca sniggered nervously. But the snigger soon became a scream as she flinched when she almost bumped into a full-size model of the Frankenstein monster with the box-shaped forehead and the electrical bolts in the neck. This was the moment that Patrick and Richie had been waiting for and they doubled up with laughter.

'Ha, ha, very funny, can we get serious now we've got that out of the way?'

'Sorry, Becca, couldn't resist it. Follow me.' Richie guided them down the hallway passing a curving staircase with four full-size resin statues of fantasy beasts either side of the bannisters.

Following behind, Rebecca stifled a sneeze as she disturbed the dust on the tail of a resin dragon. At the end of the hall they entered the living room. There was an original Victorian fireplace on one wall and the peeling wallpaper looked as if it was original too; faded green leaves on a faded grey background. This was obviously the room where Rich spent most of his time. But this living room was nothing like one she had come across before. It was full of dummies of Universal monsters and various framed posters of famed shock-horror movies. On the far side, there was a work station with all the latest technology, looking more like a control centre than a simple workstation. It would have been more impressive if the dining table and chairs next to it hadn't been littered with empty pizza boxes and takeaway cartons.

Rebecca did her best not to be too sniffy but she couldn't stop a quick dig. 'You obviously live here alone, Richie?' But Richie didn't pick up on the sarcasm.

'Yep, 'cept for my two babies, Ripley and Sally.'

'His cats,' Patrick muttered in her ear.

Richie began scratching his head. 'Sorry, guys, I don't get many visitors, where are my manners?' Shovelling empty pizza boxes on the floor, he dragged a couple of the dining chairs out for his two guests to sit on.

Patrick and Rebecca checked to see that the chair seats were not decorated with bits of cheese or tomato before sitting down. They watched with amusement as Richie spun himself around on his leather office chair like a spinning top. After he had had his fun he got down to business.

'So here we go. I have managed to uncover some pretty interesting stuff based on what Patrick has told me. Oh, hang on!' he jumped up bumping his knee on the corner of his desk. 'My salmon and broccoli bakes are burning in the oven.' Then he shot off to the kitchen.

Rebecca sighed and looked sceptical. 'Listen, maybe this wasn't such a good idea, after all. Are you sure we're doing the right thing?'

Chewing his lip uneasily Patrick came clean. 'OK, I'm going to own up, I've had to tell Richie everything.'

'You what?' Rebecca gasped.

'I had to, otherwise there was no point trying to get him to help us. He had to know everything so he could get the necessary info.'

'I can't believe you did that without telling me first.'

'Becca, we have to trust him, he's all we've got. There's no point messing about being secretive otherwise we'll get nowhere.'

'Oh yeah, and what happens if he goes blabbing online to his other conspiracy nutters and it starts a pandemonium?'

'Come on, it's Richie. I have confidence in him and so should you. Besides, you told the whole world about Blue after he killed your father, and nobody took any notice then. Look, if there is anything out there which the public is not supposed to know, believe me, he'll find it. He really knows his stuff.'

Picking a dried coil of spring onion from the leg of her chair Rebecca warned, 'You'd better be right.'

Wiping his mouth, Richie returned from the kitchen. He was still hurriedly chewing and was obviously flustered. 'Guys, where are my manners tonight? I haven't even offered you a drink. I got some beers and wine in.'

Rebecca and Patrick locked eyes; they both wanted to crack on and get down to business.

'Thanks, Richie, but Rebecca has to get back to keep her mum company. She's a bit upset about things.'

'Fair enough, if you're sure.' Richie didn't push it and went over and sat in his chair. He stretched out his long legs, burped and patted his stomach. 'Right then, the problem is that I can't find anything on this Olsen person, nothing on the Internet and no paper trail at all. However, with regards to the human-ape-type hybrids, I've uncovered some very interesting stuff.' He scratched the back of his head.

'Let's go right back to the very beginning; back to the turn of the twentieth century and this Russian guy named Ilya Ivanovich. He was a Soviet biologist who specialised in artificial insemination and the interspecies hybridisation of animals. During his time he was involved in some controversial attempts to create human-ape hybrids. In 1920 he conducted a series of cross-fertilisation experiments to create a species of these human/non-human hybrids. But unfortunately all his experiments with ape sperm and human volunteers failed. Then, fast-forward to the 1950s when Ivanovich's work was taken up by other biologists and they created this half-human, half-chimp who they named Oliver. It was believed that he was one of the first Humanzees to be developed. By the way, Humanzee is what they called a human/chimpanzee hybrid. Roughly speaking that means that they inseminated a female chimp with human semen and she conceived the human/chimpanzee hybrid called Oliver.

'Oliver could walk upright, and his face resembled that of a human. Yet, despite his unusual appearance and behaviour the biologists involved claimed that he was just an ordinary chimp from the Gabon Region. But what makes that difficult to believe is the fact that biologists have been performing illegal experiments like these for the last eighty to ninety years and it is not beyond the realms of possibility that Oliver was the result of one of those experiments.'

'What happened to Oliver?' Rebecca asked.

'He had a bit of a sad life at the end but he died peacefully in his sleep at the age of fifty-four. Since then things have changed and those experiments have been permitted to continue.'

Patrick wanted to know more. 'But why were they allowed to continue if it was illegal? I mean, how could they carry on and be allowed to tamper with nature like that?'

'As it happens, since the 2008 Human Fertilisations Embryology Act, it's illegal to impregnate a female human with animal semen but it's not illegal to implant a female animal with human sperm.'

Contemptuously, Patrick shook his head.

'And do they perform these experiments here in the UK?' Rebecca wanted to know.

'Not quite but there are some laboratories in this country that do research with animal embryos which are implanted with a small amount of human material; although, they don't go the whole nine yards and create human-animal hybrids.'

'What is the point of doing it then?' Patrick burst out as he smacked his hand down hard on the arm of his chair.

'I think the purpose is to develop embryonic stem cells to treat a range of incurable diseases. But elsewhere in the world they still conduct illegal experiments with humans and animals, although not necessarily for the same purposes.'

'Where else in the world?' Rebecca jumped in.

'There are certain government research centres in America, one in particular which works under the guise of a research centre doing vivisection experiments on live animals. Yet, secretly, they are actually creating these Humanzee-type creatures.'

'That's despicable.'

'But why are they creating these, these mutants?' Patrick spluttered.

Richie shrugged his shoulders. 'Who knows what they're planning to do with them?'

Rebecca was getting agitated and blurted out the sixty-four-thousand-dollar question, 'Well, tell me, do you think that Blue is the product of one of these secret government hybrid experiments?'

Richie gave her an apologetic look. 'So far that's all I've managed to dig up but give me a bit more time and I'll see what I can find. I've got my contacts,' he winked cannily.

'Thanks for what you've managed to find out for us so far.' Patrick smiled at his friend.

'My pleasure.' Richie grinned broadly and lounged back in his chair.

'So what do we owe you?'

Ignoring Patrick and without any warning Richie sprang forward and made a leap at Rebecca. 'Tell me about this Mr Blue. I can't believe there is a real live para-human out there. Tell me, why do you call him Mr Blue?'

'Because when I was a child, he saved me and all I could see when he came to my rescue, was the clear blue sky behind Him.'

Richie wasn't really sure whether Rebecca was joking or not but he was hooked and wanted to know everything. 'Makes sense; tell me what he looks like.'

Seeing that Rebecca was uneasy about discussing Blue, Patrick took over. 'He's big, very big.'

'Bigger than me?' Richie punched his chest.

'Bigger and twice as wide.'

'Man, that's awesome. That's a very unusual size for these para-humans. From what I've learned so far, they don't normally exceed the size of an average human male. Shit, I would really like to see what breed of primate he originated from and who the male sperm donor was.'

'Unfortunately, they killed his mother.' Rebecca's voice was barely above a whisper.

'Why would they do that?'

'That's part of the puzzle that we're trying to find out,' Patrick sighed.

Richie gazed thoughtfully at them both. 'Looks like I'm going to have to dig a bit deeper. I think I might need the help of my associates in the States for this one.'

Patrick cut in, 'But you will keep everything about Blue's existence out of it, won't you? Promise us you will, Richie?'

'Of course I will, trust me.'

Patrick seemed satisfied that he could bank on Richie's discretion but Rebecca wasn't so sure.

'If I come up with anything else, you'll be the first to know. I might find out something important, something that will help Blue to get out of this mess. Hell, you never know, I might get the chance to meet Him for myself.'

Rebecca became even more uneasy. 'I don't think that'd be a good idea. He doesn't take kindly to strangers, especially human strangers.'

'Yeah, take it from me he can be a bit of a party-pooper,' Patrick added.

'Suppose you're right; don't want to get on the wrong side of a 400-pound primate.'

* * *

As Patrick drove Rebecca back home, she was very preoccupied but kept her thoughts to herself.

'What's on your mind?'

'We're still really none the wiser about our problem, are we? I mean, we know it was Olsen who placed Blue and his mother in Claydon Woods and we now know that they were probably part of some scientific experiment. Talking to Richie has made us aware that this kind of experiment has been going on illegally for decades. But what does it all point to?'

'Let's give Richie a chance, Becca. Believe me, once he gets his teeth into something he never lets go. Remember in school when he had that trouble with one of his teachers and as payback, he dug and dug. He found out that a girl had been bragging about having it off with the teacher and then Richie stole letters that the teacher had written to her.'

Rebecca screwed up her face. 'I don't remember that.'

'Yeah, he phoned up the teacher's house and told him that if he had any more hassle from him he would go straight to the headmaster with the evidence and then post the love letters to his lovely wife.'

'And, did it work?'

'Oh yeah, Richie got an A-plus for all the assignments he did for that teacher.'

Rebecca couldn't help smiling. He didn't go to university, though, and ended up working in a local computer shop. Perhaps that fall affected him. She began to sing out loud, 'Dick fell out of the window, Dick fell out of the window…'

Patrick joined in. 'And landed on his… Dick fell out of the window.' And they were both convulsed with laughter until the car nearly swerved off the road.

'How did he really get associated with that song? Did he actually fall out of a window?' Rebecca asked.

'Sure did, he fell out of someone's bedroom window when he was drunk.'

'Yeah, but did he land on his…?'

Patrick gave her a knowing grin and let her figure it out for herself.

'Ouch! …' she winced. 'Has he always lived alone? Looking at the state of the place, you would reckon that he's never had a partner living there.'

'I remember him seeing some girl from one of the villages. She was tiny, only four-foot ten,' Patrick scoffed. 'I think her name was Mel. Imagine how the two of them must have looked walking down the street together hand in hand. She would have been better off putting a saddle on him and riding him instead.'

'So, what happened, then?'

'She went off with a university student and broke his heart.'

'That's sad.'

'Yeah, it was. It took him ages to get over it. I suppose it knocked his confidence quite a bit. I think that's why he's become so obsessed with all this fantasy and conspiracy stuff. It's become his kind of comfort zone, away of protecting himself from the harsh realities of life. I suppose that's what happens to some people when they get their hearts broken or suffer a trauma. I suppose they take refuge by crawling into their shell and shying away from forming relationships.'

Was Patrick just making general observations, or was he subtlety hinting about Rebecca's heartbreaking and traumatic childhood experiences or even the way he had dumped her? Or, maybe he was still uncomfortable about the way she had reacted after he failed her in their briefest of brief sexual encounters?

She gave him a surreptitious glance but she couldn't read him. Nevertheless, the companionable mood was broken and they drove the rest of the way in silence.

When they arrived Rebecca was about to get out of the car when Patrick stopped her.

'Listen, Becca, with everything that has gone on lately, the stress, the tensions, the murder on Claydon Head playing on your mind, I think it might be a good idea for us to just get away from it all. We could spend the day together somewhere, just chilling. Just one day to relax and recharge our batteries. I think we need to take a day out because something tells me that soon, very soon, things may turn pretty intense. What do you think?'

Rebecca traced the letter B on the car's misted window. 'I don't know if I could just go off somewhere right now. It wouldn't feel right.'

'Well, I disagree. I think it'll do us the world of good and I think you'll be glad that you did it, so my mind's made up. Tomorrow, I'm going to take you out, it's going to be a bright, sunny day, we are going to have a lovely time and I don't think Mr Blue will mind you going, either.'

'Patrick, I don't know.'

'Rebecca, I'm not going to take no for an answer. If I left everything to you, you wouldn't do anything to give yourself a break. You would just stay at home and fret. I'm going to pick you up at 10am sharp, all right?'

Rebecca finally gave in. 'OK, if it makes you happy I'll go.'

'Excellent, right then, just make sure you get a good night's sleep. You need it.'

Rebecca managed a weary smile. 'I will. Goodnight, Patrick.' She gave him a peck on the cheek and got out of the car. As she walked up the driveway she could hear the crunch of tyres on the gravel as Patrick reversed and drove off. The night air was a bit nippy so she thrust her hands in her pockets as she speculated about the day trip with Patrick tomorrow.

CHAPTER SEVENTEEN

The clogging yellow smoke choked her as she ran blindly through the war-torn streets, passing burnt-out overturned shells of cars and fire-blackened buildings. Behind her, she could hear low-murmuring growls of the beasts as they wrecked total havoc. Frantically, she searched for somewhere to hide, somewhere to escape from the approaching monsters but there was nowhere.

Desperately, she ducked down beside a wrecked car. She wondered if she should dive inside the ramshackle vehicle, but she was more worried about becoming trapped inside if they found her there. Instead, she screwed herself into a quivering ball and listened to the beasts as their growls escalated into thunderous howls. They drew nearer, and her ears were also assaulted by the awful screams of the victims as they were being torn to pieces. Rebecca closed her eyes trying to block everything out, praying that it would all go away but her prayers were not answered.

CLANG! Making a noise like a giant sledgehammer whacking against metal, one of the monsters threw itself on the car, the impact almost making Rebecca fall forward onto her knees. Then two massive, hairy feet landed in front of her, thudding onto the tarmac. Transfixed by terror her eyes moved up the torso of the monster. Her eyes stopped when they reached its huge head and she met its yellow eyes as they blazed down.

Its jaws opened to reveal a stinking cavern of a mouth with

flesh-ripping teeth dripping with sticky, stringy saliva. Glaring at her the terrible beast reached behind its body and brought out a bloody, severed head and then dragged the rest of the decapitated corpse into view.

Rebecca's eyes dilated with shock as she recognised its features; it was the head of the old woman who had been murdered on Claydon Head. She could not take her eyes off the mutilated remains and gagged at the sight of the mangled trachea; the torn oesophagus and the dangling sections of the vertebrae spilling out like the grizzly remains of a Jack the Ripper victim. But just as she clasped her hand to her mouth and swallowed to stop the vomit rising from her stomach the corpse suddenly cried out. 'Rebecca. Rebecca,' it repeated. 'All this has a meaning, my dear. You have to stay strong, luv. You have to stay very strong.'

'What? What?' Rebecca cried as she held onto the bonnet of the car.

'Look for the truth, Rebecca, find it, find it.'

Rebecca was drenched in perspiration and was gripping the headboard when she woke up. Her heart was hammering nineteen to the dozen and she thought she was going to die with fright. She felt for the switch and turned on the bedside lamp. The familiar bedroom materialised and all she could hear was a whispering breeze rustling through the eaves of the roof. It had been a nightmare, a bad nightmare. She collapsed onto her pillows as her body convulsed with an uncontrollable tremor. She was convinced that the beast who held the severed head was Mr Blue.

* * *

As promised, Patrick picked her up on time and they drove off for their planned day out together. They headed south and followed the direction of the morning sun. Soon they reached the Arthur Stanley Expansion Bridge and crossed over to Sealand Island. They stopped for lunch at a welcoming roadside pub and then went for a stroll along the mile-long beach nestling below rolling dunes.

As they walked, Rebecca kicked at the sand and breathed in the sea air. 'That was a lovely lunch, thanks, Patrick.'

'You're welcome,' he replied.

'I didn't expect you to pay for it, you know. I would have gladly paid my own way.'

Patrick gave her a reassuring grin. 'Really, it's no problem, my treat.'

'I have to admit it is nice to get away from everything, especially on a day like this.'

'I told you that you would appreciate it, didn't I?'

Rebecca nodded and lifted her face to the sunny sky unaware that Patrick was watching her. 'I don't know where this thing with Blue and Olsen is going to go,' Rebecca announced. 'Whatever happens, though, it's not going to end well, is it? And I don't know how long I'm going to have to stay here. I told my uncle that I'd have everything sorted out by the end of the month. I can't stay here forever; I have to get back to work.'

Patrick started to say something but changed his mind.

'What do you think?' she asked.

'Why don't we give Richie another day and see what he can come up with? Maybe he'll find some information on that Olsen that'll help us out?'

'I wouldn't trust Olsen as far as I could throw him, and he's certainly got some strange men working for him.'

Pausing for a second Rebecca confided, 'I had a terrible nightmare last night.'

Patrick gripped her firmly by her shoulders. 'Rebecca, forget all that for now. You're supposed to be relaxing, a day off, remember? And I don't want to see you getting yourself worked up today.'

'No, you're right, I just can't seem to help myself.'

'Let's enjoy ourselves then, shall we? Whatever problems we have they will still be there when we get back so let's leave them alone until then, yes?'

'OK, let's do that.' Rebecca picked up a shell and they strolled on.

Leaving the beach behind they doubled back and made their way over to a belt of open fields fringed by hedgerows and trees. Before she could stop herself, Rebecca remarked that it resembled Claydon Woods. But Patrick thought it would be best to let that risky remark go and they strolled through the grass towards the wood. Patrick pulled Rebecca down beside him and they sat near one of the trees. He smoothed the grass down around them and he lay on his side while Rebecca leant back on her hands. Snapping off a blade of grass, Patrick chewed it at the side of his mouth. A long silence made them both uncomfortable and Rebecca fidgeted with her jacket zip to give herself something to do. She hoped he didn't have any ideas about repeating the disappointing fling they had the last time they lay on the grass.

But Patrick did not make a move on her. Taking the blade of grass out of his mouth and throwing it away he inquired, 'Do you mind if I ask you a personal question?'

'It depends how personal,' Rebecca replied dubiously.

'Do you ever plan on settling down and starting a family? Or is the single life what you want?'

Rebecca wondered where this was going and wasn't sure how to answer.

'What I'm asking is this. Is the single life something you have chosen or something life has forced upon you?'

'A bit of both, I suppose.'

'Then I'll ask again, do you ever want to settle down and have a family?'

Rebecca shifted her position, giving herself more time to think. 'Yes, I would love to settle down and start a family. I suppose, up until now, I've been living in the past, spending too much time trying to analyse where I ended up and why. It's no wonder I've made a complete mess of things, letting my past dominate my life. For me it's like being in a time warp; you're struck in that particular time, stuck in your own particular world while life still goes on around you. It's all been holding me back and preventing me from moving on and living the kind of life I see other people my age living.'

Patrick selected another blade of grass and chewed on it meditatively as he listened. 'Well, if I can help in any way, I will.'

Rebecca laughed mirthlessly. 'Do you really think I've got what it takes to handle a husband and children of my own?'

'You'd be surprised how resilient and adaptable people can be. I don't think you'd have much of a problem.'

'Do you know, I've always wondered what it would be like to have a baby of my own; to hold it in my arms, care for it, nurture it, feed it; protect it. I mean, what else can give you that same kind of loving purpose, responsibility and feeling of accomplishment?' Rebecca paused. 'What about you? How come you didn't have any children when you were married?'

Patrick snatched the blade of grass from his mouth as if it suddenly gave him a bad taste.

'It just didn't feel right for us to bring a child into the situation, not at that time. We should never have got married in the first place, it was too quick. We were more or less pushed into it by her parents. You see, they were the typical traditional family unit. Her brother was married, her sister was married and even her younger brother was engaged. Marriage to them was an inevitable step when you reached a certain age. The thing was, you not only had to marry their daughter; you virtually had to marry the whole bleeding family as well. After a while, I just felt suffocated by it all and one day I woke up and decided there and then that I had to get out.'

'Did you love her?'

Patrick took a moment. 'I thought I did. She and her family did their best to convince me that I did but their manipulation and constant pressure made me feel like I had no choice and I was being swept away by a powerful current. The frightening thing was, I didn't know where this current was going to take me and whether or not it was going to drown me in the process. In the end, I started arguments on purpose to try and get her to go off me. I hoped that she would ask for a divorce. I knew I was being a coward, but I didn't want to take the blame and deal with the fallout from her family. And that's what I meant when I told you that we just drifted apart; we did but it was all my doing.'

Rebecca hadn't expected Patrick to be so honest. There was nothing for her to say so she tried to lighten the mood. She spotted a daffodil lying in the grass. 'Hey, that's flowered early.'

Patrick snapped off more blades of grass. 'Well, it won't be too long before the spring kicks in.'

'Do you know this field reminds me of one of the dandelion fields that Blue and I used to go to, so we could hang out together and play our games. We were so young and so clueless.'

Patrick studied her for a second. 'Blue again; he's always on your mind. You're still very close to Him, aren't you?'

'I suppose I am. He was more family to me than my own parents.'

'In the bad times as well as good?'

'Yes, but not always great times; even he could be a bit of a pain now and again, but when I needed comfort and support, TLC, he was always there, unlike my parents.'

'What do you mean?'

Rebecca was getting pins and needles and she rubbed her leg. 'He had this way of either sitting or lying down facing me with his forehead touching mine. I remember Him doing this whenever I was very upset or if I was in any pain. And when he did it, the distress and the pain used to go away. It just did something to me.

When I felt better, I used to thank Him by picking a bunch of dandelions for Him.'

'Did you? What did he do with them?'

'At first, he tried to eat them until I got Him to understand that they were a gift, to be kept, not to be eaten. But even then, he still didn't know what to do with them.' She chuckled as she stared at the daffodil lying in the grass then something struck her.

'Flowers!' she blurted out. 'He did get it.'

'What's that?' Patrick asked.

'Flowers; I've just remembered that I have a box of flowers back home. According to my mum, Mr Blue has left a flower on the driveway for me on every one of my birthdays since I moved away.'

But Patrick wasn't following, 'Say that again.'

'I forgot to mention it. Maybe that's why he left them. He remembers the flowers I gave to him as gifts; perhaps he was doing the same for me on my birthday.'

Patrick was idly wrapping a blade of grass around his little finger when he saw her shoulders slump.

'No, no, it's too simple. There's got to be more to it than that. He would have given up leaving flowers after the first few years. There must be another reason why he left them there for me – it has to be some kind of message.'

'So, what are you going to do?'

'Go home and try to figure it out,' Rebecca said scrambling to her feet.

Patrick didn't move, he just carried on sitting there looking dejected. The day had not gone the way he had hoped.

CHAPTER EIGHTEEN

Rebecca reached under her bed and pulled out the white cardboard box. She flipped off the lid and stared down at the flowers inside. She picked out a chrysanthemum and laid it in her palm as she tried to work out if it had some sort of meaning. Had Blue been using it to send her a message? But nothing came to mind. Then she tipped out the whole box and decided to try again with a different flower. She chose a daisy and held it up, saying, 'Now what's so special about a common daisy?' Dropping it back into the box she had another idea.

She put all the flowers back and carried the box downstairs into the living room where her mother was sitting reading a magazine.

'Mum, these flowers that you collected over the years for me, can you remember which one I got for every birthday?'

'Goodness me, no, my memory isn't that great.'

Rebecca sat with the box nestled on her knees. 'Well, can you remember some of them at least, maybe just the last four or five years or so?'

Mrs Samuels let the magazine fall on her lap. 'Why? What do you want to know about the flowers for?'

'I don't know exactly but I'm guessing that Blue didn't just leave them there as a birthday present. Knowing Him, there could be some deeper meaning but for the life of me I can't think what it could be.'

'Don't you think you're reading a bit too much into this? Surely he can't be that intelligent. Why don't you just ask Him the next time you see Him?'

'I will when I get the chance, but I am not sure when that will be, and I need to know now, I really do. Try to remember, Mum, please. Which flowers did I get for the last four or five years?'

Her mother cast her mind back. 'A rose was the very last one, I'm sure of that.'

Rebecca opened the box and rifled through it until she found a squashed red rose.

'Elderflower, tulip,' her mum was on a roll now and flying through the names as her memory came flooding back.

'Hang on a minute.' Rebecca slowed her down as she looked for an elderflower and a tulip to place them alongside the rose.

'A snapdragon, yes, definitely a snapdragon because I remember thinking what a strange-looking flower that was for someone to leave.'

'What does a snapdragon look like?'

Leaning over, Mrs Samuels rummaged through the box until she found a slender stalk bearing tall spikes of faded flowers. Rebecca regarded it thoughtfully before placing it next to the others. The last two flowers her mother remembered were the ivy and the sweet william although, strictly speaking, ivy wasn't a flower.

'That's six altogether,' Rebecca totalled.

'Yes, the reason why I remembered them was because those last six were left right outside the front door, but the rest were left further down the driveway.'

Patting each one in turn Rebecca declared, 'Then that might have some kind of significance.'

She studied all six flowers lying side by side but still couldn't fathom what they could mean. Grabbing a pen and paper she pulled out her mobile phone and started to tap the screen. 'I'm going to Google these plants to see if they have any special meaning.'

One by one Rebecca went through the list and wrote down the meanings of each of the six flowers. 'Right, the rose symbolises love in its various forms but that certainly isn't Blue's cup of tea. He hates all that mushy stuff, so I don't know about that one. The elderflower symbolises zeal; that could mean anything. The tulip…'

'Oh, this isn't getting you anywhere. Do you fancy a cup of tea?' her mum asked. 'It might inspire you.'

Not taking her eyes off the screen, Rebecca mumbled, 'Yeah, thanks,' and continued writing. 'Tulip means fame or a perfect lover – no, definitely not Blue, either. The snapdragon means grace but could also mean deviousness. The ivy signifies affection and friendship and the sweet William suggests gallantry.' Rebecca did a quick tally: 'Rose – Love in its various forms; elderflower – zeal; tulip – perfect lover or fame; the ivy – affection or friendship. Then, there's the snapdragon – grace or deviousness and the sweet william – gallantry.' She bent over and tapped her head with the palm of her hand in frustration.

'They could be meaning anything. And even taking the first letter from each flower, it spells RETSIS.' She couldn't make any sense of it at all and was beginning to agree with her mother; maybe she was wasting her time. For now, it would be better to give it a miss. She went into the kitchen to get her cup of tea and wandered out into the garden.

Relaxing in the summer house, Rebecca took a tentative sip of tea and found herself reflecting on her trip out with Patrick. What stuck in her mind was Patrick's interest in whether or not she wanted to settle down and have a family. Was he testing the waters? Was he trying to find out if she wanted a relationship with him?

Of course, Rebecca was still attracted to Patrick. That had been obvious from the moment they met up again in the cafe. She certainly enjoyed his company, but it wasn't only that, there was something else about being with him that made a difference. Rebecca tried to put her finger on it but the only thing she could come up with was the simple fact that there was a connection, she felt safe with him and she trusted him, for now anyway.

Rebecca never thought she would ever hear herself admitting that, especially after the way he dumped her.

In all fairness, they were only kids at the time and he was more or less ordered by his parents to finish with her. No, she couldn't possibly hold that against him, not now, not after everything they had been through so far. From what she had seen lately Patrick had proved that he could be reliable and supportive in a terrifying crisis. But was she sure enough that he could fulfil her sexual or emotional needs? *What happens if we survive all this?* She posed the question to herself. *If we both manage to get through it and then try to settle back to normal life, will Patrick still care the same way he does now, or will he feel suffocated just like he did with his ex-wife, and bale out once more?* So many questions, so many possibilities.

Her speculations were interrupted by the buzzing of her mobile and she saw it was Patrick's number. 'Speak of the Devil,' she quipped pressing the call button.

'Hello, Patrick.'

'Hi, Becca, I've just had a call from Richie and he wants us to pop over to his house again, tonight.'

Rebecca was all ears. 'Why, what's up?'

'He's come up with some more interesting but disturbing information.'

Rebecca's mouth went dry. 'OK.'

'Can you be ready for about seven again?'

'Definitely, I'll be ready with knobs on. Has he given you any idea what it's about?'

'No, he just said we need to get over there. I don't think he wanted to discuss it over the phone.'

'It sounds serious.'

'Well, there's only one way to find out, isn't there?'

'I suppose.'

'I'll see you about seven.' Patrick paused. 'By the way, I really enjoyed spending the day with you, today.'

Rebecca couldn't stop herself softly murmuring into the phone, 'Me too, me too. See you later.'

* * *

Arriving at Richie's house, Patrick rapped on his front door.

Stamping her feet impatiently on the step, Rebecca was eager to get inside. 'I can't wait to hear what he's found out.'

The door creaked open and they were greeted by Richie's red-bearded grin again. 'Hey, guys, come on through.'

When they reached the living room they saw that he had already placed the two dining chairs beside the computer workstation. Throwing his arms out expansively, Richie nodded at the chairs. 'Take a seat, guys.'

Hurling himself into his swivel chair, he rubbed his hands together. 'As you know, I've been doing a bit more research on this and I've been checking out that research centre in America, the one I told you about, the one that conducts animal-human experiments. I've been in touch with my transatlantic pals on chat room and between us all we've uncovered some pretty interesting stuff. The centre is actually called Berkis and is located in Florida near the border with Georgia. Berkis is actually under the umbrella of a much larger corporation called Tarbo in Washington DC and it's not the only one.'

'Tarbo?' Patrick questioned.

'Yes, Tarbo is a top-secret development centre that deals in behaviour modification plus weapons and defence technologies.'

'Where did you say Tarbo is located again?' asked Rebecca.

'Washington DC. Apparently in Washington DC they conduct top-secret programmes for the CIA, the Central Intelligence Agency. Among other things, the CIA make decisions relating to national security and these programmes have been devised to create assassins.'

Not surprisingly, Rebecca was baffled. It was a case of too much information in too short a time. 'You've lost me now.'

'Haven't you seen any of the Jason Bourne films?'

'Yes, but what's the connection?' Patrick frowned.

'I'll get back to that. Just let me digress for a while. In Berkis, Florida, they have these slaughterhouses and live pigs, sheep and even cows are selected from the animals that are due to be slaughtered. They then inject human stem cells into them and grow human organs. The selected animals are then housed in a separate unit. The idea is that these parts, these spare organ parts, can be removed when they are ready and used to treat a range of incurable diseases.'

'Growing human organs in pigs and cows? That's gross,' Rebecca grimaced.

'But that's just a cover,' Richie explained.

'A cover for what?' asked Patrick.

'They're really growing these organs for something else.'

Patrick and Rebecca were all ears.

'Stay with me now... remember when I told you that these experiments to create human and animal hybrids were conducted by these government agencies?'

They both chorused, 'Yes.'

'Well, the word is that they're trying to create an army of super-soldiers to take over the human race; a race of para-humans or Manimals, human-primate hybrids; we could be talking about a real-life *Planet of the Apes*.'

Patrick and Rebecca were too flabbergasted to say anything, but they had the words, "THIS IS CRAZY," written all over their faces.

'These places like Berkis are secretly developing Humanzees or Manimals and these hybrids are being fed on these organs, injected with human cells, so they can develop a taste for human blood which will make them become more efficient killers; killers of people. That's not all: Tarbo, the Pentagon agency in Washington DC, is using Black Ops-type agencies to brainwash these Manimals. I'm not sure what methods they are using to brainwash them, but I do know that they are doing it so that they will become these super-soldiers.'

'How the hell can they do that?' Patrick cried.

'I think they inject specific human stem cells into the brains of these Manimals which develop human-type attributes, giving them more astute and efficient warfare intellects but not any feelings of association with the human race.'

'Do you think it may be possible that Mr Blue has been developed for this type of purpose?' asked Patrick.

'Who knows? But I have something just as interesting. Listen, there happens to be a university in Alabama which has a laboratory that specialises in evolution and behaviour. Wait a minute.' He dived into a pile of papers and began trawling through reams of printouts and notes. 'Where is it? Where is it…? Ah!' he announced holding up a sheet stained with coffee. 'This information dates back to the late 80s, by the way. The faculty mentor at this particular university was a Dr Craig Hammer and his assistant was…' Richie handed the paper over to Patrick so he could see for himself.

Patrick read the name on the paper and choked. Then he passed it over to Rebecca. The name printed clearly under the title of Faculty Mentor Assistant was Dr Samuel Olsen. Wordlessly, pointing at the name, Rebecca waved the paper at Patrick and he snatched it back to double check it was true.

Recovering her power of speech, Rebecca snorted, 'So, Olsen IS involved in all this.'

'That's unless it's referring to another Olsen,' Richie replied.

'Unlikely, and how are they managing to get away with this?' Patrick asked.

'Apparently, there is supposed to be this regulatory body called Bioethics whose job it is to advise these secret government centres as to how far they are allowed to go into Frankenstein territory. But at the end of the day, even if Bioethics turns down these experiment proposals, it's still perfectly legal to carry them out.'

'Well, Bioethics sounds as if it is as useful as a chocolate teapot.' But Rebecca was anxious to bring the conversation back to the problem in hand. 'How does Blue fit into all this? First, they create Him then they place Him within a controlled environment so they can study Him, and now they're trying to destroy Him. Why would they do that if he was part of this illegal programme? What's the point?'

'It is like the Frankenstein story,' Richie tried to explain. 'You ignore all the moral and ethical implications to create this kind of monster simply to prove it can be done. But when the monster starts thinking for itself and starts claiming its own rights to determine how it lives, then the creator becomes more acutely aware of the moral ramifications together with the potential dangers and then tries to destroy it. They must have factored this scenario in as a possibility and planned what they would have to do. They can't have feral monsters roaming free around civilised countries, can they? It maybe that Blue has forced them to act because he doesn't want to go along with this plan of joining some super-army of hybrids so they're trying to get shot of Him.

'These hybrids, that we believe are being created in these laboratories as we speak, can be extremely dangerous. From what I have been told, they are four or five times stronger than normal human beings. And once they have been groomed to develop a taste for human blood there will be no stopping them.'

'But Blue is not much of a meat-eater. He eats plants, berries and a kind of mushroom stew and only the cooked meat he finds outside takeaways. Years ago, I did see some raw meat outside his cave but he threw it over the cliff,' Rebecca protested.

'Have you thought of this? What if that instinct is buried deep within Him waiting to come out at any time?' Richie argued. 'It could be that the Black Ops may have realised that their brainwashing techniques are flawed and they can't predict or completely control what Blue thinks or does.'

Rebecca stood up and paced the room. 'Well, then what in heaven's name can we do? More to the point, can we do anything?'

Folding his arms, Patrick announced, 'First, I think we should expose this Olsen and his whole damned so-called scientific mob.'

Rebecca turned on him.' And just how are we going to do that?'

'Try the press,' Richie chipped in. 'I have quite a few friends who work in the media. I can give any one of them a call, they would jump at it. They would wet themselves. It would be the biggest news story to hit the headlines ever.'

Rebecca stopped pacing. 'You haven't thought this through, Richie. Once something as horrific and unthinkable as this becomes public we don't know what will happen. It will probably be hyped up, sensationalised and would whip public opinion into a frenzy. I mean, blowing something like this wide open could prove to be very dangerous for everyone involved, Blue in particular. Mobs of vigilantes would hunt Him down.'

Catching Rebecca's hand as she came to stand beside him, Patrick gently squeezed her fingers. 'Perhaps the best way to help Blue is to expose Him to the world ourselves. But we don't reveal where he is living. We keep his habitat a closely-guarded secret. That would make it much harder for Olsen and his team to get rid of Him. There would be too much press coverage.'

Loosening her hand, Rebecca's gesture indicated her deep reservations.

'Tell you what,' Patrick added hurriedly to Richie, 'give us a day to think it over and we'll get back to you.'

* * *

As Patrick drove Rebecca back home, they carried on trying to find some sort of agreement on how they should go forward.

'I think Richie might be right, Becc. If he can get hold of a reputable reporter to back us up, we'll have the whole power of the press behind us and that'll put us in a much stronger position than we are right now.'

'No, it won't, Patrick. If we expose Olsen to the press where will it leave Blue? He won't be safe from the public. He won't be safe in the hands of some government body either. They would probably destroy Him, or subject Him to a lifetime of cruel and damaging experiments before they destroy Him.'

'I know, I know, I heard what you said back at Richie's but what else can we do? Would you prefer Blue to be left in Olsen's evil hands, or in the hands of the proper authorities? Or, do we help him escape and risk a full-scale man-ape hunt by the armed forces who will surely destroy Him on sight.'

Rebecca sighed wearily. 'I don't know. The thing is, who are these proper authorities? We are not sure if any authority has the kind of crisis measures in place to deal with such a unique situation.'

Parking at the bottom of Rebecca's driveway Patrick left his car in neutral.

Taking her front door key out of her pocket, Rebecca turned to towards him. 'Patrick, I just want to say that I appreciate everything you are doing to try and help me. Without you I don't know what I would have done.'

And before Patrick had the chance to say anything, she leant across and pecked him softly on the cheek.

The kiss was only light yet to Patrick it packed a fair punch and he was stunned for a second. 'Only too glad to help. That's…that's what I'm here for,' he stuttered.

Rebecca smiled coyly and opened the passenger door but Patrick stopped her. 'Listen, Becca,' he was bursting to say something mushy but he was tongue-tied… 'I'll give you a ring tomorrow after I've had another chat with Richie, OK?'

Rebecca nodded back at him and climbed out of the car. As Patrick watched her walking up the driveway he felt her peck on his cheek again and grinned like an overgrown schoolboy.

* * *

Richie ambled back into his living room with a dustbin-lid-sized pizza box and a large carton of Diet Pepsi. He opened the pizza box, popped the can of Pepsi and sat down. As he was taking his first bite he searched for some Indie music to play on his smart phone. He found something he liked and began nodding his head to the beat. Manoeuvring his chair closer to his computer he locked onto the home screen which had a giant face of Uncle Fester from the film, *The Addams Family*. After keying in a question about the CIA, he licked his fingers and took out another slice of pizza with pineapple, ham and olives on it. Without warning, there was an ear-splitting bang. The sound came from above and was like a satellite falling from space and crash-landing on the roof of his house.

'What the f…?' he muffled with a sliver of pizza dangling from his mouth and he jumped so violently that his chair nearly tipped over. Quickly he turned down the music and listened for a moment and then there was another crashing thud. Alarmed, he threw the pizza back into the box and glared up at the ceiling to try and figure out what was going on. Above him, the noise changed and seemed to reverberate through the whole house. It was as if King Kong was trampling over his roof using cars as shoes. Richie followed the heavy clumping sounds with his eyes until they stopped midway across the roof. As soon as they did, he darted out into the hallway to investigate.

When he reached the stairs, he looked up at the dark landing but there was nothing to see, only shadows and nothing to hear but the drumming of his own heartbeat. But then he heard something; a laugh, a laugh coming from one of the bedrooms upstairs. At first, Richie was intrigued; he'd been watching this type of thing in the movies all his life. But this was not the movies, this was real and when the laughter became painfully high pitched his curiosity quickly turned into apprehension. The sound drowned out the noise coming from the roof and was so unpleasant that he had to pin his hands over his ears to try and block it out. He had to get away from it and he began to back away from the stairs until he reached the front door. With a trembling hand he lifted the latch and backed over the threshold. He continued backing out of the house until his feet crunched onto the gravel path. He chanced removing his hands from his ears and was relieved when all he could hear was his own laboured breathing. Behind him something hit the ground heavily. It landed with the impact of a massive bag of cement. Richie didn't even have time to turn around to see what had come for him.

* * *

The following day, just before teatime, Rebecca received a very anxious call from Patrick. 'What's up?' she asked.

'I'm a bit worried about Richie.'

'Why is that?'

'He's not answering any of my calls. I've phoned him three times today already and I just can't get through to him.'

'Perhaps he's gone out or something.'

'No, I don't think so. He may have missed the first and second calls but surely not all three and he should be back by now, anyway. I'm going to go around to his house to check on him, just in case.'

'OK, then I'll go with you.'

'I'll pick you up. I'm on my way.'

* * *

In broad daylight Richie's house didn't appear quite so spectral. Patrick impatiently rapped the door knocker but there was no answer. He tried again, this time hammering his fist into the wood but still nothing.

Rebecca watched as he knelt down and pushed open the letterbox to peer inside. 'Can you see anything?' she asked.

'Nothing; no sound, no nothing.' He straightened up and tried turning the weighty black door handle but the door was locked. He stepped back onto the gravel drive and stood scanning the front of the house for any clues. Rebecca went and joined him.

'Maybe he has been called out and he just hasn't got back yet,' she repeated.

'That doesn't prevent him from answering his phone though, does it? I know Richie, he always gets back if he misses a call.'

'Maybe we should try again later,' Rebecca suggested just as her own mobile started ringing in her jacket pocket. Rebecca pressed the phone to her ear. 'Hello?'

'Rebecca?' was all her mother said. She sounded strained and then the line went dead.

'Mum?' Rebecca cried with alarm.

'What is it?' Patrick asked.

'It's Mum, she called me then the line clicked off.'

'Did she just lose the signal?'

Rebecca had to fight to keep control. 'No, I don't think so, it sounded like she was distressed. Maybe she's collapsed or something?'

Patrick tried to calm her down. 'No, hang on a minute, if she had collapsed the line would still be connected.'

But Rebecca's gut was telling her that something was wrong. 'Patrick, I know you probably think I am worrying about nothing but I need to get back home. Do you mind?'

'OK, it's probably nothing but we'll check on your mother just to set your mind at rest.' He took a last look at Richie's house. 'We'll come back later.' The tyres on Patrick's car squealed, kicking up the stone chippings as they headed off back to Rebecca's house.

When they arrived, Rebecca was out of the car before Patrick even had the chance to pull up. 'Mum,' she cried racing through the hall to the kitchen but the house was deathly silent. Rebecca rushed back through the hall towards the living room, half-expecting to find her mother collapsed on the floor but there was no sign of her. She dashed into the living room and stopped dead in her tracks. They were all sitting in there – her mother, her Uncle Jim and Dr Samuel Olsen.

CHAPTER NINETEEN

Taking in the unimaginable spectacle before her, Rebecca literally rocked back on her heels. 'Mum, are you OK?'

But Mrs Samuels didn't look capable of answering her daughter. She just sat there, still as a statue, with an expression of utter hopelessness on her face. Rebecca hadn't seen her like this since her father had died.

'What the hell's going on, Mum?'

Her mother was in one of the armchairs while Uncle Jim sat beside Olsen on the couch.

Patrick appeared in the doorway and was gobsmacked by what he saw.

Rebecca wheeled around to her uncle. 'Jim, what's all this about?'

'I'm sorry, Beccs,' was all he managed to say.

Olsen took over. 'Rebecca, please let me explain.' He stood up. He was wearing an expensive, well-cut grey suit; there was no long raincoat in evidence today. 'Please sit down, we have a lot to talk about.'

'Why should I?'

'Please, Becca, you need to hear this, believe me,' Jim implored.

Rebecca's eyes were steely as she glowered at her uncle, but she did as he asked.

'You too, Patrick; have a seat,' Olsen instructed, and Patrick went and perched on the arm of Rebecca's armchair.

Giving everyone a moment to adjust to the situation, Olsen moved over to the fireplace. He was in command and he leant against the mantelpiece as if he was a latter-day lord of the manor. He gave a polite cough and addressed his audience. 'Allow me to start from the very beginning. Have any of you heard of the Venezuelan ape man?'

Nobody answered, and it was obvious that Olsen hadn't expected them to.

'OK, in 1920 an American geologist by the name of Dr Merrion Cooper was on a three-year expedition to try and locate profitable oil reserves. The expedition party itself started out with about twenty people including Dr Cooper but only half a dozen of them survived.

'Officially, the rest of the party was ravaged by disease or killed by hostile tribes. Unofficially, many of them were torn to pieces by unrecognisable creatures in the forests near the Tarra River where the expedition was camped.

'To defend themselves, the men had to use their guns on this small group of creatures, who were only trying to guard their home territory. During the attack the survivors of the expedition did manage to capture a male and female member of this extraordinary species. Unfortunately, the male eventually died from gunshot wounds but the female survived, and it was carrying a child; it was pregnant.

'Great care was taken when they flew the female to Europe. To keep their cargo secret, a special plane was chartered, and the creature was housed in a spacious cage. It was kept warm and once it was established what she liked to eat, it was well fed. She had no noticeable adverse effects from the flight and the Academy of Science in Paris was tasked to study this great anthropological discovery. What they established was astonishing. The female creature was an anthropoid, an ape-like mammal that walked on two legs and stood about seven feet tall. At first, it was thought that this creature was a member of an ape family, but the fur was distinctly different from that of an ordinary simian. Also, instead of fingers it had powerful claw-like digits.

Their initial findings suggested that the creature might be a Sapajon, a type of New World monkey but these Sapajon monkeys only grow to the height of about a metre and they also possess a tail so it was therefore deduced that it was not of the same species.

'But there was another contradictory feature of this anthropoid that baffled the scientists. They observed that the shape of its face was oval rather than triangular and there was an absence of a prognathism, or the marked protrusion of the lower jaw as is found in some other ape species. Plus, it had a very high and prominent forehead. Finally, the scientists concluded that they had indeed discovered a distinct new species of primate and they brought in a team of anthropologists to verify their findings. Both the scientists and anthropologists agreed that it should be named Ameranthropides in honour of the American discoverers.

'Eventually, this creature did give birth to a female although at this point the gestation period remained unknown. It was decided that it was essential to the field of anthropology that further research was crucial. It was further decided that all additional research should not be carried out in a laboratory; there would be more to be gained by studying the creatures in an undercover, semi-wild but controlled environment. A large area of land was purchased and converted into a top-secret safari park-cum-training camp. It was completed some time ago and now has administration buildings and a laboratory. It also has comfortable accommodation for the research team, trainers, trainees and animal keepers.' Olsen paused and paced up and down before them as if he was giving a lecture at the National Geographic Society.

'So, this is where it all started off from,' Patrick snarled almost sounding like a wild creature himself. 'This is where all this irresponsible, barbaric interbreeding began. Don't you idiots know what you have done?'

Olsen ignored the outburst. 'Now this is where things get very interesting. Allow me to elaborate, Mr Farrell, if you will? I'm quite aware what you and Rebecca have found out and I understand that you both must be wondering what is behind it all. First and foremost, I don't have to remind you all that there will always be the threat of war and whether it is fought with nuclear or chemical weapons is immaterial. The devastation that a nuclear or chemical war would bring about would be disastrous to our planet. Therefore, we must have global uniformity. We must have law and order to govern our societies in order to guard against such cataclysm. We must find a way to maintain a ruling body to preside over our global population. Instead of indulging in power struggles and risking the destruction of the Earth we must come together to preserve it. That is why certain factions of our governing bodies have come up with a... let's say, a more ecological way of herding the flock so to speak.'

Incensed, Patrick couldn't contain himself. 'He means divide and rule, controlling the populace, maintaining a Fascist regime.'

With a superior smile Olsen held up his hands. 'Not quite so drastic, Mr Farrell, there's no need to be so pessimistic. Let's simply describe it as a more congenial deterrent.'

'You can say what you want, it all means the same thing.'

Mrs Samuels was visibly wilting. 'I don't understand any of this.'

'Mum, Patrick and I are pretty sure that Dr Olsen and his scientific cronies are developing human-animal hybrids as super-soldiers, so they can take over the world.'

'What?' Jim practically vaulted up from the sofa.

'Only to police our society,' Olsen corrected.

Curling his lip at Jim, Patrick sneered, 'Yeah, they want us to obey them like a herd of docile cows.' He turned his attention to the professor. 'Your time is up. We know all about it now, Olsen, so don't try and deny it. My mate has found you out, all right. By the way, what has happened to him? Have you got rid of him too? Did he know too much?'

'Please, Mr Farrell, I don't know what has happened to your friend.'

'Yeah, I bet you don't. Well, I'm telling you now you're not getting away with all this. The game is up on you and all your illegal scientific experiments. We're going to expose you and everyone else involved. If my friend doesn't turn up soon I am going to the police to report him as missing and I will tell them all about you; what you have done and what you and your lunatics are planning to do.'

Collapsing back onto the sofa, Jim broke in, 'What is he talking about, Olsen?'

Rebecca began to suspect that there were things she didn't know about Olsen and his association with her uncle. 'Uncle Jim, do you already know Olsen?'

'Of course he does, and your mother knows me, too,' Olsen explained.

Rebecca glared across at her mother and waited for her to deny it. But Jim and Mrs Samuels didn't say anything.

Not wanting to get sidetracked by his revelation, Olsen persisted,' Please allow me to continue. Where was I…? Ah, yes, we have been experimenting with human-animal hybrids for about a hundred years and in many countries around the world. We have also carried out long-term experiments involving humans from different cultures and with differing physical disabilities in order to establish if the results of these could be factored into our programme. I won't go into details about those results now; suffice it to say that the latest results have not proved anything conclusive as yet.

'However, while all our experiments involving inseminating a woman with primate sperm have also failed we have found that reversing the process and injecting a female primate with human sperm appears to be more successful. Our own experiments began with the female offspring of Dorothy. Remember, Dorothy was the original Ameranthropidis primate that was captured in Venezuela back in 1920.

'By the time our generation of scientists and anthropologists took over we were already creating the progeny from Dorothy's great-granddaughter, Emily. Emily was the product of a third generation of human-animal interbreeding. Yet, while she retained most of her original ancestral traits and features she also displayed a remarkable human-like intelligence, a problem-solving intelligence. We then injected her with human stem cells to enhance her intellect even more. We also noticed that Emily communicated with her offspring using what appeared to be an instinctive form of primate sign language.

'After we had artificially inseminated Emily with two human male donors she became pregnant and gestated for about 250 days giving birth to triplets. In fact, this was the first generation of triplets born in human-animal history. Emily bore two males and a female. But first let me explain the science behind the conception of triplets.'

'Olsen, we don't have time for a biology lecture, here,' Patrick protested but Olsen wasn't going to be deterred; he was in his element.

'Triplets can be either Monozygotic, meaning that the egg has split into three identical embryos. Or triplets can be Dizygotic. This means that they are formed from separate eggs. However, Emily produced Polyzygotic triplets which in simple terms means, a pair and a spare. That is, two identical twins from one egg plus another offspring from another egg, which was fertilised by sperm from a different donor.

'The identical twins share the same sex and the same physical attributes, but the spare offspring could conceivably be of the opposite sex and not share any of the physical characteristics of the two twins. This is something that I need to emphasise so that we are completely clear. The spare egg may be completely different from that of the identical twins; in many ways a disconnected sibling, a different being altogether.'

Like her mother, Rebecca was having problems absorbing all the facts that Olsen was coming out with.

One by one, Olsen focused on each person in the room before he dropped his bombshell. 'Emily gave birth to two males and a female. Sadly one of the twins, a male, died just after birth but the other two survived. The male survivor we named Rassimus.'

Suddenly Rebecca was on red alert. 'Blue?' she exclaimed. 'My Blue.'

'Yes, I believe you refer to him as Mr Blue Sky. Rassimus was born a healthy eleven pounds two ounces of muscle and matted black hair.' Olsen involuntarily ran a hand over his own thick black hair. 'The female survivor weighed in at eight pounds three ounces and we named her Sister, which was what she was to the other surviving sibling. Rassimus and Sister did not share any physical attributes. They were completely different, almost like two separate species. Contrary to our expectations, Sister was born a healthy baby with human characteristics and whose only biological connection to her own mother and brother was less than twenty-five percent of their DNA. Of course, this shook the very foundations of our research even though we were fully aware how she was conceived.'

'What happened to this so-called human baby?' Rebecca asked.

'She was placed with adoptive parents,' Olsen replied.

'And where is she now?'

With a dramatic pause, Olsen stared fixedly at Rebecca. 'The child who was reared as Sister is now called REBECCA and she is sitting in front of me as I speak.'

'What? What are you saying?' Patrick yelled.

There was a rushing in Rebecca's ears and the room tilted. Then her knees folded as she passed out. Taking charge Olsen pushed the others aside. 'Give her some air,' he ordered as he leant down beside her and loosened the waistband of her jeans, 'and get her some water.'

He gently patted her cheeks and rubbed her hands. As she started to come to, he stroked her hair and whispered to her, 'You are the third child, the offspring of a simian primate and a human; you are an anthropological miracle and you are the true sister to Rassimus. You are truly remarkable. We could call your creation an inert coil of chemicals or slight variants expressing different proteins in an embryo – who knows how it happened, but it did, and you are here.'

All sounds around her were distorted like they were coming to her through a wall of water. Rebecca wanted to immerse herself in the water. She wanted to swim away, swim down into the depths to escape from the nightmarish reality on the surface. And as she swam down, further and further into the watery abyss, two questions reverberated around her head and she kept saying to herself, *Who am I? What am I?* Finally, just before she reached breaking point, she was jolted back to reality by the sight of Olsen stroking her hair.

Gathering all her strength, she struggled to her feet, pushed Olsen away and bolted out of the living room.

She tore upstairs and into her bedroom and slammed the door behind her. She felt like a frightened animal, an animal like Blue, who went to ground when threatened with danger.

Patrick started to go after her but was stopped by Olsen pressing his chest and forcing him backwards.

'No, leave her. She needs time; time to adjust, time to come to terms with the earth-shattering news of her parentage.'

Patrick protested vehemently but Olsen reasoned with him and guided him over to Rebecca's vacant chair. 'It would be in Rebecca's best interest if she was not put under any more pressure at the moment.'

His air of authority still intact, Olsen took up his position by the fireplace and continued with his discourse. He was obviously completely unaware that his revelation about Rebecca had lost him his audience. 'For centuries, the superpowers have governed this world and by the way, I'm not referring to your duly elected prime ministers and presidents who are merely puppets; I'm referring to the very top of the pyramid, the heads of the elite organisations that run everything from the governments to the police, the banks, even the military and the media. It is these globalists who have been formulating a plan to create a world with one law, one religion, even one single currency; in effect, a super state.'

'Yeah, I've heard all those conspiracy theories, too, but it'll never happen.' Patrick tried another sneer, but he didn't quite pull it off. He was still in shock. It wasn't every day that you were told that the person you fancied was descended from a Venezuelan primate.

Olsen sensed his advantage and couldn't disguise a sardonic grin. 'Have you also heard of the term, Hegelian Dialectic, named after the philosopher Friedrich Hegel?'

He wasn't going to admit it, but Patrick was struggling, his concentration had gone to pot, and he couldn't place the term. 'It sounds vaguely familiar.'

'Of course, you are a school teacher.' Olsen couldn't have been more patronising. 'Well then, let me refresh your memory. In simple terms it means thesis versus antithesis, or problem-action-solution and can be adapted to influence the general public. When two opposing sides are forced into a conflict and then a third party is introduced into the situation, a synchronisation, a synthesis occurs. In other words, let's say there is an existing approach to a problem – the thesis. However, you have a particular plan that you wish to initiate to solve the problem, but you know full well that the general populace will never accept it. The solution to this is to propose a far more extreme solution, creating fear and desperation in the population – the antithesis. Then, you propose your original, more acceptable plan and it is seized with open arms and hey presto you have become the hero for saving the situation. In essence, that is how the populace can be manipulated into accepting the policies of the powerful.'

Mrs Samuels, Jim and even Patrick had been subdued by Olsen's rhetoric and Rebecca's agonising distress had left them all feeling desolated. They were drained of emotion and curiosity. They sat there like brain-dead students in the middle of an incomprehensible double philosophy lecture.

Not deterred, Olsen warmed to his subject. He loved the sound of his own voice too much to acknowledge that what he was saying was falling on deaf ears. 'Let me give you an example of a modified Hegelian Dialectic. Soviet Communism and Nazi Fascism resulted in the conflict of World War II. Now, an elite body of globalists engineered those political factions in such a way that they would cause a war. This was stage one of their conspiracy for world domination. When the war ended, they were then able to put forward their plan for the United Nations, arguing that such an assembly would act as an arbiter and stop another war occurring. This then led to the formation of the European Union; stage two of their conspiracy.

'Now, today, all the countries who are members of this European Union have surrendered their sovereignty, their democracy and their independence. They have opened up their borders and allowed unlimited numbers of immigrants to infiltrate their nations, all in the name of so-called multiculturalism; cohesion; diversity?

'The globalists predicted what would happen when all these different cultures were thrown into the mix together. They predicted conflict, unrest, battles in the streets, gang warfare, no-go areas as each ethnic group formed their own segregated areas of the towns and cities.

'They then addressed the problem of how law and order could possibly be maintained in these circumstances. It could not and that is where the globalists want our organisation to step in. Stage three of their conspiracy is that, under their ultimate control, we will provide an army of highly intelligent super-strong, military-trained simian hybrids who will police our nations, and a New World Order will have been achieved. A world order with a bureaucratic, totalitarian world government that controls all the significant occurrences in finance and politics and will put an end to international power struggles.' When Olsen finished speaking, his face was flushed, and his eyes were lit with the frenzied blaze of a fanatic.

Patrick snapped, 'But that is not the whole story, is it? Your world order can only be gained at the expense of anyone who protests. They will be eradicated, won't they?'

'Wait a minute, Olsen,' Jim jumped in. 'You hoodwinked me, my brother and his wife. You haven't been honest with any of us, have you? You didn't say anything about all this when we agreed to go along with you and we still don't know what the hell you are going on about.'

Patrick rounded on Jim. 'Tell me, because I really want to know, just where do you, and Rebecca's mother and father, fit into all this?'

Olsen didn't give Jim a chance to explain. 'They agreed to be a part of this groundbreaking and exciting experiment.'

'Not all of it, we didn't,' Jim retorted.

Olsen cut in. 'You see, we thought it would be beneficial for Rebecca to be reared by her blood relatives.'

'Blood relatives? I thought you said Rebecca was conceived by a primate,' Patrick argued.

'Born from a primate but not purely conceived by two of the same species. Don't forget what I told you, she had to have human sperm donors.'

Patrick glowered back at Jim. 'You agreed to participate in this sick, deplorable experiment. Did you even consider the consequences for Rebecca?'

Jim's head dropped in shame. 'Rob and I agreed to become the sperm donors. We did it for the money, we both needed it. But we were told that all we were going to do was rear Rebecca and they were going to study the monkey and that's it. There was nothing about all this super-army crap.'

'Yes, and you were both financially compensated for this service,' Olsen pointed out. 'This house and all the land was provided free of charge and don't forget that large injection of cash into your business.'

Patrick's utter contempt for everyone involved including Rebecca's mother was plain to see. 'So, where do we go from here, Olsen? Just what are your plans for Rebecca and Mr Blue or Rassimus?'

Olsen took a moment. He had to choose his words carefully. 'Over the years we have been preparing Rassimus. We have been training Him to lead an elite fighting unit and here on Claydon Head is where his training has taken place.'

Patrick stabbed his finger towards Olsen. 'Trained to obey and perform just like all your other mobsters and monsters?'

'No, not like all the others. Rassimus was born a thoroughbred. He is a direct descendant of the Ameranthropic primate Dorothy and the amazing Emily is his mother. The first step in his training was to deprive Him of Emily's protection so he would learn to become completely self-reliant. We also had to ensure that his natural aggressiveness would not be weakened by a relationship with his mother. And even more importantly we had to instil as much anger in Him as possible. We had to do everything we could to make sure he could tap into his animal aggression; the kind of aggression he needed to kill when necessary. That could only be achieved by killing and removing his mother.

'To this end, they were both sedated and transported from the research facility to Claydon Woods in our custom-made horsebox. Rassimus was not as heavily sedated as his mother and when he came to for a brief time he thought she was dead because she did not respond to Him. When he fell asleep again we placed Emily on a stretcher and took her back to her home at the research facility. Understandably, she displayed considerable distress at the loss of her remaining offspring, but we gave her a course of tranquillisers and provided her with a substitute. A human child, with learning and physical disabilities, was found abandoned in India. He was brought back and introduced to Emily; she reacted well and began to bond with him.'

Mouthing a string of obscenities, Patrick hurled himself at Olsen. 'You are a heartless, evil bastard Olsen; you did that to a vulnerable little boy. I dread to think what has happened to him in your so-called research facility. And you made Blue think that his mother has been dead for all these years.'

Dodging Patrick's attack Olsen was scornful. 'Oh, work it out, Mr Farrell. We would never have killed Emily. She is indispensable to our research and Rassimus did succeed in becoming self-reliant and capable of killing. Now, he is in line to become my general. But first he must face the ultimate test to prove he is up to the task, that he is worthy of that status.'

'What test?' Patrick asked.

'What else; in the field of combat, of course.'

'What field of combat?'

'Everything has been meticulously planned to prepare Him for the test; from the food he eats to his living conditions. Of course not everything has gone according to plan. For example, we tried to introduce certain drugs into his food in order to increase his aggressive tendencies. Unfortunately, Rassimus did not react to them the way we expected Him to. He worked out that the food had been tampered with and threw it away. We were particularly disappointed that he didn't accept the raw meat as we had hoped to build up his appetite for bloody flesh; in other words, make Him bloodthirsty.

'His reaction turned out to be a double-edged sword. On the one hand, we were impressed and pleased that he had caught on to what was going on so quickly but on the other he was displaying a more self-determining intellect than we had anticipated.' Olsen gave an admiring chuckle. 'He is certainly a quick learner. We gave him potassium permanganate powder and it didn't take Him long to figure how to make a fire with it by adding some sachets of table sugar. He found the sugar on the outside table of a cafe during one of his night-prowls.

'We were aware that his uncontrollable actions could cause a severe set-back so we decided to keep testing Him with a continuous series of hunting exercises. Rassimus has adapted so well to all our attack strategies that he is almost the complete warrior. But if he does prove to be up to the task of commanding my forces he will have to wear a uniform. Along with the objects and books, I left different types of garments for Him, so he could get accustomed to the feel of clothes against his fur. By the way, we also studied the response to wearing clothes on some of our other experimental subjects. The outfit they seemed to like best was a long raincoat and a Stetson hat. I found this particularly gratifying because that was what I often wore. You know what they say, imitation is the greatest form of flattery.' Olsen couldn't have looked more pleased with himself if he had tried.

'We also had to keep Him stimulated so we made his living quarters as interesting as possible. We rigged up an electric light system and as I said, we placed a variety of objects and books in the caves. We added the objects to the smugglers' booty that had been stowed away there many years ago. A cache of weapons was also included, and we let Him find weapons that he thought his hunters had discarded. For obvious reasons, Rassimus would need to learn as much as possible about weapons; what they were for and how they worked. We supplied Him with military manuals with clear and simple diagrams showing the mechanisms of each weapon and how each weapon could be used.'

'So, you do know where his cave is?' Patrick was incredulous.

'Oh yes, I was the one who selected the caves as a home for Rassimus. The location has been a closely-guarded secret, but it was necessary to divulge it to the two men who set up the electrics and carried the objects and books there. Sadly, they are no longer with us and Rebecca and I are the only two people who know the extent of the caves and where they are.'

'And what about Rebecca, Olsen,' Jim intervened. 'You promised that she would come to no harm.'

'She will not be harmed but we still need her; she is very much an integral part of our plan. Now Rassimus is ready for his final test, we need Rebecca to help draw Him out of hiding. Of course, I can find Him without Rebecca but we don't want Rassimus to think he is being coerced at this stage. We want Him to believe that the decision to take the test is his own choice.'

Patrick shook his head violently. 'Rebecca won't help you trap Him, Olsen, I can tell you that now.'

As always, Olsen was ready with his reply. 'You see, Rassimus and Rebecca have a very strong, natural bond because they are both from the same set of triplets and they share a percentage of the same DNA. That is why we needed them to maintain contact and interact when they were young. We had to foster that bond at an early age so the connection between them remained strong even if they became separated. And when that did happen we were pretty sure that the bond would not be broken. However, we were not sure how Rassimus would react when the time came to complete his training. We estimated that he would have developed an understanding of our strategies, but he may have also developed his own ideas about how to proceed. Now it is time to implement the final tasks and put the pressure on by increasing the violence of the hunting exercises. But we suspect that Rassimus has become paranoid and feels persecuted, so he has turned to the person he cares about most, for support.

'Because of their special bond Rebecca experiences his distress and has been compelled to return home to be there for Him. Many twins and triplets share telepathic powers and they have a compulsion to rush to the side of a sibling in trouble when they receive a telepathic cry for help. Rebecca and Rassimus certainly share the pull of strong telepathic power so there was very little she could do to resist coming back. It was inevitable, and we were counting on it and – Mr Farrell – she will help us.'

Patrick snorted with disdain. 'You think you have got it all worked out, don't you, Olsen? Rassimus, Rebecca, the house, the off-limit woods, the Gas Mask Men all components of your sick plan?' The self-righteousness radiating from Olsen's eyes was so repulsive that Patrick had to look away before he leapt up and smashed his face with his fist.

'You must be so proud of what you have created, Olsen,' Jim declared.

'We should all be proud,' Olsen replied.

Jim's sagging face had aged even more since Olsen had started talking. His skin looked grey and his body was scrunched up as if he was in pain. 'No, no, Rob was right, I should have listened to him. He wasn't happy about any of this right from the beginning.'

'But he was happy enough to accept the money,' Olsen retorted.

'Yes, but he would have turned it down if he had known what we were letting ourselves in for. He was the only one who had any sense, he wanted to pull the plug on this whole despicable charade. He gambled all your money away, he didn't want it because he knew everything was going to end badly. That was why he went after Rassimus. He went after Him, so he could put an end to it once and for all. But he never made it, did he? No, your precious monster killed him.'

'Rassimus simply did what any animal would do to protect itself or a member of its family.'

With all this talk about her husband opening up old wounds, Mrs Samuels stood up and quietly left the room. They could fight it out amongst themselves. She didn't want anything more to do with any of them.

In her bedroom Rebecca was lying on her bed staring up at the ceiling. When she heard a gentle rapping on the door she kept on staring. She knew who it was and when the rapping started to sound frantic she turned on her side, away from the door.

'Rebecca,' her mother called softly, and very delicately she opened the door. She went over and sat gingerly at the foot of the bed. She reached over to touch her daughter but pulled her hand back in case it made matters worse.

'Don't bother trying to explain, I heard everything else from the landing. All I want to know is why you agreed to do it and why have you and Uncle Jim carried on lying? Lie, upon lie, upon lie.'

It was time for another confession, but this one was going to be harder to justify. It was time for her mother to look deep into her soul and face up to the fact that her compliance might have ruined her daughter's life. Mrs Samuels wiped the tears that were trickling down her cheeks and she tried not to wallow in self-pity. This was not about her pain, it was about Rebecca.

'Back then we were desperate to have a child but unfortunately I was unable to have any children. The medical term for my condition is polycystic ovarian syndrome. Then this opportunity came along with Olsen and it seemed too good a chance to miss. Everything was laid out for us; we didn't even have to get a house of our own. They gave us this house as part of the deal. We thought that all we had to do was to bring up a baby girl as our own. It sounded like an answer to our prayers. Even when Olsen told us that we had to allow her to interact with her brother, an ape-like creature who lived in the woods, we didn't hear the alarm bells ringing.

'But to be honest that was probably because we heard what we wanted to hear. We went into a kind of denial. We buried any reservations we had about the baby's connection to the ape-like creature. When I say we, it was mostly me. All I could think about was that I was going to be given a baby to love and cherish.

'All Olsen told us was that you were both being studied for medical research. We were sworn to secrecy and in exchange we would be paid to bring up the baby, the baby that we always longed for. Plus, we had a nice place to live in as a family. But as you and Rassimus grew older, Olsen and his team started making more research demands. He wanted us to let you live with Blue full-time to see what effect that might have. Then finally, Rob had had enough so on that fateful night he planned, along with your uncle, to put a stop to it by killing your Mr Blue.'

Falling forward, her mother hammered her fists on the duvet. 'Rebecca, why didn't you stay with your uncle? You'd have been safe, he was there to protect you. It was the only way to give you some kind of a normal life.'

With her head buried in her pillows, Rebecca mumbled, 'What does it matter now? My life was just one sick experiment; a charade, a pantomime. All I am is an unwitting part of Olsen's megalomania, an anomaly, a freak; how can I ever possibly live a normal life?'

'You're still our daughter.' Even to her own ears, her mother's words sounded hollow.

Mrs Samuels leant over her daughter. 'Please get away from here right now. Go with Patrick. Get away while you still have a chance and just try and live as normal a life as you can. You're still young and healthy and you can still have a life. Just because you were adopted it doesn't mean you can't live like everyone else. Lots of people have been adopted and they still manage to enjoy a fulfilling life. That's why I took you to the cafe. I knew Patrick went there. I recognised him, and I wanted you to get together so he might take your mind off everything and hopefully take you away from it all.'

Her mother's attempts at trying to console her daughter were pitiful. Her desperation was making her irritating and blinkered. She failed to mention the circumstances of the adoption, let alone the implications of such a pact. Rebecca had to bite her lip so she wouldn't say something she might regret. She didn't have the energy, anyway; her tank was empty. There was nothing left inside except the belief that the only thing to do was to leave; leave the house, leave them all.

Patrick was the first to hear the clattering of footsteps tearing down the stairs and then the front door being flung open. As he dashed out of the living room to try and stop Rebecca he was stalled by the two burly minders standing guard outside. Patrick was just about to bulldoze his way through when he heard Olsen shout through the living room window, 'No, leave her, Mr Farrell, we were expecting something like this to happen.'

In the darkness and with tears coursing down her face she tore through the dandelion field and headed towards the edge of Claydon Woods. Once she was inside the woods everything was blurred by night shadows.

She was exhausted and felt like a worn rag doll. She was just about to collapse onto the ground when suddenly he caught her and she was enfolded in the arms of her childhood friend; her seven-foot Ameranthropic sibling.

CHAPTER TWENTY

The thick, viscous liquid tasted and smelled disgusting and she had to turn her face away to avoid another sip. In a matter of seconds most of her senses started to return to normal and she saw Him looming over her wearing what could only be described as a kind of long black cloak. He was holding the same clay drinking cup he always used for the reviving brew. This time, they were not in the Sky Chamber. This cave was much larger, more like the size of a small auditorium and there were dozens of candles to provide sufficient light. There were also two fires burning, one either side of Rebecca.

'Blue, I wish you wouldn't keep making me black out when you want to get me to your cave. Surely you can trust me by now. You don't have to keep giving me that horrible stuff to bring me around once I am here. It's revolting.' Pausing and looking around, Rebecca forgot about the foul drink. 'Hang on, this isn't your cave. Where are we?' she asked.

Blue took the cup and swished back his cloak to sit beside her on a slab of rock. *Where did he get his outlandish clothes?* she wondered.

He paid no attention to her questions about the noxious drink, but his fingers busily started to sign an answer to her question about the cave they were in. *This is part of the forbidden area, that area that I never allowed you to set foot in.*

Still a bit groggy, Rebecca struggled to sit up. She gazed around but there was nothing much to see except the inside of a damp, cold cavern. 'So, what's so special about this place? It's big but basically it's just a cave like the others.'

No, this is one of the central caves that lead into all the other caves that run right through this mountain. The Sky Chamber is only the tip of the iceberg. From this one you can get through to dozens of different shafts and tunnels that stretch for miles. There are still many more tunnels that I have to explore. But it is dangerous because there are open wells, pits and sheer drops that go straight down to the sea. That is one of the reasons why I never allowed to you to come down here.

'Why have you brought me down here now?'

It's time you learnt a bit about this place. But I still won't let you come down here alone. I will show you as many chambers as I can, and you will see many interesting things.

Rebecca rubbed her face with her hands. After what she had discovered back at the house she was in no state for a tour. At the moment, she couldn't get the gut-wrenching fact that Blue was her blood brother out of her mind. Blue stood up and had to duck under a rock overhang as he prepared to lead the way. He stared down at her and his tangerine-coloured eyes glinted in the candlelight. He looked uneasy, as if he was aware that she was hiding something from Him.

Rebecca didn't know how to explain; all she did know was that she had to try. 'Blue, there are some important things that I think you should know.'

Holding up his massive hand, Blue signalled, *Tell me later.* Then he reached down and swung Rebecca to her feet as if she weighed no more than a feather.

She followed Blue over to three exit tunnels and Blue signed that if she ever became lost she should take the middle tunnel. To make it easier for her to identify, he had poured white paint over one of the stones at the entrance. His finger signs were slow and deliberate as he impressed on her that this was the only safe route back up to the Sky Chamber.

Blue reached down and produced a torch made from a rod-like piece of wood with a rag wrapped around it at one end. The rag smelled as if it had been dipped in some sort of flammable fluid; he lit the torch from a flickering candle. Nodding at Rebecca to follow he stepped into the tunnel on the right.

Trying not to become over-wrought at the improbability of the whole situation, Rebecca resorted to making a weak joke as she entered the tunnel after Him. 'Christ! Now I know how *Alice* felt.' But her reference to *Alice in Wonderland* was lost on Blue.

Slowly they made their way down a long, twisting passage, the light of the torch creating a flaming glow around them. Down they walked in a seemingly endless concentric circle until they reached the bottom where the sides of the passage were much narrower. Blue bent down to a metal box that had a small lever attached to it. He flicked it down and immediately dozens of light bulbs bathed the passage in a bright white light. From where Rebecca was standing she could see another long, winding tunnel that also had light bulbs laced into a black cable that ran down the jagged rock surfaces.

Impressed, Rebecca's voice echoed around the cave. 'Wow! Did you set all this up?'

Blue signalled back to her, *No, all this was already here before I came.*

'Who did it?' she asked but Blue didn't reply. Instead, he motioned for her to carry on following Him. They curved around a few bends until the passage opened up into a huge dome-shaped hollow illuminated with more wall lights and stacked with piles and piles of fantastical objects.

'What the...?' Rebecca gasped. It was like an Aladdin's cave full of treasures. 'Where the hell did you get all this stuff from?'

The shadow of Blue's large fingers danced on the walls of the cave as he replied. *From what I have learned, the local humans say these caves were used by smugglers that used to operate along these coasts. Some of the stuff that has been left down here is very old. I suppose it was* the smugglers who hollowed out some of the caves and passages, so they could use them to stash their treasures.

Rebecca walked over to examine some of the contraband and as she came across a splintered, wooden box, she asked, 'Is this cave connected to Bishop's Cave?' But she was much more interested in the contents of the box than Blue's answer. There was a pile of World War I Webley service revolvers inside and next to it was another wooden box, half-full of Brodie helmets. Beside the boxes of war relics were several barrels. If all the stories about smuggling were true they were probably full of rum or wine. Behind them, partially draped by a rotting, water-stained crimson cloth she saw peeling gold-leaf frames surrounding, what looked like, works of arts by old masters. Sadly, the paintings had deteriorated in the damp atmosphere of the cave and it was difficult to make out what the artist had actually painted.

'My God, Blue, some of this eighteenth and nineteenth-century stuff is worth an absolute fortune but the guns and helmets are from World War I. I don't think much smuggling went on by then. I wonder when they were put here and why. And who, in heaven's name, rigged up the electric light system?'

I don't know but this is only a part of it,' Blue explained. *There are still many other chambers with many more treasures. I have also discovered piles of books, volumes and papers with pen writing on them. Many of the books have drawings and photographs. They make it easier to understand all about the human species. Over the years I have studied these books and have even managed to make out some of the simple words. I remembered what you tried to teach me when we had our reading and writing lessons and I have learned many new words on my own.*

'Well done.' Rebecca smiled admiringly at her half-brother. 'And where are these great books?'

Not here. They are kept in my own cave. I must take great care of them because they have opened up a different world to me. The books are more valuable than anything else that may be down here.

'You're not even going to let me see them?' Rebecca wheedled.

In time, Blue signalled staring broodingly over his hoard of secret treasure. When he noticed Rebecca shivering against the cold he drew her into the folds of his robe.

'Can we go back now?' Blue nodded and he guided her back the way they had come.

* * *

The fire in the Sky Chamber had taken the chill off and Blue and Rebecca sat down to eat. Blue had a huge dish of berries and wild mushrooms and he gave Rebecca an apple, some red berries, broken bread and a wedge of cheese. Rebecca gazed down at her food. It wasn't posh nosh but it was better than nothing.

'Where did you get this food from?'

The travellers leave food for me every week, so I won't harm them. I wouldn't harm them, anyway, even if they didn't leave food for me.

Rebecca froze before taking a bite out of her apple. 'You're telling me that I'm eating a vagrant's left-overs?'

Their food is good but some of it is not for me. It gives me bad air. Anyway, I don't eat all of it because I don't know where it's been.

Rebecca guffawed, spraying crumbs in Blue's face. 'Oh, thanks very much. It's not good enough for you but it will do for me.' She was hungry, and she debated whether or not to eat the unwashed apple. In the end, she decided to risk it.

While they were eating, Rebecca told Blue almost everything she had learned from Olsen, everything except for the shocking revelation that Blue was her sibling. She wasn't quite sure how he might react to the news and she was worried it might confuse Him and complicate the situation, especially with everything else he had to deal with. She also neglected to tell him about the third twin who had not survived. That would only distract Him even more and he had to stay focused at all costs. If he was to get away from Olsen and his team he had to have all his wits about Him.

You have to stay here with me now, Blue ordered. *Only here will you be safe.*

'I can't stay here, Blue.'

For now, you must. If what you have said is true, there is more danger than I first thought. Now you know why I have to escape.

'But how will you ever be free from this? Even if you did get away, Olsen won't give up until he finds you. You'll either end up dead or a part of his super-army.'

Blue stopped eating. *I'm not going to become one of his soldiers, they will have to kill me first.*

'One of the last things I heard Olsen say was that you had to prove yourself in the field of combat. What did he mean?'

He means no more games. Now we play for real. I must fight to prove myself worthy. I must fight for my survival.

Rebecca couldn't bear the thought of it. 'You know they'll find us here eventually, don't you?'

Like I've already told you, there are miles and miles of tunnels beneath this cave. You have seen some for yourself. If I wanted to, I could disappear from the surface of the world forever and nobody would find me again.

Rebecca was not convinced that Blue knew what he was up against. Olsen had so many resources at his disposal. He would find Him no matter what it took but she went along with his delusion. 'Why don't you do just that? Why go through all this and why do you need my help?'

Humans say that the best things in life are free but to me the best thing in life is to be free.

'That doesn't answer my question though, does it?'

All in good time.

❋ ❋ ❋

Rebecca lay awake on the rock bed staring across at the flickering flames of the fire. If Patrick could see her now he would probably tell her that she looked like Wilma, the TV cartoon character from *The Flintstones*, although she was a lot warmer now that she was snuggled under her fur blanket. In spite of everything, she still wished she was back in the comfort of her own bed at home. But perhaps not; that would mean that she would have to deal with Olsen, her mother and Uncle Jim.

Outside on the Sky Ledge Blue was sitting with his legs crossed, studying the stars. Rebecca knew that sleep was out of the question for her. She told herself that nobody would be able to sleep if they had just heard Olsen's disclosures about their own parentage. There was also the matter of all the lies she had been told. She couldn't get over what her mother, father and her uncle had agreed to do for money and then there was Olsen himself. What sinister plans did he have for all of them? How was all this going to play out? She tossed and turned on the hard rock as everything crowded in on her. Through it all, Patrick's face suddenly cropped up.

Would he still be there when all this was over? Of course he wouldn't. How could he be? She was related to an ape. Who would want a relationship with a freak like her? She needed to speak to him, to test the water and find out what he was thinking. 'If only I had my blasted phone,' she moaned.

In her blind panic to get away she had forgotten to take anything with her, even her mobile phone and a jacket. As her frustration at her own carelessness began to spill over, she began to whimper, 'Why is all this happening to me?'

As she wiped away her tears with the back of her hand she saw Blue standing over her with his head tilted to one side. He had the same expression on his face that he used to have when he knew Rebecca was upset but wasn't sure what to do about it. It made Him look young again, like a confused and faithful dog.

He snuffled her hand and licked away the salty tears. Leaning down he clasped her wet hand in his and drew her up from the bed. He led her out onto the Sky Ledge and Rebecca had another blast from the past as he pointed to the canopy of twinkling stars above. She remembered that they always seemed to be in some sort of alignment with the soothing sounds of the waves hitting the shore down below. Blue motioned for her to sit down on the ledge facing Him and she did as he instructed. She didn't have the energy to resist even if she had wanted to.

Once she had settled down he gently cupped her face with his huge hands. His hands were so big that they covered her eyes and ears almost blotting out her ability to see and hear. Tenderly, he drew her head closer and closer until their foreheads touched.

Rebecca closed her eyes and resting against his bony forehead, she was transported back to more innocent times. He still smelled like a mountain goat, but she found the familiar smell comforting and let herself go. Almost immediately she began to unwind. It was like pulling the plug in a basin and letting the water drain away. The anxiety and the tension began to swirl down some imaginary plughole. They were youngsters again and Blue was consoling her the way he did when she was a little girl when something had scared or upset her.

* * *

Early next morning Rebecca woke from a surprisingly deep sleep. She could feel the warmth of the fire penetrating her fur covering and she lazily stretched her arms and legs. Blue was shuffling about wearing a poncho made from a king-size tartan blanket that had a hole cut out for his head. He was obviously preparing to leave the cave. She sat up. 'Where are you going?'

I'm going to fetch the food left by the homeless people. If I don't take it they'll think I'm angry with them and I have to feed Little Shit.

'Who, who's Little Shit?'

Blue let bough-like arms flap to his sides. *Come with me and I'll show you.* He went over to the far rear of the cave and bent down.

He gripped two iron handles set in the shadow of the back section of the cave and gave them a sharp push. Immediately early morning daylight flooded in and hit their faces. The sudden contrast with the light in the cave made Rebecca blink rapidly and she shielded her eyes from the glare.

They stepped out from this concealed entrance to the cave directly into a small hollow full of tall, thick evergreen bushes, the same type of bushes that grew at the edge of the woods on the west side of Claydon Head.

Blue quickly replaced the rock cover and rearranged the evergreen bushes so it was completely hidden, and raised his strong jaw to the pale grey sky. He was checking for any strange scents and Rebecca watched with amusement as his nostrils flared out to their full width. When he was satisfied that they were safe he gave her an all-clear signal and they moved out of the hollow. Blue led the way over to a narrow recess just below a crop of overhanging rock. At the base of the rock face there was a handful of fist-sized stones stacked neatly together. Blue squatted down and moved them aside until he uncovered a cloth bundle about the size of a cooked chicken. He picked up the bundle and went to sit on a grassy mound. Rebecca stood watching curiously as he began unravelling the cloth.

He uncovered a cracked bowl containing food. The food consisted of two stale-looking pasties, half a pizza, some cheese and the heel of a loaf of bread. Breaking off some of the cheese and splitting one of the pasties in two he placed them down on the wet grass and waited. Rebecca found all this intriguing and moved a few steps closer until Blue halted her with a stern hand. After waiting a few seconds Blue began to make some odd hooting noises and stopped.

Rebecca found herself involuntarily holding her breath and a moment later she spotted the beautiful rusty fur coat of a fox emerging from the bushes. Rebecca's mouth fell open and wordlessly she watched in wonder as the fox padded a few paces closer, sniffing the ground as it advanced towards Blue. Reaching the food, it ran its black wet nose over the chunks of cheese and then began to nibble the bits that Blue had placed on the grass. Slowly, Blue leant over and stroked the soft fur on the fox's head. Rebecca couldn't quite believe what she was witnessing and a tender smile touched her lips. But if that wasn't magical enough the bushes rustled once more and three small cubs scampered over to join in the feast.

Rebecca couldn't stop herself quietly cooing at the sight of these adorable creatures. She had a problem controlling herself because she desperately wanted to rush over and scoop each one up in her arms but she knew that she would only frighten them. Blue broke off some more pasty and cheese and scattered the scraps on the grass. Soon the little cubs were greedily chomping away at all the food. After the vixen had finished eating she ran her long, pink tongue over her lips and licked Blue's fingers and Rebecca was sure she saw Him smile.

Finally, the fox decided it was time to go, her bushy tail bouncing as she scampered back towards the woods, the three cubs following closely behind. But before she disappeared back into the bushes the fox stopped and turned as if to thank Blue and then they were gone.

Moved by this captivating scene Rebecca ran over to Blue. 'That was beautiful, those three cubs were gorgeous. So that's one of the reasons you scavenge for food and save what the vagrants leave you. But I still don't understand why you threw away the food that used to be left outside your cave. I know you did throw it away because I saw you do it when I stayed with you after I ran away.' Blue waved her question aside so Rebecca let it go and asked Him about the foxes. 'How often have you been feeding them?'

Blue's fingers danced in front of her. *Three or four years ago I found her abandoned in the forest yelping for her mother who had probably been killed, just like my mother was. I took her home and let her live with me until she was old enough to look after herself. It was good for me to have some company and she became my pet. Then when she was ready I started to take her into the woods. I wanted her to be free so I used to leave her there but she always found her way back to my cave. After a while she started to take longer and longer to return until one day she didn't come back at all. After that she only came occasionally but I still wanted to look after her so now I make sure she has enough to eat.*

Rebecca found Blue's story charming. 'You had her as a pet. What did you call her?'

I told you, Little Shit.

'Little Shit? That's not very nice. Why did you call her that?'

Blue sat back on the boulder with an indignant look on his face. *Because she kept shitting in my cave and I had to get rid of it.*

'Oh dear, that's foxes for you,' Rebecca chuckled.

Ever since I let her go, she comes back to see me about once a week and I give her some food. Those cubs are only about six weeks old and Little Shit brings them along to see me and gets fed as well. At first, they were wary but they're beginning to accept me. In time they will accept you, too.

Rebecca loved the idea of making friends with the foxes but wasn't sure if it would ever happen. Nevertheless, what she had witnessed that morning was the first time she had been able to take a real pleasure in something. The woodland scene had been like an oasis of enchantment that had lifted her tortured mind out from the maelstrom of chaos coming at her from all sides.

The morning's excursions weren't over and Blue took Rebecca to the tip of the knoll overlooking the farmer's fields so they could sit and watch the rabbits chasing each other over the grass bunkers. It was still early enough in the morning so they didn't have to worry about anyone spotting them sitting there. As they watched the rabbits hopping about together Rebecca could see that Blue was mesmerised by their antics.

'Why are you so fascinated by the rabbits?' she asked.

Drawn out of his reverie Blue jerked his shoulders. *Sometimes I like to watch them play and if you're lucky you can actually see them trying to trick one another. They actually use simple traps and diversions to have more fun. I think it's important to know that little creatures, as ordinary as this, can show that they can plan as well as play. They don't just eat and have babies; they actually care about one another. They protect their young and they stick together.*

Rebecca thought about what he was saying and wondered if he was trying to tell her something more. Was he trying to tell her that humans, even humans as clever as Olsen, had always underestimated the mental capacity of animals? Maybe he had his own powers in mind; the telepathic powers that connected Him to her and could send her into a trance-like state when he wanted to bring her to his cave. She wondered if she would ever get to grips with the complexities of Blue's character and abilities.

The morning was moving on and the locals would be preparing for the working day. It was time to go before someone saw them. The sky was a crisp shade of arctic blue and the air felt fresh and uncontaminated by the presence of the inhabitants of Claydon. Rebecca could see why Blue found this part of the day so pleasurable as well as safe.

* * *

Finishing bowls of hot mushroom soup that Blue had cooked in a battered pan over the fire Rebecca's heart sank when she realised that they were going to carry on with their tour of the caves. She could have done with a break and her feet hurt. But Blue's telepathic powers didn't stretch to such mundane matters and he took her much deeper into the bowels of Claydon Head. This time, they almost reached the very core of the mountain where there was no electrical light system. Blue's torch gave enough light to illuminate the way and he had a spare one hung around his neck. It was more claustrophobic down here and Rebecca felt like the whole weight of Claydon Head was bearing down on them. Even the sound of her voice seemed as if it was being throttled as it faded in the long, narrow rock corridors. The tour seemed never-ending and she stuck as close to Blue as she could. Finally, he stopped and stepped into a high crevice and Rebecca couldn't hide her relief. 'What are we doing here?' she panted.

Blue passed the torch over a human grave-sized pit, lighting up a couple of dozen dirty cloth bundles.

'Great, a priceless collection of filthy clothes.'

Taking no notice of her sarcasm, Blue squatted down and unravelled some of the cloth revealing gold and silver ingots, the gold winking at them in the wavering flame of the torch.

Forgetting her cynicism, Rebecca's face also lit up at the sight. 'Oh, what's this? More treasure?'

Blue nodded and he moved the ingots aside to expose a much larger object underneath. This one was draped in yellow canvas. He peeled away the folded material and uncovered a large golden cross with a red ruby set in the centre.

Blue's fingers danced animatedly in the torchlight. *From what I've learned from the pictures in my books this cross could well be part of the lost treasure of an army of god soldiers. They had a special name that looks like Kite Temples.*

'I think they were called the Knights Templar but you did well to work out as much of their name as you did. The word Knights is hard to read because you don't make the sound of the letter K. Anyway, I don't know much about them. Who are they?'

Not sure but they were fighting a long time ago.

'How on earth did their treasure find its way here and why has no one ever found it? If you are right, it's been here for hundreds of years. It's even older than all the other stuff. One more mystery that will never be solved.'

Blue wasn't listening. He was too busy carefully wrapping the golden cross back in its canvas shroud. He had worked out that he had to protect it from tarnishing in the dank air.

'That lot must be worth millions of pounds.'

Blue pulled her hair. *They're all precious but not just because they are worth millions of pounds. Why has it always got to be about money with humans?*

'Pardon me! I bet you wouldn't be so high and mighty if some of it was sold and the money could buy us out of this mess.'

Blue's eyes flashed as he stood up. She had hit a nerve but he didn't sign a response. He just moved away taking the torch and plunging the cave into total darkness. 'Hey, wait for me,' Rebecca called after Him.

* * *

Back in the Sky Chamber Rebecca rested on the stone bed while Blue sat at his rock table. He was copying drawings and words from one of his books. With his long tongue sticking out of the corner of his mouth he was slowly and carefully replicating the shapes and lines on another large sheet of curling paper. She remembered that he used to try and draw with bits of charcoal from the fire. But he couldn't use charcoal any more. His hands were much bigger and stronger now and the charcoal kept breaking. Now, he had a giant souvenir pencil. He must have been pleased when he found a pack of them in one of the local gardens when he was prowling around at the dead of night.

Sitting with her knees pulled up to her chest Rebecca broke the silence. 'Blue, tell me something.'

Blue grunted to let her know that he was listening but he didn't stop drawing and writing.

'You're obviously very intelligent and you clearly have a tender side to your nature.'

Blue uttered a low growl as if he was warning her not to go too far with the soft side of his nature. Even if he did rescue a fox, make friends with her and say he didn't want to fight his enemies, that didn't make Him a pushover.

'No, don't get all defensive. I know how brave you can be, I have seen you in action, haven't I? I'm not saying you're a bit of a softy or anything. All I'm saying is that, on the one hand you can show a reason for preserving life and on the other hand, you can kill as if life means nothing to you at all.'

Blue glanced up and twiddled his fingers. *You're not quite as dumb as you look, are you?*

Rebecca flicked him the "Vs" and waited for a reply. Realising he wasn't going to get any peace, Blue dropped his chunky pencil on the page. *I never really wanted to kill at all. All I wanted was to be left alone so I could live without fear. I wanted to enjoy the stars, the trust of the wild creatures and our friendship. But all I have ever known, ever since I can remember, is dread. The dread of being hunted all the time by these men in masks and uniforms. I hated them because they made me kill to survive. Killing has become a part of my life. Those men know that you can turn anyone or anything into a killing machine if you keep showing them, or it, the face of death.*

Rebecca was chilled by his honesty but she plucked up the courage to push Him further and ask Him about something that had been hammering away at her. 'Blue, tell me the truth. Last week they found an old woman decapitated at one of the caves on Claydon Head. Blue, did you do it? Did you kill that poor old woman, the same way you killed those Gas Mask Men that were hunting us in the woods?'

Blue lowered his heavy brow and his tangerine eyes glittered with fiery darts. For one, uneasy moment Rebecca thought he was going to turn on her.

Just when did this happen?

'I told you, last week.'

I have never killed anything that has not been a threat to me or you and I never will. Blue then drew a finger across his lips and carried on with his own version of a literacy lesson.

Rebecca wasn't going to get any more out of Him so she decided to back off. As far as Blue was concerned the conversation was

definitely over. Feeling unsettled she got up and left Him to his
studies and went to sit on the Sky Ledge to clear her head. Outside,
a cool breeze was stiff enough to ruffle her thick hair. She looked
over to the horizon were a bloodshot sun was about to sink into
a bed of mauve-coloured clouds. Down below she could hear the
seagulls and the cormorants squawking on the rocky cliffs. She sat
well away from the edge, her back against the rock behind. It was
still fairly warm from the weak heat of the vanishing sun.

Rebecca tried very hard to enjoy the moment but she just
couldn't get the conversation with Blue out of her mind. She wanted
desperately to believe Him, to believe he was telling the truth. But
she couldn't come up with any logical explanation to prove that he
didn't do it, that he was innocent of the murder. As Patrick had
already pointed out, only something of Blue's immense size and
strength could have inflicted such terrible injuries on that poor old
woman. 'There's more to this than meets the eye,' she told the birds.'
There has to be a missing link. There just has to be.'

Shivering as a sudden sea breeze swirled around the ledge,
Rebecca wished she had a jacket. Then, as if her mind had been
read she felt a fur blanket being draped over her back and shoulders.
She turned to find that Blue was stooping over her. She patted his
hand and gave Him a grateful smile; he could be so thoughtful. Not
wanting to miss the glorious sunset, Blue sat down beside her. They
sat in silence and let the vibrant colours on the horizon sooth their
minds.

* * *

Later, lying on the rock bed, Rebecca stared, trance-like, at the
candle flames as they flickered from a draught coming in from the
Sky Ledge. All she could hear was the crackling of the fire and the
muted sound of the waves. Then an almighty roar reverberated
through the tunnels and chambers. Frightened out of her wits,

Rebecca leapt up and banged her head against a protruding rock. Swearing, she staggered as she made a grab for one of the candles. Blue was nowhere to be seen. She had to find Him. Taking her courage in both hands she ventured out of the Sky Chamber. Tiptoeing through the middle tunnel she could see a soft glow coming from another chamber just up ahead. Another roar rang out and it was evident that it was coming from this other chamber. Flattening herself against the sides of the tunnel she edged her head towards the opening and peered in and there he was. So, nothing to be scared of; it was only Blue. He was lying on a flat rock snoring his head off and his tartan blanket was spread out underneath Him. Relieved but exasperated she snorted like a horse. *He might have warned me that he made so much noise these days, he knows how jumpy I am.*

It was the first time that Rebecca had seen where he slept and she was intrigued. She stepped in to get a better look. It was all so clean and tidy and it even had furniture. Blue must have built it all himself. Everything had been made out of sturdy fence panels and the pieces of wood were joined together with metal screws.

Not for the first time, she asked herself how he came by this stuff. There were shelves on one side and a crudely-made wardrobe on the other. Eventually it dawned on her, the whole layout was a carbon copy of her bedroom at home. But as far as she knew, he had never been in her bedroom: another mystery. But what really caught her attention were the murals he had painted on three sides of the cave. Blue had made crayon drawings which charted the journey of his life, from when he was an infant right up to when he became an adult.

On the jagged rock of the remaining side, were all the coloured paintings Rebecca had given to Him when she was a child. She felt a catch in her throat; she was genuinely moved. He had kept all these pictures; every one. They had obviously meant a lot to Him. She studied the murals and was interested to see that he had depicted scenes of his life here in Claydon Woods. There was one of the infant Blue with his mother and another one of Blue and Rebecca playing in the dandelion fields.

Next to it was an image of Blue standing alone in the woods. He had managed to make himself look confused and sad. In this mural, he was the same age as he was when Rebecca's father was murdered and the setting was the same as the actual murder scene. Was he so upset at the murder of her father that he had to make a record of it? She swallowed to get rid of the lump in her throat and turned to watch Him sleep. He was on his back and completely out of it. A rush of emotion engulfed her and she bent over Him and whispered, 'You big, blundering bastard. Why did you have to come into my life and mess it all up?'

Jerking her head back she reached out and touched a long plastic tube that was lying by the side of his head. She pulled it up to the candlelight and saw that it ran down the edge of his bed and down into a large clay pot which was partially covered with a thin tarpaulin. Rebecca trained the candlelight over the pot so she could see what was inside. It was half-full of a dark liquid. 'What the hell is that?' Blue's response was to snore louder than ever and break wind at the same time.

The smell of the liquid and his fart gave her the answer; it stank of alcohol. The liquid in the pot was probably some kind of moonshine that Blue had taught himself to make and he had got drunk on it. Yet another human skill that he had mastered – but how? She shook her head. In so many ways he behaved just like a man would when the pressure was on. 'Poor, poor bastard, I suppose you had to have something to help you hold out against Olsen and pass the time away.' She carried on listening to him snore for a while longer then, gently tweaking one of his ears, she left Him to sleep it off.

CHAPTER TWENTY-ONE
(THE LEGEND OF MR BLUE SKY)

Rebecca woke the following morning with a start. For a few moments she didn't know where she was then it all came back to her. Beside her rock bed she found a clay dish containing some pieces of fresh bread, white crumbly cheese and a banana. There was also a bottle of Volvic mineral water and a large carton of orange juice. She hoped that Blue hadn't given her the travellers' left-overs again. But where was Blue? He must be around somewhere because he had brought her something to eat and drink. Perhaps he was nursing a hangover? She let out her breath not even realising she'd been holding it since she had woken up. Wearily, she swung her legs off the rock and gingerly pushed herself upright. Her back was aching. The hard surface of her rock bed was not doing it any good. Standing there she caught a whiff of her own body odour. She was still wearing the same clothes she had worn yesterday and the day before. 'Shit, I wish I'd brought a fresh set of underwear with me,' she grumbled.

By the fire she saw a plastic bucket of warm water. Blue must have left it for her to wash in. Maybe he had noticed that she was smelly. She did her best to wash and dry herself with a couple of fairly clean rags. Feeling more awake she settled back on her bed to eat. As she pressed some of the cheese onto the bread she began to wonder where Blue was most likely to be. Tearing off another chunk of bread she headed out onto the Sky Ledge to get a bit of fresh air and check on what the weather might be doing.

Outside it was cold and windy and the sea below was choppy. The seagulls wheeled around in the winds squawking fitfully. All of a sudden two familiar hands appeared on the edge of the ledge, a bunch of long-stemmed flowers held in one. The hands were gripping the metal handles which were set at the top edge of the cliff face. These hands were immediately followed by a shaggy head rising above them. Rebecca folded her arms as Blue hauled himself up. 'Jesus, Blue, just what the hell do you think you're doing hanging off the cliff like that? You do know you could have fallen?'

Clumsily, Blue stood up and flashed her an indignant look before marching towards the cave mouth. He looked the worse for wear after his binge the night before but Rebecca was more curious about the wrought-iron handles bolted into the rock than his hangover. 'I suppose those handles were used by the smugglers to winch up all their spoils from the beach?' Getting no reply, she followed him inside and watched as he dropped the mangled yellow flowers on his table.

'Where did you get those flowers?'

On the cliffs. They were getting in the way. He signed with his hands.

'Getting in the way? Getting in the way of what?' Before he could answer the flowers had triggered another question and Rebecca butted in. 'Oh, by the way, what were all those flowers for? You know, the ones you left for me every year on my birthday?'

Blue stopped what he was doing. Finally she had got his attention. Sniffing scornfully his fingers danced in her face, *You still haven't figured it out yet?*

'No, I haven't, so tell me.'

Blue wagged his head. *You don't need my help with that, you need to use your brain and figure it out for yourself.*

Irritated, Rebecca stamped her foot. 'You can be such a pain in the arse.'

Giving a little skip Blue didn't let the offensive comment annoy him, he just beckoned her to follow Him.

'What now?' she griped. 'And by the way, you kept me up last night snoring and farting.'

But her whining was lost on Blue; he had other things on his mind and he had already disappeared down one of the tunnels. She only found out which one when she saw torchlight dancing on the sides near the entrance.

Scurrying after Him she wasn't too surprised when he revealed yet another chamber. It was roughly the size of the Sky Chamber with a heap of something in the centre. Blue had put on a loose jacket but the seams of the sleeves had come apart. She guessed that they had been ripped when he tried to force his massive hands through the lower arms and cuffs. He pulled back a mouldy canvas cover and showed Rebecca a stack of weapons. There were sharpshooter rifles, revolvers, handguns, a pile of gas masks and about a dozen distress flares.

Now Rebecca was surprised, really surprised. 'Where did you get all these from?'

Some of them were here and I've collected some of them from the hunters over the years.

'Do you know how to use those guns?'

Blue didn't have many facial expressions but Rebecca could have sworn that he looked very pleased with himself as he signed, *Of course I do and I'm going to show you how to use them, too.*

Throwing her hands in the air, Rebecca took a step backwards. 'Whoa… wait a minute, I'm not getting involved in using guns. If you want to end up blowing your enemies' heads off that's your choice but leave me out of it.'

But I may need you to use one in case I can't protect you.

'What…? Are you saying that I might get shot at?

Well, they're not going to launch an attack with flower petals, are they?

'Blue, what the hell are you talking about?'

Removing the rest of the cover Blue's expression and body language changed from smug to serious.

They're coming for me – for us. The time has come. All those years they have been hunting me it's all been leading up to this day. They want to destroy us and we have to be prepared for them. That's why you had to come back and that's why I need you here to help me.

Rebecca swallowed hard and her legs felt as if they were going to give way. 'I don't know if I can do this. This is not what I expected. I knew there were going to be dangerous times ahead and I wanted to help but I didn't realise what was actually involved.'

You have to be here, there is no escaping what is going to happen. You're not safe wherever you go. They want us both and being here with me is the only chance you've got to fight for your life. Your only chance to beat them and survive. That's why I called out to you. We have to be prepared. We must be ready. We have to fight them together. It's the only chance we've got.

Blue picked up one of the handguns; a semi-automatic 9mm Glock, and slapped a 17-round magazine into the handle. He angled the gun away from her and pulled back the slide on top of the nozzle and pointed to the safety catch beside the trigger. With one chunky finger he flicked it off, squeezed the trigger and made a "boom" sign with his hand. It was obvious that he must have been practising to be able to get his hefty hands and fingers to work the mechanisms so easily.

Nervously, Rebecca nodded that she understood how to use the gun but Blue wanted to make sure. He repeated the process a few more times until he was satisfied she had grasped it. He gestured for her to show Him that she would be able to defend herself when the time came. Hesitatingly, she took the gun from Him and repeated the action. She felt as if she wanted to throw up and dropped the gun on the ground before she squeezed the trigger.

Blue didn't try to force her to do it again but he was not letting her off the hook. He snatched a handful of distress flares and a few of the other weapons from the pile and glowered down at her with a determined glint in his orange eyes. She waited for his next instructions but all she got was a signal for her to follow him back to the Sky Chamber. Back in the chamber Rebecca watched as he unloaded all the items, including the Glock gun, on the flat rock table. Then, without a sign or signal, he left her alone once more.

While he was gone Rebecca gazed at the gun with dread. With trembling fingers, she was about to reach over and touch it when Blue returned with even more weapons in his hands.

'What have you brought now?'

Blue laid down the first object and started to sign. *This is my idea for that thing the police use to stun people. I think they call it a taster.*

'They call it a taser, Blue.'

Oh! OK, but now you need to let me tell you all about it. I will have to sign some of the new words I have learned from one of my weapon books. I haven't signed them before because I only worked them out from the pictures when I knew I was going to fight. So, this is going to be hard for me. I also used the words and pictures in the books to teach myself how to make a taser and I will try to show you what I did. It took a long time but I did it in the end. Slowly, Blue began to sign and explained that his taser was made out of an old disposable camera. He had taken out all the plastic components and replaced them with a circuit board, batteries and a capacitor. Pointing at the end of the camera he showed her two short screws that were attached to some cords inside. In between the plastic seam of the camera's casing was a small strip of brown film. Very carefully Blue started to demonstrate how to activate his taser to make it work. First, he gesticulated to her that she must pull the strip of film, sticking out of the casing, which instantly charged the capacitor inside. Once this had been done the taser would be ready to use. Then all she had to do was stab the two exposed screws into the enemy and they should receive a direct, paralysing shock.

Next, he showed her a second object which he called the Flash Device. Blue's fingers began his second demonstration. *I have already used this one before and it's very effective, especially if you have been cornered and need a quick escape.* Blue showed her that the Flash Device was basically a lighter with the flash shroud, the striker wheel and the flint with the flint spring taken out. The idea was that it could be used when she needed to create a diversion. He explained that one of the springs was wrapped around the flint and then the flint should be heated by a flame for around thirty seconds. Once that had been done, the hot flint should be hurled to the ground with some force, causing a brilliant spark of light. Blue showed Rebecca where to light the flint and how to hold it until it was ready to be thrown to the floor. Again, she nodded that she understood although she was still not happy about having to use any of them. After he stopped signing Blue gave her a handful of the flint coils.

'Wait a minute, how am I supposed to light them?'

I use this special powder mixed with table sugar but I'm also lucky enough to have these. He unearthed a box of Cook's Matches from under the jumble on the table.

'Where did you get those, the local one-stop shop?'

My traveller friends gave them to me as a present.

'And there was me thinking that you could have been using a tinder nest and two sticks to rub together to light the fire and the candles, just like a real caveman.'

Blue retorted, *I may look primitive but I'm not stupid.*

Rebecca managed a rueful smile then pointed at the distress flares. 'What do you use those for?'

If you happen to get lost in the caves they will help you find your way around.

Rebecca ran her hands over all the weapons. 'You need to tell me exactly what this all for, Blue. What is going to happen? You have got to let me know.'

Something is not right out there. This morning I had a peep around like I always do. But this morning there were no animals, no singing birds, there were no sounds. It was deathly silent. The animals know something is coming. I have always taken notice of their behaviour. I have used their instincts to tell me when I needed to hide away. The animals are warning me that danger is on its way so I've checked all the secured areas and so far, they're still OK.

'What secured areas?'

There are many secret entrances to my cave. Any one of them could be used to get in and I wouldn't know.

I've tied thin strips of birch bark to the surrounding trees to form a ring or barrier. If any of the bark has been disturbed I will know that someone has used one of the entrances to get into my cave. I have set the strips at an average, human-height level so they won't be broken by any of the woodland animals. The thin bark is a kind of camouflage because it blends in with the bushes and trees and that makes it more difficult for my hunters to spot it. So far none of them has been broken.

'Well, who do you think is coming?'

Who do you think? Olsen and his men; who else? Blue signed.

'Sounds to me as if we haven't got much of a chance. I can't see how we can make much of a stand. We will be outmanoeuvred, outnumbered and they will have the latest weapons.'

Blue made signs urging her to come back to the Sky Chamber and drink some water before following Him again. While they were there he lit a fresh torch and then led her to another chamber. It was next to the one they had just been in. He had chosen to use this chamber to store another armoury of weapons that he would use to defend himself. Rebecca watched in awe as he fixed a switch-blade hunting knife into a special holder under the tattered sleeve of his jacket. Once this was secure he tested the mechanism by thrusting his wrist in a downward motion and the blade shot out with a sharp click. With great care he pinched the tip of the blade between his finger and thumb and pushed it back into its coiled-spring catch.

Rebecca gulped and stammered stupidly, 'That's dangerous.'

In the far corner of the chamber there was a stack of long wooden spears. Blue picked up two of them and spun them through his fleshy fingers. He must have gone through the routine day after day because he was almost as good as a cheerleader twirling a pair of batons. With a flourish he then slotted them into two thin rubber tubes attached to a body harness he was wearing under the front of his jacket. Picking up an army-style knife and some flash-flint coils he clipped them all into the special pouches he had also fixed inside his harness.

'I didn't know you had one of those things under your jacket.'

Blue flattened out the bulges in his jacket and stood to attention like a sergeant major. *You stay here for now, you'll be safe in here.*

Rebecca seized his forearm. 'What? Wait, where are you going? You can't just leave me here.'

This is the way it has to be done. I have to be ready for them. They're coming, I can feel them.

Rebecca was losing heart. 'Why even fight them? Why don't we just hide in the caves until they give up?'

Blue shook his head despondently. *Like you've already said, he will never give up hunting me until he wins. For years it has been planned this way and today it ends. I win or I lose. Whatever the outcome I would rather die fighting than spend the rest of my life running.*

'But what about me? What am I supposed to do if you don't come back?'

Gently, Blue peeled Rebecca's hand away from his forearm and his orange eyes became piercing. *You don't know how important you are to me yet. I cannot defeat them without you and when the time comes you will know what to do – trust me. Trust me now and we will have our lives back – I promise.*

Not for the first time Rebecca was frightened of losing Him. But this time the fear was more immediate and it snaked through her, twisting down to the pit of her stomach. It lay there throbbing like an uncontrollable seizure. Blue saw pinpoints of tears glistening in her eyes and had to leave before he weakened and lost his edge.

She wasn't sure exactly where she was supposed to wait. Was it in this chamber or was it anywhere in the caves? She decided it was anywhere in the caves and she went back to the Sky Chamber. Feverishly biting her nails, she stood, gazing desperately over the table of weapons.

The time ticked by. She didn't have her phone or a watch but she estimated that he had been gone for about thirty minutes, then fifty minutes, then an hour. After about an hour and a half had passed Blue still hadn't returned. The suspense was excruciating. Pacing up and down the Sky Chamber she couldn't handle it any longer; she needed to know what was happening.

Rebecca contemplated taking the handgun with her but she couldn't bring herself to do it. Instead she opted for the flash-flints and the taser-camera thing. Finding one of Blue's old jackets she put it on, rolled up the sleeves and taking a deep breath set off into the unknown.

With a sharp thrust Rebecca managed to force the cover off the cave's secret entrance and found herself in exactly the same spot where Blue had taken her the day before. However, she was so scared and distracted that she forgot to replace the cover before she headed off into the woods.

When she plunged into the undergrowth the eerie silence made her stop in her tracks. Blue had been right, there was something ominous in the air. There was no birdsong, no sounds of any woodland life at all. It was as if all the animals had left or gone into hiding.

Placing a trembling hand on the taser in her jacket pocket she crept forward on her hands and knees making the bracken snap and crackle, her eyes constantly darting from side to side as they scanned the woods for any sign of danger. As she crept through the bushes, the menace in the air was palpable. She could almost taste it. The sense of isolation and desperation made her think of the way foxes must feel when they are being chased by hounds.

Keeping her voice low she called out for Blue but there was no response. She knew he would be incensed to find her out here but what did he expect? She couldn't just wait and do nothing. Up ahead she heard a loud rustling coming from a clump of bushes so she knelt down behind a cluster of tall nettles. Straining her eyes and avoiding touching the stinging leaves she peered through the stems. Was that a movement just ahead?

She froze like a terrified hunted animal, her instincts telling her that it couldn't be Blue. Blue was too good at evading Olsen's team and wouldn't be careless enough to crash through bushes and alert them to his presence. Perhaps it was one of the Gas Mask Me? Her heart began to thump like a double bass drum in a street parade.

'Rebecca?' a voice hissed.

Rebecca couldn't believe it; she knew that voice. Forgetting the danger, she sprang out from her hideout stinging her hand on a nettle as she did.

'Patrick! Is that you?' she called softly.

And there he was, in full view for anyone to see. He was standing between two trees just ahead. As soon as she was sure it was really Patrick she ran headlong towards him. She couldn't get to him fast enough and when she did she buried her head in his chest and squeezed all his breath out of him.

'Patrick, Patrick, how did you get out here?' She snuggled into his thick cotton shirt, stroking his face, his shoulders and his arms.

Rebecca's enthusiastic reaction was more than Patrick could have hoped for. He held her close but he had to keep a grip on the situation. 'Olsen wanted me to come to look for you. I don't know why, he just said I could be a great help.'

Reluctantly, Rebecca peeled herself away. 'Why would he suggest something like that?'

Patrick shrugged. 'I don't know.'

'How're Mum and Jim? Are they OK?'

'Yeah, they're fine but they're really giving Olsen a hard time because they feel he betrayed them, too.'

Nuzzling into Patrick's shirt again Rebecca tried to gather her thoughts. 'What's going on? What does Olsen want now?'

'He won't say but I honestly don't think he sent me in here just for your benefit. When you ran away I tried to come after you but Olsen's men stopped me. Olsen said that he expected you to run off to Blue. He made it sound as if it was all part of his plan.'

'What part of his plan?'

'I don't know for certain but I think it's likely that he is leading us all into some kind of trap. I wouldn't put it past him. By the way, where's Mr Blue?'

'He's already out here but I don't know where. He told me to stay in his cave but I couldn't stand not knowing if he was OK or not so I came to find out.' Rebecca reached into Blue's jacket pocket and pulled out her improvised taser.

Patrick drew his head back. 'What's that?'

'It's a taser. Blue made it for me.' Then she showed him the flint coils and explained what they were for.

'Well, that's very inventive but I don't think it's going to do much against Olsen's mob of thugs, do you?'

Firmly taking her arm Patrick shoved her forward. 'Come on, let's get away from here while we've got the chance.'

But Rebecca dug her heels in. 'No, I can't just leave Blue to fight Olsen's men on his own.'

'Becca, what can you possibly do to help Mr Blue? How can you possibly go up against trained fighters? You'll get us both killed.'

'Let's find Blue and then go back to the cave and hide,' she suggested.

Patrick shook her. 'Becca, listen to me, we have to get away right now before it's too late.'

But Rebecca was adamant. 'I'm not leaving Blue.'

'Remember Blue killed your father. Have you forgotten that little detail?'

Rebecca rubbed the sting on her hand and eyed him coldly. 'I'm not leaving… you go if you want to.'

'OK, fine,' he sighed. 'But you've just thrown away the only chance we might have.'

Moving past Patrick, Rebecca started to run back the way she had come. 'I don't care; we have to find Blue.'

'Oh, bollocks!' Patrick muttered. He had no choice; he couldn't leave her to deal with Olsen's murderers on her own. 'Hang on, Beccs, I'm right behind you,' he called as he followed her. He had only taken a few steps when there was an almighty CRACK. It was like the sound of a giant tree being felled. They both shuddered to a stop and froze.

Whirling around in a circle Patrick slipped and nearly fell over. 'Oh God! What the hell was that?'

An ominous silence descended then it began. In the distance they could hear the thrashing and tearing of bushes and trees. It sounded as if they were literally being torn out from the ground by their roots. Whatever was causing the upheaval was advancing towards them, growing closer and closer. It stopped just beyond a row of tall, thick bushes. Patrick and Rebecca waited with their hearts in their mouths. Then tearing aside a swathe of leaves and branches, it revealed itself. It stood over seven feet tall and wore a long trench coat and a Stetson hat. There were no ripped seams in this coat; it had obviously been tailor-made for its colossal body. Rebecca faltered and her legs nearly went from under her as she cried with relief. 'Blue, you're safe.' Recovering her strength Rebecca stumbled towards him.

But Patrick pulled her back. 'Wait a minute, is that Blue?'

The beast standing before them bowed its head and tugged off its hat. Rebecca clasped a hand over her mouth to stop herself screaming. In a strangled voice she stammered, 'Oh my God, Patrick, that's not Blue.'

'Are you sure it's not Him? If it's not Him, who the hell is it then?'

Rebecca had thought that she would be ready for most things that Olsen and his men were going to throw at her but she wasn't ready for this. She grabbed at Patrick for support. This monster was larger and broader than Blue. Although its ape-like characteristics were similar it had much coarser features. The brow was heavier and the thicker mandible jaw jutted out making it look more aggressive. And unlike the longish hair on Blue's head, this creature's head-hair was cropped short except for a tight plait clinging to the back of its skull. Overall it was more powerful, uglier and more menacing than Blue. Still holding its hat in its grasp, it stopped and watched them with the persistence and patience of a meat-eating predator.

'Patrick, what do we do?' Rebecca shrieked.

'The only thing we can do... RUN!'

Once her brain had managed to engage with her body Rebecca's legs moved faster than she ever thought possible. Both she and Patrick tore through the woods. Patrick only slowed down to risk glancing back and he discovered that the Thing was nowhere in sight.

'Shit!' he cried coming to a sudden stop and tugging Rebecca to stop with him.

'What? What?'

'Wait, it's gone, I can't see it.'

Rebecca's chest heaved and she had the taste of ashes in her mouth.

Shoving her onwards Patrick gasped, 'Let's just keep going; it's our only hope.'

They expected the Thing to leap at them at any time but to their relief they made it all the way into a clearing in the woods. They stopped and doubled up, hands on knees, their chests and lungs burning as if they were on fire. Rebecca was in a worse state than Patrick and she sank to the ground. The clearing was about the size of a golfing green and was surrounded by low-growing shrubs.

When she got her breath back, Rebecca straightened up. 'Where are we? I've never been here before.'

'Perhaps we should keep going. Maybe we lost it,' Patrick panted.

His optimism was short-lived. In one mighty leap from nowhere it landed with a thundering thud in front of them. Too terrified to move Rebecca and Patrick could only cling to each other.

The Thing had ditched the hat and trench coat and was standing up to its full height. It lowered its head and looked as if it was going to make a charge at them as it glared from under its hefty brow.

Its eyes, cockroach-black and bulbous, were blazing with deadly intent. The sheer evil that this monster exuded meant that it had one purpose and one purpose only. It was going to attack Patrick and Rebecca and rip their bodies apart until they bled to death. Looking at the monster, Rebecca realised that she was looking at the face she had seen in her nightmares. She was looking at the face of death.

Shaking, she sank her fingers into Patrick's arm. 'Patrick, it was him, he killed that woman traveller. It wasn't Blue; Blue didn't do it.'

'And Richie? Oh no! … Did he…?' Patrick choked up. 'That, that bastard Olsen; this is his Thing, his monster. That's why he sent me in here to find you. First, he got rid of the old woman traveller who tried to warn you, then Richie and now he wants to get rid of us.'

But Rebecca wasn't ready to accept her fate. She wasn't going to go down without a fight. She had endured and survived years of emotional turmoil and it had given her an edge. With all the air she could hold in her lungs she pursed her lips and whistled. The high-pitched shrill tone reverberated around the woods causing the birds to flap into flight from their sanctuary in their treetop perches.

The Thing lumbered towards them. It had Patrick in its sights and was focused on doing what it was programmed to do. But just before it was about to strike, in a kind of cinematic slow-motion action and with virtually no sound, Blue flew through the air and landed on the ground in front of them. The Thing stopped in its tracks and roared as its heavy head swung from side to side. Blue roared back and advanced towards it, his body coiled like a spring, ready to attack; ready to attack his hitherto unknown simian twin.

CHAPTER TWENTY-TWO

Despite the terror she was experiencing pride shone in Rebecca's eyes when she saw that her brother had come to their rescue. Blue tore off his jacket and harness and moved forward for the attack. He was tilting his head in much the same way that the Thing was tilting his. But Blue's was not an aggressive action. Rebecca knew that he was trying to figure out what this creature was and she hoped that his confusion would not give the Thing the upper hand.

'This is what Olsen wanted, this is the plan,' Patrick spat. 'This is the Battle of the Generals, and the winner will command Olsen's army of Manimals. They will rule the world and we will just be collateral damage.'

The Thing glared at Blue. There was no confusion in its bearing. It had been well-trained to expect this showdown. However, it regarded Blue with a warrior-like respect. It waited and watched as a snarling Blue swept Rebecca well out of the way. With its breath steaming through its jaws the Thing planted its feet square on the ground. It knew what it had to do on this day; it was what it had been born and bred for. The oldest, most primordial instinct had been drilled into it over and over again; kill, kill, kill.

Patrick shoved Rebecca further back from the two opponents momentarily distracting Blue as Blue chanced a look over to them to make sure she was safely out of harm's way.

Gaining the advantage, the Thing rugby-tackled Blue and pitched Him to the ground. They both hit the earth with a heavy thud and rolled around, each one trying to pin the other down. The Thing appeared to be the most skilful fighter and managed to keep Blue underneath its powerful torso. They were both growling and snarling as they wrestled and tested each other's strength.

Rebecca was unable to watch. She could only pray for her Blue. He had to beat this hideous monster but he didn't have the same indiscriminate killer instinct. With one of its vast hands the Thing seized Blue's neck in a steely grip. With the other it started bludgeoning the side of Blue's head. Rebecca could hear agonising grunts and she stole a look through her fingers. She winced in anguish as Blue took more and more hammer blows to the head.

Patrick edged towards them. 'Come on, Blue,' he rallied. Realising that he was getting caught up in the intensity of the fight and getting too close to the fray he quickly backed away.

On the verge of becoming concussed Blue smashed the Thing's choking hand away and delivered brutal, clubbing hooks to its face. The Thing shook its head and seizing the chance, Blue was able to loosen his stranglehold. Scrambling to their feet they squared up to one another roaring. As they moved around in a circle they threw rapid jabs at the upper body to try and force a mistake from the other. Around and around they charged until the Thing made a rush at Blue, its arms flailing wildly. The heavy blows were finding their mark and Blue caught another one on the side of his skull sending Him down on one knee. The Thing sensed a bloody victory and doubled his frenzied attack. But Blue wasn't done yet –his own rage gave Him a super-strength and he wrapped his huge arms around the Thing's legs. With one colossal effort Blue hoisted it up and slammed his adversary to the earth.

'Yes!' Rebecca punched the air jubilantly.

With the wind temporarily taken out it, the Thing rolled out of Blue's reach and clambered back to its feet. Blue couldn't get close enough to pin it down and once more they paced around each other baring their incisors. Bellowing, Blue then charged in with a flying leap but the Thing caught Him by the waist in mid-flight and rammed Him back down onto the ground. Enraged that his attack had been thwarted, Blue managed to roll the Thing over and over until they reached the long grass at the edge of the clearing.

Patrick clutched at Rebecca's arm. 'Quick, now's our chance to make a run for it.'

But Rebecca snatched her arm back and snapped, 'NO!'

'Listen, Becca, what if Blue loses? We'll be next.'

But Rebecca was losing her temper with Patrick. 'When will you get it into your head? I'm not leaving Blue.'

Taking matters into his own hands Patrick hoisted her up into a fireman's lift and bolted, as fast as he could, back into the woods. Rebecca beat his back, screaming, 'Put me down! Fucking put me back down!'

Still grappling on the ground Blue heard her cries and the sight of her being carried away made Him drop his guard.

Once they were at a safe enough distance Patrick put her down but as soon as Rebecca's feet touched the ground she took a swing at him. 'Get out of my way, get out of my way now, I'm going back.'

But Patrick pinned her arms to her sides. 'Listen, Becca, I have to get you away from here. That's why Blue wanted you to stay in the cave; so you'd be safe.'

'Patrick, I'm warning you, you had better let me go.'

As Rebecca was trying to free herself from Patrick the bushes parted and a group of men stepped through.

'Rebecca, Mr Farrell.,' Olsen announced smoothly. He was leading half a dozen or so armed troopers in black balaclavas with sharpshooter rifles.

Patrick and Rebecca stopped grappling with each other and glared at Olsen and his men. Nonchalantly, he lit a cigarette from his gold Colibri lighter and squinted as he took a drag. After exhaling the bluish smoke he grinned at his victims. 'The plan went swimmingly, even though I say so myself.'

'Olsen, you sodding bastard.' Patrick went for him but was quickly grabbed by two of Olsen's soldiers.

Rebecca was past being scared for herself. Blue was fighting for his life, fighting to save her. She went up to Olsen and spat in his face.

Shaking himself free, Patrick followed her. 'So, we were used as bait to draw out Blue for your Frankenstein monster to challenge Him?'

Olsen put up a hand to stop his men from interfering and wiped his face with a white silk handkerchief.

'Well, it was until you came on the scene and then we had to amend our plans to include you; no loose ends, you see. We were going to send her out into Claydon Woods alone and once Victor had hunted her down Rassimus would come to her rescue.'

'Victor.' Patrick sneered. 'Is that after Victor Frankenstein?'

Olsen appeared genuinely impressed that Patrick was able to overcome his fear enough to make a witty remark. Under the circumstances it was quite impressive. 'That's why I wasn't too bothered when Rebecca ran away. We knew if we sent you in there, one way or another, we would still get the same result.'

Rebecca was incensed by Olsen's complacency. 'It was your Victor who murdered that poor old woman traveller, wasn't it?'

Olsen's eyes narrowed as he took another puff from his cigarette, he said nothing.

'You are worse than evil. You made me think it was Blue to try and convince me that he was a psychotic killer so you could get me to set Him up for you, didn't you?'

Olsen threw up his hands and laughed. 'Hey, I just wanted to get you all together. I didn't want to ruin this great family reunion.'

'You really are a complete bastard, aren't you?' she seethed.

Through gritted teeth, Patrick asked the obvious question. 'So what now, Olsen? Now everything is out in the open what are you going to do – shoot us?'

Olsen made a pretence of frowning at them. 'No, nothing so dramatic and crude, we're not the animals. We are sophisticated humans and I would never do anything to harm Rebecca. She still has a major part to play in my wonderful experiment.'

Tiny red sparks flew from Rebecca's eyes. 'What major part?'

Olsen's face suffused with a sinister delight. 'You'll see. But for now, shall we take our ringside seats for the battle of the century.' He extended his arm to her. 'Shall we?'

With as much contempt as she could muster Rebecca turned her back on him.

* * *

The two combatants had fought their way out of the glade and into the surrounding woods. The Thing crunched Blue into the trunk of a stout tree and the impact was so forceful that it almost snapped it in two. A dull mist clouded his eyes as he tried to climb back onto his feet but the Thing was ready. It free-kicked Him back against the same tree. Blue was now beginning to weaken and had to dig deep to gather the strength and all his will to get back onto his feet. Yet, before he had the chance, the Thing hoisted Him up by his legs and Blue was turned upside down. He just had the chance to catch a blurred glimpse of the woods, the wrong side up, before being hurled against the trunk of another tree.

He was badly hurt and winded as the Thing came thundering towards Him but he was too dazed and weak to do much to protect himself. He was grabbed in a front choke-hold and then his neck and windpipe were crushed by the Thing's death-dealing hands. Blue couldn't move and he began to feel the life being squeezed out of Him. He knew that it would be all over for Him if he didn't find some energy from somewhere.

But just as he was slipping into unconsciousness Blue had a hazy vision of a familiar area nearby. Groggy as he was he recognised it as the spot where he had once knelt over the lifeless body of his mother after she was mercilessly murdered by Olsen's men all those years ago. Blue thought that it was almost fitting that he should meet his own fate near the same place where his mother had taken her dying breath.

It all came back to Him. Once again, he recalled the terrible agony and the trauma he felt after losing his mother; it had been unlike any pain he had ever experienced in his young life. Over the years that anguish and pain had been dimmed but had never been erased from his memory. It had become a pilot light of dormant rage, always there, always alight; ready and waiting to flare into a ferocious flame if it was ever fanned by the right touch-paper. And here in this deadly arena that time had come; the right touch-paper had been lit. This beast was not only killing Him, it was killing his mother all over again... no... not this time. The flames began to burn into a fire until every muscle, every fibre in Blue's body was ignited with an all-consuming, blazing fury.

No longer trembling under the weight of the Thing Blue felt a powerful energy force flooding through his limbs. He reached up and curled his fingers over the meaty arms around his neck. Growling, he began to tear through the vice-like grip and he broke the hold on his throat. His blood began to circulate and his brain cleared. Getting back on his feet he lifted the entire weight of his enemy and shrugged it up onto his shoulders. With an almighty shift Blue then turned his body and slammed the Thing back against the tree trunk hard enough to almost snap its back in two. Not giving it a chance to recover Blue was on it, roaring as he rained a frenzy of hammer blows on his stunned victim. The Thing rallied and fought back but Blue's anger had made Him into an unbeatable super-beast. Soon the ferocity of his attack began to take its toll and the Thing began to weaken.

Blue dived headlong onto his near-unconscious prey and wrestled it into a position where he could get a stranglehold on its throat; a gurgling sound came through its jaws as it choked. Sensing that it was close to its downfall the Thing made a last lunge but it did not find its mark. And as Blue crushed its windpipe even harder the flailing limbs of the beast started to drop. Its power slowly seeped away and as it collapsed it started to look like a garden hose after the water pressure has been turned off. Finally, the Thing's body twitched and went still. All Blue had to do was to square his mighty shoulders so he could get enough leverage to snap the Thing's head from its spinal column and total victory would be his for the taking.

* * *

When Olsen and the others eventually reached the spot where the fight had taken place there was no sign of the Thing or Blue.

'Where are they?' Rebecca fretted.

'I don't know,' Patrick replied.

But Olsen wasn't fazed. He was wearing his usual superior expression and standing coolly waiting. He always looked as if he knew something that they didn't and he didn't bat an eye when they heard the sound of heavy footfalls coming towards them. Out of the dense woodland the hulking figure of one of Olsen's ape-men appeared. It was half-dragging another ape-man on its back. At first, Rebecca couldn't tell which one was Blue because both were injured and bloody. But Blue limped forward and stopped in front of Rebecca. With his remaining strength he lifted the Thing high above his head and held it aloft.

Rebecca held her arms out to Him, too many emotions to get a handle on how she felt. She was so proud, so relieved and also worried about Blue's injuries. Blue had won the battle for survival but he was obviously badly hurt.

Patrick couldn't get over what had happened. 'Fuck, shit, he did it.'

In a feat of incredible endurance Blue still held the Thing above his head. He eyed everyone in turn. He was a gladiatorial warrior, a warrior who had won the right to be saluted for his victory. But then he lowered the unconscious monster to the ground. For reasons only known to himself Blue had not delivered the death blow. He had not killed the Thing, after all.

'Very well done, Rassimus.' Olsen applauded but then added, 'But why didn't you kill him like you were supposed to?'

'Because he's not a corrupt monster like you!' Rebecca shouted.

'Oh, but he is,' Olsen replied. 'You see, in order to turn Him into a cold-blooded killing machine we first had to isolate Him and fill Him with nothing but hatred. That's why we had to get rid of his mother and give Him drugs.'

Blue pushed the body of the Thing away from his feet and glowered at Olsen. With a red brilliance in his orange eyes, he emitted a low, murmuring growl.

'Abandoned or orphaned offspring make far better assassins and soldiers. But one thing troubles me. Despite the fact that we provided Him with all the necessary training, the drugs, the nutrition, stimulation, isolation, the exercises and mind manipulation, he still didn't complete the task he was given. He didn't kill Victor – that was what he was trained to do– that should have been the end result.'

Blue, with his chest still rising up and down, never took his eyes off Olsen for a second. Concerned that he might attack, Rebecca moved even closer to Him. She avoided looking at the Thing and focused on Blue. She could see how much he wanted to kill Olsen so she took his bruised and battered hand in hers.

Olsen hadn't noticed the gesture and continued patronisingly, 'For you to be in sole control of my army I need to have complete confidence that you can take orders and that you will accomplish the missions without any hesitations. Kill Victor right now and you will command the greatest and most powerful army that has ever existed.'

Rebecca gave a sharp intake of breath and shook her head at Blue as she waited anxiously for his response.

'You have to prove to me that you have the back-bone and determination to lead such a formidable military force.'

But there was no reaction from Blue; only a stone-cold stare. Olsen repeated his order, 'Kill Victor or you cannot rule as my general.'

Blue's stare dropped to Victor still lying in an unconscious heap then it darted back to Olsen.

Pointing at Blue, Olsen delivered his ultimatum, 'Kill Victor or we will kill you.'

'No!' Rebecca cried clutching Blue's hand even more tightly in hers.

Blue took his hand away and fiddled with something behind his back. In one deft movement he hurled one of his flash flares in Olsen's direction. A phosphorescent white light flared up in front of Olsen and his men.

They were unprepared for the blinding glare and they all drew back. This was their chance. Blue wrenched Rebecca by her arm and headed back into the cover of the woods. Olsen's men cocked their rifles but Olsen stopped them. 'Get them,' he ordered, 'but I need the girl alive.' Then he pointed at Patrick. 'Keep hold of him; we might still need him yet.'

Patrick stiffened as two rifle barrels were shoved in his face.

Blue and Rebecca reached the hidden entrance to the cave and that was when Blue discovered that the cover had been left off. He turned to sign his anger at Rebecca but changed his mind when he realised that it would just waste time. He jostled her through the narrow opening in the rock but Rebecca pulled back. 'No, Blue, I can't leave Patrick with Olsen. You'll have to go back for him.'

Blue snarled back at her.

'No. I don't care what you think about him. If you don't go back they might kill him, too.'

Blue knew that if he did go back it would jeopardise their escape and he punched the limestone rock above the entrance. Rebecca wasn't deterred and with time running out and only minutes to spare Blue had to give in and he shoved her through the hole. Then he dragged his exhausted body back the way they had come to rescue Patrick.

'Blue, be careful,' Rebecca shouted after Him but he had already gone.

Inside the dank tunnels, Rebecca did her best to remember which tunnel was the right one that led up to the Sky Chamber. But without any of the matches or flares that Blue had told her to carry she could only feel her way along the cold, jagged stone surfaces. She inched her way through and soon a familiar smell of a sea breeze filled her nostrils and ruffled her hair. This was a good sign; it must mean that she was heading in the right direction. By now, her eyes were becoming accustomed to the darkness and she could make out a left turn. After a few paces she reached a bend and the tunnel appeared to brighten up ahead. She was becoming more confident and expected that she would soon find her way straight up to the Sky Chamber. But just as she was beginning to quicken her step, a ghostly face leapt out at her. Rebecca fell back and screamed, her voice rebounding off the tunnel walls.

The apparition, or whatever it was, held one of Blue's fire torches under its chin. It made its grotesque grinning face even more chilling. Rebecca knew who this was. It was the smiling clown, the Joker-like imp who had stalked and terrorised her back in Benarth; the figure she had named the Smiler. She cowered against the side of the tunnel and tried to edge her way past but the Smiler dodged about in front of her and in a squeaky voice spoke for the first time. 'Finally, Rebecca, we get the opportunity to meet. It was very careless of you to leave one of the entrances to the caves uncovered. Luckily I came upon it just by chance.'

Rebecca's heart thumped even harder than it already had that day, and she elbowed him out of the way and inched her way down the tunnel. But the Smiler followed and taunted her with his ghoulish torch mask. 'Rebecca, I've been dying to meet you. I feel I've known you for years.'

'What do you want?'

'We want you back, back where you belong, my dear.'

'Back where?… What do you mean?'

'Back in the family fold, Sister, because that's where you should be. You are not just the sister of Rassimus, you are also the sister of Victor.'

Gasping in disbelief Rebecca stopped. 'What? What are you saying?'

'Oh, yes, that's why Rassimus could not kill him in their great battle in the woods. His instinct told Him that he could not kill Victor. His instinct told Him that he could not kill his own brother, your brother.'

'No, no, that can't possibly be. Olsen said that one of the twins died in childbirth.'

'No… that was one of Professor Olsen's little lies. He lived and he grew up to be another magnificent specimen just like Rassimus. Don't worry if you can't take all this in at once. There is so much for you to understand and accept. On top of that, we had to mess with your mind and telepathic powers in order for it all to work and I have had the satisfaction of being part of that. I have played mind games with you, my dear. It has been so much fun.'

By now Rebecca's brain had been so overloaded with each new revelation and all the terrible events that she couldn't think straight anymore. All she could understand was that she was caught up in something, something abominable and she didn't know how it had come about without her having any idea. And now this. 'What do you want with me? Why am I so important in all this?'

The Smiler flashed another one of his mocking looks. 'Rebecca, you will be the mother bearer, you will give us the next generation of human-animal hybrids.'

Rebecca's face registered horror and revulsion.

'You will be impregnated to produce the next superb spawn of Manimals. You will be Phase Two of this great experiment; this time we're going to reverse the procedure with a human female with primate sperm. That's why Olsen has made sure that nothing has harmed your body. He wants you alive and he wants you physically fit.'

Rebecca spat out the bile that filled her mouth. 'I would rather die first.'

The Smiler's grin almost touched his ears. He was enjoying doing Olsen's bidding, he was enjoying her torment. 'Stay away from me,' Rebecca warned.

The Smiler ignored her and began to sing and dance, jerking like an out-of-control puppet. She had to get away and forcing herself into action she shoved past him and ran blindly back through the dark tunnel.

* * *

Patrick was escorted by three of Olsen's men; two either side of him and another, following behind. Stealthily they moved along an overgrown path in the woods, the soldiers using the barrels of their rifles to flick the shrubbery aside. Suddenly the soldier at the back let out an agonised howl as his foot was almost sliced in two. He had stepped onto one of Blue's traps. It had two metal claws and they worked like a giant Venus flytrap, clamping down on anything that stepped onto them. Blue had laid the trap in the hope that Olsen and his men would use this old path. While the two other soldiers were preoccupied with the injured soldier, a screen of leaves and shrubs opened up behind them. Blue sprang out and he leapt on top of them crushing the two soldiers' skulls together with such force they both crumpled to the ground. He snatched the rifle away from the soldier who had his foot impaled by the metal claws and turned to Patrick. Giving a contemptuous growl Blue gestured for him to follow quickly.

* * *

Rebecca had no idea where she was going but she had to keep moving. The air inside the dank tunnels was so foul that she could actually taste it. Visibility was also limited so she had to resort to feeling her way along the tunnel walls again.

'Rebecca.' The voice snaked through the dark chambers.

Rebecca stiffened and held her breath. Anytime now she expected to see a probing shaft of light from the Smiler's torch seeking her out.

'Rebecccaaaa… that wasn't very nice running away from me like that. Not very nice at all but don't worry, I won't hold it against you.'

His voice sounded like it was coming from some distance away, so she hoped she was safe for now, although she wasn't sure where she was or where she was supposed to go from here. She knew she couldn't go too far in case she got lost or fell down one of those deep potholes that Blue had warned her about. She even thought about waiting until the Smiler was close enough so she could go on the offensive. She could try and overpower him. After all, she was bigger than he was.

'Rebeccaaaa.' The high-pitched voice made her jump.

Tormented she screwed her eyes shut, a cold sheen of perspiration forming on her forehead and upper lip. When she opened them he was before her but how had he got to her so quickly?

'I suppose I owe you an explanation about the way your father died. I don't have to tell you anything, of course, but I will out of the goodness of my heart. You see all this time you thought you actually knew what happened to your father on the night he was killed. You really thought you knew, didn't you? You believed what your childish eyes told you when you saw Rassimus standing over the body of your father.'

Rebecca was listening now, listening intently. She was too intrigued to be frightened and all thoughts of escape had vanished.

'But as you have recently discovered things aren't always what they seem. Yes, your father went along with this whole experiment for the money until it began to play on his conscience. And then when he couldn't take it any longer he decided to kill Rassimus. But we couldn't stand by and watch that happen, could we? No, no, we couldn't have him wrecking our agenda for a magnificent New World Order. We couldn't allow him to kill one of our most prized creations so we had to take drastic measures to prevent it from happening.'

The Smiler chuckled giving himself hiccups and explaining in between spasms, 'So I killed him. I waited in the woods and stabbed him in the heart. As I plunged the knife into his chest he looked at me as if I had just stuck it up his arse.' Putting his hand over his mouth in an exaggerated gesture, the Smiler then burst into uncontrollable giggles.

'It was you...you killed him, not Blue!' Rebecca whispered.

'When Rassimus found him he thought that one of his vagrant friends had done it.' The Smiler became even more crazed and went into uncontrollable hysterics.

'Bastard, you bloody sick bastard.' It took every ounce of Rebecca's self-control not to hit out at the insane fiend. But then her nostrils twitched. She thought she smelled smoke in the darkness. Where was it coming from?

'Boo, surprise!' the Smiler yelled in her face and Rebecca screamed as if she would never stop.

She was left with no other choice but to run and run she did. She charged through the tunnels, expecting to fall down one of the potholes. She didn't really care anymore. If she did disappear into the bowels of the caves never to be seen again it would just be her hard luck. Behind her she could hear the Smiler's shrill voice echoing, echoing.

'Oh, don't worry about the fire. I just thought I'd try and warm up the place a bit. I know you're feeling a bit cold.'

Was this one of her nightmares? It felt like it; it was unreal. Surely, she would wake up soon. But no, this was not a nightmare, she was actually running through the dark tunnels of the caves, running from a maniac and now there was a fire. Not only was she running from mortal danger, running for her life, but she didn't know which way to run. She was completely lost. Whichever way she chose there was a chance that it would be the end of her.

As if some self-fulfilling prophecy was being acted out Rebecca tripped and fell face down. She tried to spring back to her feet but her ankle twisted and she winced in pain. She hobbled down another tunnel where the smoke became much thicker and she had to open her mouth to breathe. Now her breaths were rasping and she was struggling for air. She had to find her way out; she had to keep going, keep going. She was so disoriented and in so much pain that it took her several seconds to realise that the bright red blaze in front of her face was not coming from the fire.

'Rebecca, it's me,' Patrick cried holding one of the distress flares in his hand.

'Patrick, oh, Patrick.' Rebecca's knees sagged, and she fell against him. 'Quick, he's behind us; the thing, that clown midget.'

'What? Where?' Patrick waved the flare about turning the tunnel walls the same colour as Blue's eyes.

'He was here, chasing me. It was him, Patrick, it was him all along.'

'Rebecca, there's nobody here now.'

'Where's Blue?'

'He had to make sure we weren't being followed. Where the hell's that smoke coming from and why are you limping?'

'I twisted my ankle and that crazy dwarf has set fire to the cave. Quick, we have to get out of here.' She yanked at his jacket, almost pulling him over. Steadying himself, Patrick gave her his arm and held the torch with his free hand. Together they went back down the tunnel that he had used.

When they reached another dead end, Patrick couldn't remember which way to go and as he swung the flare about they could see tendrils of smoke curling after them. Rebecca started to cough and her lungs were beginning to burn. 'Patrick, if we don't find a way out of here we're going to suffocate.'

'Don't worry, we'll get out. We haven't come this far to perish in a cave fire.' He hooked his arm under her armpit and half-carried her down the nearest passage.

Yet, the further down they went, the thicker and blacker the smoke became until both of them were coughing and spluttering. Rebecca couldn't make it any further and she had to stop; she was done for. She turned to Patrick and her shoulders slumped. 'Patrick, we're lost, we're…Blue, Blue, is that you?'

Yet again, Blue had come to their rescue and as always, he appeared from nowhere. He bundled them into a passage with fresher air and it began to ease their coughing and cool their lungs.

Blue could see that he had got there just in time and he didn't waste precious moments trying to sign. But his attempt to lead them all back up to the Sky Chamber was obstructed by the fire so they had to backtrack.

Whichever way they turned the fire prevented them going any further. Blue had to take them along a narrower and more hazardous passage because it was the only way to escape from the smoke. He struck the cap of a flare and as the flame fizzled he made some quick hand gestures to Rebecca. Once she understood she turned to Patrick.

'Blue thinks that you should travel down this passage for about 200 yards and it'll take you right through to the west side of

Claydon Head. Once you have reached this point it will be safe for you to follow the road down into the town.'

Patrick frowned. 'Wait a minute, aren't you coming with me?'

Blue had to use his sign language to reply and Rebecca had to translate.

'No, Blue says that I need to stay with Him because he needs my help to finish this.'

'But…?' Patrick protested.

'Blue says there's no time to argue, you must go now.'

Blue shoved another couple of flares into Patrick's chest but Patrick looked doubtful.

'Blue says keep to the left and you will be safe from any potholes.'

'Potholes? OK, watch out for potholes, but what about you two and what about Olsen and his soldiers?'

'Blue says that Olsen and his men are going in the opposite direction. They are carrying Victor to a horsebox so you will be safe.'

Patrick protested but Rebecca would not be moved. She said her place was by Blue's side, the way it had always been when she had been in danger.

Saying goodbye to Patrick was heart-wrenching and Rebecca wanted to dive into his arms and kiss him while she still had the chance. But once more she was unsure of herself, her lack of confidence let her down and her chance was lost. Instead she murmured a soft goodbye and told him to get help.

Patrick knew there was no point in trying to argue so he reluctantly made his way down the passage, looking over his shoulder as he went. Impatiently, Blue flapped his hand forward and growled at him to hurry up.

'Don't have a go at him, Blue,' Rebecca sighed. 'He has done his best; more than most people would have done.'

It was time to go and Blue tugged at her arm, but Rebecca couldn't take her eyes off Patrick as he disappeared down the tunnel enveloped in a halo of flaring red light.

With most of the ducts and passageways obstructed by the fire the only way left open to them was the one that led out onto the shore directly below the Sky Chamber. Blue didn't have the space to carry Rebecca and she winced as she clambered out of the cave's exit. She was immediately showered with salty spray from the waves as they crashed against the rocks. Blue poked her in the back to indicate that they were going to have to climb right up to the Sky Ledge. Rebecca looked up to the rock overhang. It was over a hundred and fifty feet high and she shouted over the waves, 'You expect me to climb up there?'

Blue signalled. *We have to. The fire hasn't reached it, it's the only safe place and I need more weapons.*

Rebecca glared back at Him with a stubborn expression on her face. 'No way. You're asking the impossible. In case you hadn't noticed I'm limping because I twisted my ankle in one of the tunnels. Plus, I'm scared of heights. You're just going to have to leave me here, Blue, I just can't do it.'

Leaving Rebecca was never going to be an option. Blue had managed to retrieve his harness after his battle with Victor and producing a tiny bottle and piece of rag from one of its pockets, he clasped his hand to her mouth. Her eyes rolled in panic then slowly began to close. He had used his magic sleep potion on her once more.

It had only been a mild dose and she came round within minutes. She began to pick up the sounds of the waves but it was the violent jerking of her body that finally woke her up. Rebecca turned her head to one side and that was when she saw the terrifying drop to the crashing surf below.

She screamed and Blue roared at her to keep still as he had her strapped to his back in his body harness and she was being hauled up the cliff like a baby in a carrier. They were now only eight yards away from the Sky Ledge and Blue had the two, lower smugglers' handles in his sights. With the agility of a professional rock climber he continued the ascent while Rebecca kept her eyes firmly shut.

Then all of a sudden Blue stopped and Rebecca opened her eyes to find out what was wrong. In the distance they heard a low-sounding thrum and they both knew that a helicopter was approaching. Blue quickly resumed his climb but because of his haste his grip slipped once or twice, giving Rebecca a series of mini heart attacks. At last they reached the base of the overhang and Blue gripped the two handles under the rock ledge and made a series of short barks at her. Rebecca's heart gave another somersault as she understood what Blue wanted her to do.

'I can't climb over you to reach the metal handles; I'll fall,' she bellowed at the top of her voice.

With one hand, Blue stretched behind to unclip the harness that held them together and freeing Rebecca to climb. Realising that there was nothing securing her any longer, she clung to Blue's neck for dear life and took deep breaths to try and quieten her hysteria.

Blue wriggled and roared again to urge her on. With trembling fingers she began to crawl up over Blue towards the overhang. Behind them the whirring blades of the helicopter chewed the air between them. Inch by inch Rebecca's quivering fingers crept over the coarse limestone rock until her clammy fingertips touched the cold metal. Once she had a good enough grip she began to haul herself up onto her knees balancing on Blue's shoulders. Blue wedged his feet into a rock crevice to give himself a secure foothold so Rebecca could put her full weight on Him. Rebecca steeled herself as a blast of ice-cold air blew up from the shore, nearly blowing her off Blue's shoulders. In the distance, the now familiar Westland Lynx helicopter whirled closer to the cliff edge. Inside the cockpit the pilot spoke to his passengers through the radio in his aviation helmet. 'I can't fly too close to the cliff face because of the updrafts.'

Olsen stared blankly ahead then issued his instructions into the microphone attached to his headset. 'Just get us as close as you can.'

Rebecca pulled on the iron bars with all her might and levered herself up. With her one good leg, she stepped up then with the other but the pain made her wince and her foot slipped off Blue's shoulder. Her grip was yanked away from the iron handles and she wailed as she began to plunge down to the raging surf below. But Blue caught her by the wrist and with his remaining strength hoisted her back up onto his back. With every muscle in her body quivering she waited for her second wind and tried again. This time she blocked everything else out. Paying much more attention, she gripped the metal bars and heaved herself up into a semi-standing position on Blue's shoulders. By now they could both feel the draft from the Westland's blades as the helicopter began side winding towards them. Then the cabin door slid open and Olsen barked out his order to his sharpshooter. 'Wait until the girl is out of the way. I still need her alive.'

With his feet still wedged into the rock crevice Blue extended his legs to their full capacity to give Him maximum leverage and as soon as he felt Rebecca's weight shift he jerked himself upwards. With this extra boost Rebecca was able to lift herself up and over the ledge in one last effort. At last she lay there trembling from nervous exhaustion. But staying there was not an option she could afford. She had to force herself back onto her feet as best as she could. Leaning against the entrance to the cave she stood on the ledge facing the Westland helicopter with the wind of the blades blasting her face. She saw the soldier in the open cabin door pointing his Sig Sauer, bolt-action sniper gun at Blue.

'No…!' she screamed at the top of her voice.

'Fire!' Olsen commanded.

The shot thudded into the rock just above Blue and showered Him with chippings of limestone. Blue roared but he wasn't hit. The updrafts were buffeting the helicopter so much that it was affecting the soldier's aim. Blue seized at the overhang and prepared to leap for the iron handles but another shot from the helicopter stopped Him.

'Closer, we need to get much closer,' the sniper yelled back into the cockpit.

'I can't get it any closer or we'll crash into the cliff,' the pilot shouted back.

'Try man, just try,' Olsen barked at him.

Frantically, Rebecca stood with her hands clasped to her head. She had to do something but what could she do? Then it hit her. She dashed back into the Sky Chamber as another shot pinged off one of the metal handles. On the rock table the rest of the weapons were still there, including the Glock pistol. Rebecca limped into the cave and went to grab the pistol but before her hand could even touch the handle, someone seized her arms and pinned them tightly to her sides.

'Got yer,' the Smiler sneered triumphantly.

'Let me go, let me go!' Rebecca kicked and yelled furiously.

'No, no, Rebecca, it's all over,' he cackled, and she could smell his fetid breath wafting down the side of her face.

Although her arms were pinned to her sides she was still able to wriggle her fingers into her jacket pocket.

Swiftly, she pulled out the piece of film from the casing of the improvised taser and charged it up ready.

'As you are going to be carrying the next generation of hybrids, we're going to keep you happy by pumping so many drugs into you, you won't even remember your own name.' The Smiler waved a crooked finger in front of her face, tormenting her.

Enough was enough. In one deft move Rebecca whipped out the taser and stabbed her tormentor in the thigh with the two protruding screws. There was a sharp electrical clicking and the Smiler began squealing like a stuck pig and immediately let go of her. Rebecca pulled away and watched as the Smiler's face convulsed from the shock. Seeing her chance, she went for the Glock on the table and flicked off the safety catch as Blue had shown her. Now it was pointed right at the Smiler's face.

The Smiler's glazed eyes stared down the barrel of the Glock pistol and he gave a lopsided smirk, but Rebecca wasn't sure if it was a smirk of defiance or a smirk of defeat.

Whichever one it was, so be it. Rebecca closed her eyes and squeezed the trigger. The shot rang out through the walls of the tunnels and the kick-back sent a thread of pain right up her arm and into her shoulder. She reopened her eyes and looked down the end of the barrel but she could only see empty space before her.

The Smiler's twisted body was lying at her feet. 'That's for killing my father,' she hissed. Her reaction to killing another living being was not what she expected. She did not feel guilty or distressed. She felt justified for avenging her father's death and ridding the world of one of Olsen's sick experiments.

From outside, Rebecca could hear more sounds of gunshots so she hobbled out onto the Sky Ledge and saw Blue slumped over the edge, clinging to the two metal handles and he wasn't moving. The helicopter was hovering thirty metres away and she spotted the sniper in the open cabin door poised to take one final shot at Him.

With a fury and focus she had never experienced before, she aimed the Glock at the cockpit of the helicopter. She didn't know how she did it but she beat the sniper to the shot and luckily managed to empty most of the magazine into the cockpit. Olsen was spared but the pilot wasn't so fortunate and it was either the third or fourth shot which punctured his carotid artery.

In an instant the helicopter began to spin and weave out of control. Inside the cockpit Olsen frantically grappled with the cyclic lever to try and regain control but it was no use. His earthly world was now literally spiralling out of control and all he could see was the cliff edge getting closer and closer and the swirling sea glinting below.

Rebecca watched dispassionately as the helicopter spun and spun, rotor tail chasing the cockpit; the roar of the engine pitching high and low until it dipped beneath the ledge. She moved closer to the edge so she could witness first-hand the downfall of the worst monster imaginable. It was the tail fin that crumpled against the cliff face first. Then the main rotors impacted, scything into the limestone rock, and sending tiny missiles of composite steel and aluminium into the air.

The machine shuddered and clanked, the metal buckling as it dropped onto the rocks below, exploding into a ball of ferocious heat. Rebecca felt a blast of hot air hitting her and the cliff face was suffused with a dazzling brilliance. A pall of dark smoke curled out from the wreck and formed into the shape of a large black mushroom as it drifted up the rock face.

Rebecca stood completely transfixed until the heavy smell of diesel fumes jolted her back to the here and now. Olsen was dead and hopefully all his barbaric experiments had died along with him. It was hard to tear her eyes away from the burning shell of the helicopter but Blue was in trouble. He was the one who needed her help now.

'Blue,' she cried kneeling beside Him.

He couldn't move his arms or legs but he lifted up his massive head and as soon as their eyes met she saw the deep, agonising pain in his eyes.

'Blue, can you climb up?' she asked but he shook his head.

It looked like he had been shot but where or how many times Rebecca didn't know; she couldn't see any blood. 'Blue, come on, we have to get you up.' Hauling at his titanic body, she strained as hard as she could to lever him back onto the ledge, but he was a dead weight.

Her arms felt as if they were being pulled out of their sockets as she persevered. 'Blue, you'll have to help. I can't do this all on my own.' But it was no good. She began to suspect that he may have been shot in the spine which would explain why he couldn't move. His feet were still wedged into the two other handles beneath the ledge so his position was steady for the time being. Frantically, she racked her brains but she couldn't fathom a way of hoisting Him back up. Her only option was to try and coax Him into action again.

'Come on, Blue, you can't stay there all night, it'll be dark soon.' But Blue was unresponsive and she sat back on her knees frustrated and exhausted. 'Blue, I can't, I...' Her words trailed away as she wept in despair.

Blue remained motionless with half of his body bent over the ledge and his two hands gripping the iron handles in the cliff. She gazed down at Him, her face wet with tears. It was poignant and tragic that this incredible, noble specimen who had survived so many attempts on his life now looked so vulnerable, so weak; like Samson drained of all his strength.

The sun was beginning to set and a deep sadness began to steal into her heart but still she couldn't give up.

'Blue, Blue, don't do this to me now. Don't let go, not now, not after everything we've been through. We've done it, we've succeeded; now we can move on together. You're free.'

She felt his hands and they were cold to the touch and faintly trembling. Rebecca's tears dripped onto his head as she was forced to come to terms with reality and start to think the unthinkable. She couldn't save Him. The only thing she could do for Him was the same thing he used to do for her at times like these. She knelt over and placed her forehead against his and remembered all the wonderful times they had played together in the dandelion fields when they were young. All those times she had sought comfort and he was the one who always soothed her pain away by simply – being there.

With their faces close together Rebecca whispered into her brother's ear. 'You do know, don't you?'

Blue lifted up his glassy eyes to meet hers.

'You know who I am, don't you?'

Blue answered in the only way he could and blinked.

'You do know I'm your sister?'

Blue gave an imperceptible nod and blinked once more.

'Why did you make me believe that you were the one who killed my father? Why did you take the responsibility for that when all along it was that evil clown who killed him? If only I had known the truth, things may have turned out different for us.' Rebecca gently rubbed her forehead against his, her love for Him pouring out in an unstoppable tide. 'My life has been a complete pantomime, a show, an illusion, a pretend life with pretend parents and a pretend future. The only real thing, the closest thing I've ever experienced to having a real family, is you.

'And for the last twenty-something years, all I've been doing is running away and trying to convince myself that you never existed. I've been blaming you for everything that has happened in my life, I was completely in denial. Somehow, I knew there was an explanation to all this but I just didn't want to face the truth.

Only now I have the truth. Now I have the answers to all those questions that have been haunting me all those years and it doesn't come as any surprise that, as always, I don't know what I'm supposed to do. I feel like I've been locked in a prison for years praying for my freedom. Now that I'm actually standing outside those prison gates I don't know where to go or even what to do. I'm scared, Blue. Before all this, I was scared of my life with you and now I'm scared of having a life without you. You're the only one that really means anything to me; you're the only family that I have right now. You've always been there for me and you are the only one who has ever truly cared for me.' Tenderly, Rebecca placed both of her hands on top of his knuckles. She used to think they were the size of golf balls but now they didn't look so big and they were stone cold.

Blue stirred and he turned his head towards the setting sun. The sky was now a canvas of magnificent pinks, reds and purples. Rebecca knew how much he adored the sunsets and she imagined how many of them he had enjoyed over the years, all alone on the Sky Ledge. This one, however, they would enjoy together, as a family.

Up there on the Sky Ledge it was so quiet, so peaceful. The sea had calmed and not even the seagulls or the cormorants disturbed the stillness with their cries. It was as if they too respected this sacred moment. A gentle sea breeze whirled around the ledge and a hank of Rebecca's dark hair rested on Blue's head and blended in with his.

Rebecca closed her eyes, warmed by the closeness she felt to her brother. That was when she realised that he was slipping away from her. She kept her eyes shut and let go. There were no sounds, nothing as Blue took his last journey down the cliff face.

Rebecca opened her eyes but she was blinded by her tears and all she could see was the blur of the sea and a haze of colours in the sky. **Blue had gone.** A pain stabbed through her heart and soul, a pain that hurt more than anything she had ever known.

She remained crouched on the Sky Ledge for what appeared to be an eternity, not wanting to move and not wishing to accept what had happened. Had it not been for the distant thrumming of an approaching helicopter she might have stayed like that all night.

'A helicopter,' she murmured to herself.

Patrick must have made it to safety and had raised the alarm. He hadn't let her down this time.

Rebecca forced herself to fetch the distress flares from the Sky Chamber and with one in each hand she stood with her arms outstretched like a human firework. Yet as she stood there, waiting to be picked up, she gazed at the horizon once more. The sky had now turned a dull greyish purple and the air had an alien chill to it. She didn't think she could ever enjoy another sunset again.

REBECCA'S DIARY

How I miss Mr Blue, my brother, a true noble warrior. I will never see Him again. It has now been two years since I lost Him and only now I am beginning to realise exactly what he meant to me and how much of a big part he played on my young life. Mr Blue Sky was real; he existed. How I hated myself for leaving Him down there in his watery grave like that. He deserved much better; he deserved to live and he deserved to enjoy the freedom that he fought so hard to gain.

After his death they came, the government officials. They sealed up the entrances to the caves and they completely cleaned out Claydon Woods, although it is still off limits to the general public. There was no enquiry, no interrogation, no official investigation, nothing; it was all hushed up. Even Richie's disappearance wasn't properly investigated and he has just been written off as a missing person.

Everything in Blue's cave, all his possessions, his drawings, his attempts at writing, all his treasures are now locked away somewhere, lost forever. All except for one. The very next day after his death, I found a cord wedged in the opening of my bedroom window and when I pulled it up there was Blue's diary, bound in that disgusting animal flesh. This was his attempt to put down his experiences with pictures and words. How on earth he had got it there I don't know. Perhaps he stuck it there on the morning of that final, fateful day. But nobody knows about this diary, not even Patrick. It will always be my secret. From what I have made out already there is so much about Blue that I never knew and so much about the capabilities and intelligence of our species; our mixed human-animal hybrid potential that I couldn't have imagined. Plus, there are plenty of Mr Blue's own thoughts and theories illustrated with more detailed drawings. I will study these when I am ready. In the meantime, I will treasure this legacy.

However, what I did find particularly interesting in his diary was the solution to the mystery about all those flowers that he left for me every year on my birthday. In his diary, Blue explains the meaning for every flower that he sent me, but he pays particular attention to the last six flowers; the rose, the elderflower, the tulip, the snapdragon, ivy and the sweet william. The meaning for each of these flowers consists of love, zeal, fame, deviousness, affection and gallantry. Now they could mean anything but when I looked back on my life I realised that I have often displayed many of those flower meanings. A coincidence? Perhaps.

Yet the most intriguing discovery I made was about the order in which the flowers were sent. If you take the first letter of each flower and lay them out together they form the word RETSIS. I already knew this but at the time it didn't make sense to me and even when I asked Blue about it he teased me for not figuring it out.

But now I have figured it out. The word RETSIS is an anagram for SISTER; this is what you get when you swap the letters back to front. And SISTER is the name Olsen gave to me after I was born as one of Emily's triplets. Obviously Blue wanted me to know the truth but how on earth did he work it out? He was so intelligent, more intelligent than Olsen could ever have imagined, even in his wildest dreams. I sometimes wonder if he was intelligent enough to work out that his mother had not been killed by Olsen; that she was still alive. I hope he did.

Another thing that I keep turning over in my mind was what Olsen said to Patrick about Blue wanting to escape his hunters. He said, "Any highly intelligent species will eliminate their enemies and never leave any traces when they escape."

Bearing that in mind, how do I know that Blue didn't fake his own death to escape his captors? Surely the most effective way of evading your enemies is to convince them that you are already dead. And the more I think about it, the more it seems possible especially when I recall the things he said to me in the cave. Things like him wanting me to help Him end his own life because he was sick of being hunted. He kept saying that it was essential that I remained there with Him to help right up until the very end. He even mentioned that he had a plan. Everything, absolutely everything, was meticulously planned on that fateful day; the traps, the weapons, he even left the distress flares on the table in the Sky Chamber, so I could direct the air rescue helicopter to rescue me from the ledge. It was as if he knew how everything would all pan out.

Some of Olsen's theory also panned out. Blue did successfully eliminate his enemies and he didn't leave any trails behind. For all I know he may have also faked being shot by the sniper in the helicopter. After all, I didn't see any blood on Blue. And he may not have fallen into the ocean and been washed away; his body was never found. He could have been hiding under the rock ledge? He had scaled that rock face regularly and was certainly capable of pulling it off. He even did a test run on that particular morning when he decided to clear some of the flower plants that had been growing on the rock face. They must have been in the way. But am I fooling myself, just grasping at straws?

Assuming that he did pull this whole thing off, where would he go? Perhaps he intended to live a subterranean life underground in the labyrinth of caves. He even said that he could quite easily hide down there and nobody could ever find Him, ever.

Yet, why would he abandon me? Why make me believe he was dead and put me through all that heartache after all we've been through, especially now that we both knew that we were family? My guess would be that he intended to grant me my one true wish, which was to have my life back. Maybe he thought that I could actually move on and put it all behind me. Blue probably realised that this could never happen if he was still around. And I'll never forget what he told me in his own language... *The best things in life are free but the best thing in life is to be free.*

REBECCA'S DIARY *(update)*

It has now been nearly three years since I lost Blue and each birthday that passes I pray that I might find another flower waiting on my driveway. But every year my heart is broken again. I have to accept that he is gone, and he is not coming back.

height

I have now moved back in with my mum as her health is not very good. I forgive her; life is too short and too precious to carry grudges. Patrick has been wonderful. I was right about him, he is the one for me. Ever since that air rescue helicopter dropped me off he was there to pick me up and he has never let me go since. He has been so supportive and understanding over the years and he is always ready to listen when I need to talk about Mr Blue. We have been engaged now for about eight months and he will move in with Mum and me when we get married next year.

For a time, I was too embarrassed to talk to Patrick about our pathetic sexual episode in the fields. But it turned out to be a miraculous episode because it gave me my baby. My baby, my beautiful, healthy baby boy, was born eight pounds and ten ounces nine months later and we have called him Peter. Mum was so proud and so happy, I had never seen her smile so much.

Everything about Peter seems to be normal, except he has a strange orange tint to the whites of his eyes but the doctor assures me that this will pass as he gets older. Our fears about what kind of baby we might have because of my complex DNA were our main concern but we couldn't let the antenatal staff in on our secret.

Thankfully, after all the scans, we were assured that everything looked normal. But what do doctors know, especially if they don't know what they are looking for? Nevertheless, I will try not to let fear dominate our lives. I have done that one and a lot of good it did me.

Peter is such a strong baby. He is growing so fast and he has a quick temper that reminds me of his Uncle Blue. It is remarkable that although Peter cannot talk yet, it looks as if he is already developing the skill to communicate with me using some of the simpler language signs that Blue used.

LAST ENTRY

March 31st– 8.56am.

It is the morning of Peter's second birthday. I am in the kitchen but I think I can hear a familiar whistle outside. It sounds like a bird or some owner calling their dog but something nags at me to have a look. I open the door and of course, as expected, there is nothing there. Nothing except... on the doorstep I find two flowers lying side by side: a single red rose and a single yellow rose. Just two flowers and what do I find when I check what their names mean?

**Congratulations, a promise of a new beginning and...
REMEMBER ME!**